Night Bites

Vampire Stories by Women

Edited by Victoria A. Brownworth

D0111784

Seal Press

Cover design by Kate Thompson
Cover photograph by Karen Moskowitz
Text design by Clare Conrad
Typesetting by Stacy M. Lewis
Copyediting by Cathy Johnson

Library of Congress Cataloging-in-Publication Data
Night Bites : vampire stories by women / edited by Victoria A. Brownworth.
1. Vampires—Fiction. 2. Horror tales, American. 3. American fiction—Women authors. I. Brownworth, Victoria.
PS648.V35N54   1996   813'.08738089287—dc20   95—43877
ISBN: 1-878067-71-0

Printed in the United States of America
First printing, February 1996
10 9 8 7 6 5 4 3 2 1

Distributed to the trade by Publishers Group West
Foreign Distribution:
In Canada: Publishers Group West Canada, Toronto, Ontario
In the U.K. and Europe: Airlift Book Company, London

Acknowledgments

Every anthology requires the work of more than just the book's editor, and this book literally could not have been completed without Judith M. Redding, who acted in many ways as its co-editor. Judith sorted through the myriad submissions, giving me synopses of the stories so I could assess which ones fit the book's criteria and which did not. She also did extensive copyediting and keyboarding and was responsible for making sure deadlines were met and authors' revisions were made. Her work on this book was invaluable, my thanks immeasurable.

The idea for *Night Bites* developed, in part, because I wanted an audience for the work of two of my writing students, Joanne Dahme and Diane DeKelb-Rittenhouse, who had written vampire stories that were very different from the ones I was used to reading. Joanne's and Diane's stories made me realize a real void existed in the genre, and I wanted to see more stories like theirs. My thanks to them both, for catalyzing this idea.

A great deal of combined effort went into the realization of *Night Bites*. I spent a lot of time and energy convincing women who are known as writers of serious literary fiction that they could create maverick works by upending the vampire genre; I want to thank those women for taking a risk on a new style of writing. I also want to thank Susanna Sturgis, Kanani Kauka and Ruthann Robson for their suggestions of other writers. Thanks also go to Meredith and Jim Baird for desperately needed computer help.

Seal Press has a twenty-year record of publishing iconoclastic works by women, and *Night Bites*, its first foray into the horror genre, is yet another risk the press has taken in an effort to make the diversity of women's writing available throughout the world. My thanks go to Seal co-founder Barbara Wilson, for her initial support for the project and to Seal's fabulous publicist, Ingrid Emerick, for her enthusiastic support throughout. Special thanks go to Holly Morris, who was never an overbearing editor and whose experience with her own anthologies made her more sensitive to the intense work involved in compiling such a book. Holly was always upbeat and excited about the project, a rarity in an editor.

Finally, I want to thank all the women who submitted work for this volume, those whose work I used and those whose work I did not.

for Magda Wallenda

Nessun dorma!... Tu pure, O Principessa,
nella tua fredda stanza
guardi le stelle
che tremano d'amore e di speranza!

Contents

Introduction   ix
Victoria A. Brownworth and Judith M. Redding

They Have No Faces   3
Meredith Suzanne Baird

Anita, Polish Vampire, Holds Forth at the Jewish Cafe of the Dead   19
Judith Katz

The Last Train   33
Linda K. Wright

The Vampire's Baby   43
Joanne Dahme

Immunity   71
Toni Brown

Sustenance   81
Susanna J. Sturgis

Apologia   97
Jan Carr

Bad Company   115
Joyce Wagner

Almost the Color of Summer Sky 127
Mabel Maney

Best of Friends 133
Lisa D. Williamson

To Die For 141
Diane DeKelb-Rittenhouse

Unexpurgated Notes from a Homicide Case File 159
Judith M. Redding

Refugio 165
Terri de la Peña

Women's Music 179
Ruthann Robson

Twelfth Night 195
Victoria A. Brownworth

Backlash 219
Nikki Baker

Contributors 257

Introduction
Victoria A. Brownworth and Judith M. Redding

Vampires. They are the supernatural icons of the twentieth century—beings both human and superhuman, natural and unnatural, of this world yet spawned by another. Creatures of the night, vampires epitomize and symbolize our most primordial fear: that the dark will steal our souls, changing us irreparably, so that even those we love will no longer know us. Vampires are members of society who have been cast out in the blink of an eye, the beating of a bat wing, the moment it takes to sink teeth deep into the throat of a victim. Anyone can become a vampire simply by being in the wrong place at the wrong time, befriending the wrong person, choosing the wrong lover, offering hospitality on a cold night to the wrong houseguest (or being offered hospitality by the wrong host). Because anyone can become a vampire, the threat is that much more terrifying. *No one is safe.*

Like all myths based on a modicum of historical fact, the vampire mythos is compelling simply because it edges so close to reality. The first reported vampires were real historical figures in fifteenth- and sixteenth-century Eastern Europe: Elizabeth of Bathory and Vlad the Impaler. They sucked or drank or bathed in the blood of their victims; each reveled in the murderous process; each spawned the myth of the vampire slayer who lived for and on the blood of the innocent.

Bathory and Vlad were people of wealth and power who preyed on peasants and political enemies; they epitomized the bloodthirsty tyrant. But as the tales of vampires spread across Europe, these original historical vampires became lost in the myth and new ones, vaguer, and hence even more frightening, took their place. The central historical elements, however, remained intact: The vampire was nearly always either a person of wealth who lived in isolation from the rest of society (and the lower classes from which he or she would cull victims) or a stranger, a foreigner, who took up lodging with some distant acquaintance and repaid the favor murderously.

At the foundation of the vampire myth is blood—*life* blood. The vampire can feed on its victim over time or kill outright. Not every victim becomes a vampire, but it is the not-knowing that adds to the fear: Victim and victimizer often are interchangeable. And that range of possibility for "infection," as vampirism was often euphemistically referred to, expands the myth as it expands the fear.

Every culture has its indigenous supernatural beings—ghosts, fairies, trolls, dragons, golems—but none has captured the imagination of readers worldwide the way the Eastern European *vampir* has. Although a relatively new creature by supernatural standards, first appearing in folklore and literature in the fifteenth century, the vampire has successfully transcended place and time. Our western image of the vampire—suave, cultured, handsome, pale, thin, nocturnal—is surprisingly different from the original vampir, who was often corpulent, ruddy-faced, decaying, slow-moving and diurnal as well as nocturnal.

Although vampire stories appeared in English as early as 1800, it was not until the 1897 publication of Bram Stoker's novel *Dracula* that the vampire appeared in its now quintessential western form. Part myth, part history, completely sensual and just as completely ruthless, Stoker's Count Dracula set the standard for modern vampires. Dracula embodies all that mortals desire—looks, intelligence and wealth—without paying the price of mortality. But he is also the perpetual outsider, dependent on his need for blood (and the means to obtain it), shunned by society. The vampire is always the "Other": outside the realm of whatever standards a given society or culture has set—sexually, racially, ethnically; a pariah.

In the Victorian age, with its repressed and repressive notions of sexuality, the vampire also became the erotic Other whose lust and sexuality stood outside the social norm. *Dracula* was not only the most popular novel of the Victorian period, it was also made into a variety of stage plays. The reality of Victorian life made the fascination with vampires explicable. Jack the Ripper was a living vampire of that era, preying on women of the streets in a way that combined sexual lust with blood-lust; he was rumored to be a member of the royal family—the Bathory/Vlad of his day. And although Victorian sexuality was straitened by social mores, the facts of Victorian sexuality made vampirism seem rather tame; there were approximately one hundred prostitutes for every man in Victorian England at the time *Dracula* was published, many of these women catering to "unusual" sexual desires.

Vampirism itself—depicted as uncontrollable desire and as a sensual swoon for both victim and vampire—stands as a euphemism for sex, forbidden by social mores. And the sex itself is not of a normative nature.

In J. Sheridan Le Fanu's classic novella *Carmilla*, published in 1872, the title character is both vampire and lesbian, luring her innocent victim with the guise of friendship. In Stoker's novel, Dracula's hold over Lucy Harker and her husband, Jonathan, is definingly erotic; Stoker defines the vampire as pansexual, creating tension between good and evil, the sexually chaste and the sexually profligate. Whitley Strieber's 1981 novel *The Hunger* and Anne Rice's tetralogy featuring the vampire Lestat also ascribe this pansexual archetype. These vampires choose their victims and partners based on character and desire, not gender.

Vampires became as popular in the art of motion pictures as they were in the novel. In 1922, Max Schreck loomed across the silent screen as Count Dracula in F. W. Murnau's chilling *Nosferatu* (released in England under the title *Dracula*); in 1931, Universal Studios made the first sound version of *Dracula*, starring Bela Lugosi. Universal was so sure *Dracula* would be a hit that they used the same sets at night (the English-language version was filmed by day) to shoot a Spanish-language version of Stoker's story, starring Carlos Villar as the count. *Vampyr*, Carl Dreyer's 1932 classic, was based on Le Fanu's *Carmilla*, and was the prototype for a later series of lesbian vampire films.

Vampire movies have been popular since these early classics, and most popular vampire novels—including Anne Rice's *Interview with the Vampire*—have been adapted for the screen.

The movies also resurrected the lesbian vampire from her historical grave—Elizabeth of Bathory transmogrified into the ultimate erotic carnivore. From 1936's *Dracula's Daughter* (based on an unpublished chapter of Stoker's novel) to a spate of lesbian vampire movies in the 1960s and 1970s—including *The Vampire Lovers, Lust for a Vampire, Twins of Evil, Daughters of Darkness* and implications of lesbianism in many other American, British, French and Italian films—to Tony Scott's lush and stylish adaptation of *The Hunger* in 1983 (starring international film doyenne Catherine Deneuve, budding American star Susan Sarandon and rock-and-roll idol David Bowie), lesbians have ruled the screen as the epitome of the vampiric Other. Film and video archivist Raymond Murray notes, "It seems that Hollywood could only understand lesbians if they were vampires."

Not surprisingly, the vampire genre, literary and cinematic, has diverged little from the roots of *Dracula, Carmilla* and *Nosferatu.* Women appear in the vampire myth in one of two ways: as innocent victim or bloodthirsty victimizer. Women with active sexuality, like Le Fanu's Carmilla, must, of moral and social necessity, be evil, while the passive honor- and love-bound women like Stoker's Lucy Harker are obviously doomed to become victims of rampant vampiric sexuality.

And the vampire genre has, despite a few notable exceptions, remained a strongly male-dominated field. Most vampire anthologies include only one or two stories by women.

Women writers, perhaps because they are more acutely aware of the status of women as Other, have always had a vision of vampires that differed from the Stoker/Le Fanu paradigms. In 1896, one year before the publication of *Dracula,* Mary Elizabeth Braddon—one of the most prolific writers of England's Victorian era—published the short story "Good Lady Ducayne" in the popular and influential *Strand Magazine.* In Braddon's story, young Bella Rolleston hires herself out as companion to the ancient Lady Ducayne. Lady Ducayne wishes to prolong her already extended life and engages the Italian physician Parravicini to perform vampiric transfusions with Bella's blood. Typifying the melding of the natural and supernatural worlds, Braddon's story was based on the medical experiments of her day. (And diverges little from the predilections of Elizabeth of Bathory for the blood of her serving girls to prolong her youth and vitality.)

On the other side of the Atlantic, American writer Mary Wilkins Freeman published the story "Luella Miller" in 1903. Set in Freeman's small-town New England, the beautiful Luella Miller causes the deaths of all who aid her—rather than sucking their blood, Luella sucks the life from her family and friends by having them do all of her housework—shopping, washing and ironing. An interesting early feminist commentary on how draining women's work can be.

In 1976, with the publication of the superb and groundbreaking *Interview with the Vampire*, novelist Anne Rice brought the by-now-clichéd and somewhat moth-eaten European vampire back from the literary dead—and into the twentieth-century (albeit, via the three centuries preceding it). Rice's novel exploded the previous paradigms of the genre; her vampire Lestat was a sensual Other with a strong sense of twentieth-century alienation; she blended the vampire myth with the politics and paradoxes of postmodernist nihilism.

Rice's best-selling account was the first to plausibly explain the evolution of the western vampire and to view the vampire from within, as a being with human emotions and a deep need for connectedness. And while Lestat is wholly male (though pansexual, in traditional vampire fashion), the popular vampire is a wholly female creation.

A few other women have attempted to break into the genre in the nineties, traveling down the path Rice carved out. Jewelle Gomez's award-winning collection *The Gilda Stories* took Rice's thinking-person's vampire in yet another direction, addressing racial issues throughout history and introducing an African-American lesbian vampire with a feminist compunction about killing. Poppy Z. Brite's novel *Lost Souls* added vampirism to the problems of the slacker generation; Ouida Crozier used lesbianism and AIDS as her metaphors in the vampire science-fiction novel *Shadows After Dark*.

Yet despite Rice's phenomenal success and the success of other women now writing in the genre, *Night Bites* is the first collection of vampire stories written only by women. The stories in *Night Bites* stake new ground and expand the boundaries of the genre while utilizing some of the most traditional aspects of the vampire mythos. The idea behind *Night Bites* was to expand the thematic structure of the vampire myth, using the concept of the vampire or vampirism to explore the range of "otherness" within society, all told from the vantage point missing in most anthologies of vampire stories—that of women. The result is a compelling mix of tales, some seemingly traditional, others completely upending everything we have come to believe about vampires and vampirism.

In choosing the stories for this collection, the editorial intent was to have a diverse group of writers and a compendium of stories that were completely different from each other in style, content and form. Thus the writers of this collection cross all lines (save the supernatural). There are stories from every geographical area in the country. Stories by women of a range of races, ethnicities, classes, ages and sexual orientations. These stories were written by young, unpublished writers as well as well-known science-fiction writers. But the majority of the stories are by women known for their "serious" literary fiction—writers who offer a fresh look at an old form; solid, impressive, engaging writing by women with a strong feminist edge—just the thing to turn the genre on its head. To that end, some of the writers here had to be cajoled into penning a vampire tale; others who had always been closet fans of genre fiction were surprised to find how expansive the form could be.

Night Bites explores a feminine and feminist perspective on the genre—the vampire myth as viewed through the female gaze. These stories reflect a distinctly female sensibility, and many of the metaphors derive from that definingly female sphere of experience—the domestic. These tales are also decidedly political—some in subtly nuanced ways, others overtly through social commentary. The diverse topics addressed by the authors range from the seemingly traditional arenas of marriage, motherhood and adolescent longing to hot-button social issues like racism, AIDS, drug and gang wars and global destruction. Each author takes a different approach: In some stories the vampire is complex villain, in others, misunderstood pariah; in still others, vampirism stands as a metaphor for society's manifold ills.

Meredith Suzanne Baird and Judith Katz take a traditional approach to the vampire myth—with slight variations. Both take us into the original geography of the myth, Eastern Europe. In "They Have No Faces," Baird's protagonist tries to save her failing marriage; a trip to Romania turns out to be an uncommon aphrodisiac. Katz follows in the steps of Isaac Bashevis Singer and Cynthia Ozick, blending Jewish myths and traditions with vampire lore to create (perhaps) the first Jewish vampire in the wickedly funny and gruesomely ironic tale "Anita, Polish Vampire, Holds Forth at the Jewish Cafe of the Dead."

Susanna J. Sturgis and Jan Carr grapple with the most draining aspects of mothering: "Sustenance" and "Apologia" both explore what can happen when a mother has too much to do—but with highly divergent climaxes.

Family history forms the foundation for Toni Brown's "Immunity" and Mabel Maney's "Almost the Color of Summer Sky." In these very different tales, two daughters learn about their own particular traditions—one Afrocentric, the other solidly middle American, both chilling.

Adolescent angst and rebellion form the foundation for stories by Lisa D. Williamson and Diane DeKelb-Rittenhouse. In "Best of Friends" and "To Die For," teenage girls search out their hearts' desire but find love and lust become complicated after dark.

Taking familiar, but less familial, paths are Ruthann Robson and Joyce Wagner. "Women's Music" exposes our tabloid obsession with rock stars and asks compelling questions about personal versus public identity. "Bad Company" gives new meaning to the term "biting satire," as conspicuous consumption meets Dracula via a most benign route.

Current social issues are at the heart of the remaining tales. Joanne Dahme takes on domestic violence and the hypocrisy of modern-day Catholicism in "The Vampire's Baby." Linda K. Wright takes a new look at homelessness versus the fast track in "The Last Train," and shows that staying late at the office may not be the wisest career move.

Nikki Baker and Judith M. Redding offer compelling portraits of drug abuse, AIDS, racism and murder in the inner city. "Backlash" features Baker's African-American detective Cassandra Hope tracking a killer on the streets of Chicago. In Redding's "Unexpurgated Notes from a Homicide Case File," the deaths of four young African-American boys baffle African-American detective Teresa Dash and lead her through the ethnically strained neighborhoods of Philadelphia.

Terri de la Peña turns her keen eye to the examination of the sometimes violent intersection of Anglo and Chicano cultures in "Refugio." How society handles global destruction—war, famine, disease—in hot spots like Bosnia, Rwanda and Haiti and how one woman chooses to make a difference is the subject of Victoria A. Brownworth's "Twelfth Night."

Genre fiction often gets short shrift for being "merely" entertaining. The stories in *Night Bites* prove there is a good deal of bite left in the vampire myth and that women writers provide the fresh blood needed to bring a rich tradition back to life.

Victoria A. Brownworth and Judith M. Redding
Philadelphia, Pennsylvania
October 1995

Night Bites

They Have No Faces

Meredith Suzanne Baird

LYDIA KNEW THE TRIP TO ROMANIA was a failure.

How could this have happened? she wondered. She'd planned the trip so carefully for her twentieth wedding anniversary with Art. It was supposed to give their marriage a much-needed infusion of romance and adventure. It was supposed to be exotic. Provocative. Erotic. It was supposed to make things the way they were before.

She'd hoped spending this time together would dispel the feelings of doubt that had plagued her recently. The overwhelming feeling that her life was slipping away from her. Her marriage. Her youth. Her sense of self. Whereas it once had all been so clear to her, she suddenly had become unable to imagine her future. She'd needed to be alone with Art to set everything right again. To reassure herself that her sense of despair was all in her imagination. That nothing had changed.

But it had changed. It was all going wrong. Spinning out of her control.

Lydia and Art sat finishing a late lunch of stuffed cabbage at an outdoor cafe in the bustling marketplace in Bistrita. The weather was pleasant—unseasonably warm if you believed the natives. They warned of the heavy fogs that such warm air created at night. The motorcoach was parked in a lot adjacent to the plaza, undergoing minor repairs before the tour could continue. Lydia found it hard to believe this was the medieval town that launched Bram Stoker's journey into Transylvania. The plaza was noisy, crowded with vendors in quaint costumes. Tourists clustered around display tables jumbled with tacky souvenirs, eagerly snapping up Dracula toothpaste, bat repellent and vampire teething rings.

Lydia and Art picked at their food, avoiding looking at each other. They sat enveloped in a bitter silence born of a terrific fight in their hotel room the night before. They were only four days into the tour, but Art was ready to call it quits. Nothing was right, he complained. The crowds, the tour buses, the Dracula hype. Nothing escaped his criticism.

Lydia had accused him of being too rigid, unable to experience anything new. Infuriated by her accusation, he'd countered with an attack on the gross commercialism of the tour. She'd reluctantly agreed the trip was more touristy than she had expected, but argued that it still could be fun—except, she added, he wasn't capable of making the best of it. He wasn't capable of having fun.

She hadn't dared bring up what was really bothering her. She'd realized in the last few days that somehow—almost overnight—he'd turned into a graying, overweight caricature of the fifty-something executive. He was always planning his next business call, his next flight, his next drink. Especially his next drink.

Before they'd left for Romania, she had been feeling more and more lonely, spending more and more evenings home by herself while he attended late business meetings, meetings that stretched long and improbably into the early morning hours. Now, Lydia noticed the easy intimacy he'd established with the young women in their tour group and the piqued air he'd assume when she attempted to join him or coax him away from each new attachment.

It hadn't always been like this, she thought. Art had once been a wonderful husband. Loving, attentive. They had no children—they had tried for years, then discovered she was infertile—but they had worked through this disappointment and devoted themselves to each other. Their relationship had been fierce with passion, excitement, discovery. Somehow, all of this had vanished over the years. Maybe, Lydia thought, forever. She hadn't shared her feelings with Art. She wasn't sure why.

"Do you wish a guide?"

The voice came from behind her. Art ignored it, drained his glass of beer and signalled the waiter for another. Lydia turned around to see who had spoken.

The tall, young man looked like someone from another century against the backdrop of the colorful baroque homes surrounding the marketplace. He wore the loose white shirt and black trousers favored by so many of the peasants with an easy elegance. He inclined his head, his narrow, alert face framed by long hair so black it seemed to absorb all light from the sun. Lydia guessed he was about thirty—at least ten years younger than she. His smile was beguiling—sharp white teeth flashing against olive skin. He looked like a gypsy prince, she thought. All he needed was a gold earring.

"We're on a tour already," she told him. She expected him to leave—to move on to another table. She was surprised when he continued to smile at her, his eyes lingering on her for a long moment. Lydia's face grew hot. At forty-three, after twenty years of marriage, she didn't usually get this kind of attention. She suddenly remembered what it felt like to feel young and beautiful. Desirable. She blushed and nervously ran her hand through her shoulder-length blonde hair.

His smile widened. He moved over to their table and stood next to Lydia, his hand resting lightly on the back of her chair. She looked up—amused and curious at her own strong reaction to him. His hand caressed the curve of her chairback, lightly brushing across the fine knit of her sweater. Surprised by the unexpected contact, she took a deep breath, inhaling an unfamiliar mixture of something earthy and wild.

"Ah, the tour," he said. "You go to Borgo Pass, Castle Bran, Dracula's grave at Snagov?" His English was lightly accented, nearly correct.

"That's right," said Art dismissively. "Like the lady said, we already have a guide."

"These places are for tourists," the young man continued. He kept looking at Lydia. "A way to take your money. I can show you the *real* vampires. The places they hide. The world they move in."

Lydia didn't want him to go away. She was intrigued by him—by his offer. They'd been approached by natives trying to lure them off the tour, but they had only proffered different versions of the glitzy Dracula hunts. This seemed different. And there was something else. Something indefinable had seemed to pass between them when he'd touched her. She wanted to know more about him, about what he could show her. She gestured for him to sit. Art looked annoyed but didn't say anything. The young man bowed his head gracefully and joined them.

"My name is Ivan," he said.

"Ivan," repeated Lydia, savoring the foreign sound of the unfamiliar name. "I'm Lydia, and this is my husband, Art."

Lydia extended her hand. Ivan reached across the table to meet her. His smooth, elegantly tapered fingers closed over hers. His hand was like ice. Startled, Lydia looked up. Ivan was staring at her. There was an understanding in his eyes, as if he could know her unhappiness through her touch. His fingers began to warm. She tried to pull away, but his grasp tightened to hold her—to absorb her—a moment longer. She felt exposed, unable to hide from the terrible sympathy in his eyes. Suddenly, he released her hand. His features shifted subtly. Once again, he was merely the friendly tour guide.

Shaken, Lydia quickly glanced at Art. She expected him to react to Ivan's strange behavior, but apparently he hadn't noticed their exchange. He had grudgingly shaken Ivan's hand and was now asking him to outline his tour.

Ivan described the villages he would take them to. Names they hadn't heard before—Tirgoviste, Mizil. Mountain retreats, cemeteries. They would meet the people who knew of vampires—who had seen them, killed them. As he spoke, Lydia found herself losing the thread of the conversation. His voice was liquid, hypnotic. She immersed herself in it.

"And just how much is all this going to cost us?" Art asked.

Lydia snapped back to attention. She looked over at Art. He was leaning across the table, waiting for Ivan's answer. He sounded interested in spite of himself.

"Nothing," replied Ivan. "Nothing if I don't deliver all that I describe and maybe more. If you are pleased with the tour, then you can decide what to pay me. I'm sure you'll be more than generous."

Art leaned back, looking skeptical, but Lydia jumped on it. She had seen his flash of curiosity. Maybe they could salvage this trip—and their marriage—after all. She had to convince him, coerce him, if necessary. She felt compelled to join this stranger who so casually offered a journey into the mysteries of the real vampire culture. To experience its fears, learn its secrets.

"This is our chance, Art," she said excitedly. "Exactly what you said you wanted last night." She held up her hand, counting off the advantages on her fingers. "No tourists. No gift shops. No hype. No money if we don't like it. We can ditch the tour and go on a real adventure. Why don't we try it for a few days? We can always catch up with the group if it doesn't work out."

Art looked chagrined. Lydia knew his mind was racing to find a way out of the trap he'd laid for himself with his complaints about the relentless commercialism of the tour. She knew he really didn't want to take any risks. She was counting on his pride to force him into accepting this daring change in plans. He hesitated a few moments, thinking. Finally, a look of defeat came over his face.

"I'm in," he said reluctantly. "This better be everything you described." He looked straight at Ivan.

"It will be," Ivan promised. He smiled at Lydia. She looked at him closely, but there was no trace of the intimate knowledge she thought she'd seen a few minutes before. He simply looked pleased—as pleased as she was to be going on this new adventure. Relieved, she felt as if they were sharing a huge secret, something wonderful. She smiled back.

∾

Lydia hurried over to the parking area to tell Alexander, their tour guide, about their change in plans. He was busy trying to correct the problem with the engine on the motorcoach and barely looked up as he responded to her request. Yes, yes, it happened all the time. They could meet up with the tour again anywhere along the route. If they chose to continue on their own, they had their plane tickets for their return. She could ask Gregor, his assistant, for their bags.

Lydia thanked him and went over to Gregor, a burly dark-eyed student from the University of Bucharest. He smiled, unlatched the luggage compartment and began searching for their bags.

"One of the locals got to you, eh?" he said. "Happens at least once a tour. Which one are you hooking up with?"

"His name is Ivan," Lydia replied. "He's over there at the outdoor cafe with my husband."

She turned and pointed. Gregor straightened up, a bag in each hand, and looked over at Art and Ivan.

"I haven't seen him around before," he said with a slight frown. "Do you want me to check him out?"

Before Lydia could reply, Alexander called Gregor to come help with the motor.

Gregor smiled apologetically at Lydia.

"If you can wait just a moment," he said as he set down her bags, "I will come over and meet this new guide of yours."

"Thank you for your concern, Gregor, but we'll be just fine. We're leaving right away. I hope to see you again before the end of the tour."

Lydia picked up their bags and crossed the square to rejoin Art and Ivan. She knew it would be more prudent to let Gregor check out Ivan, but she didn't care. She felt reckless, free, ready for anything.

Lydia could barely see through the fog. They'd left Bistrita hours before in Ivan's old Volvo. Art sat next to Ivan in the front passenger seat. They drove along quickly, headlights stabbing through the heavy mist. Ivan seemed to know the way, expertly negotiating the twists and turns of the mountain road he'd chosen. Lydia had no idea where they were going, only that they were climbing. The air had grown chillier with their ascent and, now that the sun was gone, had turned cold. She pulled her jacket closer around her neck and peered out the car window.

The landscape—what she could see of it—was thickly forested. The dense fog seemed to creep out from between the trees and rocks lining the road, reaching across their path like skeletal fingers. Lydia shuddered and turned her attention back to the conversation in the front seat.

Even Art seemed to have come under Ivan's spell. He chatted with Ivan amiably during the drive, and showed increasing interest in this unexpected sidetrip. Earlier, he'd pored over an historical map Ivan had given him and was now eagerly questioning him about the ancient legends of the remote mountain regions they were entering. Lydia was encouraged by his enthusiasm, one of the things she'd always loved about him. She began to feel hopeful about the trip. About the possibility that her marriage might survive.

Then she saw it. Out the window, a shadowy figure by the side of the road. The headlights caught it briefly. It threw up its arms, as if to ward off the light. She quickly shifted closer to the window, wiped off the condensation with her glove, looked again. Nothing. The figure had vanished. She smiled ruefully and leaned back in her seat. This trip is really getting to me, she thought as she closed her eyes. I'm beginning to see things.

Suddenly the car stopped.

"We are here."

The voice. There was something in Ivan's voice that Art would never hear. Could never understand. Something deep. Slightly wicked. Lydia knew he was talking only to her. She looked up to find Ivan staring at her in the rearview mirror. She forgot about the figure in the roadway.

"They have no faces—these creatures of the night."

Ivan slammed the bolt closed on the window shutter as if to emphasize his mysterious words. The sudden noise made them jump. Lydia shivered deliciously, enjoying the brief scare. Art looked irritated and extended his glass for his third refill. Lydia recognized Art's sudden mood change. He was getting drunk.

She watched Ivan cross the rough plank flooring of the ancient cottage. He carried a dark bottle of peach schnapps, a nameless local brand. His walk was liquid, as if he didn't touch the earth when he moved. He glanced over at her and winked. Lydia looked away, embarrassed to be caught staring, yet delighted by the mild flirtation.

She smiled and shook her head when Ivan proffered the bottle. He deftly refilled Art's glass, set the bottle down on the table next to him and walked over to throw more wood onto the roaring fire. Lydia could feel the heat brushing her face as she looked around the candle-lit room. She felt as if she'd landed in the middle of a stage set for a 1930s horror movie.

The small cottage reeked of garlic. Ivan had strung ropes of it across all the windows and doors. Crucifixes covered the tables and mantle. Fragments of white cloth, each one sewn with dozens of crosses and scraps of religious relics, were tacked over the shuttered windows. Bits of straw, tied in complicated knots, were scattered around the room. The effect was almost theatrically amusing, yet she couldn't shake a slight sense of uneasiness. As soon as they had entered the cottage and bolted the front door, Ivan had secured the house—every surface and opening—with these talismans. His manner was matter-of-fact. This was no act for their benefit. She knew this was his usual evening routine.

She took a small sip of her half-finished drink, savoring the subtle infusion of warmth.

"What do you mean, 'they have no faces,' Ivan?" she asked. "I've always heard that vampires look like everyone else—that they stop aging the instant they are bitten."

"That's a neat trick," said Art with a nasty laugh. "We should have taken this trip ten years ago and introduced you to the local bloodsucker."

Lydia gasped. Her face stung as if he'd slapped her. He wasn't usually this blatantly vicious. Never in front of others. It was the alcohol talking, she thought. Not him. But it didn't help the humiliation or the pain. She sat up straighter, hugging her arms across her chest.

Ivan looked up from the fire.

"I would not make fun of things you do not understand," he said.

"And what would that be?" Art said. His voice was a drunken challenge.

Ivan straightened up. His black hair fell loose to his shoulders. The fire leaped and swirled behind him, throwing long shadows across the room.

"In our country we value a woman of certain years. Her blood—her life—flows rich with memories and emotions. The same is true of the Old Ones—the ones you call names. They have lived for centuries in grace and harmony with their surroundings. They are the repositories of wisdom, the aristocracy. They choose who will join them, who will live forever. They have nothing to do with your foolish stories. You do both your wife and the Old Ones dishonor. That is not a good thing."

Lydia couldn't believe what she was hearing. She braced for the explosion, but Art was drunker than she thought. He ignored Ivan completely, fumbling for the bottle of schnapps. He managed to pour half a glass before it fell, shattering against the table and cutting his hand. The remaining liquor, mixed with his blood, spilled across the tabletop and onto the floor. He slumped down in the chair, passed out.

Lydia jumped up. She looked around for a cloth, anything she could use to stop the bleeding from the ragged gash. Ivan crossed the room, staring at the blood that continued to drip from Art's hand.

"Wait," said Ivan. He gestured for Lydia to stand back. Pulling the white shirt from his waistband, he tore off a narrow strip of cloth and began wrapping the wound. "I will attend to this. In this land—in these mountains—it is dangerous to allow another's blood to touch you. This is bad blood, a bad soul."

"I'm sorry," she said to Ivan. She kept her head down to hide her tears. "He's only like this when he's drunk."

She recognized the lie the minute she told it. Alcohol may have exaggerated his actions, but thoughtless behavior and cruel remarks had become a daily fixture in her life with Art. Lydia realized she'd been holding on to the memory of who Art had been, not the person he had become. She'd been holding on to the memory of a marriage that had ended. Of a world that had fallen away.

Ivan reached out and touched her face where the tears glistened against her pale skin.

"All will be well," he said.

He picked Art up and carried him into the bedroom.

Lydia was numb. Drained of all emotion. She sank down onto the heavy sheepskin rug in front of the fireplace and rested her head against her knees, grateful for the solace of the fire.

"It is finished."

Lydia raised her head at the sound of his voice. Ivan had returned to the room and stood next to her in front of the fire.

"Will he be all right?" she asked.

Ivan nodded.

"The spirits always have a strong effect the first time," he said. "He will sleep like the dead tonight."

"Of course," Lydia said softly. "Why should tonight be any different?" She sighed and pushed her hair away from her face.

"Do you wish to go to bed?" he asked.

Lydia's eyes moved to the doorway of the bedroom. Ivan followed her gaze and pointed to a door she hadn't noticed hidden in the corner next to the fireplace.

"There's another room," he said. "Another bed. Do you wish to sleep?"

Lydia shook her head wearily.

"No," she said. "I just want to sit here for a while."

"May I join you?"

"Please," she said and moved to make room for him on the rug.

She didn't want to be alone. There was going to be plenty of time for that in the future. Right now she needed the comfort of another human being, even a stranger. She watched him as he sank down onto the soft fur, his movements strangely graceful for such a tall man. He handed her the glass of schnapps she'd half finished. Impulsively, she pressed her fingers against his as she took the glass from him.

"Thank you for what you said," she said.

"You are a beautiful woman," he replied. "Strong with life. Curiosity. Knowledge. You should be with someone who respects you." He leaned over and kissed her fingertips.

Lydia pulled her hand away, fingers burning at the imprint of his lips. Her heart was pounding. She wasn't ready, or able, to acknowledge the feelings he was awakening in her. She pressed her hand to her mouth as she struggled to regain control.

Ivan seemed to sense her confusion. He shifted away from her. Their bodies were close, but not touching. Lydia relaxed. She wanted to know more about Ivan, about the world in which he traveled. The words he'd used to defend her from Art's drunken attack haunted her.

"Tell me about the Old Ones," she said, suddenly nervous.

He turned toward her. The firelight played over his face, changing the shape of his high cheekbones and forehead.

"What do you wish to know?" he replied.

"Are they like other vampires? Can they see themselves in a mirror? Enter without an invitation? Tolerate daylight and garlic?" She gestured around the room at the bizarre charms guarding the doorways and windows. "Are they evil?"

Ivan smiled at her and took a swallow of his drink.

"They are not evil," he said. "They are subject to the rules of the undead, but they live to preserve what fragile peace and beauty that may be left in the world. Their only fault, if they have one, is that they require blood to exist."

Something still wasn't right. Then, she remembered.

"You said they have no faces."

"Only when the hunger is upon them. Their faces—their features—shift, blur, disappear as the fierce craving for blood commands their bodies. Some say it is the faces of their victims fighting to leave. Only their eyes and mouths remain—for feeding. Once they're satisfied, their faces return to normal. They can move among people undetected—until the next time."

"But you said they choose who will join them. Who are the victims caught in their bodies?" Lydia wasn't sure she believed that any of what he had told her was more than myth, storytelling. And yet, he made it all seem so real, so . . . unnerving.

Ivan turned his attention back to the fire. He lay another log at the edge of the flames and waited for it to flare up before he answered her question.

"They share their blood with the chosen ones—the ones who will walk with them. The others are drained of their blood, prevented from ever roaming the earth again in any form. The Old Ones will not allow anyone they perceive as evil or even worthless to continue."

Lydia took a sip of her drink. Ivan had brought out another bottle of schnapps and refilled her glass. She had no idea how much she'd had. She didn't feel drunk, just removed from her own life, caught up in the drama of Ivan's tale. She wanted him to continue talking. As long as he talked, she could disconnect from reality, immerse herself in the legend, in his voice. Forget the other voices in her head.

"How have they managed to stay undetected all this time?" she asked.

"There are those who have dedicated their lives to helping them," Ivan replied. His eyes were fixed on the fire, watching the flames leap up the chimney.

"How do you know about them?"

"These stories have been told to me since I was a small child," he said. He turned to face her. "According to family legend, my ancestors are among the Old Ones."

Lydia smiled and lay back on the rug. The story was marvelous. Superior beings walking the earth in search of beauty and harmony. Striking down evil in their path.

"It's a beautiful legend," she said. "Like one of the fairy tales I dreamed of living as a child." She was no longer nervous, no longer afraid.

"Yes," he agreed. "It's a wondrous tale."

Suddenly, Ivan's arms were around Lydia, pulling her close. His loose shirt had opened at the neck. She could see the smooth muscles of his naked chest, the plain gold cross that rested against his heart. A strange birthmark or tattoo on his neck caught her eye. Then his mouth closed over hers.

The kiss took her breath away. Her senses were reeling, but she had no anchor to hold on to, nothing to stop her from giving in to her intense yearning. He was above her, the weight of his body pressing urgently into her own. Helpless, she stared up at him, seeing only his mouth and the dark desire burning in his eyes. Her body came alive, arching against him as his long fingers slowly unbuttoned and then pushed the sweater from her neck and shoulders.

Lydia wanted him, but the last sane part of her said it couldn't be in the main room. She managed to move out from under him and struggle to her feet.

"Not here," she whispered and opened the door to the second bedroom. It was dark, lit only by a single candle Ivan must have set on a table on the far side of the room. Lydia crossed over to the bed and sat down. She turned, expecting Ivan to be next to her. He stood in the doorway, his silhouette etched by the light of the fire in the room behind him. She couldn't see his face. She held out her hand to him.

"Are you inviting me in?" he asked.

"Yes," she said.

Lydia was asleep, a small smile curving her lips. Her hair, damp and tangled, curled against her forehead.

She looks so young, Ivan thought as he stroked her cheek. Sleep, like death, so often restores the youth that life steals away.

"I promise," he whispered, "you will be lovely forever."

Ivan pulled the covers away from her neck and breast. He stared, mesmerized by the translucent whiteness of her skin, the delicate flutter of the blood moving beneath. He leaned over and pressed his lips to the heat of her pulse. Lydia gasped, suddenly awake, and pulled him to her.

The shards of glass on the table next to Art's chair glittered in the firelight. The mix of blood and alcohol had dried into an ugly red stain. Ivan began cleaning up the blood and broken glass, carefully checking the floor for spatters of blood that might have dripped from Art's hand when he'd carried him into the bedroom. There were none that he could see, but he compulsively rubbed a wet cloth over the path to the closed door of the main bedroom. At last, Ivan was satisfied that he'd cleansed the room of blood. He stripped the windows and doors of the ropes of garlic and threw them into his bag, along with the crucifixes and other charms. His work was done now. He sat down to wait.

The knock came a few minutes later. Soft. Not loud enough to wake even the lightest sleeper.

Ivan leaped up and hurried to open the door. The night mist swirled in, eddying around his feet. Two cloaked figures stood before him. The Old Ones. The crucifix Ivan wore grew hot, as it always did when they were near. He placed a hand over it, drawing comfort from its warmth. He hesitated for a moment, thinking of the woman lying asleep in the next room. The Old Ones shifted impatiently, waiting for the invitation that would allow them to cross the threshold.

He stared at them. At their eyes and mouths, the only features that remained in their dissolving faces. Their eyes burned into him. He had no choice.

"Enter," Ivan said.

They drifted past him in a rush of cold, damp air. Ivan knew there wasn't much time left, that his window of safety depended on getting out as quickly as possible. He pulled on his cloak and picked up his bag. Repelled by the contents of the case, they drew away from him.

Their faces shifted, melting into countless shapes. Ivan could never tell their sex when they were seized by the hunger. Their desire washed over him, the sickening craving that threatened to pull him into their eternal lives. He knew one day —when they no longer needed him—he would be the feast. He looked away.

"There are two this time," he said. "A man and a woman."

They nodded, faces glowing brighter with their terrible need. They moved toward the inner rooms. Ivan watched them, knowing what would happen next. He pictured Lydia's face against the pillow. Her neck, exposed—defenseless. For the first time, he was sickened by the fate to which he'd led her and all the others. He'd never asked the Old Ones for anything before. Maybe, this one time, they would let her go.

"Wait," he said.

But they kept moving.

Ivan had to break their concentration, their focus on what waited for them. There was only one way. He strode toward them and threw down the bag filled with garlic and crucifixes. The Old Ones jerked back as if burned, hissing at the abominations blocking their path. Furious, they swung around to face him, eyes blazing out of amorphous flesh. The frenzied heat of their blood-lust seized him. Suddenly dizzy, Ivan staggered. His vision blurred—fragmented, sharpened. All he could see was their eyes, their mouths. They became his world, his universe. Fear drained from his body. His will to resist vanished. Now, Ivan thought as he moved toward them, now is the time to join my family.

"Forgive me," he said and held out his hands in supplication.

The Old Ones swayed toward him. Ivan welcomed the closeness, craved the embrace that would make him immortal. He shivered when he felt the hands on his shoulders and then cried out when they pushed him to the floor. He looked up. They were staring at him as before. Their craving was there, but back under control. It had nothing to do with him. He was free.

They waited.

Shaken, Ivan passed his hand over his sweat-soaked forehead. He felt empty. They would not take him. It was not his time. The Old Ones held dominion now. There was nothing left for him to do here, no one he could save. He stood up and faced them.

"The woman," he said.

They nodded briefly.

"Be kind to her."

"The man?" The voice was hollow—dead. It came from another time.

Ivan shrugged. He pulled his bag from their path, crossed the room and stepped through the open doorway into the mist. He turned back. They hadn't moved. He could barely make out their dark figures in the flickering light of the dying fire.

"Savage him."

The door began to swing closed. Ivan stopped it with his hand.

"Next time?" he asked.

"She will be with us."

Ivan let go of the door, heard the latch fall into place. He smiled and disappeared into the night.

Anita, Polish Vampire, Holds Forth at the Jewish Cafe of the Dead

Judith Katz

T WAS RAINING IN KRAKÓW WHEN I arrived, the ride from the station into Kazimierz district treacherous, for the streets were wet and slick, and even the *droshky* driver for whom these streets were daily bread and butter seemed to lose his grip from time to time as he reined back his horses against the hill. It poured as I have only seen it pour in Kraków, the rain falling in long, cold drops, so loud that one could barely hear the *clop clop* of hooves against cobblestone, and there was no one, not even an ecstatic Hassid, to be seen when we at last arrived in the Jewish part of town.

The little carriage stopped in front of my hotel, and I gathered my skirts about me when the driver fetched me from the cab. He held an umbrella in one hand, my carpetbag in the other, and there was something oddly familiar in the way he took the few *groschen* extra I handed him as he opened the door into the tiny lobby. An elderly woman sat at the desk and rang for her daughter, who showed me straightaway to my room. I changed out of my wet things and was just about to settle into a hot bath when the innkeeper's daughter knocked again with a pot of tea and a sealed letter. I thanked her and handed her some coins, for I had been expecting the letter, but not the tea.

I took both to the tub. The tea was strong and sweet, the letter short, as it had been when I dreamed of it one month before: a simple set of directives in a well-educated hand. It chilled me a bit, even in the hot bath. I pulled myself from the tub, climbed into my bed and slept my long train ride away.

In the morning, as it was still raining, I took breakfast in my little room. I made notes in my diary as to the nature of my journey, then made a list of what I was to do. This completed, I wrote letters to my skeptical colleagues until noon, when I wrapped myself up for a walk. I left all but one letter with the innkeeper to post and then asked for the loan of an umbrella. The old woman handed me an ancient one, which she told me she kept for just such purposes. "It was left long ago by a young lady such as yourself," she told me. "It's old, but you will see, it keeps the rain off good as new." So armed, I made my way to the Vistula and remained reasonably dry as I wandered along its banks, nearly to the castle. Then I doubled back to Kazimierz and made my way to the Remuh cemetery. This was years, of course, (but not many) before the Germans came and used these grave markers for paving stones. They were all still intact, so beautifully carved, some with deer jumping blissfully across their tops, some with two hands reaching straight up to heaven.

I followed the instructions in last night's note to the letter, and sure enough, I found the marker I had been searching for all these years. In bold Hebrew letters I read her name: ANITA LIPSKY. The legendary Anita, I whispered, as I drew my last note from inside my coat. This I placed on her marker and secured beneath a fist-sized stone. Almost immediately the ink began to bleed in the rain. I touched my gloved fingers to my lips and then against the stone. "Tonight," I whispered in Yiddish and then went along my way.

❧

That evening the innkeeper prepared lovely foods for me, the likes of which I had not eaten since I left to study in England. Before me were laid cabbage rolls and borscht, *kreplach* and roasted potatoes, yet even these delicious morsels could not raise my hunger. To be polite I took small bites of everything, but mostly I sat with the old woman and her daughter and drank the strong black tea they made at my request.

At nine-thirty, I retired to my room and made further notes in my diary. I took out the ancient photograph I carried with me. Even in its faded state, one could plainly see how beautiful she was, this Anita, and how mysterious. If all went well and my dreams had not lied to me, if my purpose had remained secret and last night's letter was not a hoax, then tonight at last my search would be over. I could prove once and for all her existence to the rest of the world, or at least to my skeptical colleagues at the university.

At a quarter to eleven I bundled up and took my borrowed umbrella to the street outside the inn. What luck! Just as last night's note had promised, a droshky was waiting for me, its driver smoking by the carriage door. He tipped his hat to me, and I saw it was the same man who had brought me from the station the night before. "*Paniq* Sadowsky?" he asked.

"I am," I answered. "You know where to take me?"

He nodded.

"Very good then." I gave him my hand, and he helped me into the cab. His hand was icy to the touch, but then, he had been waiting for me for who knew how long. He wrapped an extra blanket around me and then closed the door. The rain had stopped at last, but now there was fog everywhere in Kraków. Yet this time the driver's hands were firm upon the reins, and all the long way I had nothing to worry about but what was to come.

At a minute before midnight, I was deposited safely outside a restaurant door. I reached into my satchel with the intention of paying my fare and a few *zloty* extra for good measure, but he would have none of it. "There's no money necessary, miss. It's already paid for."

"By whom, may I ask?"

"In there." He pointed with his thumb to the restaurant. "The first trip is always complimentary."

"Come back in an hour," I wanted to tell him. But when I looked up he was gone.

A dust-covered valet opened the door for me, and I found myself at last in Poland's best-kept secret, the Jewish Cafe of the Dead. I had spent my entire twenties reading about it, accounts in Polish and Yiddish, Russian and Hebrew, by farmers and tradespeople who swore it existed, and rabbis and scholars who insisted it did not. Yet here it was, that legendary place that existed not only in my imagination but in hard, cold reality, far beyond the Kraków city limits. It sat like a villa facing the river, but true to the legend, only those invited were allowed to see it. If the driver of my droshky had not brought me here, who knows how long I might have wandered the back roads of the Kraków villages, how many months I might have walked in circles through the forest and along the riverbanks?

I knew the journey I was about to embark upon might change my life forever. And yet, I reminded myself that, in the name of scientific research, no matter what happened, I must at all times appear to be nonchalant and unsurprised. Even so, when I went to check my coat and borrowed umbrella, I must admit I was taken aback when the girl who took them from me was to all appearances a skeleton. The ball gown she wore was faded and blue, and as far as a bony skull can smile, she smiled at me and handed me a worn wooden square on which was written no number at all. I thanked her and kept my composure just long enough to keep her from taking my satchel, for here were my notebooks and pens, and I must be certain to document every minute of this night.

A maitre d' in a moldering tuxedo made his wobbly way toward me. He clicked his heels together and nodded. "This way, miss," he told me, then spun around toward the dining room. Together we made our way under cobwebs, through the dingy bar and into a dining room where an ancient trio played chamber music with nearly stringless violins on a broken-down stage. There was a candelabrum on each table, but still it took me an eternity to get used to the dim light. And then the maitre d' swept open his decrepit arms, and there she was before us: Anita, alone at a well-appointed table here in the Jewish Cafe of the Dead, more beautiful than that old and faded photograph, more gorgeous than I had dreamed her. Her wispy hair was tied in a loose knot atop her head, and her long neck was naked but for a cameo on a black ribbon. Her low-cut satin dress was red and, I must admit to my pleasure, revealed every inch of her lovely cleavage. She wore black fingerless gloves, which allowed me to see not only her bright red nails (which matched so well her lips), but also her marvelously long fingers, which were just now curved around a tarnished silver knife and fork. And just above her left breast was a heart-shaped red mark, barely discernible in the candlelight, and yet, impossible for me to ignore.

Anita's face was pale, pale; her eyes were yellow. And one could not help but notice her teeth, so crooked and gray, but for two, which were sharp and glinted white in the candlelight.

How well-laid her table was, even in that gruesome place. Yes, even here, the tablecloth was white, and on it a single red candle burned in a polished silver stick. She appeared to be in some kind of trance, tapping her cutlery to the strange music the trio was playing. Then all at once she seemed to see me. Ah, that Anita! Immediately she put down her cutlery and motioned to the chair opposite, just as she had in my dream.

"Well, here you are, my darling, at last, at last! I was beginning to think you weren't coming. I'm embarrassed to say I ordered without you!" She gestured to the chair again. "*Shev yashav, cum zitzen*—sit down!" Before I even had the chair pulled out she was calling, "*Proszę, Pana!* Waiter! Some wine for my friend!" She looked at me and winked. "Your trip from England, I trust it was fine?"

I nodded.

"And that little dive hotel where you stay in Kazimierz, is it to your satisfaction?"

"It's far from a dive—" I started to tell her, but she waved me away.

"No matter, dive, *schmive*, a hotel where a woman feels safe on her own is a rare thing these days. I seem to remember the beds are quite soft there."

"Very soft," I said.

Anita winked at me again. "That's all that counts." Then, "*Pana!*" she shrieked, and out of nowhere the waiter appeared. Who knew where he had come from, how old he was, how long he'd been there. His white hair flew in every direction, his vest had soup stains everywhere, and around his waist was an apron smeared with dull red splotches. Absently he filled our glasses with a brilliant substance that frightened me with its redness.

My hostess took a long, languorous sip. She licked her lips and drank again. Then she looked across the table at my glass, untouched. "Ah!" she slapped her head, "How barbaric of me. Of course we need a little toast!" She lifted her glass, gestured to me to lift mine, which I did reluctantly. Then Anita stood and said with great charm (and it seemed to me not a little restraint), "To the lovely Miss Professor Sadowsky. *L'chiam!* To your health!"

"L'chiam," I offered back and slowly sipped my wine.

"It's good, isn't it? You won't believe this, no one does, but this excellent wine is domestic! From Gdansk! Like you, I thought such wines could be obtained only in Paris or Spain . . . but for those one has to pay an arm and a leg, which just at this moment I am no condition to do . . ." She drained her glass and set it sharply on the table. "I must have more! *Pana!*"

In an instant the waiter was at our table. He poured Anita a new glass. He offered to top mine off, but I shook my head. Then he wiped the rim of the bottle with his finger and offered those last drops to Anita. I watched as she considered for a second and then waved the man away. "No, no, you go ahead."

The waiter sucked his finger but lacked Anita's enthusiasm.

"Magnificent, no?" she asked him.

"It's very good, madame," he said.

Anita grabbed him by his grimy tie. "It's better than good, it's magnificent . . . magnificent, do you hear me? And where is my dinner?"

"Just here," announced the waiter, who snapped his fingers and brought forth a large white plate on which sat a battered silver cover. "*Voila!*" he shouted, then lay down the plate and removed the cover all in one move.

And here before Anita it sat—what I can tell you now quite calmly (although to be quite honest, it shocked me then) was a bloody human heart. It was the exact color of the wine in our crystal goblets, and I am not certain, but for an instant I was convinced it was beating still. Anita's yellow eyes became wide, and for a minute she seemed absolutely alone with her dinner. She stabbed her silver fork into the bloody thing with one hand and cut into it brutally with the knife, which she was strangling in the other. She was about to take a huge bite, might even have swallowed that steaming red heart whole, had she not noticed me again as I sat there staring. "How rude of me, my dear, you travel all this way to meet me, and I begin without you. Shall we have our friend the waiter bring another plate?"

I shook my head. "I'm fine," I said, though I felt far from it.

She raised an eyebrow. "You're certain? Because the food here is quite marvelous. Some say the very best this side of Warsaw. This heart here," she pointed to her plate with impatience and love mixed as one, "this heart is a pure, kosher heart. Not mine, of course..." She tapped it with her fork. "I'm certain it's quite good." Anita ran a finger over the heart, stuck the piece already on her fork in her mouth, sucked long and loudly and then smacked her lips. "Yes, this is an excellent kosher heart. Absolutely delicious. Almost impossible to come by in Poland these days. One literally has to find oneself in New York or South America to have a Jewish heart like this!"

"Where did it come from, then?" I ventured.

"Trolley accident in Buenos Aires, I think. Are you certain we shouldn't have the waiter bring another plate?" She lifted her eyebrows again. Was it a dare? Was it seduction? "Well, drink your wine and see if it whets your appetite." With that Anita dug in a second time with her knife and fork, cut off a chunk of the heart and began to chew ecstatically. Blood trickled down her chin. Carelessly she wiped it away with the back of her hand and then licked the blood from there. "Dear friend, I insist! You absolutely must try this! No, really, we must have the waiter bring a second plate—a second heart—no?

"Ah." Anita took another ecstatic bite, followed it with a joyful gulp of wine, smacked her lips lavishly. "My darling," she purred, "you've no idea what you are missing! Ah! Marvelous! Marvelous! Last chance for a taste of this marvelous heart!" She raised her eyes to me expectantly. "Very well then!" And in one huge bite she greedily gobbled down the remains. She was lost in her own reverie now; I might as well not have even been there. The waiter appeared and took her plate, and then, almost demurely, she said to him without raising her eyes, "*Proszę*, Pana ... bring me another?"

"Straightaway, madame," he told her with a little bow, and then he disappeared.

Anita stared after him blankly. "In good time he means ... a heart like this, it's very hard to come by. Sometimes a person waits for years ... centuries ... I could go out and try to find one for myself, but then, I've decided to have a little treat. Let another do the hunting for a change ... isn't that what one pays for, after all?" She chuckled then and sipped her wine. She did it almost delicately. She was about to lift her hand and call for the waiter when she stopped herself. "No," she decisively pushed her glass away. "I'll smoke instead." From out of nowhere she procured a tarnished cigarette case and then a dainty, although by no means tiny, black cigar. She smiled and offered the case to me. I shook my head.

"No? *Panią* Professor Sadowsky, have you no vices at all? Ah well, we'll see about that later. Have you by any chance a light?"

"I'm sorry to disappoint, madame, but no."

"No matter." With that Anita snapped her fingers, and the little case disappeared. "Proszę, Pana!"

Our waiter appeared. "Yes, madame!"

"Light my cigar."

The old man dutifully snapped his fingers, and from their tips a flame appeared. He touched it gently to Anita's cigar.

"*Dziękuję,*" she told him.

"*Proszę bardzo,*" he answered. "Your second heart should be here momentarily, madame. Our people are just now plundering the scene of a Swiss avalanche where we are told the Baron von Rothschild was entertaining a party of friends." He clicked his heels and walked away.

"The Baron von Rothschild, *hoo ha,*" Anita said as she smoked. She tried to remain cordial, but I could see she was impatient. She was too polite. She looked about her nervously, it seemed to me, and then pulled in a breath of smoke and forced another smile. But her stare lingered at my throat, and all at once I could see it—she was riveted by desire: Her yellow eyes became wide and hypnotic; her incisors, long. In that moment they glistened with saliva, and her fingers opened out slowly as if to grab me by the neck. Then, in another instant, she pulled herself back and smiled at me as if we were the best of old friends. But I could still see that wolfish glint in her eye, the trace of saliva on her teeth. I must tell you, it excited me.

"Why, Professor Sadowsky, you've brought along your notebook. Put it away."

"But I was promised an interview—"

"Did I promise? I thought you wanted to meet me for myself."

I was embarrassed then, for in truth, just at that moment I was using my diary as a shield. Indeed, I had come to Poland to hear Anita's stories of the vampire life. But right now, here in the Jewish Cafe of the Dead, with the gorgeous Anita before me, I cared very little for historical facts and scholarly documentation. I wanted Anita for myself, and although I felt the danger, I hardly cared.

She saved me herself, though, by humoring me. "All right. I'll tell a sad story . . ." Anita leaned back in her chair. The room transformed around her. "Chelmnicki and his boys came through here a dozen years ago. Oh yes, it was a terrible thing . . . blood and feathers everywhere . . . broke up my sister's wedding party in this very cafe, as a matter of fact. I was the maid of honor . . . those Cossacks actually rode in through the door, sabers flashing, horse shit everywhere. First they smashed up the furniture, and then they started working on us. My sister, her spanking new husband, everybody's parents . . . sliced to ribbons, run through like stuck pigs . . . and nobody stopped them. Me they cornered right over there, one skinny-as-a-rail Polack with ham hands and one guy young enough to be his son. I don't even want to tell you what they did to me. Let's just say that when it was over the only thing still attached to me was my head, and that just barely. Why do you think I wear this little cameo around my neck? If I take it off, I'm not responsible for what happens. Write that down in your notebook, why don't you." She reached for my wine glass. "Do you mind? I'm feeling rather dry."

"Not at all," I said, although at that moment I became extremely thirsty.

"To us," she winked and knocked the wine back. Some of it dribbled down her chin, but she didn't bother to wipe it off, even with the palm of her hand. "They treated all the women and the little girls the same, you know. I don't know what they did to the men—I was too busy screaming and scratching their eyes out—but I know it wasn't pretty. The whole village was here, all of us wiped out in less than an hour. We tried to stop them, we yelled at them, we waved our forks at them and ran at them with our knives, but they weren't about to let a few happy Jews with steak knives stop them... When they were done, that was the end of our little village.

"There were no survivors ... wait, there was one ... a crabby old widow who was invited to the wedding but refused to come. She had had a fight with my brother-in-law about chickens, and she swore she'd never dance at his wedding, even if it was destined to be the best party in all of Europe. But then, spite paid off for her, didn't it? Except I think she was the only one left to bury us ... and I'm not sure she got to all of us ... in fact, that couple over there?" She pointed across the room, and sure enough, at a little round table there was a couple in blood-spattered party clothes leaning into each other and holding hands. Anita looked at me knowingly. "They've been that way since our very waiter brought in the matzo ball soup for the wedding dinner thirteen years ago. Don't pity them. They're very happy." She sighed a deep vampiric sigh, drew deeply on her little cigar. "One has to envy them..." Anita looked about the cafe, suddenly anxious. "Where is that waiter? Proszę, Pana! I'm starving!" Out of breath and out of nowhere our waiter appeared, but alas, for poor Anita, he was empty-handed. "Proszę, Pana—gdzie są serce? Where is that heart?"

The waiter lowered his head and said something so quietly I could hardly hear him. Anita also lowered her head and whispered back to him. The waiter shrugged and shook his head. And then Anita grabbed him by his collar. "Macht es gich! Ich bin hungerik!" After which our waiter quickly spun away and disappeared. Anita leaned into me and told me confidentially, "I hate to speak to them in Yiddish the way things are these days, even in a place like this, because it upsets people. They hate to be reminded of their past. But in an emergency, trust me, it's the only way to get things done. I happen to think Polish is a hateful language. And the way they speak it, always in a whisper . . . it isn't natural to whisper. I am a native Yiddish speaker, and Yiddish, as you know, one yells. One bangs the table with a fist, and no one is upset or offended. The Jew slams the table and asks frankly and with much emotion, 'Where is my heart?' The Pole, on the other hand, is always averting the eyes and whispering, 'I'm sure I don't know.' For such a blood-soaked people they certainly like to act polite . . . Not me. Ask for what you want, that's my motto."

Anita looked at me, and her eyes began to spin a bit; she just barely began to reach out to me, but then pulled her hand back and bit her finger. She sighed. "You know," she said sadly, "I could never really find my place after that pogrom. Sadly, I began to develop odd appetites— odd by your standards, I mean, you younger generation. By my own *vampirishke* standards they are quite natural. I mean, what does a Jew do all day long but eat her heart out? You must admit, it's the tastiest of morsels. You don't agree? Oh, yes, the heart is the tastiest morsel, no matter what the nationality. But the Jewish heart—the kosher heart— this is the most lovely delicacy of all. Think of it—just the size of the Jewish heart alone! It's an established fact, the unafflicted Jewish heart is enormous . . . well, all right, there are some Jews whose hearts are tight and tiny. But typically—I mean, the Jew like you and like me—the heart looks like this"—Anita balled her hand into a fist and made it throb—"it's bigger than this! And for the typical Jew—the Jew like you or me—the heart is more than just a muscle—it's an intellectual organ, an emotional organ! It loves the complicated violin solo by Paganini and the simple *kazatzke* tune all at once!" She lowered her eyes and stared frankly at my breasts. "You have a lovely heart, Panią Sadowsky. I can sense it."

I had to work very hard just then to keep from throwing myself across the table at her, for in that moment Anita's eyes began to glaze, then focus almost hypnotically upon my own. I wanted to succumb to her that instant, but for science's sake, I held myself back as she continued. "Yes, I feel it . . . you love small children and have great empathy for people who have nothing to eat . . ." She leaned forward, her teeth glistening. "You are interested in women's suffrage and even free love— but I sense your desire to hide this." She reached toward me; I could barely resist. "You have a great love for women, and yet you so often feel alone in that love. Poor thing, you cannot see into the future. You do not know that in this same century, a great love awaits you, the love of many women in many countries ... Yes, three or four decades from now, that great love you have for a woman will flourish! You might live openly and freely with one special woman. ..."

Anita licked her lips, and I felt myself moving toward her, submitting, melting into her vision of my long future. Her voice was warm and soothing. "You are heartbroken at the constant and daily suffering of your sister human beings, but listen to me, there is solace. There will be love and delicate kisses, passion the likes of which you have always dreamed of but never seen—" Ah, Anita was just about to reach out and grab the very heart from out of my breast when, curse him, our waiter appeared, carrying another silver-covered dish. As he placed it before the lovely Anita, she jerked away from me, startled. Immediately, I missed the warmth of her beautiful yellow eyes, and we both stared dumbly as the waiter lifted the tarnished silver cover.

With great flourish he offered the plate to Anita: "Madame, your heart!"

"Why yes," she answered with a false smile and forced restraint, "it's beautiful."

And even I must admit, it was a beautiful heart, so red and alive, it was practically beating.

The waiter smiled. He held the bottle over the lovely vampire's glass. "Madame, more wine?"

Anita looked at him, but sadly. "I'd love some ... but how can I drink alone?" She looked to me then. "Won't you join me?"

How could I resist her sorrow? "Please."

The waiter filled my glass, and the wine he poured smelled wonderful, tasted wonderful, and was red, more red than any I had ever seen, even here, even tonight.

"Will madame have anything else?"

Anita looked questioningly to me, gestured openly with her hand. "I am fine at last, Pana, but perhaps my ... friend here, Pani Sadowsky, would like something more?"

I was speechless. Anita's heart there on the plate, her tear-streaked cheeks, her sad yellow eyes, all made me want and want more, yet I could ask for nothing.

Our waiter left at last. Anita and I watched him until he was all the way out of our view. When we were at last alone together in the Jewish Cafe of the Dead, Anita tentatively reached for her fork and knife, but then pushed them aside. In one swoop she grabbed for the heart with both hands and took an enormous bite. Then, holding it in her palm, Anita Lipsky, Polish vampire, offered that bloody, warm heart to me.

I took a bite. It was tough—I had to chew on it for an eternity—but the taste of it pleased me beyond my wildest imagination ... and yet I am hard-pressed to describe it for you now. Let it suffice to say that together we gobbled that heart down, and our moans of pleasure, our sighs of delight filled the ruined cafe. When at last we were through, we sucked our fingers, licked the plate. We licked each other's lips, drank down our wine as if we would never have more. When all was gone, we looked at each other with our bloody lips and then smacked them. We were flushed and full, but we were not satisfied.

Anita leaned across the table and reached for my hand. How glad I was for her to touch me—how it chilled and calmed me, livened and deadened me all at once. I was in her power gladly then, would have done for her anything she asked. "I wonder, Panią Sadowsky ... should we have another?"

"If that is what you desire, Madame Anita—"

Our eyes met, and Anita ran a finger across her mouth. "Perhaps not ... perhaps ... "

Oh, anything, I thought, ask for anything.

The waiter appeared out of nowhere, but even he could not break Anita's spell.

"*Kawe,* mesdames?"

Anita looked me in the eye as if our waiter were nowhere near. "We can get coffee in that dive hotel of yours, can we not?" she asked. She did not wait for my answer. Without taking her eyes from mine, she told the waiter calmly, "No coffee, thank you. *Proszę o rachunek.* Just the check."

The waiter rubbed his hands together, and the bill appeared before us. Anita snapped her fingers, and it burst into flames. "Dziękuję, Pana.

Thank you. Thank you. And now, if I'm not mistaken, there is a droshky waiting for us. Will you tell the valet to bring the lady's coat, and also my own—"

"And an umbrella also," I added quickly.

"Yes, and that awful umbrella. That's fine with you, isn't it, Pani̜a Sadowsky?"

"Oh, very fine," I told her, all the time wishing for nothing more than a long, lovely look into her sad and yellow eyes.

The Last Train

Linda K. Wright

INALLY. NICKI THOMPSON HAD finished her last sales report. She leaned back from her hunched position over the computer keyboard and put her arms above her head. She stretched long and luxuriously, enjoying the momentary relaxation of her body, cramped too long over her work. As she brought her arms back to her sides, she glanced at her watch. Ten-fifteen.

Ten-fifteen? Damn. She'd have to rush if she was going to catch the last commuter train out of the city tonight. She hurriedly closed a straining folder and forced the folder into her worn and already too heavy briefcase. Taking off her heels, she threw them into the bottom drawer of her desk and quickly slipped into and tied the laces of her sneakers. She didn't have time to remove the pearl necklace and matching earrings she'd made part of her business attire. She *had* learned the trick of buttoning the sturdy coat that protected her from the biting March wind over her shoulder-strap purse. That coat would also hide the pearls, and the chemically relaxed hairstyle she had adopted in the last six months would hide the small earrings. She grabbed her briefcase and dashed out of the long-empty customer-sales department.

Nicki was betting the fourteen-hour days she'd been putting in, as well as her politicking with upper management, would pay off in her bid for the manager position that had just become available. Those fourteen-hour days had already gotten her a first interview, scheduled for next week. If she got the job, she'd be the first African American to have that title at Kramer Chemicals.

But, for now, she had to make that ten-thirty train, the last one tonight that would stop at the Brentwood Farms station, not far from where she lived. Her home. A two-room apartment whose bathroom did not include the luxury of a tub, and a kitchen whose only appliances were the toaster oven and a tiny refrigerator. Nicki knew if she got the promotion, she could move into Center City and leave the commuting nightmare and the apartment behind.

She walked quickly down the dark street, not only to make sure she caught the train, but also to keep her distance from the furtive shadows that populated Center City at night after all the businesses closed. Street people—flesh during the day—became shadows at night. If she couldn't distinguish them, how could she avoid them?

Nicki ran down the steps of the entrance to the train station and, as she turned a corner, came face to face with a young man. Her nostrils flared, her eyes blinked as the man's odor assaulted her. His black face was covered with several days' growth of beard, and he was very thin, as though he hadn't eaten on a regular basis. Still, Nicki was not sure she would be able to defend herself if he decided to grab her. He was so close, and she was aware they were alone. She backed up and tried to step around him. His braided hair swayed as he moved to block her path and said, "Don't take this train, lady."

"I'm not interested," she said, as she stepped around the man and quickened her pace forward. He called out, "Lady, come back." Nicki did not look behind her but walked straight to the train platform and sat down on one of the benches. Realizing suddenly that she was alone, she checked her watch to make sure she had not missed the train. It was only 10:22. She looked around—she knew she could not let her guard down, especially at night. She had been raised in the city or, more accurately, in one of the insular neighborhoods the city contained. When she was growing up, she had been protected. People looked out for each other. She knew better than to expect that in today's world. Out of the corner of her eye, she noticed a movement. *Him again.* The man who had accosted her at the entrance was walking down the train platform toward her. He had an ambling walk, as though his legs were too long for his body. He wore a yellow and green plaid shirt that hung half way out of his jeans, making his flesh an easy target for the windy draft of the train tunnels. She watched as he approached and tried to get her attention. "Lady," he said.

Nicki raised her hand as if to ward off an unruly child and stated, in what she hoped was a firm voice, "I said I'm not interested."

He spoke slowly, "Allow me to tell you—"

"I said, *leave me alone.*" Nicki made direct eye contact and enunciated so there would be no misunderstanding. At the same time she wondered fleetingly where he'd learned to speak like that. Like she did.

"Lady," he said plaintively, "take the train tomorrow, okay? This train is bad. People go to sleep on this train."

Nicki noticed he held both his hands out in a begging motion. She looked at him. How to get rid of him? She tried not to breathe; his stench, so pervasive, was of something spoiled, rotting even. She could explain that this was the last train out of the city. She could explain that she was tired and in no mood to be bothered by him. But she had to be tough. "Look, if you don't get away from me . . ."

"Nicki, dear, is that you?" The welcome voice came from her left, and she turned to confirm its source. "Yes," Nicki sighed in relief. "Mrs. Erdman, how are you?" Nicki warmly greeted Mrs. Erdman, one of her neighbors in the Brentwood Farms apartment house. She turned back to the young man. He looked at her and at Mrs. Erdman, and then, shrugging his shoulders, continued down the train platform. Nicki watched him make his way toward two people who had just come onto the platform, a blonde-haired young woman wearing a pair of ragged jeans and carrying a knapsack and an older gentleman in a rumpled suit that did not hide his protruding stomach. Good, let them handle him, Nicki thought.

Nicki turned back to the comforting figure of Mrs. Erdman and said, "Boy, have you got great timing!" She patted the bench on which she was sitting to encourage her to put down the package she was carrying and share the seat.

Mrs. Erdman was famous—sometimes Nicki thought infamous would be a more fitting word—among the residents of the Brentwood Farms Apartments. No one knew where she came from or even what her ethnic background was. She had lived in the apartment house for as long as anyone could remember. Mrs. Erdman was known as much for the mass of thick gray hair she wore full and loose as for her willingness to speak her mind for just about any cause, the latest two being women's rights and animal rights. Nicki was not sure which held the greatest interest at the moment. Mrs. Erdman was a little eccentric in Nicki's view, and she did not have much contact with her, but right now, she was glad for Mrs. Erdman's presence. After a day of being on guard at the office, she needed the kind of closeness Mrs. Erdman usually demanded.

"Seems like I came by at a good time. Was that man bothering you?" Mrs. Erdman gently touched Nicki's shoulder.

"He was trying, but he didn't succeed. How are *you* doing? I haven't seen you in a while."

"Oh, I've been a little under the weather, but I'm fine now. Besides, I had to get better. Who would have taken care of my little ones?" Well, that answered the question of which cause was currently the stronger. Mrs. Erdman's "little ones" were the stray cats that had wandered onto the apartment complex property. Actually, Nicki was pretty sure the strays belonged to a couple of the new people who had just moved in. They probably didn't want to take care of the animals anymore, so had put them out. But Mrs. Erdman would not let them starve. She fed them every evening. Which reminded Nicki. What was Mrs. Erdman doing out at this time of night? She didn't work outside the home and could do her errands during the day. At her age, she must be even more nervous than Nicki about traveling this late alone.

Nicki was distracted from that thought by the sound of the approaching train. After it had slowed to a stop, she and Mrs. Erdman entered the last car of the two-car train, along with the woman with the knapsack and the man Nicki had dubbed the paunchy business suit. He looks like the man who would be my boss if I get this new job, thought Nicki, pasty-faced, and he even has a Band-Aid on his neck, just like Mr. Woolery, who always cuts his neck shaving. Except this guy doesn't have Mr. Woolery's ever-present cigar. Behind the fake Mr. Woolery ambled the derelict, his braids swinging as he walked.

Nicki slid into a triple seat in the middle of the train car and sat nearest the window. Mrs. Erdman sat closest to the aisle, putting her packages between herself and Nicki. Nicki noticed out of the corner of her eye that the street person had taken a seat in the front, facing them. He was watching her and Mrs. Erdman. She made a mental note to herself to tell the conductor about him when he came to collect the tickets. As they settled down, Nicki's question returned to her mind.

"So what are you doing on this train? It's a little late for you, isn't it?"

Mrs. Erdman eyed Nicki frankly and said, "You're one to talk. The hours you've been keeping lately." Mrs. Erdman stretched her hand toward Nicki and sympathetically touched her hair. "They working you too hard at the office again?"

Nicki explained the reason for her long hours, but as much as she enjoyed Mrs. Erdman's sympathetic listening, the exhaustion caused by the last several weeks was catching up with her. She had to keep blinking her eyes to stay awake.

"You know, dear, you're looking a little tired," Mrs. Erdman said, seeming to read Nicki's mind.

"You're right," Nicki said, smiling ruefully. "I can hardly keep my eyes open, and I've got some work I want to do when I get home tonight. I think I'm going to catnap for a couple of minutes to get my second wind. Do you mind?"

"Actually, dear, I think I'll do the same. We'll wake up when the conductor comes to take the tickets."

"Right," Nicki said, sliding down into her seat to rest her head. Just before she closed her eyes, she contented herself that the offending street person was still seated where she had seen him last.

But then suddenly he was coming toward her. She tried to move away, but something prevented her. Her legs and arms were so heavy.

He kept coming closer, hands outstretched, fingers long and grasping. She had to move. She had to. She could feel his breath, smelling like spoiled milk, caressing her face. *Dammit, move,* she told herself.

She woke up gasping. A dream. She saw the man was still seated in the front of the car, looking like he too was asleep, his head tilted. She had only dreamed he had been a threat to her, probably because she was so tired. She sat up and looked out the window. *Where were they?* The darkness outside revealed no clue. But, Nicki thought, this is a local train; we'll be stopping at a station soon.

She stretched and looked over at Mrs. Erdman, who was still asleep. Nicki wondered why she hadn't been awakened by the conductor when he came by to collect the tickets. He had to have come through the train by now. She was confused. Maybe Mrs. Erdman had been awake when the conductor came through. But that didn't explain why they hadn't wakened Nicki. Nicki frowned; she really should find out where the train was.

She reached over and gently shook Mrs. Erdman by her coat as she whispered, "Mrs. Erdman ... Mrs. Erdman?"

There was no response. Mrs. Erdman's head had fallen against her coat collar. Nicki thought she would wake up if she felt Nicki's hand on her cheek. She leaned sideways and stretched out her hand. Mrs. Erdman's cheek was cold. And there was a thin trail of blood running from her mouth. Nicki pulled back her hand and shivered, wanting to erase the feel of that cold cheek from her fingers and the sight of the blood from her mind. Was this a dream, too? Was she awake?

"Mrs. Erdman," she said in a loud voice. "Wake up." She heard her own voice echo in the train car. She *was* awake. But Mrs. Erdman didn't respond.

Silence. Nicki could not bring herself to touch Mrs. Erdman's skin again, but she gave a gentle shove to her body and watched horrified as it slid slightly at the push.

Oh my God. She's dead. She must have had a stroke or something. Calm. *She needed to be calm.* She needed to get help. She looked at the street person still seemingly asleep. He wouldn't be any help. She looked around to see who else was in the train car. The blonde-haired woman and the businessman were in separate seats behind her. The woman looked as if she had fallen asleep, too, but the businessman was facing the window. Nicki would ask him to get the conductor.

Crouching so as not to hit her head on the overhead baggage rack, she climbed over the back of the seat she shared with Mrs. Erdman. She couldn't stop shivering. She made her shaky way to the seat where the businessman sat, staring out the window. He seemed so still. Nicki leaned over him and said, "Excuse me, sir."

He didn't move. Nicki tried to swallow the fear she felt rising from her stomach. Slowly she reached over and touched him. He fell forward in the seat. She screamed, the sound louder than the roar of the train.

The scream woke the dark man with the braids, the street person. He stood slowly and started to move toward her. Nicki, backing up quickly toward the seat where the blonde-haired woman sat, held up a hand and said, "Don't come near me." She took a quick glance at the slumped-over body of the blonde-haired woman and fought to swallow the bile that rose in her throat as she noticed the blood on the woman's neck.

Has he killed them all? Where is the conductor?

Nicki looked around the car. She might have to fight this guy who stood between her and the next car. She didn't carry mace. She had always figured that if she did and got attacked she'd end up spraying herself in the face. *Her keys.* Nicki fumbled for them in her coat pocket. Keys were sharp. If she had to, she would cut him with the keys. Her hand gripped them tightly.

"Lady," he said, coming closer. "I don't want to hurt you."

"Then stay the hell away from me," Nicki said fiercely.

"I told you not to take this train. I told you. Now I don't know what to do." He looked at her, looked at the blonde-haired woman.

"You can leave me alone and get out of my way." She raised the hand that held the keys and brandished them in front of her. "You may have killed the others, but you're not going to kill me. Now get out of my way. I want to get to the door. Put your hands where I can see them, and keep away from me or I swear, I'll cut you."

The door. That was her first goal. She walked past the bodies of the blonde-haired woman and the businessman, keeping the street person constantly in her sight. He remained motionless, except once when he looked at the body of Mrs. Erdman. This reminder of Mrs. Erdman's death brought tears to Nicki's eyes, tears she wiped away hurriedly so they would not blur her vision. She took a deep breath and walked past Mrs. Erdman's body, gripping the keys so tightly the metal teeth cut into her hand. Her legs seemed to become very heavy. *Come on, kid, you can do it. Just keep this bastard at bay.* She kept her eyes on him and told herself that all she had to do was to get to the door. She would get help from somebody in the next car or, if she had to, she would jump from the train. At least she'd leave this madman here.

The door. As she divided her attention between the street person and the door, she saw his eyes dart to something behind her. Reflexively, she turned, and she dropped the keys as, shocked, she saw Mrs. Erdman standing in front of her.

"Mrs. Erdman," Nicki rushed to her, "thank God, you're all right." She turned quickly back to face the street person. "I think he killed the other two people on the train." She turned back to Mrs. Erdman. "I thought he'd killed you, too."

Silence greeted her words, and Nicki noticed the trace of blood still remained on Mrs. Erdman's mouth, a contrast to the bloodless pallor of her face, which held a smile. *A smile?*

"Mrs. Erdman?" Nicki said, her voice unsteady.

"Yes, dear," Mrs. Erdman replied. "Did you have a good nap? I was rather busy as you slept. Seems I got a little hungry, had to drink my fill of what was here, then fell asleep after my meal."

What was she talking about? Nicki looked back at the street person as if he would provide an answer to this puzzle. Mrs. Erdman saw her glance. "I don't take any blood from our friend here," she said, gesturing to the man. "Too little food, too much alcohol. His blood is too thin."

Nicki looked at Mrs. Erdman, not believing what she had heard. Mrs. Erdman had gotten hungry. So she had what, drunk the blood of the two other people on the train? Nicki shook her head, laughing.

"I must be more tired than I thought." Her laughter quickly turned to a plea. "You drank their blood? This is another dream, right?" Nicki's laughter had an hysterical edge.

"No, dear," said Mrs. Erdman, as she snatched Nicki's wrist with one hand and brought her down to her knees in pain. "Does this feel like a dream? Do my little ones look like a dream?" She nodded her head back toward the blonde-haired woman and the businessman, both of whom had risen from their seats and come to stand behind Mrs. Erdman.

"But . . . but," Nicki stuttered, "I saw them. They were dead."

"No, dear," Mrs. Erdman kept a firm grip on Nicki's arm. "I ride the ten-thirty train all the time, and so do they. I have visited them before, and tonight they have become part of my growing family. And they are quite hungry. So, while your blood may be a little tired, you do have a full complement, don't you, dear?"

Nicki looked at the pale faces of the blonde-haired woman and the businessman. They held no compassion. They smiled at her as they nudged each other in anticipation. She turned her head to look at the street person, tears flowing from her eyes, as Mrs. Erdman, not so gently, bent her wrist backward. *Help me*, she mouthed silently. *I didn't know, help me.*

The street person looked at her and said, "Lady, I tried to tell you." He turned his back and walked slowly to the next car.

The Vampire's Baby

Joanne Dahme

HEN MARCY CALLED, NORA'S reaction had been shock—a shock that dissolved into a disturbing sense of panic. The voice on the other end of the phone was from her past: Nora and Marcy had been college roommates for four years. One of those lucky, random combinations, they had become inseparable. But sometime after graduation, the lock on their friendship had been picked. By what, Nora never knew.

At school, Marcy had been an exciting discovery for Nora—a kindred spirit in a world from which Nora sometimes felt separated, as if an infinite, crystal-clear pane of glass allowed her to see perfectly, without really hearing exactly what was going on. But Marcy, in her quirky, almost childlike way, seemed to have an instinctive understanding of her, always knowing the right questions to ask when Nora had something on her mind she felt too self-conscious to talk about. Sometimes it seemed that all Nora had to do was look at Marcy and out popped the question that allowed

Nora to open the gates to her cautious heart. This connection Nora felt to Marcy made it all the more mysterious and painful when Marcy seemed suddenly to let go.

In the beginning, it was Nora who made the excuses for Marcy. After all, they did live three hours away from each other, and after all, Marcy had just started a new job in advertising, which everyone knew was an extremely demanding field. Marcy had said that her boss was a tyrant, a monster who treated them all like highly expendable dirt. He wanted his employees at the office day and night, at his beck and call, even on weekends. When Nora had asked Marcy why she just didn't look for another job, Marcy had answered her as she would a naive little girl: "Nora, this is the world of advertising. You don't quit. It's the same way everywhere. And besides, I like my job." That was the first time Nora had felt their fine antennae for sensing one another's feelings needed tuning, as if some wall, large and unseen, were interfering. Nora, who was teaching at a grammar school near her home, couldn't imagine liking working for anyone who treated her badly—it was another point of separation between her and Marcy.

And now, six years later, when Nora had finally allowed herself to let go of or at least put aside the hurt of this lost friendship, relegating Marcy to the lost souls area of her Christmas card list, Marcy had called.

And what a strange call it had been. Marcy's voice had been bare of emotion, tiny, a voice Nora had had to strain to hear. January was coming to an end, and Nora had looked out her kitchen window as Marcy spoke, watching the skeletal tree branches being blown back and forth by the callous touch of the bitter winter winds. Nora had found herself shivering, and she wasn't sure if it was from the winter chill or the dead calm of Marcy's voice.

She needed Nora, Marcy informed her in that scary monotone, a voice so alien from that of the old Marcy. She was pregnant and had to talk to Nora. She needed Nora. She didn't trust anyone else. Never had. Could Nora meet her tomorrow night in Lintonville, the next small town over from their college, where they used to go to drink a few beers or shop at the Woolworth's? Could she make it?

If Marcy hadn't sounded so lifeless, Nora would have allowed herself to be furious, would have opened the floodgates of long pent-up anger and hurt. But Nora was numbed by the call. Sure, she promised Marcy. She would meet her at five o'clock in front of the movie theater. They'd go to dinner, get a room at the Budget Lodge near the college and spend the night. She could cancel her weekend plans. "Thank you," Marcy had flatly responded, ending the conversation quickly, saying she was on a pay phone and could not talk.

Nora had been left with too many questions on the tip of her tongue when Marcy hung up, after squeezing in the news that she was pregnant, in that same threadbare voice. Marcy, pregnant? But what about that long ago conversation they'd had, in which, despite the many beers they'd drunk, Marcy had made Nora swear on her mother's grave she would never repeat to anyone that Marcy would never be able to have children.

Nora remembered that she had laughed at first, thinking, well, there goes Marcy making some medical problem sound weird and full of doom. She probably missed a period once or twice in her life. Nora remembered saying, "Bad uterus? What the hell is a bad uterus?" Marcy had looked at her, wounded, curtly insisting that she was not joking. She would say no more, and Nora was left to promise that she would never repeat Marcy's secret, nor ask any questions later. Nora had often regretted that promise, whenever something reminded her of their strange conversation.

Nora was thinking about the "bad uterus" when the bus pulled up in front of the old Fireside Diner in Lintonville. The early winter darkness was already descending, but even the soft gray twilight could not mask the shabbiness of the old town.

Stepping off the bus, she looked across the street to the old Woolworth's and the discount drugstore she and Marcy had periodically visited back in college. They looked the same, even down to the faded displays that leaned haphazardly against the windows. She remembered joking with Nora back then that the displays had not been changed since the 1950s. Nora knew without looking closely that they were still the same displays.

For a moment, she just stood there on the sidewalk, not wanting to move just yet, allowing the bus to pull away so she could get a better look at Lintonville's Main Street. She stood almost wistfully, looking up the avenue to the worn, faded facades of the once stylish, deco-style storefronts. Christmas decorations, oversized candles and tree ornaments that had probably done their best to make Lintonville look festive for decades swung dejectedly in the wind.

Below them, swirls of trash, mostly papers and cellophane bags, followed the whims of the wind playing along the street curbs. Directly beside Nora was the Fireside Diner, where she and Marcy had spent countless weekend mornings eating big, cheap breakfasts. A dying orange sky provided the background for the brown diner. The scene made Nora think of bread in the oven. Nora pulled her jacket a little more tightly about her neck and began to walk up the block in the direction of the movie theater.

Nora thought it was odd that though it was still relatively early in the evening, really just late afternoon, Main Street was empty except for the few bodies she could see almost furtively stepping in and out of doorways, only to scurry up or down the street as if they were already late for their destination. She looked at the shops to see if any had changed. No, there was Helen's Beauty Parlor, and next to it the Lintonville Book Store. Across the street, the old Church of Scientology building still stood, the garish red lettering screaming out its messages on the building's storefront windows. In the past, she and Marcy had giggled at the church's glass promises and messages. Today, Nora was glad there were no scientologists staring in animated enthusiasm from behind the glass, beckoning at passersby.

The record store still adjoined the church. She had always thought they made odd neighbors, especially in the warmer weather when the record shop would open its door and blare some untamed lyrics into the street. From what she could see, it looked like records were displayed prominently, as if to spite the arrival of CDs. On the other side of the record store, however, was a noticeably new building, a one-story number with a modern, black marble facade. Above the doorway, in large, red block-lettering, it said BLOOD BANK. Here, at least, there were a few people coming in and out of the building. But Nora thought it was odd how all of them seemed to keep their eyes on the ground, as if they didn't want to be recognized, or perhaps, to recognize anyone either. Maybe they're selling their blood, Nora thought. Times in this town were certainly hard.

Except for a heightened sense of shabbiness and the new blood bank, everything else in Lintonville seemed oddly unchanged. It was as if the six years Nora had missed here had also been missed by the town, as if time had sped by too fast to affect the town, leaving in its wake only the small spirals of trash. To Nora, the town seemed to be missing a sense of life, or maybe, Nora thought, trying to pin down her feeling, a sense of what normal life should be.

She was glad to reach the movie theater. Although the theater's doors looked closed and dark, an old man sat hunched over a black-covered book in the ticket booth.

Nora stood a few feet away from the booth, mainly so the old man wouldn't get the impression she wanted to buy a ticket. But Nora looked at him, just to perhaps give a smile and get one in return. She was feeling alone in Lintonville today, and she would have welcomed a little human contact. But the old man never looked up.

Suddenly, a tall man dressed in black rushed out of the pawnshop next door, allowing the glass door to bang in the wind. He ran to the entrance of the movie theater, blocking the way between the theater doors and Nora. When he turned to face her, Nora could see he was a priest, his white collar rising above the blackness of his clothes.

He was large and strong-looking, his black hair, flecked with white, was blowing wildly in the wind, and Nora was startled to see that he had a terrible, almost crazed expression on his face. He was looking right at her.

When the priest suddenly reached inside his coat, for a moment, Nora thought he was going to shoot her. Scenes from hundreds of TV shows flashed through her mind as she stepped back in alarm. But, the priest pulled out a shining silver crucifix, pointing it at her as if, indeed, it were a weapon. "Do not enter this place of sin!" he screamed at her. At first, she only stared blankly back at him, in shock. She looked to the old man in the booth for some reaction, but he never raised his head from the book. "Go! Get away from this place!" the priest yelled again. And then, lowering his gaze to Nora's flat stomach, he asked suspiciously, "Are you with child?"

"I beg your pardon," she sputtered, almost too shocked to believe this was happening. Now the priest was walking toward her, stretching his arm out in her direction, the crucifix glinting in the street light.

"What is the matter with you?" Nora yelled back, her own anger overcoming her bewilderment. She instinctively pushed his outstretched arm away from her face. After staring speechlessly at her for a few more minutes, the priest pushed past her and moved in the direction of the pawnshop, turning once to thrust the cross back in her direction. Again, she looked to the old man for some sign, some acknowledgment of this bizarre scene, but still he did not look up. It was then that Nora noticed the movie poster displayed in the case beside the entrance doors.

The Vampire's Baby. The words in the title dripped with blood. A stark wooden cross lay broken in two below the words.

If Nora hadn't been cold before, she was cold to the bone now. She ran her hands up and down the sleeves of her coat, feeling an intuitive wave of panic washing over her.

Okay, get a grip. Nora calmed herself, hoping to quell what might be unnecessary anxiety. The world was full of weird people, and she had just happened to stumble into a cluster of them, she assured herself. The cold wind was whipping her long brown hair about her face, snapping at the strands, stinging her face. *Marcy, please, where are you?* she pleaded silently.

Suddenly, the theater's set of glass double doors banged open simultaneously, and a stream of people pulsed out of the theater, silently gushing through the exits. Nora still stood a few feet away from the ticket booth, but now she found herself caught in the flow, fighting to anchor herself firmly to the ground. The crowd was actually trying to move past her, almost through her, as if she weren't even there. She felt elbows and shoulders jarring her, shoving her with soundless urgency. She looked in desperation at the faces in the crowd. "Hey, be careful. Watch it!" she snapped at them. But the crowd was silent, unspeaking. She focused on individual faces. No one was looking at anyone else. No one was smiling, or talking, or looking miserable about being in the midst of a claustrophobic's nightmare. Their faces were blank, empty as the starless night. Many wore black, all black, and under the muted light of the street lamps, their faces looked strangely pale.

Nora felt herself losing ground, caught up in the undertow of this human tide, which was pulling her up the block. She turned to see where everyone was going. The leaders of this soundless parade were already crossing the street, streaming toward the Roy Rogers restaurant on the opposite corner. They didn't bother to look for traffic. The few cars or buses coming down Main Street simply stopped and waited patiently. It was only after Nora let her sights go beyond the crowd that she noticed the almost billboard-sized sign propped on the roof of the fast-food restaurant. "Don't Miss Our New Juicy Blood-Red Burgers." Nora felt her stomach protest in revulsion. She grabbed onto a street sign to keep herself from being dragged farther.

It was while she was clinging to the sign like a lifeline that Nora saw Marcy near the theater waving frantically to her. Marcy was on the edge of the crowd, standing closer to the pawnshop entrance.

"Marcy!" Nora yelled, releasing one hand to wave frantically in return. But as the last of the crowd was going past Nora, she saw two men suddenly grab Marcy by the arms. "Marcy, watch out!" she yelled too late.

She could see the men practically lift Marcy's slight figure off the ground, her feet kicking at the air. Nora tried to keep her sight trained on Marcy's short blond hair, as if her head were a beacon in the wave of black. The men pulling Marcy toward the alley were extremely tall, their svelte, well-toned bodies accentuated by their tightly fitting clothes. Nora was struck by their long dark hair, which both wore pulled back in tight ponytails. They reminded Nora of the transvestites she saw on morning talk shows.

One of the men looked Nora right in the eye before disappearing with Marcy into the alley. His eyes were brilliant, outlined in thick black eye-liner so that Nora could almost measure their size against the other features of his face.

Nora pushed against the last bodies flowing by her, struggling to reach the alley that separated the theater from the pawnshop. She paused a moment when she reached the alley—no street lamp revealed what might be lurking in the dark corners at the alley's end. She took a deep breath and plunged down its length. Only because she was concentrating on her steps was Nora able to prevent herself from tumbling into the yawning excavation half way down the alley.

A surprised gasp was the only sound she made as she stared down into the hole. Two figures in jeans and hardhats were huddled over a thin piece of pipe, a small spotlight illuminating their work. She stared at them for a moment, seeing only the tops of their white hardhats, hardhats with stark black crosses stamped upon the crowns and sides. She paused, straining to pick up some scent of goodness or evil, and sensing neither, she directed her question into the hole. "Excuse me, did you see two men dragging a woman through here?" When neither of them looked up to acknowledge her, she added urgently, "She's my friend, please!"

"Gas leak here," one of them intoned, without looking up. "Had to evacuate the theater."

"You mean the movie wasn't over?" she asked in surprise. Those people weren't exactly leaving in a frightened stampede, she thought, distracted by the odd piece of information.

She shivered at the memory of that crowd. "Did you hear anyone in the alley?" Nora tried again. "You must have seen them. They couldn't have gotten by you!" she added insistently.

"Ma'am, you're going to have to leave this area. Gas leak, you know," the other unseen face answered her.

Suddenly Nora spotted a purse in the ditch, about two feet away from the bigger man's foot. It was a small clutch purse, brown like the dirt under their feet. "Excuse me," she commanded. "What's that by your foot?"

"Looks like a purse, ma'am." Finally, the bigger man reached for it, turning to Nora with a wary, oddly fitting smile. He stood up to hand her the purse.

"What are you smiling about?" she demanded, exasperated. She heard her schoolteacher voice sliding into her tone.

"It's the gas, ma'am. Sometimes gas makes you smile. You know, like a baby." He knelt to go back to his work, leaving only the sight of the two black crosses staring back at her.

Nora stepped back. She didn't know what to do. She was cold and extremely confused. She felt she was without a compass—so out of sync with the people in this town. Were they all crazy? Surely, she wasn't the crazy one. She ran back to the front of the theater, searching the sidewalks up and down. No sign of the men or Marcy. No sign of *any* life on the streets. She looked across the street to the packed Roy Rogers, dark figures moving within the lighted interior of the restaurant like a swarm of bees on honey.

"Oh God," she shivered. Why had those men taken Marcy? What was going on? She needed to take some sort of action she told herself. She opened the purse. All it contained were a set of keys, a comb, some loose change and a photograph of a man with shiny black hair, shoulder length and slicked back, revealing a stark widow's peak over his expansive forehead. He was standing at attention beside a hair stylist's chair, the mirror behind him bouncing off a fireball of light from the flash. Could this be Helen's Beauty Parlor? But where was Helen?

Otherwise, there was no wallet. No ID. No way of knowing the purse was Marcy's.

"The police!" The idea jolted Nora like an electric shock. *Of course!* Nora approached the ticket booth. The old man was still hunched over what Nora noticed was the Bible. Nora rapped hard on the glass booth to get the old man's attention. "Please," she shouted at him, "where is the police station?" Nora was lasering her gaze at the top of his bald head, but instead of looking at her, the man turned the small sign that was hanging by a tiny chain above the exchange window so that it now read Closed.

"Please!" she shouted again, banging her fist with all her might against the glass. The air inside the booth remained undisturbed by movement.

"The police can't help you," she heard a man's voice snarl. She swung about in the direction of the pawnshop to face the disheveled priest. This time he simply stood on the sidewalk, his arms hanging limply by his sides. His hands were empty. "Only God can help you here," he continued darkly, his eyes watery and intense.

"Listen," Nora took a few cautious steps toward him. "You must tell me where the police station is. My friend was kidnapped by two men. I need help," she nearly screamed at him.

An insane smile captured the priest's face suddenly, a transformation that left Nora staring at him with repulsed wonder.

"You're all jezebels," he croaked through a wheeze that perhaps at one time had sounded like laughter. "The apprentices of the devil himself." The priest quickly turned to look in the other direction, maybe for more wayward jezebels, Nora thought.

"Are you here to celebrate the spawning of the devil?" His eyes burned as he spit the question out.

"Listen, I don't know what you're talking about. I'm just here to find my friend!" she shouted back in exasperation. She couldn't understand why no one would listen to her.

"Father, get in here this minute! What is the matter with you?"

Nora and the priest both turned to look at the old woman who had opened the pawnshop's door. She stood in the doorway, filling its frame. She wore what Nora's grandmother called a housecoat. Her stockings were thick and bagged around her knees and ankles, her gray hair pinned in some sort of bun. She held a broom in one hand like a weapon.

"What are you trying to do, Father?" she scolded him. "They'll see you. Now, get in here, and stop all this nonsense."

The priest turned, shoulders slumped like a naughty boy's. And then he looked at Nora with eyes full of fire and brimstone and for perhaps a split second, regret. He then squeezed past the old woman to get into the pawnshop.

"Miss, please, can you help me?" Nora hurried toward her. "I need to find—"

"Shoo, shoo!" The old woman interrupted Nora, making sweeping motions with her broom, as if Nora were a mangy mutt. The woman wrinkled her nose in disgust, quickly blessed herself and slammed the pawnshop door.

"Wait!" Nora heard herself wailing now. "Wait!" Nora banged on the pawnshop window, watching the retreating backs of the old woman and the priest. "Wait," Nora whispered, mainly to herself, her numb fists suspended above her head, pressed against the glass. For the first time she noticed the shelves over the pawnshop counter stacked with gleaming chalices, crucifixes and crosses of all sizes and materials, and plaster statues of saints and Holy Family members.

Nora stared at the collection of religious articles, as if by staring hard enough at them, she might find some answers. *But I don't even know the right questions,* she wanted to scream out loud.

A sound—not exactly the sound of a buzzsaw, more like the overwhelming hum of a generator or motor coming to life—pulled Nora's attention back to the street. Turning from the pawnshop window, she saw the Roy Roger's crowd flowing back onto Main Street. They were headed in her direction, still one huge silent mass made up of hundreds of marching legs, like some monstrous centipede. A full moon shone down on the crowd, and in the moonlight, their eyes gleamed like cats' eyes and their lips shone red.

Nora struggled to get her bearings. She looked at the Roy Rogers crowd, trying to imagine exactly what would happen to her if she held her ground. But instinct kicked in, and Nora broke into a run, down the block, in the direction of the diner. The image of the bus stop beyond gave her incentive. *Get on the bus,* something inside of her screamed. But then the image of Marcy flashed before her—Marcy yelling for help while those creeps carried her away.

She had to stay, Nora realized. She had to find Marcy.

When she heard the piercing screech of a police siren, she turned in time to see a blue and white police car cut through the crowd as if parting a black sea. Nora jumped in front of it, waving the police car to a stop.

Two cops sat in the front. She ran to the driver's side and frantically banged on the window. But before rolling his window down, the cop shined a light in her face, blinding her momentarily. He cracked his window maybe an inch. "Okay, get in the back, fast," he ordered. Nora opened the back door, glancing at the crowd only yards away from the car, and jumped in.

A middle-aged man, with thinning brown hair combed over his bald spot, sat beside her in the back. In his rumpled suit and tie and holding a bulging beat-up briefcase, he looked like a salesman. He glanced at Nora, embarrassed, and turned away.

"Not a nice night to be out on the street, babe," the cop at the wheel said, addressing the windshield.

"Actually, in this neighborhood, no night is!" quipped his partner, turning to look at Nora. He was young, all-American looking. He gave Nora a wink.

"I need help!" Nora was long past any pretensions of politeness. "Where are you going, and why aren't you guys doing something about those people?" she yelled, looking in the direction of the zombielike crowd.

"Those people?" the cop at the wheel spat at her. "What's the matter with those people, babe? So, they ate at Roy Rogers. So crucify them."

"Bad taste isn't against the law in these parts," the cheerful partner winked at her again. "It's you two we're taking in."

"What are you talking about?" Nora felt as if she were reaching some sort of mental brink. She clasped her trembling hands in her lap. "Those people," she continued, "they—"

"Were walking in your direction, babe?" the driver yelled. "So sue them!"

"But my friend Marcy," Nora added desperately. "Two men grabbed her and took her away. You have to . . ."

"Marcy!" Both cops whipped around, the police car screeching to a halt. And then quickly recovering, the cheerful cop noted, "She was past curfew. And so are you two. That's why we're running you in."

"Past curfew! But I'm twenty-six years old, and it can't be even eight o'clock yet!" The shrillness in her voice alarmed her.

"Listen, sweet thing. It's not how old you are, or the fact that the night is still young," the winking cop explained patiently. "It's the quality of the blood that runs through your veins. It's your scent, your internal temperature."

"Mike, can it," his partner growled, nudging him with his elbow.

"Oh, sorry, Joe. I got carried away. Let's turn the siren back on and get back to the station."

"But what about my friend?" Nora was frantic and chilled by this interrupted explanation. She leaned forward and grabbed the metal screen that separated the back seat from the driver and shook it hard. The salesman then thrust his arm in front of Nora's body and shoved her back against the seat. She looked at the salesman, incredulous.

"What is your problem?" he whispered almost hysterically. "Do you want them to just dump us back on the street?" His face was bloated and red from his efforts to contain Nora. A thin sheen of perspiration veiled his forehead.

"I want them to find my friend. What the hell is the matter with everyone around here?" she whispered back furiously, pushing his arm away. "And what if they *do* dump us back on the street? What are you so afraid of?"

His eyes widened at the thought. "Geez, what are you doing in this town if you don't know?"

"Don't know what? What is going on? And what did he mean—all that stuff about blood?"

"Hey, guys, we're here," the smiling cop announced, as the car came to a screeching halt in front of St. Vita's Church. "Now when I open the door, I want you two to sprint up those steps. No dawdling, right, Stanley? You know how it works." The salesman nodded in embarrassment.

"So, we lose a tourist or two. What's the big deal?" the driver growled.

"But this is a church," Nora protested, as the back doors were opened and she and Stanley were shoved in the direction of the large oak doors. Nora stopped with a sense of dread when she noticed the primitive black cross spray-painted across the doors. It looked like a childish version of the crosses that covered the hardhats of the gas men.

"Just get in." The grumpy cop pulled open the doors and pushed them through.

Nora and Stanley stood in the back of the barely lit, musty church as the two cops busied themselves off to the side. St. Vita's had obviously once been a proud, meticulously ornate church, its gothic ceilings vaulting toward the heavens. Now, however, the church looked like a prodigal angel—dirty and decrepit. The pews, a hundred rows on two sides paving the way to the altar, were dusty and moldy. The stained-glass windows adorning both sides of the church were grimy and cracked. The cold interior of the church gave Nora the shivers, and she drew her coat tightly around her.

The sound of something heavy being dragged across the stone floor behind them caught Nora's and Stanley's attention.

"Need any help?" Stanley asked without conviction.

"No, don't want you to strain yourself, Stanley," the cheerful cop replied. "Just pick your pew."

The two cops were heaving a heavy board into the medieval-looking latches on the sides of both doors. They dropped the board with a thud into the latches.

"Is this really necessary?" Nora asked. Between their conversation about blood and their attempt to turn the church into a fortress, Nora was beginning to doubt her own sanity. Her thoughts ran to what the unspoken secret of the town might be, what the policeman had meant. But the idea seemed too ridiculous, too crazy, too horrifying. And everyone around here was acting as if this were all routine.

"No, it's not really necessary. We just need the exercise," the grumpy cop snarled. "Pick a pew, both of you, and stay put," he barked.

"But not in the same pew," the cheerful cop added teasingly. "We don't want any footsie-playing going on in church."

"Come on," Stanley said, roughly grabbing Nora by the elbow and leading her up the church's center aisle. "Sit in this one."

"Stanley," Nora whispered pleadingly, "sit in front of me, please. I need to talk to you. I need to hear what I'm up against. I need you to explain."

"No," Stanley whispered nervously. "It's not allowed. Now sit there and be quiet."

"Stanley, if you don't talk to me, I'll sit next to you, right in your very own pew," Nora shot back. It was the only threat she had. Stanley peered quickly over his shoulder to see if the cops were watching them. Nora turned to look too, and for the first time, noticed the two Lazy-Boy recliners crammed back by the confessional. An oversized TV was balanced atop two file cabinets. What sounded like a hockey game suddenly filled the silence of the church as the TV was turned on and the cops each popped a can of beer.

"All right," Stanley agreed. Nora noticed his left eye was developing a tic.

Even with all of the noise from the game, Stanley still faced forward. Nora had to practically lean over his shoulder to hear him.

"Every night, as soon as the sun sets, this town closes down. I mean literally. You can't get in or out until the sun rises again." Stanley wiped his forehead with a well-used handkerchief. "I wouldn't be here now if it weren't for that damn bookstore, that Melvin haggling over extra copies for crissakes. But a sale is a sale."

"But Stanley," Nora interrupted, "what about those people out there? What are they exactly?"

"They're the people who come out at night. They're allowed to," Stanley interjected quickly. "The rest of the town knows to stay in their homes when it's dark. They know it's not fair to tempt the others."

"Stanley . . ." Nora paused to get the words out, to say them slowly so that there could be no mistake. "You mean, they only come out at night because they are—"

Stanley whipped about to face her, then looked back at the cops. His eyes were bulging. "Yes. Yes," he whispered, his voice harsh. "But outsiders are not supposed to know." He was twisting his handkerchief in his hands.

"Not supposed to know! Maybe somebody should inform them what a big secret it is. They're hardly what I would call an unobtrusive group." Nora shivered involuntarily.

"Don't make light of them. They know you're here. They know I'm here. Our blood doesn't smell like the regulars'. It has an outside scent. Fresh."

"But why don't the people do something to get rid of them, to beat them? They could do it during the day." Nora was trying to draw from the limited knowledge she had culled from old movies and Anne Rice novels.

"It's not that simple. They and the town have a pact." This time Stanley pressed his handkerchief to the top of his bald head. "You see, a few years ago, this town was dying, economically that is. A few of them showed up one night, looking for asylum. No one knows from where. But they're quite wealthy. So they bought the town and gave it a new life. They paid its debts and municipal fees, and they left the townspeople alone. And the townspeople agreed to keep their secret, as long as they were left alone. Outsiders, however, are fair game."

"But what keeps them here, I mean, at night?"

"Their self-discipline, I guess. They know they're safe here. This is where their coffins are. And at night they cut off all communication with the outside. Roadblocks go up, phone lines are out of service. Surrounding communities think it's just some kind of archaic blue law that the town enforces."

"I still don't understand what all this has to do with my friend Marcy. Why did they take her like that? For what reason?" Stanley's story was too surreal. Nora didn't understand how she and Marcy had gotten caught up in this nightmare. All she was convinced of now was that she had to get them both out of Lintonville.

"Naughty, naughty, Stanley," the cheerful cop teased as he clamped his hand down hard on Stanley's shoulder. "Not good for business," he singsonged.

"Look," Nora turned on him, indignant. "I have a right to know what I'm up against. You have no right to keep us prisoners here."

"Mike!" The grumpy cop suddenly sat up ramrod straight in his chair, snapping off the TV. "Listen," he commanded.

They all listened, and they all heard the dull thudding noise reverberating from the belly of the basement. It sounded like a battering ram being taken to the door.

"Battering ram?" they all said out loud in unison. Nora was shocked that for the first time, her response equaled theirs.

"Let's go, Mike. We better check it out. Grab your cross and gun," the grumpy cop ordered in a stage whisper. "You two had better stay where you are."

Stanley grabbed the arm of the cheerful cop. "Please, don't leave me here. Take me with you."

"Come on, Stanley old man. You know the drill. Chill out. We'll be right back." And shaking Stanley off, he joined the grumpy cop. One hand on their holstered guns, the other gripping bare black crosses, the two disappeared down the basement stairs.

Nora stood up immediately, hurrying into the aisle. "Stanley, how do I get out of here? I'm not waiting here all night to become somebody's dinner. Besides, Marcy needs me."

"Are you out of your mind?" Stanley nearly screamed, forgetting himself. His tic seemed to have infected both eyes now. "Didn't you hear a word I said?"

"Yes. Of course I did. But like you said, we're trapped here. And it appears that we're not really safe here either. Do you just want to wait for them to batter down the door? And," Nora emphasized, "they're not after the police. If what you said is true, it's you and me they're after."

Stanley seemed to crumple into his own lap. "This is all your fault," he cried. "Go ahead. There." He pointed at the altar. "The door behind it leads to the sacristy. They won't come in that way."

Nora approached him gently. "Stanley, thank you." And then, as a guilty afterthought, "Do you want to come with me? You and Marcy and I can try to get out of this town tonight. We might not last till morning if we just sit here."

"No," he wailed like a child awakening from a nightmare. He grabbed Nora's wrist. "But you must stay away from your friend," he advised through his sobs.

"Marcy? Why? What do you mean?" Nora drew in a breath at the new surge of dread filling her.

"They say," he said, a little more softly, "that she's carrying Stefan's baby."

When Nora just looked at him blankly, he added, "Stefan, the top man. He's the leader of their pack."

Nora pulled away in shock. The idea was unimaginable. Could those creatures actually have babies? Weren't they the undead? She shook off the thought to concentrate on her next plan of action.

Nora buttoned her coat. She noticed the battering sound had stopped. "Be careful, Stanley," she said, trying a reassuring smile on him as she headed through the sacristy door. Inside, the sacristy was small and dark, but a heavy metal door on its opposite wall had a dimly lit exit sign above its frame. She pushed hard against the handle and let herself into the schoolyard. The door locked with a click behind her.

Nora pressed her body close against the stone of the church. The schoolyard was in the back of the church, enclosed on two sides by a cyclone fence and, on the opposite side, the school. The January night was quite dark, and Nora waited for her eyes to adjust, squinting to discern shadows or shapes outside the fenceline.

Nora had realized her destination while talking to Stanley. She had thrust the photograph of the hairdresser into the pocket of her coat in front of the movie theater and could feel it now between her fingers. The beauty parlor was beside the old bookstore, across from the Church of Scientology. Mimicking the old lady at the pawnshop, Nora blessed herself, listened for night noises and ran as quietly as she could toward the fence bordering Main Street. She scaled it with the fearlessness of a child and began her run back up the street.

Main Street was again completely deserted. She ran along the sidewalk even though the street was empty of cars. The only sign of habitation was the soft glow of light bleeding through the shuttered windows of apartments and storefronts.

But when Nora reached the empty bus stop, she again heard that sickly humming sound, which this time sounded almost like a Gregorian chant. She darted across the street, hoping to lose the sound. But on the other side, it was worse, louder, buffeting her eardrums. She peered around the corner of the building she had braced herself against, down the small street that intersected Main Street.

And then she saw them, about a block away. A group of them in a parking lot, with their backs toward her, their heads tilted up as if they were howling like coyotes at the land beyond their reach.

The hairs on the back of Nora's neck stood on end. She realized the group was gathered by the town's border. And that they were probably staring off in longing at fresh meals they couldn't sink their teeth into.

Nora was suddenly aware of her own blood throbbing in her temples. The sound of her blood seemed to be getting louder, drowning out the humming sound, as if her blood were whooshing through her like a rain-swelled river. The whole town must hear her blood pounding, announcing to all that she was here and alive, Nora thought. And then in horror, Nora saw the group in the parking lot slowly turn, in unison, in her direction. They looked right at her. Even at this distance she could see the glint of greedy hunger in their eyes.

They began moving toward her, almost gliding, as if their feet were not actually touching the ground. Nora put her hand to her throat to strangle what felt like a scream.

Before she realized it, Nora was running again, blindly, across the intersection. She wasn't thinking about where she was going, or why, just that she had to get away from them. But she was still heading in the direction of the beauty parlor. If she had the time to think about it, she wouldn't go. But, what were her choices? Nora heard somebody whimpering like a child and was surprised to realize that it was herself.

She was almost at the shop, passing by the bookstore, when an arm shot out in front of her, blocking her path. Before Nora could even scream, someone pulled her through the bookstore door, throwing her hard to the floor.

"You stupid, stupid girl! Are you trying to ruin everything? Do you want to give them a taste of fresh blood after all these years?" a dark little man squeaked at her. In his brown sweater and pants, with his brown skin and hair, the little man reminded Nora of a fieldmouse. His nose actually twitched with rage, and his eyes were reduced to tiny balls of light.

Nora was a bit dazed, having had the wind knocked out of her. Her heart was still in overdrive, the force and weight of it in her chest pinning her to the spot where she had landed. All she could do was stare at the mousy man, in awe of the fury directed at her.

His back was to her now as he scrambled to the door, sliding its many latches and chains into locking positions. Next he dimmed the lights. When Nora finally made a practice clearing sound in her throat in an attempt to speak, he put a scrawny, knuckled finger to his lips, waving his free hand in irritation to keep her quiet.

At first, all Nora could hear was the sound of her own heart. But in a moment, she heard the humming sound again, this time accompanied by the sound of footsteps—footsteps that were unhurried, searching. The intensity of the humming grew, until Nora could swear the group was right outside the door. The mouse man was glaring at her. Nora tried not to breathe. Finally, the humming moved on, becoming only a faint echo before fading into silence.

"Who are you?" the mousy man snarled at her. He walked toward her with the hunch of a man trapped in a cramped room. Nora did a quick, backward crabwalk until she bumped into a bookshelf. She was alarmed by his anger.

"Nora! My name is Nora!" she almost shouted at him. "Look, I'm sorry for causing you any trouble." She leaned against the bookcase to shimmy herself up. "I'm just looking for my friend, for God's sake," she blurted out, the frustration of being surrounded by crazy people nearly bringing her to tears.

"Outsiders are not allowed here after sundown," he said, pointing his crooked finger at her accusingly.

"Look, I've learned that . . . Melvin. May I call you Melvin?" Nora began tidying up the books she had knocked askew. "Really, all I want to do is find my friend and get us both out of here."

"How do you know my name?" Melvin sniffed at her suspiciously, grabbing a book from her hand as if she were planning to steal it.

"Ah, Stanley told me . . . he mentioned how well your business is doing." Nora took a quick look around at the shop. For the first time she noticed how many shelves were only sparsely occupied, as if the store were having a going-out-of-business sale.

"Oh, he did, did he," Melvin sniffed. "Did he also tell you what a thief he is, the prices he's trying to charge me, just for coming into this town!" Suddenly, Melvin seemed preoccupied with his books. "Look at this place! The, uh, people here are voracious readers. I can't keep the shelves stocked."

Well, they had little else to do at night, Nora thought.

"Actually, just before closing, my, uh, neighbor's young wife practically bought every book I had on parenting. And, here I thought it was just a rumor that . . ." With a sudden jerk, Melvin stopped talking, as if someone might be listening.

It was Marcy, Nora thought. "What did she look like?" Nora came closer to him, to look into his face. "Was she small, blonde?" Was she terrified? she wanted to add.

"Look, I don't know. I shouldn't be talking about my customers like this. Now be quiet, and find a spot to . . . sit through the night." Melvin started edging Nora toward the stairs leading to the second floor.

"Wait, please. Marcy's next door, isn't she? She's your neighbor's wife, right? You know, don't you?"

Melvin was extremely agitated now. He looked erratically about the room as if someone were watching them. "Yes, but be quiet," he whispered nastily. He moved closer to her, speaking into Nora's ear. "She's right next door. But you don't want them to know you're here, do you?

You must stay here, until morning. You'll be safe, upstairs . . . with me."
Nora didn't like the nasty glint in his eyes. His closeness made her
shiver in revulsion.

"What's out back?" Nora asked, surprisingly controlled. She just
wanted to get away from him. She wanted to find Marcy, to bring all
this to an end.

"A parking lot," Melvin said slowly, suspiciously. "All of us shop
owners share the back parking lot." He scratched his head, nervously,
as if he were trying to think fast. "Tomorrow, though, you can go out
the back and knock on their back door. I'm sure . . . your friend . . . will
be there."

"No, I've got to go now." A terrible loathing fueled Nora with the
courage to act. She ran to the back door, Melvin frantically scrambling
after her. "No! Don't go!" he squealed. Nora pushed him away, opened
the door and practically threw herself into the parking lot, Melvin
slamming the door loudly behind her in fury. Nora was left standing
in the darkness, only a street lamp providing a washed-out glow
around its bulb. She stared at the building next door.

It was brick, two stories, like most of the shops on the block. The
second floor, which was dimly lit, had an outside deck, the stairway of
which led to the parking lot. Nora could see curtains were drawn across
the sliding glass door that opened onto the deck. She quietly approached the back door on the first floor landing, put her hand on the
ice-cold knob and turned it as if it were made of eggshells. The door
was locked.

Cursing the darkness softly, she turned, with apprehension, toward
the stairs to the deck. Each step she took felt leaden, loud in the eerie
silence of the night. A faraway train wailed as if lamenting its own
heavy burden, and the sound made Nora draw in her breath. She was
all too aware of her heart pounding in protest as she drew closer and
closer to the deck. With each cautious step, Nora feared that the furious drumming of the blood between her ears would alert the entire
town of her whereabouts. *Please God, please God, please God*, she
chanted to herself, pleading for whatever help He could offer.

When Nora finally reached the floor of the deck, she froze. For
what seemed like an eternity, she simply stood there, looking at the

curtained glass doors, mesmerized by the suggestion of movement within.

What was she going to do? she asked herself in a frenzied whisper. Did she really expect to catch them unaware? And now what? Did she simply knock and tell them it was time for Marcy and her to go home? Nora pelted herself with questions, furious that now, when she was this close, she felt all too vulnerable and powerless.

Her question and answer session abruptly ended when the curtains on the door suddenly whisked to one side, and a tall, powerfully built, darkly handsome man stood on the other side, smiling sinisterly at her. He took his time sliding the door open, the sound piercing the noiseless vacuum of the night. The man in the photograph stood before her. She couldn't mistake the pronounced widow's peak that crowned his pale, intense face.

Nora felt herself gaping at him, into his black eyes, which hinted at eternal secrets and uncharted darkness. The cut of his nose and cheekbones were those of the privileged and strong—kings, princes, lords. His thin lips, the color of dried blood, curled into a wicked smile as he whispered her name.

"Ah, Nora. We've been anxious about you, especially Marcy. We all worried we might not get the opportunity to meet you." His voice was deep, wintry like the wind. He reached out and took Nora by the elbow and guided her through the door.

Nora stood in shock for the moment, simply taking in the scene before her. There was Marcy, looking tiny and crushed against the overstuffed couch, like a cried-out child. Marcy's face was streaked with tears; her eyes looked sunken, resigned. Nora saw Marcy mouth her name in sorrow. The two men Nora had seen grab Marcy earlier sat at a counter that separated the small living room from the kitchen. They were munching on something, and one gave Nora a quick wave of recognition. Crumpled Roy Rogers' bags lay on the counter.

The man in the photograph sauntered over to Marcy and placed his hand on her head as if she were a naughty child. "You must be Stefan," Nora said without question. "I've heard so much about you." She hoped her voice did not tremble like her body.

"What a pity," Stefan said with a nod and a patronizing smile. "In the past, I tried to rein in my taste for the beautiful ones. And," he added, seeing the look of terror on Nora's face, "you are the best friend of my wife." His hand closed hard on Marcy's head, and she winced at the pressure. "But your scent, Nora, has captivated me since your arrival, and I've been, shall I say, champing at the bit."

Nora struggled to pull her eyes from his face. She was surprised at the calmness of her voice. "I promise your secret is safe with us, Stefan. Just let me take Marcy home. That is all I came to do. I didn't mean to . . ."

"Do you think I would let your stupid little friendship interfere with the birth of my child?" Stefan suddenly seemed to grow larger with his fury. "I've been waiting for centuries to find a woman whose womb could nurture one of our own. This will be an extraordinary event."

"But how can that be? Marcy told me years ago that—she couldn't have children. I don't understand," gasped Nora.

"Not human children," Stefan laughed mockingly while Marcy began to cry softly again. "My wife's womb is abnormal, inverted, an impossible journey for any human sperm to complete. But for my seed, the perfect, nurturing environment. We are in the process of creating an immortal, living being—a virtual god."

Stefan's eyes shone with delirious excitement, his men beaming their approval of his words with meat-moistened smiles.

Suddenly Marcy grabbed at Stefan's wrist, pulling his hand from her head.

"Get out, Nora, run!" Marcy screamed at her as she tried to hold Stefan. And then turning to Stefan, she yelled, "And I will kill myself and your baby if you hurt her!"

Stefan shoved Marcy with restrained fury back onto the couch, and before Nora had even blinked, he was pushing her backward out the open door, onto the deck. He kept walking right at her, causing Nora to stumble backward until her back was against the deck's railing. He held Nora by both shoulders, unbuttoning the top buttons of her coat, never taking his eyes away from hers.

"Nora, Nora, such an appropriate name for a beautiful woman," he whispered close to her ear. Nora felt her resolve to fight him slowly draining, ebbing away, as he continued to whisper in her ear, stroking her shoulders and neck. She was aware of her head bending back as if she were offering her neck to him. She felt her body wanting him to press against her. She wanted his hands about her neck and face. She would soon cry out in frustration if he didn't kiss the vein throbbing in her neck with his lips.

It was Marcy screaming her name again that brought Nora back, that caused her to push Stefan away from her just as he was about to bite into her unbroken skin. But Stefan grabbed her viciously now, intent on getting the blood he desired. Nora freed one arm and jammed her elbow into Stefan's side as hard as she could, causing him to choke at the precise moment he was ready to strike.

Suddenly, Stefan fell away from Nora and onto the deck, his body shaking with spasms as if he were having a convulsion. Nora looked at his stricken figure in shock as she placed her hand about her neck, feeling for any violation. All she felt was the loose chain of the little gold crucifix she always wore. In his frenzy to bite her, Stefan had swallowed it.

Marcy stood in the open doorway, looking down at Stefan uncomprehendingly. Nora could see Stefan's men getting up from the kitchen counter.

"Marcy, come on!" Nora yelled, motioning for her to get to the stairs. In a flash, they were both pounding down the steps, their adrenaline in high gear, the possibility of escape giving them new hope.

At the bottom of the stairway, they grabbed each other's hands and paused for a moment to choose a direction to run in.

"Let's go across the train tracks, through the parking lot. I think it's the town border," Nora urged. Marcy nodded in agreement.

They were halfway across the parking lot when an old black Chevy came barreling down at them, cutting off their path. Nora was shocked to see the passenger side door swing open, revealing the crazy priest at the wheel. "Get in!" he roared at them. "I'll take you out. We don't want that devil child here!"

Nora looked back toward the deck to see Stefan weakly sitting up, pointing his men in the direction of pursuit. "Okay, Marcy, get in. We don't have any other choice," she yelled, pulling Marcy into the front seat with her. She reached over Marcy to slam the door. "Go!"

The priest did a quick reverse, his wheels screeching against the cold, hard asphalt. The jerking motion flung Nora and Marcy into the dashboard, and their hands knocked over a number of magnetic Marys and Jesuses in their attempt to keep their balance. As they straightened themselves back into their seats, the glove compartment popped open, and a large ball of something rolled onto Marcy's lap. Instinctively, she screamed, flinging the ball into the back seat. Nora looked at her petrified. The smell of garlic permeated the air.

"Evil creatures. Are your eyes burning? Are your throats screaming for water?" the priest queried, laughing his demented cackle.

"For God's sake! When are you going to realize we're not one of them? And what are you waiting for? Drive, for crissakes, they're coming!" Nora's fear of the priest evaporated at the sight of the crowd suddenly surrounding the car.

About ten of Stefan's gang had their moon-white palms pressed against the windows, and they were chanting as they rocked the car, as if performing a soft lullaby. In the darkness, their eyes stared like red lasers.

"Please!" Nora screamed. "Drive!"

The priest slowly turned to Nora. He stared into her eyes. His own showed a sudden, clear intelligence, which just as quickly slipped below surface. "Please," Nora whispered, grabbing Marcy's hand.

And with that the priest stomped down hard on the accelerator. The figures before them had no impact on the car, but instead, dissolved, as if they were vapor. The priest drove like a charging bull, with no regard for the concrete dividers in his path. As they approached the parking lot's exit, the looming figure of Stefan stood blocking their path. This time Marcy screamed "Kill him!" above the roar of the car as the priest floored it. Stefan, like the others, dissolved.

"Father, watch out!" Nora yelled, pointing at the police car bearing down on them, its emergency lights flashing and its sirens wailing. The priest was shooting down Main Street, blurring the barely lit scenery into a collage of stores, diner and apartments. When they passed St. Vita's, the cops pulled up right alongside of them, the grouchy cop again at the wheel. He was trying to run them off the road. The cheerful cop was still smiling and winking at them, waving his gun as if it were a bottle of beer. The priest remained oblivious.

"When I reach the border, which will be in about two minutes, I'm jumping out. Be ready to grab the wheel." Marcy and Nora both looked at him in shock. His voice was calm, in command, reassuring.

"What do you mean?" Nora asked, again searching for his eyes. "They'll kill you. Don't be . . . foolish."

"No, they won't kill a crazy old priest. I'm their biggest weapon in keeping the Catholics out of town. Would you want to become a member of my parish?"

"You mean, all along, it's been an act?" Nora asked. But before she could get an answer, Stefan again appeared, this time in the car, sitting smack in between Marcy and Nora. They both screamed, swatting futilely at the air.

"Ignore him. It's simply a projection. He can't hurt you in this form," the priest commanded them. "Now get ready to take the wheel!"

The look of pure hatred and fury that twisted the image of Stefan's face scared Nora more than all of Stefan's marching legions and threats put together. It was a look Nora knew would provide her with plenty of nightmares if they managed to escape.

"Now!" the priest screamed, slowing only enough to open his door, pushing himself out and away from the car. The police car swerved just enough to miss him and suddenly slowed, as if accepting defeat. Nora grabbed the wheel and ran the car right through the barricades that separated the town from the outside world.

Nora and Marcy both took a quick look at the town behind them before Nora pressed her foot down hard on the accelerator. "Marcy, check to see if anyone is coming after us." Marcy nodded, squinting in the direction of the shrinking town border. Nora looked for the flashing red signal of the police car in her rearview mirror. The red light did not appear to be moving. There were no signs of Stefan or his people.

"Marcy," Nora said, slightly above a whisper. "I think we made it."

Marcy leaned gently against Nora, crying softly in relief.

They sat in silence for a few minutes, Nora automatically looking back to make sure no one was following them.

"Do you think the priest will be all right?" Marcy asked, as if reading Nora's thoughts.

"I don't know. I hope so. The cops should protect him." Nora prayed that it would be true. "And they do have a pact with Stefan and his people."

Marcy nodded.

"Nora, you've always been my best friend, and I owe you everything, my life and . . . the baby's. I have an explanation, for whatever it's worth, for it all, all those years. But I can't talk about it tonight."

"I know, Marcy. None of this seems real anyway. I'm still waiting to wake up." Nora tried an encouraging smile, but it just wouldn't come.

"You know, he was so wonderful at first," Marcy said, looking straight into the road ahead. Other cars were beginning to pass them periodically. Their headlights seemed brave and comforting. "He said that I was the one for him, his special one." Marcy smiled wistfully. "And when I got pregnant, it was like a miracle. Me, pregnant."

Nora turned apprehensively toward Marcy. Was that affection she had heard, if only for a moment, in Marcy's voice?

Nora couldn't say anything. She didn't know if it was the cold vinyl seats of the car that made her shiver, the black loneliness of the January night or the sight of Marcy, her hands cradled protectively over her barely swelling belly. Later, Nora thought; we'll talk about the baby later. In the morning, in the harsh January light, where she could stare into Marcy's unblinking eyes, for a clue, for an answer. She touched Marcy's hand and drove toward home. They were safe. For now.

Immunity

Toni Brown

AIT, MOM! LOOK AT MY mosquito bite. I think it's bleeding!"

Celeste leaned into the doorway of her six-year-old daughter's room and clicked on the light. Out of the darkness appeared four lavender walls decorated with pictures made with crayon and water paints. There were wooden shelves, on which books leaned and stuffed animals haphazardly slumped. From the ceiling, a balsa wood pterodactyl hung on fishing line. The bed's ebony headboard was trimmed with a border of speckled cowrie shells. Carved into the center of the headboard was a yellowing ivory mask from the Nigerian province of Benin.

Nia, round faced and the color of dark plums, sat up in bed. She had kicked the covers aside and was closely examining her right wrist. She wore white pajama bottoms and a T-shirt that barely covered her baby-fat stomach or the thumb-tip belly button that protruded from it. Printed on the shirt in red block letters was the word *Monster!*

"I could bleed to death," she said plaintively. "It's over a vein, you know."

Her mother smiled slightly as she crossed the room to the edge of the bed. She seemed to float over the floor, making no sound. She looked at the bump on her daughter's wrist, rubbed it gently, then kissed it.

"It's not bleeding, sweetie." Celeste knew the small raised bump was not a mosquito bite. She pulled the covers up, making a tent, into which Nia automatically lay down.

"It's time for sleep now, Nia." Celeste tucked in the covers and then kissed her daughter's warm cheek. Nia seemed comforted. She hoped Nia would quiet down and that this would be her last trip into her daughter's room tonight.

"Mom?" Celeste crossed the room, headed for the door.

"Mom, can I have another glass of juice?" Celeste's hand reached for the light switch. Nia lifted her head from the pillow expectantly. Her mother turned off the light.

"Good night, Nia." Celeste used her tired, final voice as she closed the door.

"I'm really thirsty, Mom!" Nia's voice pleaded, slightly muffled.

"Good night, Nia." Celeste walked along the dimly lit hall and slowly descended the stairs.

Each night the ritual was the same. Nia would try to engage her in last-minute bedtime conversation, and Celeste would respond by monotonously repeating good night until Nia finally gave up and went to sleep. Usually Nia got the message after two or three tries, but this was Celeste's fourth trip to her room and Nia still looked very much awake.

Nia had come home from school that afternoon talking about Dracula and vampires. "Could garlic really keep them away?" "Were they really afraid of crosses?" "Can't we have just *one* cross at our house?" This gave Celeste a bad feeling, stirring up anxieties she had tried to keep pushed to the back of her mind.

Celeste sat right down with Nia, and they talked about it. She thought she had convinced Nia that these were just stories made up to frighten and amuse, like at Halloween. Nia listened intently, taking it all in. She seemed fine until bedtime, until the lights were turned out. Celeste sucked her teeth in irritation and her stomach growled. Tonight was not the night for her to have problems with Nia falling asleep.

Celeste's dark fingers slid along the polished mahogany banister. Her knuckles, wrinkled and gnarled like ancient tree roots, belied her fortyish-appearing face. In the foyer, she passed an old, gilt-frame mirror. It reflected the ornate front door and nothing more. She passed through an arched doorway and into the living room, where she settled into a pale blue wing chair. The supports had given way long ago, so sitting down in this chair meant sitting nearly on the floor. Still, it was cozy and it faced the French doors and the courtyard. This was her favorite room, with its high ceiling and stone block floor. The walls were painted a neutral eggshell color, but sometimes when the light was right she could see a wallpaper pattern underneath. There was a large fireplace. Inside it, carved in the stone, were images of joyous women dancing with wolves and snakes and birds. When there was a fire blazing, the scenes seemed to come alive. Last year at this time she had needed a small fire to take the chill out of the room, but this October night there was no need, since it was unusually warm and raining gently. She wondered what the room had looked like when the Victorian mansion had all sixteen rooms intact, before being renovated into three spacious apartments.

They had come to this town when Nia was an infant. This house, on the outskirts of a large university campus, was just right for them, an older single woman and her child. The other apartments were always filled with busy, preoccupied students who moved in and out again with regularity and anonymity. Sometimes there would be someone willing to baby-sit for her during an infrequent evening out or someone willing to listen through the wall for the sound of Nia's voice. Generally she left her student neighbors alone though; things seemed to work better that way. And as Nia had grown older, Celeste had found it possible to leave Nia alone for short periods at night.

The rain softly pattered against the windows and the side of the house. She looked through sheer curtains at the full moon rising, reflecting silver on the surrounding clouds. There were many windows in this room; most were sparkling clean and bare. From early morning until late in the afternoon, the sun visited here, and while Nia was in school, Celeste would bask. Tonight she lit candles and let the room fill with moonlight. The French doors rattled against the intermittent wind.

She curled into the chair and relaxed, loosening the turban that was wound about her head. The day had been long, and she still had the night ahead of her.

She thought about Nia and this new fear. Celeste knew that this was only the first of many misrepresentations of people, distortions of history that Nia would learn. The vampire stories were just children spreading tales, but this was only the beginning. Anger flashed through her quickly, then dissipated as she sighed, resigned that despite her efforts Nia would learn about the world from those who knew the least about it. She wondered how long she would have before Nia began to question the difference between the world inside their home and the one outside.

The wind slapped a loose shutter against the house, distracting her. She heard a car drive past. Her breathing slowed. The blood began to drain from her face. She sank back in the wing chair until all that could be seen from the doorway were her dark hands gripping its thick blue arms. Her eyes closed. Her breathing became a rhythm that echoed the beating of her heart. The vision began.

She felt herself moving through a wooded patch of land. It was dark, and the last clear rays of sunlight seemed weak and cold. The ground was littered with pine needles. She could see the road in the distance. She was a snake from the belly down. Her head, shoulders and arms were bone and skin and hair, while the rest of her was rounded and thick and covered with glistening black scales. Ferns and stiff grasses grazed her sides. Her body rippled like the ocean meeting sand as she moved swiftly forward. In her mouth, the acrid taste of hunger. Saliva began to well beneath her tongue.

A short distance ahead was a disabled car, a man and woman standing by it. The woman, with her arms crossed over her chest and her back to the man, looked up the road.

The wind whispered, "Faster," and she plunged on, eyes focused on the figures ahead. She could smell them now.

First the man just glanced in her direction, then riveted his attention on the terrible apparition looming before him. He pressed himself against the car. He raised his arm as if to protect his face. He took in one sharp breath, and then she was upon him. She pinned his arms to his sides as she coiled her constricting body around him. He screamed, and the woman wrenched around—

"Mom! Mom!" Nia's bedroom door slammed. Celeste heard her daughter's footsteps as Nia ran toward the stairs. She blinked rapidly, trying to focus. She rubbed the goose flesh prickling her upper arms. Nia burst into the room and climbed into her lap.

"Mom, I heard something." She buried her face in her mother's chest and curled against her. Celeste hugged her. Nia was shivering. Celeste stroked her daughter's thick hair and then rubbed her back comfortingly. She began to rock Nia gently. Nia sat up and stopped her mother's rocking.

"I'm not a baby, you know."

"I know," Celeste sighed, and Nia rested her head against her shoulder again.

"It's all right, Nia," she patted her. "What's the matter?"

Nia looked down at her knees and picked at a scab, bumpy, beneath her cotton pajama pant. Celeste pulled her hand away.

"I heard something."

"Like what?"

"I don't know, something scary."

"Scary like a dog or thunder?"

"No, like a scratchy, growly sound. I don't know. It woke me up." Her voice had become an annoying whine.

"Nia, you have school tomorrow."

"I know, but I'm scared."

"Honey, there's nobody here but me. What is there to be afraid of?"

She already knew her daughter's answer, but waited patiently for Nia to whisper, "Vampires." She felt anger rise in her again like heat waves.

"Nia, listen. Those stories about dead men who walk the earth were made up to scare you. All that stuff about stakes through the heart"—she shuddered and wrinkled her nose at her daughter—"is just silly lies. The dead cannot walk, the dead cannot be killed. Once you are dead, you are dead. These are tales made up by people who don't know anything about being dead, since they obviously are still alive themselves."

She smiled at her own joke, but Nia was not amused.

"You, my young pup, should be in bed. Don't you see that big, beautiful moon? Can't you hear it calling you to sleep?" Her voice was soft and low, yet heavy. The weight of it was meant to pull her daughter's eyelids down. The rain dripped slowly off the edge of the roof.

"But where did all those stories come from? Why would anyone want to scare me?"

Celeste slid Nia off of her lap and guided her out of the room.

"Nia," Celeste said, taking her hand and leading her slowly toward the stairs, "you have nothing to fear from vampires. Let me tell you a story. Long ago when our ancestors still lived in Africa, another people came to visit us. These people were from a place called Greece. They came to visit our tribe and brought us gifts and told us all kinds of strange and wonderful things. They called themselves Lamia. The Lamia were a people similar in some ways to the ones they now call vampires. But they were not dead men. We danced with them and showed them our ways. We showed them our magic, and they were impressed. We decided to become as one tribe. We made an agreement with these Lamia." She paused as if trying to remember.

"To never hurt each other, to be as if sisters. All African people are protected by that agreement. That's why there are no stories about black people being bitten by vampires, Nia. Have you ever heard of any?" Celeste paused briefly.

"That agreement from so long ago keeps us safe. We have immunity. You are protected."

Celeste stopped. The story was over. They had reached the top of the stairs. Nia looked around as if confused.

"Honest?" Nia asked after a moment. She looked into her mother's eyes, searching for a lie. Celeste's eyes were dull black almonds. She turned her gaze away.

"Honest," she answered.

Nia was silent. Celeste led her into the darkened bedroom.

"Good night, Nia." She kissed her cheek. Nia scratched sleepily at the lump on her wrist.

"Mom," Nia yawned noisily, "what else did we get in the agreement we made?"

"That is a long story for another night, sweet. Sleep tight now. And Nia—don't get out of bed again." There was no fatigue in this final voice. She closed Nia's bedroom door.

As Celeste moved slowly down the stairs, she thought that in a very short time Nia would no longer be a child. When she had grown to be a young woman, maybe then Celeste could share the whole secret of her people.

Before the coming of the Lamia, in the villages south and far west of the Sudan, her kind were called *Awon Iya Wa Aje*—our mothers, the witches. In the spring, when the rains came, the Yoruba people held festivals celebrating the season. Members of the Gelede cult carved masks of dark wood and ivory. They danced to invite the witch mothers, or *Aje*, into the village. They courted good favor with music and chanting. They offered appeals for fecundity of fields and wives. They prayed for the continued good health of the children already born. They left caches of cowrie shells and precious stones and gold hanging from the low branches of trees.

When the Lamia came, they told tales of their kin the great Medusa and her immortal Gorgon sisters. They sang songs about their great strength and the curse that left them with an appetite for human flesh. They spoke of Greek cities reduced to ashes, burned by humans provoked by the sight of a nest of snakes.

The Aje complained of the loneliness of immortality, the precariousness of a shifting noncorporeality. The Lamia and the Aje exchanged magic: from the Aje, the ability to change form from human to cat to jackal to bat to smoke. From the Lamia, a physically material body and the possibility of the blessed sleep of death. From the Aje, the secret of fecundity, the ability to bring about fruitfulness of soil and of women. From the Lamia, the terrible hunger for human flesh. Ironically, the very babies that the Aje had helped birth, the Lamia were devouring with delight.

Soon the seasonal dances of life were replaced by rituals of appeasement for the new spirits who made the children disappear. And it wasn't just the children who were eaten—anyone wandering the bush in the night or sleeping in an outlying hut could be taken. In time, the hunts became a rite of passage into manhood. Many of Celeste's ancestors were killed. Some escaped, disguised by shifting form.

For Celeste, Nia brought a focus to her eternity, a consanguinity. She remembered bringing the infant home. Home then was a battered old structure at the edge of a dying town. She rested in the shadows and held the wriggling stolen bundle at arm's length. The baby wailed, yet there was not a single tear on her dark face. Her little hands were balled into hard fists, which she waved uselessly in the night air. But as the child shook with fury, Celeste stared down at her hair. Her thick aureole of black curls seemed alive in the moon's bright light. The baby's hair looked like tiny, shiny snakes. Celeste had never been moved in this way. She felt a conflict between the instinct to eat the sweet, warm-blooded creature and the urge to somehow suckle it.

Celeste had not lied about Nia's protection. Nia was protected by her. She would not be harmed by the tiny sips of blood Celeste sometimes took from her wrist. As for the other people of African descent, Celeste could honestly say she had not feasted on their flesh since she left her native land.

Celeste was perhaps the only one of the joined beings, Lamia and Aje, still left. She had not seen one of her kind since she left her home in Africa. She had lived for centuries. She might live forever, but at least for a time in this foreign place, she would not be alone.

Deep in her chair again, she looked out at the swirling fog. She closed her eyes. Her breathing began its slow cadence. A rhythm that had become a rattling hiss echoed against the walls of the moonlit room. Her scalp began to tingle as her kinky, corded hair began to move, transformed into pencil-thin snakes that writhed sinuously. Her skin deepened to a shiny black. Her fingernails also blackened and grew long and pointed. She dug them into the arm of the chair. She opened her mouth to accommodate the sharp row of teeth that grew there. A cloudy thread of spittle spun slowly to her chin.

She looked past the flimsy glass door into the lights of the small town. Its sleeping people awaited her. The moon rose victoriously in the sky. The rain had stopped. Slithering out of the chair, she moved to and opened the French doors. The wind blew cool and sweet across her face. Her massive serpentine body glistened in the night's bright luminescence. She was hungry. She surged forward, undulating toward the low garden wall. Hair hissing in the damp autumn air, she stopped and listened. Had she heard a small voice call out from upstairs? No, it was only the wind. She murmured, "Good night, Nia," as she disappeared into the night.

Sustenance

Susanna J. Sturgis

L ILLIAN KRAMER SLUMPED AGAINST the bathroom door. Now the kids were squabbling over who got the last of the Cocoa Pebbles. Thank God they'd waited till Steve left for work. Steve, after smacking one or both of them, would have been ragging on her the rest of the week because she didn't buy enough of the rotten cereal last Saturday.

Lillian squinted at her image in the big mirror, still fogged over from Steve's shower. The gray bath rug was clammy under her bare feet. Once, just once, she thought, I would like to step into a dry, orderly bathroom and shower for ten blessed minutes—twenty if I want—behind an unlocked door.

Here she was: Four months shy of forty, as Steve was forever reminding her, and her dearest wish was for an uninterrupted shower.

She rubbed her palm across the mirror. There she was in miniature, in a bloated drop of water: a refugee from Tobacco Road, thirty-nine going on a hundred. The smudges under her eyes were more pronounced than usual. Even the faint, faint scars from her case of adolescent acne had staged a comeback. Pathetic. Lillian hated all mornings, but Mondays were the absolute worst. She couldn't wait to get to work.

She turned on the shower. Immediately the water started to back up in the tub. "Damn him," she muttered, pushing the handle that opened the drain. Steve's idea of a practical joke: leaving the drain closed when he finished his shower. Ha ha ha.

When she was a little girl, she had loved to watch the water spiral down out of the tub when she finished her bath. How her mother glared whenever she imitated that liquid rasping sound! A few years later Lillian was filching lipstick, eye shadow, blush and eyebrow pencil from her mother's hoard and locking herself in the bathroom to try on different faces. When she grew bored with beauty queens and pretty princesses in disguise, she turned to sultry seductresses with red, red lips and brows that swept back to her temples. She was going to be an actress when she grew up and wear wild makeup all the time.

Then her sister, Evelyn, three years older, caught her early one Sunday morning when she was putting the final touches on the Dragon Lady Who Stopped the Sun in Its Tracks. After a startled instant, Evelyn burst out laughing. She laughed so hard she slid down the wall and sat helplessly on the tile floor. "Oh, *Lillian!*" she said. "Here, I'll show you how to do it."

After that Lillian didn't know what to be when she grew up.

Now, after ten years of motherhood, she hated the bathroom, everything about it: cleaning it, bathing the kids in it, rushing in and out of it. Not including the lavatory on the first floor, the Kramers' house—the one they were always going to trade up from, or add on to or, at the very least, renovate—had only one bathroom, and it was a permanent war zone.

The Sunday night after Thanksgiving, year before last, when Terry was eight and Nina six and a half, the two of them had started squabbling before supper. That part was nothing new; neither was Lillian having to bathe them separately—which took even more time—while fending off Steve, who wanted her to find something he'd mislaid. Lillian had held herself tightly as she stared at the gray sudsy water receding from a grayer ring half way up the tub. Before her eyes the funnel above the drain had turned rusty and then red. It was blood, hers, trickling with growing assurance from her vagina, over the cool porcelain rim and down the side of the tub. *Her blood.*

My period already? she wondered, panicky. *Oh God, I must be bleeding to death.* She shut her eyes. Opened them warily. The water was gray. Her tan chinos were damp around the knees but otherwise spotless.

She had seen the blood. Now the blood wasn't there. She had to be going crazy.

That night she had gone to bed early and in the morning gone straight to the health food store, where on the advice of the cashier, she bought a two-month supply of B-complex vitamins and a general women's supplement with extra iron.

It hadn't helped.

That New Year's Eve, while Steve snored away, his feet pressing hers to the very edge of the bed, Lillian had lain awake, too tired to sleep, watching smoky moonshadows play on the ceiling and dreading the beginning of another miserable year of feeling her life drain away. As she watched, something had moved between the windows: the ripply tendril of an unseen plant was growing up the wall. As it rose she felt a wrenching inside her, as if a baby were being tugged unready from her womb. The trickle of blood branched and expanded as it rose up the wall to the ceiling, where it mingled with the shadowy images of bare tree branches above her.

This can't mean I'm pregnant. Please don't let me be pregnant, she had prayed.

She hated being pregnant. Morning sickness gave way to weeks of listlessness. Night and day the alien inside her sapped her blood, contorted her body into the cartoonish shape she barely recognized in the mirror. Terry, once born, had been no less voracious. Why hadn't anyone told her she would go for months without even three hours of uninterrupted sleep? When the doctor confirmed she was pregnant again, less than a year later, she had sat for hours on the kitchen floor, a carving knife in her lap, while upstairs Terry howled in his crib.

But she hadn't really wanted to die. Back then Lillian still believed that this bone-deep exhaustion would pass, that someday her body and her life would be hers again. Now she half-wished she had not replaced the knife in its butcher block holder. Years had passed, but her sole ambition each day was to survive till the next.

Evelyn claimed that her children were the joy of her existence, while Lillian wondered if she had been the unwitting surrogate for an alien race. Obviously her kids wanted something from her, and just as obviously she had no clue what it was. They were floating up there, among the moonshadows on the bedroom ceiling, like little astronauts linked to the mother ship. Nina's red plaid "best" dress had grape jelly on the white collar; its hem was half torn out. Terry wore camouflage pants and that stupid Simpsons T-shirt. Together they were hauling the blood out of her body, hand over chubby hand.

Take, take, take, you hungry bastards! she told them. *Take till there's nothing left. See who feeds you then.*

Steve could tell when her reserves were low; then his barbs, always sharp, lodged deep in her flesh and left ugly wounds when she pulled them out. Steve's nose for blood was as well honed as the next man's. Lillian's took much longer to develop—which was strange, come to think of it, wasn't it? Women were supposed to be closer to nature. But the secret of survival hadn't come to Lillian till the previous Easter, almost a year ago now. Holidays always pushed her to the brink. Everyone had pressing demands and unvoiced expectations, which she was supposed to figure out and meet. But last Easter she actually got something back.

It had been the Kramers' turn to host the extended family: Evelyn, her husband, Lou and their three kids, and Steve's long-divorced mother. The holiday ceasefire was looking shaky; Lillian had served ham instead of steak, so Steve was smoldering in front of the TV. Then Cleo, the calico cat, weary of being tugged and hugged, scratched Evelyn's two-year-old son, Jimmy. A thin line of blood appeared on the boy's plump cheek. Jimmy started to bawl. Steve rose raging at his wife for not putting the cat out. His mother rushed for the phone to call a doctor and was intercepted by Evelyn, who insisted it was no big deal.

"Cat scratch fever!" wailed Steve's mother.

"For God's sake!" Evelyn burst out laughing. *Thanksgiving* dinner, she told Lillian, would be at her house.

Jimmy howled.

Lillian got to him first and lifted him up. Once Steve realized he was ranting in the face of a two-year-old, he shut up. Lillian carried the squalling Jimmy out into the hall, fumbling through her cardigan pockets for Kleenex. She blotted the cut with her right forefinger. Rather than wipe off the blood on her good dress, she sucked her finger clean.

She licked Jimmy's cheek, like a cat. The bleeding stopped. So, after a few whimpers, did the boy's crying. He wrapped his left arm around her neck and stuck his right thumb in his mouth. She walked down the hall and out to the front yard, where Lou was throwing a baseball for Terry and his cousin Mike to catch. She watched him bounce a steaming grounder to Mike, who snapped it back, and then a high pop-up to Terry. Evelyn's nine-year-old, Suzy, had drawn Nina into a Wild West game that involved a red wagon and most of Nina's stuffed animals. The daffodils in the yard had never been so yellow.

That night Steve went to bed before nine, after feeding on leftover ham, pecan pie and three more Budweisers. Lillian put the silverware and good dinner plates away, mopped the kitchen floor and had the house to herself. An hour or two of quiet—what should she do with it? Read? Read *what?*

The Sunday paper was still on the floor beside Steve's brown leather lounger. She found the chair big, hard and not at all cozy but sat in it anyway. She switched on the lamp and reached over the arm for the Living/Arts section.

Evelyn looked great, she thought. Lou was wonderful with the kids. Lillian envied the way they caught each other's eyes across the room and smiled, how Lou touched Evvy's shoulder and said, "Ready to go, hon?" Lillian looked at her murky reflection in the dormant TV screen. What was wrong with her?

Once upon a time she and Steve had been like that, back before making love had given way to having sex. Before Terry was born, or conceived, before they were even married, they would illuminate the dark bathroom with candles and shower together, lathering each other all over and shampooing each other's hair. Once they had even made ridiculously slippery love in the bath—an experiment they didn't repeat after Lillian, in an ecstatic moment, nearly cracked her head on the faucet.

She smiled, remembering. How very long ago! For a couple of years she had shared a house with two other girls, all in their mid-twenties. By the luck of the draw she occupied the master bedroom and didn't have to share its bath with anyone. But she had wanted to share with Steve, not just candlelit baths, but the whole rest of her life.

Lost in wonder and regret, she didn't notice the thick stream of blood till it reached just a few inches above eye level. Nor did she recognize it at first or know what it was. It looked like an old bell-pull. Was the paint peeling off in strips already, was the upstairs plumbing leaking through? But though it eddied and rippled like water, it threw off droplets that never fell. She reached out with both hands. It was warm, viscous, not unpleasant to touch. She drew it to her lips, tasted, sipped—drank and drank till the whole river was gone.

In the morning she rose feeling that the world had been created just for her. She filled the tub with iridescent bubbles and admired her toes, ankles and fingers till the water turned tepid. The kids knocked on the door, tried the knob and then pounded: Nina wanted hot cereal for breakfast, Terry couldn't find his social studies book. Lillian ignored them.

But the next morning had been like every other miserable morning, and the next was just as bad. And Mondays—after a weekend of being sucked down the family drain—were still the worst.

The hospital's child-care center rang with gourd rattles, triangles, sleigh bells and blocks. Cheryl, the head preschool teacher, was leading a rousing parade of three- and four-year-olds around the big room. She looked like an oversized kid herself in her denim jumper and plaid shirt, her hair in two stubby braids tied with green ribbons.

The woman in the doorway looked like a celebrity entering a swank detox incognito: oyster-gray trenchcoat, black scarf, sunglasses, the works.

"You lead, Brian—can you make a figure eight?" Cheryl stepped out of line, paused, looked quizzically at the door. "May I help you?"

The woman removed her dark glasses and untied her scarf. It was Lillian Kramer, the toddler-room aide since last June. Cheryl gasped, pressed her knuckles to her mouth and laughed. "Oh, I'm so sorry!"

"No problem," said Lillian. "It must be the glasses. My eyes feel hypersensitive this morning, can you imagine—in this drizzle?"

Lillian hung up her coat in the office and proceeded down the short hall to the toddler room. *Of course Cheryl doesn't recognize me,* she thought. *I don't look like myself. I don't even know what "myself" looks like. The mirror is always fogged over.* Little Annie was squalling on the floor. *The child is all mouth,* thought Lillian. *All children are all mouth.*

"Thank God, you're here!" Barbara said. With her long blonde braid and animated features, Barbara seemed so young. All the teachers were absurdly young, even the two who were older than Lillian. "It was about to start spreading."

Lillian was already cradling Annie in her arms, stroking her hair, heading toward the nursery. No one could quiet a cranky toddler the way Lillian could. Annie was sound asleep, thumb in mouth, before Lillian put her down in the crib. Lillian smiled at the nursery room aide; the aide smiled back.

All the rest of that day, Cheryl got visibly flustered whenever Lillian encountered her in the hall or the washroom. After lunch, Lillian sat on the toddler-room floor, laughing with several kids as they rounded stuffed animals into a building-block corral. Something bright moved in Lillian's peripheral vision. She glanced up: Cheryl had paused in the doorway to watch. The younger woman waved and continued quickly down the hall. *Don't worry about me,* Lillian thought. *I'm fine.*

"You're so good with the children," Cheryl told Lillian at the end of the day, as they shrugged on their coats. "Have you thought about getting certified in early childhood education?"

Lillian managed a little laugh. "Maybe someday," she said. *Right. I'd have to take courses at the community college, thirty miles away. When would I find the time, or the money?*

∾

Whoever thought blood would be so difficult to obtain? Lillian, who had believed her problems were over once she had made her discovery, soon learned otherwise. How many adults would stand still to have their arms pricked? One morning when Steve cut his cheek shaving, Lillian made a point of kissing him off to work. It revived her somewhat, but even that small taste made her cough. Not long after, she seduced him—he would have been suspicious if he hadn't been drunk—and managed to prick his forearm with a sharpened fingernail after he had fallen asleep. His blood made her woozy.

So: no smokers, no drinkers. No one under the influence of any kind of drug, and no one with a blood-borne disease. Lillian had volunteered to work at the Red Cross blood drives, but you had to be a nurse to get anywhere near the blood, and besides, those drives only happened every few months. Not often enough.

Sucking her own blood had no effect at all. Her children? Now that would have been poetic justice, but when she sampled first Nina, then Terry, both in their sleep, their blood offered no sustenance. This mystified her at first, but then she had stared down her reflection in the bathroom mirror and laughed: Of course! Their blood was her blood, sucked right out of her body from before they were born.

It would have to be other people's children. Children didn't ask questions. They gave what she needed, and then they forgot. No one thought twice when a child wrapped her arms around your neck or noticed when you kissed the new needle mark on his inner forearm. When you brought the child back calm and drowsy, they were grateful; they said you worked miracles.

Aide at the local hospital's day-care center was the perfect job. Even the pay, poor as it was, gave her a lift. Every week she put fifty dollars into her own savings account and dreamed of adding on a new master bedroom—with its own bath, of course!—to the ground floor of the house.

Auntie 'Bella came to tell the kids stories one Thursday and was drafted immediately into the regular-visitors lineup. Auntie—Arabella Finch—was eighty-six and recuperating from hip surgery in the hospital's long-term care unit. She walked slowly with two canes, which fascinated the children, but she radiated such energy that she seemed quite spry.

"Shall I tell you about when I was a little girl?" she asked fourteen sprawling, slouching and sitting three- and four-year-olds.

"Okay," said one of the bolder ones.

"Let me see," said the storyteller, closing her eyes and holding one hand over her spectacles. With the other she snatched a tale from the air. "I'll tell you about the very first time my mother set me to watch my little brother and sister. Mrs. Hamilton in the village was laid up with a broken ankle, and my mother wanted to take her some soup and fresh-baked bread for her lunch . . ."

Perhaps Mrs. Finch had had stage experience, amateur at least; her voice was strong, rippling with mischief and promising plot twists to come.

"She's totally with it," Cheryl whispered to Lillian as they stood at the back of the room. "I was afraid . . ."

"I know what you mean," said Lillian.

Mrs. Finch caught their eyes just long enough to assure them that they could relax.

"Gimme that back, Willy!" shrieked a little girl's voice in the toddler room next door. A chair fell. A wail rose like a siren.

"Oh, *Willy!* Excuse me," murmured Lillian, who had slipped over from the toddler room to hear the storyteller.

Most of the children, thank heavens, remained at their little tables. A small boy in denim overalls and a miniature rugby jersey howled on the floor next to the fallen chair. An angelic curly-haired brunette in a green corduroy jumper stood by gazing up at Barbara, whose very stillness conveyed her displeasure.

Willy had swiped Jadellen's chocolate chip cookie. Jadellen, no shrinking violet, had shoved him over in his chair. "I asked first!" sobbed Willy. "You pig!" raged Jadellen.

Lillian scooped Willy up off the floor while Willy thrashed and struggled and screamed "I hate you!" at Jadellen. She carried him toward the office, whispering as she walked. By the time she got to the end of the hall, Willy's bellows had become sniffles. Nevertheless they walked up and down the hall a few times; anyone looking on would have thought them deep in conversation.

When the cookie thief and his comforter returned, Barbara was effusive. "Lil, you must have the magic touch," she said. "How do you do it?" She lifted Willy from her co-worker's arms.

"I'm sorry I pushed you over," said Jadellen, looking up.

Willy yawned as if waking up from a long night's sleep.

Early March was brown and gray; all the cars in the parking lot were dingy with road salt and mud. But within the fenced enclosure bright colors flourished: Small children in magenta, blue, red and teal jackets and equally vivid, often mismatched hats swarmed up and down a corkscrew slide of green and yellow, rode a purple dinosaur, wriggled through the portholes of a white and orange ship. Shouts and laughter came out in steamy puffs, but no one pushed or shoved, no one cried.

"Lord," said Lillian, pushing two little girls on their side-by-side swings, "eleven o'clock and not a crisis in sight."

Barbara laughed, her vigilant gaze encompassing both the slide and the even more garish gingerbread house beside it. "What do you expect? Willy's not here!"

Lillian's breath caught in her throat. She really hadn't noticed. "Is he sick?"

"Didn't you hear? One at a time there, kids—okay, Jason, you go first. His mother had to call the EMTs yesterday, around suppertime. He'd stopped breathing."

Mechanically Lillian kept pushing the swings, now slightly out of synch. Push *push* (pause), push *push*. "No," she said.

"Oh, he's fine—she gave him mouth-to-mouth, said it only took two good breaths before he started again. Doctor said keep him home a couple of days, just to be on the safe side."

"But," Lillian hardly dared ask, "why?"

Barbara shrugged. "It happens sometimes, that's all. Like SIDS—crib death. No one really knows why."

Push *push* (pause), push *push* (pause). "He's lucky she noticed," Lillian said. *What if she hadn't? It would have been my fault . . .*

"He's lucky she didn't just freak out. Some of these mothers, wow! They just don't have a clue."

One of Lillian's small swingers wanted to play on the slide; Barbara went to head off an impending squall by the big boat. Maybe it was coincidence, Lillian thought, unclasping the safety bar and holding the swing steady so the little girl could slide off. Maybe it was—but she knew it wasn't. Willy was a strapping little kid. She would have to be more cautious.

Never greedy, now Lillian took less. If she could skip a day, she did. But Steve, Terry and Nina—and even Cleo the cat—still sucked up all her energy, all her time, and they never replenished a drop of it. And she was uneasy: When a child she had drawn blood from was out sick for a day or two, even with a minor sniffle, Lillian noticed. Was it her fault? Had this been happening all along without her noticing?

On top of it all, Arabella Finch was watching her. While she told her stories, the old lady's eyes tracked Lillian around the toddler room; they even followed her down the hall. They weren't hostile eyes, not at all. Hostility wouldn't have thrown Lillian so off-balance. Arabella Finch's eyes were *wise*.

Just before the kids had lunch, Lillian sought refuge in the director's washroom—the only bathroom in the wing with toilets and sinks at adult height. The face in the sink-to-ceiling mirror seemed more wan than usual, the smudges darker under the eyes. Steve's current job would be complete by the end of the month, and the one scheduled next suddenly looked chancy; Terry had been caught cheating on a test, his math teacher said, and Terry's surly response had been "So what?" Winter was a terrible time.

Another face appeared beside hers: silvery hair, every wave in place, clear blue eyes, high color in the cheeks with the faint smell of powder.

"Lillian," said Arabella Finch. "I didn't mean to startle you."

"Oh, you didn't," Lillian replied, a little flustered. "I was, well, pre-occupied."

Mrs. Finch held up her two hands, with diamond and wedding rings on the left, a black signet on the right. "Modeling clay!" she said. "My mother, God rest her soul, was forever telling me I couldn't stay presentable for five minutes. I swear, I'll go to my grave with dirt under all ten fingernails."

Lillian smiled. Mrs. Finch ran water into the other sink. Lillian rubbed her hands on her skirt—had she washed them or not?

"I think you are troubled," Mrs. Finch said. "Am I right?"

"Oh," Lillian shrugged, "no more than most people. My husband doesn't know where his next job is coming from, and my son seems to be having trouble at school. That's all."

"Winter is hard," Mrs. Finch agreed. "I've lived here all my life. There's more work than there used to be, but there are more people wanting it, too."

You're at least twice my age, Lillian thought, and you look more alive than I do.

"I don't mean to pry—I know, I sound just like one of the old church ladies!—but if I can be of assistance, will you let me know?" When Lillian remained silent, the storyteller added, "Promise?"

"Sure," Lillian lied. Alone again, she glanced at the mirror. Her gaze rebounded off that bleak face and dropped to the shiny faucets. *Assistance, old woman? How could you be of assistance? Can you make my children stop stealing my blood? Can you take me back to when I infuriated my mother with schlurp-sucking sounds, or when I could be the Dragon Lady or Cleopatra, Queen of Egypt, whenever I wanted? Can you make Steve remember that once we washed each other's hair by candlelight?*

After that, before she left the house, Lillian applied a ruddier foundation and brushed on a little more blush. Whenever Mrs. Finch noticed her, she vowed, she would be smiling, attentive, vivacious—as if everything were fine, as if Steve's spring construction job had been confirmed at last, as if Steve had promised that this summer they really would build that new master bedroom suite.

It didn't work for long. Arabella Finch seemed always to catch her leaning back against a wall, taking a deep breath, or carrying a wailing child up and down the hall. *She knows!* Lillian thought wildly. As her adrenaline surged, subsided and surged again, Lillian grew desperate. Her body demanded more than she dared give it, yet she dared not deny it either. She might as well have been addicted to heroin.

One night, after loading the dishwasher and scrubbing a skillet and a saucepan that wouldn't fit, Lillian saw blood seeping from her wrists, turning the last greasy soapsuds a watery pink, trickling into the garbage disposal unit. *Christ, I slit my wrists!* She reached for a length of paper towels.

Only then did she realize there wasn't a knife in sight. The blood vanished, leaving no trace of a wound on either arm.

Could I try to kill myself and not even know I'd done it?

"Hey, you look like you're about to faint," Barbara said. "You coming down with something?"

"No," said Lillian. "No, I hope not. It's just Monday." *Get a grip, Lillian. Get a grip.* "Mind if I go down to the office for some fruit juice?"

"Go ahead." Barbara's extravagant wave revealed several small children coloring at one table, the rest building a castle in the far corner—all intent on their work. "As you see."

Once out of sight Lillian turned left, not right, and went to the nursery, not the office. The stout gray-haired aide glanced up from her book—bodice ripper, Lillian knew without looking—and marked her place with a wad of Kleenex. "I thought you might be ready for a break," Lillian said.

"I swear you're a mind reader, honey," the woman said, rising carefully. "My bladder just don't hold as much as it used to."

When the aide returned, Lillian's breathing was relaxed, her heart steady.

"Don't ever get old, dear," said the other woman good-naturedly. She settled back in her seat and reopened her romance novel. "Thank you so much."

Late that afternoon an eighteen-month-old girl was found dead in the nursery. Crib death, they said. What a terrible thing, but these things happened. No one knew why.

Lillian Kramer stretched out in her bathtub, her toes barely visible above the lavender-scented bubbles. The little lamp above the medicine cabinet was on, the overhead was off. In two candlesticks ornamented with fake holly and snow—all she could find in the dining-room cabinet—two white tapers had burned down about an inch. Centered between her feet was the stainless steel medallion with the drain toggle in the middle. Lillian's legs were lean and alabaster, though she couldn't see them; her hips were wide, her pubic hair sparse and blonde, her belly soft. Her ribs stuck up higher than her breasts.

That wasn't quite true.

The phone rang and rang and rang. Nina pounded on the bathroom door: "Mo-om, pho-one!"

"Later," said Lillian. She was not going to answer any more questions.

Steve was next. The locked door vibrated with his pounding. "Lillian, where did you leave the pliers?"

Lillian was not going to answer any more questions, not from the kids, the doctors, the other teachers or her boss, not from Arabella Finch and not from Steve above all.

She felt the first tug between the bottom of her ribs and the small of her back. Then a harder yank. She braced her feet and pushed against the front of the tub. Her torso rose out of the water at the other end, bubbles clinging to her dark nipples.

"God damn you," she hissed through gritted teeth.

Blood flowed out from her thighs, toward the drain. Even in the dim, flickery light she could see it: nearly black at the heart, burgundy as it blended at the edges with water and suds. It seeped under the edge of the drain cap, circling lazily like a cyclone making up its mind.

God damn it! They were down there, pulling hand over hand, like kids in a tug of war. She could hear them: *Pliers, Lillian. Phone, Mom! My homework, breakfast, lunch, supper, Girl Scouts, soccer practice, doctor's appointment, teacher conference.* Hand over hand.

She sat up, furious at last. "You can't," she vowed, "you can't keep doing this to me." She reached for the blood rope. It slid through her hands. She forced her fingers to close around it. It kept sliding through her hands. The cyclone gathered momentum. She heard them all down there, calling, demanding, cajoling. She could no longer tell the voices apart.

"Parasites, every damn one of you!" Her voice sounded too loud; she lowered it. "I'm sick of it!"

She would stop them, silence them all. She would track them to the source and force them to stop stealing her blood. It was hers, not theirs; they had no right to take it. She followed the trail through the water and away, down into the dark of the drain.

Her husband found her face down in a tub half full of pale gray water, with a froth of bubbles on the top. On the toilet tank two white candles had burned almost down to the nubs.

Apologia

Jan Carr

I CAN NO LONGER KEEP A JOURNAL. There are too many things that are better left unred. Unread, I mean of course. Though at this point, what's the difference? Just so much blood under the bridge.

When Rosie was an infant, she'd thrash and flail at my breast, unable to get any milk. She'd wail in hunger, her face worked crimson. "Rose, Rose, why are you so red?" I'd ask, as frantic as she, helpless to set things right.

The doctor told me I didn't have enough milk. "Stress can do that," he said. "Are you under stress?" He wrote down the name of a brand of formula, tore it from his prescription pad and handed it to me. So. A father was not the only thing I failed to provide for Rosie. I was—I am—Rosie's mother. I should have been able to give her mother's milk.

One muggy, buggy day, Rosie and I sit on the porch, a rickety, unpainted affair, Southern Gothic. Rosie is drawing a witch, while I cut out the pattern for the costume Rosie has requested for Halloween. A shepherdess this year. All bloomers and ruffled caps and innocence. Rosie has always been drawn to the romantic. Other years she's begged to go as a princess, an Indian maiden.

"I want ruffles on the bloomers," she instructs me. Apparently this is something she's seen on TV, or perhaps in some quaint illustrated Little Bo Peep at school.

A mosquito lands on Rosie's arm. She slaps it. Where the mosquito was, there's now a splotch of blood.

"I hate Florida," Rosie says, her face a pucker of distaste. "You know what I mean, Mom? I hate living in a state where you still have mosquitoes on Halloween."

Which is how I know she's read my journal. The mosquito/Halloween sentiment was mine, and I'd noted it just that morning. I must've left the journal open on my desk. I look sidelong at her. How much more has she read?

"Mosquitoes, posquitos," she singsongs. She wipes the blood from her arm with one impatient swipe. "Mom, can I have a big bow on my bonnet?"

"Anything, anything, my little shepherdess," I say. I plant a lipstick kiss on her cheek. A substitute for all the things I cannot give.

"Are you coming with me for Halloween?" she asks. She knows I can't.

"No, pumpkin." I avert my eyes. "I'm going to have to stay home to work."

Rosie stares out at the quiet, wooded street, overhung with moss. I've moved us to the outskirts. I can't bear to live in a city built around a theme park. It's bad enough I have to work there.

"Well, who will I go trick-or-treating with then?" she asks, a catch in her voice.

"Mr. Varna said he'd take you. He said he'd take you with Terez." Rosie hates Terez. I think she is going to say this, but she doesn't.

"I wonder what kind of candy people give here for Halloween?" she asks instead.

"Chocolate-covered mosquitoes," I say, to tease.

Rosie laughs, and I am relieved.

The Florida air sits on us. It's heavy and sodden. I wonder what they do give out here for Halloween.

"Mom," Rosie asks, her eyes trained carefully on her paper, "did I really suck you until you bled?" She picks a crayon out of the box and outlines her witch in red.

So she did read the journal, much more than just the passage about mosquitoes.

"You did, Rosie Posie," I say.

How much more can a mother explain?

The drive home from work seems endless. The traffic on the interstate drones unconsciously, like a dream. I have not yet shed the concerns of the day, and the bright, eager faces of the kids I have to costume cavort before me. Sometimes, to put myself to sleep at night, I recall the figure quirks of each one. The boy with the long torso, the girl with the flat buttocks and wide hips. Somewhere between childhood and adulthood they are, dancing for dollars, stars of their local dance school, now thrown into the entertainment mill as surely as I.

The traffic on the highway reasserts itself, a car cuts too closely into my lane. The car, I notice, is full of blondes. The whole state is unbearably, relentlessly blond. The Sunshine State. I honk the horn, then lapse into thoughts of patterns and fabrics. They want me to use sateen. Thousands of dollars in the budget, and the costumes will look like a neighborhood recital. The concerns of the day drive noisily through my brain, honking, angling for attention.

I exit the interstate and turn off onto a long, marl road that borders an orange grove. Shells and sand crackle smartly under my tires. The scent of citrus wafts into the open window of the car. I pull to the shoulder and breathe deeply. Some oranges have fallen to the ground. I open the car door and reach for them. Oranges for the taking. They will be ours for breakfast.

Farther down the road I stop to pick up Rosie. Mrs. Baker is fussing around her kitchen, wiping the stove where something in a pot has bubbled over. Rosie is at the table drawing pumpkins that look like oranges, a recent corruption. Mrs. Baker smiles as I push open the screen door. The cotton flowered dress she wears is stained at the armpits. The bodice of her dress sags, as do the breasts underneath. Still, Rosie likes her. Mrs. Baker keeps pigs. Rosie has named them all after characters in the theme park and has adopted one as a favorite.

"Did you hear the bats last night?" Mrs. Baker asks as I collect Rosie's things.

"Bats?"

"In the cemetery."

Between our house and Mrs. Baker's there is an old graveyard. The weathered headstones tell the stories of the families they recall. In one family, four children died—three in one winter, and a baby a year later. The mother died in childbirth. The father took another wife. She died in short order, too.

Bats. In the cemetery. I did hear bats the night before. I thought it was a dream.

"Screeched all night, they did," says Mrs. Baker. "Like to wake the dead."

"Bats eat bugs," Rosie chimes in. "Bugs like mosquitoes. Bats come out after dark." She has learned this at school and tells us with a teacher's pedantic tone.

I hustle Rosie into the car to drive the short stretch home. Before I leave Mrs. Baker's kitchen, I glance at the simmering pot on the stove. Rosie and I can look forward to pizza for dinner. Frozen. It is all I can manage to make.

"Good-bye, Goofy!" Rosie shouts in the direction of the backyard. She waves wildly, though the pigpen is blocked from sight by the house. "See you tomorrow, Goofy!"

How am I even going to make the pizza, I wonder. I am already bone-weary with fatigue.

There had been a time in Rosie's infancy, brief though it was, when I had milk. After Rosie would feed and drain my breasts, she'd drop off to sleep quietly, satisfied. I would feel satisfied, too, the heavy fullness emptied. I would feel, in my breasts, a sort of afterglow. And then Michael left.

I don't know what it is about the night. Thoughts of the past creep in as surely as the shadows. When Rosie is tucked in bed, I am left alone with the dishes and the past. Michael was not supposed to leave. And I was supposed to be working in the theater, not a theme park. But income from the theater turned out to be scant, as dry as my milk.

"Mrs. Daniels? Are you in home?"

Mr. Varna takes me by surprise. He often does. He has the habit—a country habit? a foreign habit?—of walking in through our unlatched door at night. There he'll be, as dark as my thoughts, his thick, Slavic accent as foreign as I feel. We are exiles, he and I, neither of us blond.

"I didn't hear you," I say, drying my hands on the dishtowel.

"I was driving past," he says. I never hear his car, old, unfashionably long and black. "And I thought I'd stop for visiting." He bows, his ways old-world, courtly. Then he unfurls a length of fabric he had folded, tucked under his arm.

"A cape?" I ask. I finger the fabric. It is heavy and black and lined in silk. He intends to wear this in Florida? I stifle a laugh. Even I am not that strange. I picture Mr. Varna at the theme park, on line at the concession stand, a villain escaped from a horror movie, children screaming at the sight.

"For Halloween," he explains. "It is custom, yes?"

"Custom, yes," I nod. Mr. Varna's syntax is contagious. Around him, my English gets as awkward as his.

I fill up the kettle at the faucet and put it on the stove. I am hoping Mr. Varna will accept a cup of tea and stay on to talk. Nights are lonely, seductively so. With Mr. Varna as company, I would still be lonely, but in someone else's presence. That, it strikes me, is his chief charm. I rattle off the names of the teas I have stashed in the cupboard. I pull out two quaint, cracked cups, bought in a back-country store.

"I must for getting home," he excuses himself, shrugging his shoulders. "Terez." He folds the cape back up deftly; he has done this before. And then Mr. Varna is gone, as abruptly as he arrived.

Everyone leaves, I think. Mr. Varna, Michael, the work I used to do in the theater, all the young, lighthearted hopes I had about what life might hold in store. A darkness shrouds me. I should be careful, I think. Every day, my outlook turns more bleak. Rosie will leave, too, I know.

You raise a child so she can leave, a parent's lonely goal.

The whistle of the kettle sounds shrilly in the still night air.

"Mom!" Rosie has awakened, startled by the sound. "I had a nightmare," she whimpers, when I go to her. I feel her bony body through the thin fabric of her nightgown. She clings to me in terror.

"What about?" I ask. "Tell me. What was the nightmare?"

"Terez's hair," she says.

Terez's hair *is* a nightmare, I think, uncharitably, though I don't voice this to Rosie. "Her hair?" I prod, instead.

"It was worms," Rosie cries, clinging tighter. "Worms in the ground."

"There, there." I rock her back and forth, a baby in arms. It occurs to me that it is actually a short jump from the image Rosie dreamed up to Terez's actual hair. Her hair is overgrown and unkempt, the way hair that has continued to grow after death might look. Terez has a dead girl's hair.

"It was just a dream," I coo, to comfort Rosie, "just a mean old bad dream. Here you are, in your bed, in our house. Everything is all right, Rosie. Right as raindrops."

We fall asleep like that in Rosie's bed, mother and daughter entwined. The next morning we will wake up to the cheerful calls of birds—egret, heron, exotic Florida birds. They will keep the darkness at bay for yet a few more hours.

The dancers at the park crowd my office, draped with the fabric pieces that will become their costumes. The young girls who work for me, their mouths mumbling around straight pins, pin the pieces to fit. Outside, the day is cloudy and windy, threatening a storm. Inside, the dancers are restless in such close quarters. Some try to stretch, some mark the steps they will do in their next big production number, a takeoff of a movie scheduled for holiday release. One girl kicks to the side without looking and knocks over a framed picture I have of a production I costumed in my previous life. I keep it there to remind me.

"Hey," I snap, "this isn't rehearsal!" I pick up the frame and inspect it for cracks.

"Sorry," the dancer says sheepishly. She's young and apple-cheeked, with a telltale Midwestern twang. Blond, sunny, like the rest. These aren't dancers, I think. They're cheerleaders.

The room quiets once I've barked my displeasure. The dancers settle and fall to talking together. One of them, I gather, is planning a party this weekend for Halloween. The others talk about what they will wear.

One girl, more earnest than the rest, announces she will not be coming to the Halloween party.

"Why?" someone teases her. "Got a date?"

"No," she says primly. "Halloween is pagan." I notice the girl wears a small gold cross at her neck.

"Pagan?" someone asks, clearly alarmed.

"It goes against the teachings of Jesus Christ."

The room hushes. I've never heard these kids discuss anything more philosophical than dance steps or diets. Suddenly everyone is gathered around.

"It's in the Bible?" presses another. I can almost see the whirring of her brain as she rifles her memory, searching chapter and verse for mention of Halloween.

At this, I cannot resist. I step in.

"Jesus isn't against Halloween," I proclaim.

"No?"

"Oh, no. He's coming to the party. Told me so Himself."

The kids are ill-prepared for sacrilege.

"Mrs. Daniels . . ."

"Sure," I continue. "He's coming as a vampire. 'Thees is my blood,'" I say, with an accent questionably Transylvanian. "'Dreenk of eet.'"

One of the girls, one who went to Catholic school, covers her mouth with her hand in a near-caricature of shock.

"Actually," I continue, on a more scholarly tack, "Jesus quite approved of Halloween. Or at least his followers did."

"It's in the Bible?"

"It's in the history books. Halloween was Celtic. The Celts worshipped gods, but not one, a variety. That's why they're called pagan."

"I thought pagan meant not religious," says another.

"Oh, no. There was religion, all right, and it was quite compelling. When the Catholic missionaries came through, they couldn't lure the people away from their observances, so they co-opted them. For instance, the spring rites honoring the fertility goddess? Those became the day to honor the Virgin Mary. Winter solstice? That became Christmas."

"Christmas!"

"And Halloween became All Souls Day."

"That's not what they taught us at Saint Anne's!" exclaims the Catholic girl.

"So why do you think they call it *parochial* school?" I ask with a smile.

This, of course, is not really the way the conversation goes at all. It is only something I imagine as I listen to what the kids actually say. In reality, I do not enter the fray. I know better than to open my mouth and brand myself as an infidel. I have a daughter to feed, a job to protect. Instead, I listen to the kids skirt the issue with ignorance and fear, then collectively come to the same conclusion I have, but by a sloppier logic. Christianity is compatible with Halloween, they decide. Halloween is, after all, a family holiday. And isn't the family Christian? I turn to the window. Rain pelts on the glass. Angry winds bend the palms outside.

In the background, the radio announces a storm warning. The storm is due to a "tropical depression," the announcer explains, which sounds, to my perverse ear, more like a diagnosis than a weather front. My diagnosis.

I am tired. I am starting to imagine conversations. Imagined conversations that border on hallucination. God, help me.

Because of the approaching storm, the park sends us all home early. I look up as I get in my car. Clouds mask the sun. The sky spits rain. Before I get on the highway, I stop at a small strip mall to pick up groceries for Rosie and me—milk, hamburger, popcorn, juice—enough food to last through a storm. Just as I step out of the supermarket, a train of toddlers passes by, herded by two teachers, one at each end. I follow the class past the clothing store (a chain), past the drugstore (same sprawling, endless aisles) and past the restaurant (fast-food take-out). Finally the children feed into a small, storefront preschool. A preschool in a strip mall? I heft up the groceries in my arms and hurry to my car, anxious to get home.

That night, against my judgment, I open my journal. I do not intend to write in it, just to look through. I do not get far when Rosie interrupts, appearing, pale and ghostlike, in my doorway. She has, in her hand, a stack of photos, bound together by an old rubber band that is worn and ready to give. They are photos of her father.

"Tell me the stories," she begs.

So I tell her that her father was handsome and funny. I tell her that he tickled her infant tummy to make her laugh. I don't know how Rosie found the photos. I'd tucked them safely away, I thought. But Rosie's been turning the house upside down, searching for her past.

"If Daddy was here, he'd take me trick-or-treating," she assures herself.

"He would indeed," I say, a collaborator in her lie.

"But Mr. Varna's taking me," she asserts, working to get it straight.

Mr. Varna, a strange father substitute indeed.

When finally I've coaxed Rosie back to bed, I pick up my journal and think of writing. Instead, I sketch a picture of a woman. She is smiling. I draw a baby in her arms, a husband at her side . . .

I close the journal quickly. It's unleashed a force that frightens me. I fight the sudden urge to get in my car and drive somewhere, anywhere. But outside, the storm now rages. Rosie sleeps. I am trapped inside.

One more day until Halloween. Rosie is giddy at the thought of a night of abandon, at the expectation of all the candy she will collect. I cannot think of anything comparable that promises to sweeten my own life.

When I pick up Rosie at Mrs. Baker's, she is caked with mud. The storm has come and gone, but in its wake has left felled branches and primordial patches of mud. Rosie has been out back with the pigs, playing with Goofy. Splotches of mud spot her face and cake her hair and clothes. My daughter looks like some uncivilized, earlier creature, a Druid come from some wallowing rite. I take her home and deposit her in the shower. I rinse off the worst of the mud, then fill up the bathtub with hot, steamy water and a generous spritz of bubble bath. I lather up Rosie's hair while she sings a song about pigs that she makes up on the spot.

"Tomorrow is Halloween!" she crows. She laughs a dark, evil laugh she has stolen from some horror show she has seen on TV. I towel her dry and slip her tingly, pink body into a nightgown. When I put her to bed, I go to the kitchen and set to work on the shepherdess bonnet, stitching on the ribbons. I feel heavy-limbed and heavy-hearted.

"Ah, she sews costume."

Mr. Varna has slipped in, as stealthily as dusk. When I see him, I start to cry.

"Dear, dear, what is the trouble?" he asks, confusing two words.

Perhaps it is his English, perhaps it is the simple fact that he is there. For whatever reason, I begin to confide in Mr. Varna. All the things that have weighed so heavily on me come flooding out. In one sniffling, tearful stream.

"I never wanted to move us here," I say. "I didn't want to bring Rosie to a city where preschools are in strip malls. The dancers I costume have never read a book. I'm tired, dead tired. And so discouraged. And the worst of it is, I feel I have no out."

Mr. Varna stares at me. It's unclear what he thinks of what I'm saying, or whether he even understands. Eventually, he shakes his head. "Dead tired," he repeats, registering the idiom.

Suddenly, I become aware of how crazed I must sound. I hurry to smooth down my hair, which has become wild in my outburst. It's exhaustion. It's begun to tell on me. Maybe I'm losing my mind.

"So what time will you pick up Rosie for Halloween?" I ask. Anything to reassert some measure of normalcy.

"Halloween," he muses. "The night the souls of the dead roam the Earth." In this, he is surprisingly articulate, not a misstep in the phrase. "Shortly after dark," he answers. He flings an imaginary cape across his face, as deftly as the Count himself.

"And where will you take the girls?"

"Back toward town, toward your malls," he says, smiling. "To the houses that border them. Toothsome families in every one."

Mr. Varna's inscrutable, idiosyncratic English presents itself once again. It occurs to me, somewhat stiltedly, in my tired, overwrought state, that a soul who is foreign is condemned to be strange forevermore.

On Halloween, Mr. Varna comes to pick up Rosie, dressed in his cape as Count Dracula. The costume is quite convincing, even to my theatrically critical eye. Rosie runs out of her bedroom, a shepherdess without her sheep, and asks me to tie the voluptuous sash that cinches her dress. She eyes Terez, who has come as a gypsy. The three of them make up a tableau from another time.

The girls bid me a high, noisy good-bye. I close the door after them and latch it. I have bought candy just in case, but I am not likely to get any trick-or-treaters this far out in the country. I have work to do, cheerful costume designs to finish for bright-faced youngsters. A sudden wind kicks up and bangs the shutters at my window. It dies as quickly as it started, no more than a shudder. Then, all is still.

All night long there is only one knock at the door. I grab a handful of miniature Snickers from the bag I bought at the Publix and run to the door, expecting to greet a cluster of young ghosts and ghouls. Instead, it is Mrs. Baker.

"Have the hooligans been here?" she asks.

"Hooligans?" I have not heard this word since my grandmother, Irish and with old-country prejudices, died.

"Hooligans. They've thrown eggs all about my yard. Ah," she says, running her finger down my screen. "Indeed. They've come and gone."

I look at the screen. Someone has soaped it. Funny, I didn't hear anyone outside. I sigh, wondering when I'll ever have time to wash up the mess. I'll have to engage Rosie to help me. Pretend it is a game.

After Mrs. Baker delivers her warning, she hikes back home through the cemetery. Under the Halloween moon, the headstones, I notice, are strewn with toilet paper. More strips of paper thread the fence that marks Mrs. Baker's property, whisper-thin scarecrows bounding a ghostly harvest.

"Kids," I think philosophically, "will be kids." I unwrap one of the Snickers bars and pop it in my mouth before returning to my sketches and swatches of fabric.

It is not long after that Rosie returns. I do not hear Mr. Varna's car pull up to the house, but I look out the window and see Rosie running up the front walk. Her sash is untied, her bonnet hangs from her neck. I go to meet her as she bursts in the door, triumphant. Rosie upends her bag over the kitchen table, a gesture that reminds me, somehow, of a cat dropping prey at my feet. Candy spills helter-skelter off the table and onto the floor. From the pile, I fish out a lone apple, some loose cookies and a doughnut and toss them in the garbage, confident, for once, in my role as protector—unwrapped treats could be laced with poison, studded with razor blades. Rosie pulls the rest of the candy toward her greedily. She looks sweaty and pale.

"Did you have a good time, pumpkin-mumpkin?" I ask. Her mouth is stained with chocolate, or is it? Maybe it's fruit juice or jam.

"Terez is a real gypsy," she says authoritatively.

"And you're a real shepherdess," I tell her.

"*No, Mom!*" Rosie is impatient. She thinks I am being condescending. "Terez is a *real* gypsy."

"I suspected as much," I say to appease her.

"How did you know?" Rosie demands.

"Well . . ." I stall, thinking. "Her hair."

Rosie nods.

"She has gypsy hair."

The next morning Mrs. Baker calls early with disturbing news. When she went to feed the pigs that morning, she found Goofy dead in the mud, killed, apparently. Mrs. Baker discovered a distinct puncture wound in his neck; though, oddly enough, there was no blood. Mrs. Baker, of course, attributes the death to the hooligans, though to me it seems quite a jump to think that the same kids who would festoon the trees with toilet paper would also kill a pig. "Couldn't the wound be due to another animal?" I offer. "Maybe a rattlesnake. Or perhaps a bobcat." These, I know, are Florida hazards.

When I hang up the phone, Rosie comes out of her room, sleepy-eyed and stumble-footed. I wonder how I will tell her. I fix her cereal, but she says she's not hungry. She climbs on my lap and absently twines her finger in a curl of hair that falls on my neck, escaped from my barrette.

"Rosie," I say. "I have something to tell you. Something bad happened. Over at Mrs. Baker's house." I take a breath, then somehow I find words, clichéd words, to tell her about Goofy. I make up a pretty story about how he's no longer living in Mrs. Baker's pigpen, how he's gone to Heaven.

"Was there blood?" she asks. A strange question. Her tone is surprisingly chilling.

"Blood?" I crane around to look at my young daughter, but she pulls me back to her and nuzzles her nose in my neck.

"As a matter of fact, there wasn't," I say. "Why?" A vague, unarticulated fear crosses my thoughts.

"I miss Goofy, Mommy," she says suddenly, disarming me.

I tighten my arms around her and rock her, a mother's age-old comfort.

"Oh, sweetie, you can still talk to Goofy. Maybe Goofy's a pig-angel, do you think? Maybe Goofy's flying around this room right now."

"Flying like a bat," says Rosie. She swats my arm.

"Rosie!" I protest, stung. "Don't hit me."

"I wasn't," she says. She lifts her hand to reveal a dead mosquito. How she'd detected it, I don't know; she'd hit my arm without looking. Rosie smiles up at me, as sweetly as an angel. She puts her fingers in her mouth and sucks.

As it turns out, Goofy is not the only animal to turn up dead. The next morning, I find a bird under the bushes in the front yard—a mockingbird, the official bird of my newly adopted state—and another in the grass to the side. I try to chalk this up to coincidence, but two days later I stumble upon a blue heron lying under our front window, its long, graceful neck now limp and lifeless.

At first I try to hide the carcasses from Rosie. I think they may upset her, so close on the heels of Goofy's death. But the morning of the heron, when I lift up the bird to examine it, Rosie walks out in her T-shirt and underwear and finds me.

"The bird died," I say quickly.

"I know," says Rosie. She strokes the bird's neck and then follows me barefoot to the cemetery, where I deposit the heron in the overgrown shrubbery.

"Buzzards will eat it," Rosie says matter-of-factly. "They'll make big circles in the sky."

I look at my daughter. Her limbs are long and gangly; she is no longer the small baby I bore and suckled. She is growing up, growing away from me. She has dark thoughts that are not mine.

It is right around this time that Rosie takes sick. She begins to sleep through the days, though at night she is restless, a hungry glint in her glazed eyes. Each day, she grows sleepier, each night, more alert. I know I must take her to a doctor. Mrs. Baker recommends one not far from our house.

As I drive Rosie to his office, I find myself aching for a partner, another adult who could help me figure out what to do in this situation, how to proceed. Another parent with whom I might share my growing suspicions.

Dr. Hinterlong is older, bespectacled, pleasantly paunchy. The shelves of his examining room are lined, anachronistically, with old-fashioned apothecary jars.

After he queries me about Rosie's symptoms, the doctor pinches the skin of Rosie's cheeks. He moves toward her eyes with a sharp, pointed light, from which she recoils. He draws some of her blood into a vial and caps it. I assume he is going to send the blood off for analysis, but he holds it up to the light, then announces a quick diagnosis, without benefit of lab results.

"Anemic," he proclaims. "The girl's anemic, nothing more."

"Don't you have to send the blood to the lab?"

He waves away my question as if it were insubstantial, no more than a gnat. "Medical hocus-pocus," he says, flapping his hands impatiently. "What do you feed her?"

It's true that Rosie's been looking pasty, her skin thin and papery. I wonder if the doctor thinks me some sort of backwoods mom, the sort who'd set out Coca Cola and potato chips for her daughter and call it breakfast. I do not tell him about the frozen pizzas.

"Should I give her iron pills?" I ask.

"Give her meat," he says, writing it down as if I am a moron. "Lots of meat."

Another doctor tearing off another leaf from another prescription pad. Another doctor called upon to advise me because I cannot manage to feed my child.

That night at home, I cook steaks for dinner, but Rosie does not eat the meat, pushing it instead listlessly around her plate.

"What do you think we should do?" I ask an imaginary husband. "Our daughter appears to be sick."

"And getting sicker," my husband agrees.

"Well, what do you think is wrong?" I wait a beat. He doesn't answer. Then I say, "I don't think steak will cure her." The rest of my fears go unspoken.

After dinner, I tuck Rosie into bed. At least she is safe in our home, I think. In the morning, though, when I wake her, I find twigs twined in her hair, grass stuck to her nightclothes. I stare at her, stunned. I want to strike my daughter, scream at her, "Where have you been? What have you done?" But the words freeze in my throat. That night, late, after I have again tucked Rosie into bed, I sneak back into her room to check on her. She is not there.

I look out Rosie's window. Her view is of the cemetery. Something propels me there. Perhaps I think I will find Rosie, asleep against a headstone, though I don't. Still, once I'm there, the moist, overgrown grass sticking to my ankles, I cannot leave. I part the bushes of the shrubbery where, short days ago, I'd dropped the heron I'd found dead in the yard. I wonder if Rosie is right, if the buzzards have gotten it. But the bird is there, fly-infested, decomposing, and on top of it are more animals. Someone has piled fresh dead atop the old. I make out some opossums, raccoons, an armadillo.

By the time I get back to the house, dawn is breaking. I find Rosie asleep in her bed, a hot bloom on her cheeks.

Because I don't know what else to do, I keep Rosie home from school. In the morning, I deposit my drowsy daughter on Mrs. Baker's couch. Then I drive to work.

Work. The very job that once seemed to sap my soul now seems a strange relief, a way to escape the dark prospects that cloud my home. I sit in my office, looking out on the crowds that swarm the park. People are dressed in loud, garish colors. Children race ahead of their parents, grappling sticky cones of cotton candy. Women search their purses for tissues to wipe their children's faces. Men corral their families together for photos. "Everybody smile," they instruct, taking aim. The bright bustle of activity reassures me.

A knock sounds at my door. It's the girl with the gold cross. "Mrs. Daniels?" she says shyly. She holds out her hand to present me with something. It's a ribbon-tied box.

"What's this?" I ask.

"I've been meaning to give you a present," she says.

"A present? What for?"

"To thank you. For the time you gave me courage."

I cannot think what she might be talking about.

"The conversation we had. About Halloween," she explains. "No one believed me. But I knew you agreed. I could tell by the way you were so quiet. It gave me the courage to stand up for my faith."

This is such strange logic that I cannot think how to respond, so I open the package. In it is a small gold cross on a chain. The girl slips it around my neck.

"May Jesus protect you," she says, as if this were some sort of rite.

"May He protect us all," I answer, surprising myself. I leave the cross around my neck. Maybe it can indeed protect me. From what I do not know.

That night, when I get home, I fix dinner for Rosie, though she does not eat. After dinner, I tuck her into bed, where she will not sleep. I lean over to kiss her. The cross falls out of my blouse and dangles on the chain in front of Rosie's face.

"What's that?" she cries.

I unhook the clasp and hand it to her. Rosie has always loved baubles and trinkets, but this she knocks out of my hand. It skitters across the bed and lands on the floor.

"Out!" She hides her face. "Get it out!"

I know what this means, of course. I pick up the cross, just as she asked, and take it out of the room. When I return, I sit down on the bed next to Rosie. I put my arm around her, as I have every night of her long childhood, to kiss her good night, to read her stories, to cuddle her to sleep. This is not the future I had hoped for us.

"Why so blue?" I say out loud, more to myself than to Rosie.

Rosie nuzzles my neck.

"Tell me about when I was a baby," she prods.

"When you were a baby . . . When you were a baby, we were a whole and happy family. We lived in a bustling city, and you had a father. I met him on a job I had, doing costumes for a quirky, interesting show . . . "

"And when you used to feed me?"

"When I used to feed you, you would come to my breast and suck and suck. You were a hungry little baby. I would look down while you were nursing, and there I'd see your sweet little face. I had lots of milk."

"And then came the blood?" asks Rosie.

The dark shadow of a figure passes Rosie's window.

"Who's that?" I ask, though I fear I know.

"Mr. Varna," my daughter reports frankly. "He comes every night. To open my window and let me out."

A stake through my heart, when it is I, I know, who should run one through Rosie's. But I cannot do that. It seems to me that I have already have. Perhaps that's why I now have a daughter who's sun-shy and pale, different from others, hungry for blood.

"Rose, Rose," I ask, "why are you so red?"

The question hangs in the air, unanswerable.

I do not want her out in the chill, dark night.

And so, without thinking, I unbutton the top buttons of my blouse, baring my neck to my young daughter. Rosie knows what it is I am offering. She puts her lips to my skin and roots hungrily until she finds the spot. I feel her teeth sink in. I hear the slippery suck of blood, the gulping and swallowing that tell me she is getting her fill. It all feels familiar, not strange at all.

The shadow at the window passes. I sink deeper into Rosie's pillow. My daughter will not go hungry tonight.

Bad Company

Joyce Wagner

PEN IT, DEAR." MRS. RENFIELD'S mouth spread wide over brownish teeth. Lucy released the tape at either end of the package, a tepid pool of anticipation warming inside of her. She picked at the center piece of tape, released the wrapping paper and swept it onto the floor. The girl's gold-brown eyes broadened as wide as her birthday cake. "Oh, Momma! Look! It's Barbie!"

"I hope you like it." Mrs. Renfield brought her leathery face close to Lucy's. "I understand all the girls have them these days."

The doll spoke to Lucy for the first time that night. "I would like my own bed."

The child's first thought was that the voice was part of a dream. It had been a long day, with too much food, too much attention, too much birthday.

"Hey, kid! I said I would like my own bed."

Lucy turned her head and faced the doll, who sat cross-legged on the pillow. She tried to blink away the remnants of sleep. "What?"

"A bed. I would like my own bed."

Lucy wondered whether dreams could be reasoned with. "Don't you like sleeping here with me?"

"No. I'm a teenage fashion doll. I need my own bed."

"Well, maybe Momma will buy you one. I'll ask her in the morning."

Barbie punched a tiny hand into the pillow, then laid back down. "You'd better."

"Momma, Barbie needs a bed."

Mina Harker looked up from her needlepoint. "What?"

"A bed. Barbie needs a bed. She's a teenage fashion doll, and she needs her own bed."

"I see. Well, you have birthday money. I suppose we can get Barbie a bed."

> Dream Glow Bed with glow-in-the-dark
> reversible pink headboard. Comforter also
> reverses; 3 lace-trimmed pillows
> N57 153 5204 (2 lbs. 4 oz.) $21.99

"Thanks, kid. Nice bed." Barbie bounced her butt on the mattress. "So now I guess I get to sleep on your dresser—in my bathing suit."

"Momma, Barbie needs clothes."

"What?"

"She needs clothes. She's cold. All she's got is a bathing suit."

Mina put down her needle and ran the side of a finger over her lips, then down to her chin. "I know, I'll see if Grandma will make her some clothes. You know how Grandma likes to sew."

Grandma accepted the assignment. In a week's time, her mission was accomplished, and she marched proudly into the Harker's kitchen and plopped a Wieboldt's gift box on the table in front of Mina.

"Oh, Mother. I can't wait to see. Looo-ceee! Grandma's heeeeere!"

The little girl bounded into the kitchen, dropped into a chair and pulled the lid from the box.

Mina reached across her daughter and lifted a tiny pair of double-knit bell-bottoms from the Kleenex-lined box. "Oh, Mother! They're beautiful! Lucy, just look at these tiny stitches. Mother, did you sew all of these by hand?"

Lucy picked up the tiny double-knit jacket, the companion to the bell-bottoms. She studied the garment, held in front of her eyes by the very tips of her thumb and index finger, as her other hand felt in the box for another atrocity. A corduroy jumper. Grandma clothes.

"Mother, these are just beautiful. Lucy, what do you say to Grandma?"

Lucy threw the jacket and jumper into the box, hopped off the chair and grabbed the clothing in two fists. "She better like these, that's all." She turned and stomped out of the room.

"What am I supposed to do with these?" Barbie tapped a naked foot on the dresser top.

"Wear them, I guess."

"Get real. A gingham party dress? Not a chance. Look at this one. Paisley! Giant amoebas all over my body. There's a new model—'Bacteria Barbie.' Swell. Is there a ball gown? No. I can't believe you even brought these in here. I can't wear this drek." Barbie blew a tiny wisp of cigarette smoke in Lucy's eyes.

"What should I do? I can't go back and ask for more clothes."

"Why the hell not?"

"Pardon me?"

"I said, 'Why the hell not?'"

"Yeah . . . Why the hell not?"

"Momma, Barbie needs clothes."

> Shushing Barbie Ski Weekend Wardrobe. 43
> colorful pieces for hundreds of combinations!
> N57 168 4507 (10 oz.) $17.50

When Lucy entered her room after school one day, she found Barbie sitting on the bed, arms and legs sticking straight out, face frozen in a dim-witted expression. She was wearing stirrup pants and a faux fur jacket. "Oh, it's you, kid." Her expression returned to normal, she crossed her legs, leaned over and searched in her jacket pocket for a pack of cigarettes. "For a moment there, I thought you were your old lady. Scared the shit out of me earlier. Can't you keep her out of here?"

"Well . . . I don't know . . . I'll try . . ."

"Look. That's not really important now. I gotta talk to you. Two things. First, now that I've got some decent clothes, we can go visiting. You have friends with Barbies, don't you?"

"Yeah . . ."

"Okay. So set it up so we can go play after school tomorrow, okay?"

A tiny crease formed between Lucy's eyebrows. "I don't know . . . I'm supposed to go to Girl Scouts tomorrow night, so I have to do home-work after school . . ."

"Bullshit. Look, this is important."

"But why?"

"Well . . . It just is, is all. Take my word for it, okay?"

The tiny crease deepened to a furrow. "Well . . . I don't know . . ."

"Look, kid, you get to see your friends all the time. What do I do all day except sit on my bed, looking at my extremely limited wardrobe. Don't you think I ought to get to see other dolls? Huh?"

"Well . . ."

"Good. It's settled. Number two. Christmas is coming up, right? I'm gonna need a few things."

"I was gonna ask Santa for a new toboggan."

"Forget it."

"Huh?"

"You don't need a toboggan. Listen. The new Christmas catalogs should be out by now. Your mom should have one or two lying around the house. Sneak them in here tomorrow night at bedtime, and we'll make a list."

∽

"Lucy, come here. I want to talk to you."

"What is it, Momma?"

"Lucy, I don't know what's going on with you, but your father and I don't like it. Your schoolwork is slipping, your room is a mess, you're a mess and your attitude has become absolutely unacceptable."

Lucy settled her skinny butt in the large wing chair near the sofa. She knew the dimensions of the chair made her look very tiny and vulnerable. She was learning a lot from her birthday gift. That doll was so smart. Barbie had seen this confrontation coming after the Girl Scouts/homework incident. Lucy and Barbie had spent hours rehearsing for just this moment.

"Lucy, is there something wrong? Your dad and I are very worried about you. Is everything okay at school?"

Her little head moved up and down without taking her eyes away from her hands.

"How about your friends? Everything okay? Are you fighting with Sarah again?"

This was going to be so easy. Lucy slowly lifted her eyes to meet her mother's. Between the long dark-brown lashes on top and the thin curly bottom ones, a little lake began to form. "Momma, are we poor?"

Mina was astonished. "Poor? Well, no. We're not poor. Actually, by some standards, we're fairly well-off. Lucy, what would make you ask such a thing?"

Lucy's eyes dropped back to her fingers. A tiny stream broke off from the lake and trickled down her cheek. She ran to her mother, snuggled deep into her arms and turned on more tears.

"What's wrong, darling? Is someone making fun of you?"

"Momma, I was playing Barbies with Sarah and Annie. And they had all this stuff, y'know?"

"Barbie stuff?"

"Yeah. Sarah's Barbie has a car and a beauty shop. (Sniff) And Annie's has a bride's dress and ballerina costume and all these great clothes. (Sniff sniff) And she has a Barbie Dream Bedroom, too."

"And they won't let you play with them?"

"Well, no. (Sniff) I mean, yeah. I can play with them . . . but . . . um . . ."

"But you're embarrassed that you don't have as much Barbie stuff?"

"Yeah. (Sniff) I guess . . ."

"Honey, those are just *things*. They shouldn't be so important. What kind of friends are they if they judge you by the things you have?"

"Well . . . they really didn't say anything . . ."

"Listen to me, darling. You just be yourself. You're a wonderful girl, and if your friends don't know that, well, they're just not very good friends, that's all. Okay?"

"Okay."

"Lucy, look at me." The little head drew back, and the deep, wet, amber eyes sought Mina's. "I want you to clean up your room and do your homework. If you're real good, I'll bet Santa will bring that toboggan you've been wanting." Mina's lips grazed Lucy's left eyebrow. "Now, go."

"Okay, Momma." The girl slid off the couch and headed toward her bedroom, pausing under the arch that divided the living room from the dining room. She ran the fingers of her left hand along the woodwork while she quietly deliberated her next move. The doll's strategy didn't work out quite the way it was planned. Barbie would be pissed. Lucy's left foot revolved until she was again facing her mother. Her right foot swung back and forth on the toe. "Momma?"

"Yes, dear?"

"I feel real funny that I get to play with all this neat Barbie stuff that Sarah and Annie got . . ."

"*Have.*"

"Have . . . but, I don't got . . . have . . . stuff to share with them. Isn't that kind of cheating?" The dam broke. Genuine tears were falling full force now. Lucy couldn't imagine having to face Barbie with the news that she was getting the toboggan for Christmas. "I don't want to cheat my friends, Momma."

"Oh, Lucy . . ."

Mina and her husband, Jonathan, glanced at each other, then at their precious daughter sitting on Santa's lap, loudly and distinctly rattling off her wish list. Barbie had made it very clear that the old whiskered man Lucy would be sitting on was not the guy in charge. Throughout her discourse, Lucy's eyes would wander away from the man in the bad costume and settle on her parents, the real targets. She finished, in a most businesslike way, politely shaking a finger in Santa's face. "Now remember, Barbie Townhouse. Okay?"

Santa, clearly enchanted, waved a finger back. "And you remember to be good. Okay?"

"OH-KAY!" Lucy kissed Santa on the cheek (as previously coached by a certain doll) and bounced off his lap. Mina took Lucy by the hand and brought her downstairs for a hot chocolate while Jonathan priced some special toys.

> **Barbie's Townhouse (furnishings sold separately).**
> **Wallpapered and prewired for lighting. Easy**
> **to assemble. On 3 levels. Crafted of corrugated**
> **wood by-products.**
> **N57 153 4700T (42 lbs.) $199.99**
>
> **Townhouse Light Kit. Includes floor, ceiling**
> **and wall lamp, chandelier. Transformer, plug/**
> **cable; 110-120V, UL Listed. (Ages 3 & up)**
> **N57 153 3140 (2 lbs. 14 oz.) $54.99**
>
> **Barbie's City Girl Furnishings. Unassembled.**
> **Plastic/fabric. Barbie's personal choices of**
> **furniture and accessories for a very special**
> **townhouse. Some assembly required.**
> **N57 153 5272 (21 lbs. 2 oz.) $189.99**

Lucy sailed into the kitchen, flung her backpack onto a chair and un-zipped her pink and white down parka. "Momma?" The jacket slipped down to her fingertips as she peeked into the dining room. "Momma?" She heard Mina's voice drifting down the front stairs. *She's on the phone.* She heard the voice getting larger and more insistent. *She's on the phone with Daddy.* The jacket fell to the floor, landed upright and maintained its Lucy shape. The little girl creeped to the bottom of the stairs, a better position for eavesdropping.

"I know it's expensive, but I also know we can afford it. I know it's a toy. I know what toys look like. The 'Beemer' in the driveway is a toy, isn't it? The Blaupunkt stereo system in the Caddie is a toy, isn't it?" Silence. More silence. "Look, I don't want to argue about this. She's going through a very difficult time right now, and I think we need to be supportive." Silence. "No, I don't think we're rewarding her for bad behavior—Oh, boy. Look at the time. Jonathan, she's going to be home any minute. I'll talk to you about this later. Bye."

Lucy quietly scooted to the kitchen. She picked up her jacket and was sliding the chain inside the collar over a hook near the door when Mina entered the room.

"Hi, sweetie. You just get home?" Mina bussed the top of Lucy's head.

"Yup, just walked in the door." Lucy outright lied to her mother for the first time. Barbie was right. It wasn't so hard.

The tiny high heels made a click, click, clicking sound on the top of the dresser as Barbie paced its length. She smoked frantically as she made her way from one end of the bureau to the other. "Okay. We've got to think this through. Your old man is a tough nut to crack. I'm gonna need help on this one. Can you play 'Barbies' with Sarah and Annie again tomorrow? Maybe their dolls can come up with some idea."

"I guess so. I'll see if it's okay with Momma."

"Just do it, okay? Set it up."

While the girls played outside, the dolls rallied and merged their vinyl brainpower. Several decades of combined experience, networking and market research had served them well. They determined that the best approach for Lucy would be the sweet-talking routine. Most fathers of little girls were considered easy marks, but Lucy's was a special case and she was well coached for all eventualities.

∽

"Hi, Daddy! Can I sit on your lap?"

"Okay, sugar-plum. Want to watch TV with your old dad?" Jonathan Harker picked up his daughter, one hand under each arm, and, with an exaggerated groan, swung her up and onto his lap. The recliner creaked, protesting the extra weight. "How are things in school, Lucy? Everything okay?"

Lucy's little shoulders popped up and released. "Okay, I guess. Work okay?"

Jonathan cracked a smile and ruffled Lucy's hair. "Yes, Lucy. Work is just fine. In fact, it's been an excellent year."

"The Christmas tree is so pretty this year. I can't wait for Christmas. Hope Santa brings me a Barbie Townhouse. I've been good."

Jonathan Harker's chin dipped, and his eyes met his daughter's over the top of his glasses. "I thought you wanted a toboggan."

"Well, I did. But a girl in my class? She got a toboggan for her birthday. She fell off. And she broke her nose. And her parents had to pay a million dollars in hospital bills. And now she's real ugly. 'Cause her nose didn't grow back right."

Jonathan's head tipped lightly to the side. "Hmm. Lucy, you know what? A man at work bought a Barbie Townhouse for his daughter's birthday. And she was playing with the lights. And she got electrocuted. And all her teeth fell out."

Lucy trilled her best giggle. "Oh, Daddy. You're making that up."

"And you're not?" Lucy's father stopped smiling. His hands once again grasped Lucy under the arms, picked her up and swung her out so she was standing next to the recliner, facing her father. "I don't know what's going on with you, Lucy, but I don't like what you're becoming. There used to be a sweet, honest, simple little girl living here. Now all I can find is this little 'gimme' monster who will do anything to get what she wants. I don't like this gimme monster. I hope she never tries crawling on my lap again."

Lucy ran past her mother, wailing all the way into her room and slammed the door. There was a lot of wailing, shouting and door-slamming for the rest of the evening. The next morning, Jonathan Harker woke up on the couch.

∾

Barbie sat on her bed, feet dangling over the sides, her face in her hands. "I'm screwed, kid. I can't believe this. I'm recycled. I'm Silly Putty."

"What? What's wrong. What's gonna happen?"

"Look. I had a job to do, and I blew it. All that training. All that net-working." Barbie's head went back and forth, her face still in her tiny hands.

Lucy's voice strained toward hysteria. "What are you talking about?"

"Lucy, did you ever hear the word 'recall'?"

Lucy stared at the doll and blinked twice.

"Look, you're a good kid and you tried hard. We both did. We're just too new at this stuff to crack a tough nut like your dad." Barbie raised her head and ran her hands up her forehead, burying her fingers in her blonde, rooted hair. "When word gets back to headquarters, they're go-ing to take me away and send in a replacement. You'll like her. She'll be top-notch. Special training." Barbie pulled herself up to full height and pushed from her cheeks the surprise of teardrops with the backs of her vinyl hands. "Everything's gonna be just fine. You'll see, kid." Lucy listened to her words, but the light from the ballerina lamp towering beside the doll caught the glistening new wetness streaming down her perfect plastic face and planted a tiny seed of doubt in the girl's newly savvy mind.

Christmas morning Lucy rose early and tiptoed in pink slippers into the living room. She noticed, with relief, a two-seater toboggan propped up against the wall, tied with a big red bow. She really did want the sled, and it gave her little heart a jump to see it there. She didn't see any boxes big enough for a townhouse and its furnishings, but she really didn't expect to and now it didn't seem to matter. There were many small boxes and one medium-sized box. She ripped the paper off each one.

Barbie Porsche 911 Cabriolet	$34.99
Barbie Hot Springs Whirlpool	$19.99
Barbie Supermarket	$19.99

Mina and Jonathan appeared in the archway, under the mistletoe. Jon was smiling. Mina had little furrows between her eyebrows. Her eyes followed Lucy from package to package.

Lucy looked up, a grinning, beaming child. "Momma, Daddy, look at this stuff! And I got my toboggan! Isn't it beautiful?" Jonathan extended his arms, and Lucy ran to her father, gem-colored wrapping paper flying in her wake. She bounded upward, and he caught her in midair. She kissed Jonathan hard and quick on the cheek, then leaned over and kissed Mina, too. Jonathan was forehead to forehead with his little girl, staring straight into her deep amber eyes. "There's snow on the ground . . ."

"Can we go tobogganing? Please?"

Mina answered. "Right after breakfast. We'll all go."

Two nights after Christmas, Jonathan Harker was settling into his recliner, newspaper in hand. Mina appeared under the living room arch, making circles on a platter with a dishtowel. "Don't get too settled, dear. We're getting company."

"Oh?"

"Mr. Van Helsing from Winsberg's Department Store is stopping by. Seems they're recalling Lucy's Barbie Doll. Something about 'substandard manufacturing' in that particular model."

"No kidding? I thought there was something about that doll I didn't like. 'Substandard manufacturing,' huh?"

"They said it's a 'difficult situation' taking a little girl's doll away, so they've created a very special limited-edition Barbie to replace the defective ones. I think that's very nice, don't you?"

"I don't know . . ."

"And they're offering very special Barbie merchandise available only to the families with recalled dolls. Isn't that great? Lucy will have Barbie stuff that none of her friends can have. I'm sure that will make up for her disappointment at Christmas."

"Hey, wait just a minute . . ."

The chiming of the doorbell lured Mina away from her husband and to the front hall. Jonathan felt a kind of sinking in his soul when he heard the swoosh of the front door opening and the sweet company-voice of his wife.

"Mr. Van Helsing? Please come in."

Almost the Color of Summer Sky

Mabel Maney

I'M ALWAYS THE SMALLEST ONE IN MY class. This year I got glasses, too, light blue because that's the color of my eyes. My grandmother says you wouldn't want to wear black glasses like the school librarian, Miss Wiggham, who's never been married and is never going to get married.

They're called cat-glasses because they're pointed on the side like cats' eyes, not because they let you see in the dark. Our cat, Fiona, cries at night if you don't let her out. In the morning when I leave for school, there are birds and mice lying on the porch. Sometimes it's just their bodies and sometimes just their heads.

My teacher says I'm to clean my glasses every day so I can see clearly. My teacher says I mustn't daydream so much. I sit up front so she can keep an eye on me. I'm always the smallest one in my class.

Each year on my birthday my mother tells the same story, to anyone who will listen: After a night out dancing she feels a contraction and goes to the hospital. "I'm having a baby," she tells the nurse at the front desk, who laughs at the skinny girl in the snug black cocktail dress stained in front and says to come back in six months. My mother goes to the waiting room to borrow a cigarette from a nice young man in uniform, and when her water breaks a few minutes later, the nurse finally agrees to admit her and, shortly thereafter, I am born.

My father, who works nights, comes by on his break.

My mother wore her street clothes the whole time she was pregnant with me. Her dresses only had to be let out a few inches at the waist, that's all, by my grandmother who specializes in the alteration of fine women's fashions. My father could still get his hands all the way around her waist even though I was in there. When my mother tires of an outfit, my grandmother covers it with plastic bags from the cleaners and puts it away.

For the first few months after they brought me home from the hospital I slept in the top drawer of my mother's bureau, where now she keeps her garters and stockings. I was so small it made no sense to put me anywhere else.

I was born the same year the first photograph of the dark side of the moon was taken. My father works nights and sleeps days. I only ever see him after supper when he comes down from his room in the attic. The downstairs rooms are all too bright, he says.

My father showed up one night at the cocktail lounge where my mother was working. She had never seen eyes so blue; almost the color of summer sky. No one knew much about him. He never was one for words. My grandmother says I'm lucky I favor my mother. Now she has a better job at a nicer place.

We live with my grandmother to make ends meet. Every day except Sunday she puts on a black dress of long-wearing worsted wool—cotton in summer—and rides the bus downtown, where she spends her days hand-stitching the hems of Better Ladies Dresses at Kringle's, one of the two department stores in town. At night she makes copies of smart outfits for my mother.

My father works nights and sleeps days. The attic is dark and cool and runs the length of the house. Nobody is allowed up there, not even my grandmother to dust. My father says there are bats up there and we're to stay away. My father is such a quiet man you'd never know he was up there. He could be right over your head and you'd just never know it. There's an old army cot in the attic that he says suits him just fine.

My Uncle Art was in the army, and when he came home he couldn't sleep for months. He said every time he closed his eyes he saw dead people. Now he works at Hank's Hardware downtown and sleeps in the back. Everybody likes my Uncle Art. He's pretty quiet.

We live with my grandmother to make ends meet. On Saturday nights after we've cleared the supper dishes, my grandmother and I cut coupons from that week's newspapers and sort them into piles. Frozen. Fresh. Canned. When we're through we play cards, then we go to bed.

Once my grandmother took me to the movies and fell asleep before the second feature or I would have never been allowed to stay. A family with a pretty daughter inherits a castle with vampires living in the cellar. The vampires appear without warning; sometimes in the bedroom and sometimes in the hallway, but always when you least expect it.

The girl's job is to roam the castle before dawn and light the oil lamps. She carries a crucifix and prays for daylight, when the vampires must return to the cellar and get back in their coffins, quickly, before they disintegrate. Even though the movie was old and scratchy and you could see the string on the bat, it scared me just the same.

At Sunday School once we saw a movie. A little girl is walking alone in a dark woods when she hears a voice call out to her from above. She is frightened but powerless to resist its pull. In a stand of juniper trees she finds a beautiful lady clad in shimmering blue. Her feet are bare. It is the Virgin Mary, mother of us all. When the girl tells people, they say, "You musn't daydream so much." Now the little girl is a saint.

When we dust the living room Sundays after church, my grandmother tells me stories. I look like my grandfather in this picture. Her son who went to war sent her the hand-painted statue of a robin perched on a porcelain branch, singing. The bronze baby shoes belonged to her other son, born on the worn red horsehair davenport and dead just four months later. Sometimes I forget and think they were mine. My mother was a child here.

Before we go to sleep each night my grandmother and I kneel in front of the red davenport and say our prayers. The nuns at school know my grandmother. She attends mass each morning at six o'clock. She is always busy praying for somebody's soul. Afterward, in her best long-wearing worsted wool—cotton in summer—she rides the bus downtown, where she spends her days hand-stitching the hems of Better Ladies Dresses.

At night my grandmother makes copies of smart outfits for my mother. Wherever my mother goes she always looks her best. When she tires of a dress, my grandmother stuffs it with tissue and covers it with plastic bags to keep the dust out. She puts it at the back of the hall closet where it's dark. Sunlight is a danger to delicate dress fabric.

My mother's purses match her shoes. Her painted nails match her bright red lips. She has a fresh handkerchief for every day of the week. Although her father had in fact been the town gravedigger, you could never say my mother looked like a gravedigger's daughter. Anyway, that's what my grandmother always says.

My grandfather would bring home deer and rabbits and take them to the basement. There's a drain in the concrete floor for the blood to run out. Before he died he taught me how to skin a catfish. Make sure your skinning knife is sharp. There's no sense looking in their eyes as they're already dead. Because they have whiskers they remind me of kittens.

I try to tell my grandmother about the scary movie and the bat and how you never know when someone's going to appear out of nowhere, but she says not to bother about it because it isn't real. I know that, I want to tell her. I saw the string but it bothers me still.

My grandmother says that once you're dead and put in the ground, you pretty much stay there. She did see a magician once at the state fair who brought a dead person back to life, but she's sure now it was just a trick.

My father works nights and sleeps days. I only ever see him after supper when he comes down from his room in the attic. No one's allowed up there, not even my grandmother to dust. My mother says she couldn't look away the first time she saw him, his eyes were so blue. Almost the color of summer sky. She didn't know much about him.

Not long ago my father put a lock on the attic door. He got it from my Uncle Art, who works at Hank's Hardware downtown and sleeps in the back. My Uncle Art was smart enough to go to college, but every time he closed his eyes he saw dead people.

My father always carries the key with him, a shiny brass key that hangs on a chain from his belt. It's the same way the nuns at school carry their crucifixes. The crucifixes slap against their knees as they walk down the hall, but my father, he never makes a sound. You'd never know he was up there, that's how quiet he is. He almost never speaks, just looks at you with those eyes, almost as blue as summer sky. He could be right above your head and you'd just never know.

I never see my father during the day. Sometimes early in the morning before the sun comes up, he moves around the house, just looking. Once I saw him gliding over the kitchen linoleum in his stocking feet while waiting for his food to cook, probably some piece of meat from the deep freeze. There's still deer in there my grandfather shot; it keeps like that, you know.

My father has sallow, pale skin that shows every vein. If you ask him a question he just stares at you with those light eyes until you have to look away. My grandmother says he has thin blood and so can't be around other people much.

I'm lucky I favor my mother. My mother is always the prettiest girl in any crowd. You'd never guess she was the gravedigger's daughter, not from her clothes, anyway. That's what my grandmother says.

I try to tell my grandmother about the scary movie, about the girl who must roam the castle before dawn, never knowing who might pop up. I want to tell her that when I close my eyes at night I'm afraid to open them for fear of who's there. She says to remember that curiosity killed the cat.

My teacher says I musn't daydream so much. This year I got glasses, light blue because that's the color of my eyes. My teacher says I'm to clean my glasses every day so I can see clearly.

We live with my grandmother to make ends meet. Every day except Sunday she puts on a black dress of long-wearing worsted wool—cotton in summer—and rides the bus downtown, where she spends her days hand-stitching the hems of Better Ladies Dresses. At night she makes copies for my mother.

When my mother tires of a dress my grandmother puts it away. "There's still some life in this yet," my grandmother always says when we cover the dress with plastic and put it in the back of the coat closet where no light will ever reach it.

At night I lie in the dark in my bed. When I awake, he'll be home, maybe right over my head. You never know. He's quiet like that. When my Uncle Art closes his eyes at night, he sees dead people. When I close my eyes, I see the bat and the string and my father's eyes, almost the color of summer sky.

Best of Friends

Lisa D. Williamson

ER DOOR WAS LOCKED. THE house was quiet. Melanie sat on the edge of the bed. She didn't know what she was going to do. She could feel panic tighten across her cheekbones, pinch the back of her neck, squeeze her chest until it was hard to breathe.

It isn't fair, she thought, closing her eyes against the pain. *Why me?* She looked at the hard plastic Princess phone sitting mute on her nightstand. Beverly should have called by now.

Melanie stood abruptly and began pacing the small room with agitated steps. She avoided looking at her desk. The test lay there.

She couldn't take it. Not yet. It had to be done in the morning.

Anyway, she thought, it was probably nothing. The flu. Maybe mono.

It isn't fair. She had watched for years while all her school friends had matured before her. She had hugged her loneliness to her flat chest and waited for her turn.

Only her best friend had stood by her. Bev would say crude things about the boys, making Melanie laugh. Bev said they didn't need those boys.

Melanie's mother didn't care that the boys weren't interested; she was thrilled. Her mother was protective, trying to keep Melanie stuffed into childhood as long as possible, even though she was already fifteen.

"There's plenty of time for all *that*," she'd say, thinking she was comforting Melanie rather than twisting the knife deeper. "You'll be beautiful someday. You're a pretty girl now. Just have patience."

"Parents," Bev said, rolling her eyes, disgusted. "They're all the same."

Melanie thought how both her mother and her own body had betrayed her. How like a spring she'd been, restrained and held down, flying out of control when she'd met Derek.

Derek. It was funny how Bev had hated him from the start.

Melanie first saw him midway through her sophomore year. He wasn't really noticeable—average height, average build. Nothing to write home about. But somehow he was everything Melanie had ever dreamed of. His hair was a clean, glossy black, swept carelessly off his forehead, falling down to his shirt collar, so different from the unsophisticated boys at her high school. He wasn't very tall, not quite six feet. He was slim and lithe and moved like she thought a dancer would, so unlike anyone she knew in her small backwater town.

But it was his eyes that had captivated her. Dark, dark brown flecked with gold, so dark it was hard to tell where the iris ended and the pupil began. They were eyes that, if you weren't careful, you could fall into and never come back.

She and Bev had met him at the one place they were allowed to go on a weekday night. The library. She thought she'd known everyone who went there, but she'd never seen him before. He looked older, maybe eighteen or more. She knew he didn't go to her school. She heard later that he was somebody's cousin, but she never found out whose.

"*Omigod, Bev, look at that guy,*" she whispered, her face flushing bright red.

Bev had looked him over, slowly, insolently.

"He's not so hot," she said with a brusqueness she reserved for the boys who ignored her.

Derek had glanced up from his book, as if he'd heard. He'd looked Melanie over, unblinking, like the panthers at the zoo, completely shutting Bev out. Bev was wrong. Derek *was* hot. But Bev never saw it.

Melanie ran a hand over her forehead. She was sweating. *It must be my room,* she thought. The stifling bedroom faced west, where the sun was setting, throwing its last rays in through her window. It was Wednesday and her mother would be working late. Bev had said she'd call. They were going to plan what to do. Melanie could not go through this alone.

Another pain hit her. She held her hand to her stomach and willed it to pass. A cramp. Just a cramp. It meant nothing. She looked unwillingly at the test, sitting in its pristine, white box on her desk. She'd have to read the directions, but she hadn't wanted to touch it after Bev had given it to her in school. Funny how much easier it was to buy when you weren't the person involved. It wasn't the end of the world for Bev.

Melanie couldn't remember how it had all started. She still couldn't explain how she had summoned the nerve to talk with Derek. Or how the first, innocent meeting had somehow blossomed into subsequent secret, nightly meetings. Still at the library—oh yes, even in her wild abandon Melanie had thought she'd been acting sanely, safely. Melanie looked bitterly around her bedroom, at all the frilly pink festooning the bed and draping the windows and thought what a pretense all this innocence was. All the things her mother didn't know.

And Bev, her friend, her closest friend, the person who knew her best, had protected her. Bev hated Derek, called him all sorts of names, told Melanie he was no good. But in the end, she helped. After all, they were best friends. Bev always covered for Melanie.

"Mel's staying the night here," Bev would confirm to Melanie's mother on more than one occasion.

And Melanie would go to Derek.

But however loyal Bev was, she was still jealous of what Melanie and Derek shared.

"What are those bruises?" she hissed at Melanie as they stood in the girls' room at school. Melanie would draw her shirt collar higher, but Bev wouldn't leave her alone. "What's he doing to you? You have to dump him, Mel. You don't need him."

But she did. That was the part Bev didn't understand.

Melanie thought back to the night Derek had finally persuaded her to go all the way, almost against her will. It had been savage, intoxicating—beyond her wildest imaginings. Beyond all her expectations. Painful, yet wonderful.

Later they talked, but she learned nothing.

"Where are you from?" she asked him, inhaling him, savoring the faint hint of foreignness that emanated from him.

"I don't belong anywhere, really," he whispered, his face buried in her hair. "My family . . ." His voice trailed off, his eyes hooded themselves.

"Why are you here?" she kept asking him, wanting answers.

"For you," Derek answered, running his cool finger down the soft flesh on the inside of her arm. "Only for you."

The blood fluttered in the vein at her wrist. Melanie got up suddenly, going to her window, pushing aside the frothy pink curtain, staring out at the driveway. Why didn't Beverly call? She had promised; Melanie didn't know what to do without Bev. Her mother would be home in a few hours. She and Bev had a lot to plan, a lot to discuss.

When Bev had handed her the white box this morning, she had told Melanie, "I'm going to talk to that jerk."

Melanie had panicked. She and Derek hadn't talked for days. She didn't want him to know anything. Not yet. Maybe not at all. But especially not through Beverly. Melanie thrust the parcel into her locker, slammed it shut and said, "No. You can't. It has nothing to do with him. Please—" she grabbed Bev's wrist. "Please. Just help me."

But Bev had been cool, practical, relentless.

"He should know, one way or the other," she said.

And pushed, Melanie voiced her worst fears.

"What if I'm not pregnant?" she whispered, leaning on the

putty-colored locker for strength. "What if it's something else?"

Melanie had told Bev when she first felt the change, when she first knew there was something wrong with her.

Bev said, "Dump the jerk."

Melanie was so scared, she listened. But then she met Derek one last time. Between the bookshelves she told him she wouldn't be seeing him again.

Derek looked down on her and smiled slightly. "You'll be back," he said in a soft, calm voice. "I'll be waiting," he murmured and ran his tongue down her throat. He bit her deeply at the slope of her neck, in the way that drove her wild. "You need me," he said.

He had almost been right. Every night Melanie had to fight the urge to run to him. Every day Bev whispered in her ear, told her she didn't need Derek, he didn't care about her, he only hurt her. But the scary feeling hadn't gone away. Nothing Bev said made it go away.

Melanie was getting angry. Beverly had made her dump Derek, and now where was she? She was supposed to call. Melanie needed her.

Tired of waiting, Melanie thought maybe eating something would help the growing feeling of nausea. She left her room and went down the stairs slowly, still sweating. If she wasn't pregnant, what was left? *Sexually transmitted diseases.* STDs. That totally irrelevant topic in that totally boring health class. Syphilis, gonorrhea, all those dreadful diseases she couldn't bear to think of, including that worst one of all, AIDS. Of course she hadn't paid attention. Those things didn't happen to girls like her.

She went to the kitchen and put water in the microwave for tea. Now ravenous, Melanie looked through the cupboards, but nothing appealed to her. Suddenly, a strong pain hit her in the stomach. She gasped and collapsed on the floor.

In the midst of her misery, an almost unbearable longing for Derek hit her, nearly as strong as her hunger—and her terrible pain. But she knew she didn't need Derek, she needed Bev.

Melanie knelt on the cold linoleum, tears coursing down her face. *I'm hungry, I miss Derek. And I'm dying.*

A stronger, sharper pain hit her. She cried out and crouched there with her head down, riding out the agony. *Where was Beverly? Why hadn't she called?* Melanie heard the kitchen door open.

Bev. Thank God, Melanie thought. The pain was slowly subsiding. She wiped the sweat from her face and looked up.

It was Derek. He stood just outside the open door, watching her.

Melanie tried to get up.

"What are you doing here? I told you I couldn't see you anymore. Did you talk to Beverly? What did she tell you?" she asked him. The questions came out in a rush. She couldn't stand. "I'm sick," she said and reached her hand out for him.

Derek said nothing. He studied Melanie's face in that quiet, watchful way he had.

"Don't just stand there," she said, suddenly feeling afraid of him. "Come help me."

Derek entered the kitchen, his movements smooth and gliding. Crossing to Melanie, he took both her hands and gently pulled her up to him.

"You're not sick," he said softly. "It's only the change. You'll be fine. I can take care of you."

His touch made her forget her pain. She stood, swaying close to him, almost swooning, breathing in the subtle smell of his body. She fought against her longing, trying to remember he had caused this pain, trying to remember what Bev had said about him. Bev said she must hate him. Melanie tried to push him away.

"You have to eat, babe," he said, nuzzling her neck. Melanie's head dropped back. She could feel his lips, his tongue, his teeth.

"Yes," she whispered. *Yes,* she thought, *this is what I want. How could I have believed Bev?*

He stood back and smiled down at her. There was a red smear on his lips. Melanie touched her neck and looked down at her hand. Red. Another pain hit, even stronger. Derek held her. The pain became more bearable, which somehow made things worse. Her choices were being taken away. Who to believe, Bev or Derek? The person she'd known all her life or someone she didn't really know at all?

"Melanie, come with me," Derek said, reading her thoughts. "You need something to eat. You need something for the pain. I can take care of you." He led her outside. She leaned heavily against him.

The pain didn't seem to bother her as much when he held her, but Melanie couldn't think straight with him so close. She thought maybe he'd drive her to the hospital. A few minutes ago, the very idea would have scared her, but now it seemed so easy to leave everything to Derek.

But there was no car in the driveway. Where was he taking her? Melanie thought again how little she knew Derek. She felt so weak, so overwhelmed. Then she saw Beverly.

Even though it was getting dark, Melanie had no difficulty seeing her. Bev was sitting in the grass, leaning up against a tree. Her round face was almost luminescent in the dusk, and she was not moving. Derek studied Melanie for a moment, then led Melanie to her.

"Bev?" she said softly.

"What's she doing here?" Melanie asked, trying to see Derek's eyes in the half light. "What's wrong with her?" She was feeling frightened again. Frightened of him.

Derek smiled slightly. He ran his hand gently up her arm. His touch made her shiver. "Your friend told me I was no good for you." He put his mouth to her ear and breathed softly, "Is that what you think?"

Melanie's head was too heavy. She rested it against Derek's shoulder while she looked at Bev. She saw the bruises. She drew in her breath. Her fingers touched the marks on her own neck.

None of this is happening, Melanie thought. *This can't be him. I passed out. None of this is happening.*

"Melanie, the pain will go away." Derek's voice was insistent, almost rough. "It's just part of the change."

Beverly still hadn't moved. She was white and waxy looking. Her eyes were fully open, but sightless. Somehow though, even in the dark, Melanie could see the faint flutter of a pulse at the base of Bev's neck. She could smell Bev's blood in the hot night air.

"I don't understand," she said weakly, although she was afraid she was beginning to. Again the pain hit. Melanie reeled. Only Derek's grip kept her steady.

"Derek, I'm sick. I think I'm dying." She almost hoped she was. "You have to help me."

"No, no," Derek said. "You're not dying. Quite the contrary." He held her briefly before guiding her gently toward the inert body.

"Beverly said she was your friend," Derek said, pushing Melanie's face down, down to the tiny, beating pulse. Telling her to feed. "I thought I'd give her a chance to help. After all, she told me she'd do anything for you. Anything for her best friend."

To Die For

Diane DeKelb-Rittenhouse

N THE END, NEITHER SICKROOM CLAUS-trophobia nor prestorm atmospheric pressure could be blamed. Sixteen years of parental limits and social taboos had simply produced the inevitable back-lash. She needed to do something risky, something to prove, finally, that all the warnings thrown out to her for sixteen years were so much authoritarian paranoia, meant to keep her a "good girl." Genevra Burke was tired of pretending to be a "good girl." She was tired of being kept safe.

Or maybe it was merely that, tonight, she was simply too restless to stay in her room.

By the time she had checked out her appearance in the hall mirror, copped the keys to Dan's bike and slipped out by the back stairs, the rain had come and gone. The downpour that had been threatening all afternoon turned out to be no more than one of those brief autumnal storms that dropped the temperature, sharpened the air and slicked the asphalt. By dark, the roadways in Peerless Falls, New York, had become dimly reflective surfaces where motor-oil stains glinted like tawdry rainbows under the illumination of the motor-cycle's headlight as Gen drove away from the Blaise Heights section of town.

Once arrived at her destination, Gen pushed away from the 900cc Harley Sportster she had "borrowed" from her oldest brother and walked the half block from the parking lot on Grace Road to Cedar Street. Although she appeared old enough to be out after midnight in the middle of the week, the petite brunette did not look strong enough to handle the bike easily.

But then, with Genevra, appearances were almost always deceiving.

At the corner of Grace and Cedar, she stopped to savor a breath of night air. It tanged of freshly washed creek bed and newly turned earth. This part of Cedar Street was only two blocks south of Blaise Creek, and one west of Rosewood Cemetery. After a good rain you could smell nature at work, breaking down fallen leaves, grass clippings and other organic residue into the compounds that would enrich the earth and allow more grass and new seeds to thrive—new life gorging on death. Spring and the triumph of life were half a year away, though: Autumn was death's season.

The pleasant odors of organic dissolution and reclamation were, she noticed, overlain by a more immediate reek: stale tobacco, old booze, fresh urine. This was, after all, the rough side of town. Gen smiled and took a deep breath.

It was just past midnight, and the action was revving into overdrive. From what she could see, the *Falls Journal*'s claim that all citizens were too terrified by the recent murders to leave their homes after dark was simply the usual media hype. Either that, or no one on Cedar ever read the papers, for the street was as crowded as a shopping mall on Satur-day. Sound systems pumped up to high volume blared an assortment of acid house, postmodern, metal and hard rock from the bars. Neon signs extolled the virtues of massage parlors, dance clubs, coffee shops and a motel that advertised hourly rates. Hookers of both sexes worked the corners while men of all ages and social classes traveled the side-walks. Almost every person she saw was sucking on one brand of oral pacifier or another: Marlboro, Colombian, even crack. Smoke hung in the air like a stripper's veil at a peep show.

As she continued down the street, her gaze winnowed through the crowd parting around her. Not everyone was moving. Some preferred to lean against an outside wall, making desultory conversation with a few companions. She watched the watchers scan the crowd as they checked out possible threats and potential opportunities.

One thing being evaluated was the opportunity she herself represented, a girl by herself, after dark, on Cedar. That alone ought to have made her nervous, but the restlessness that had driven her out into the night still made her feel more excitement than fear.

If appearances counted for anything, they ought to work in her favor. Gen was neither as heavily made-up nor as suggestively garbed as the hookers. She had dressed with an eye to practicality: denim skirt short enough to allow freedom of movement on the Sportster, but longer than any hemline on Cedar, black lambswool sweater, dark tights and denim jacket against the chill, leather half-boots to protect her feet. Every item was well cut, neatly crafted, declaring her an escaped deb from Blaise Heights as clearly as if she had had her address in the town's most exclusive section emblazoned on each article.

Her makeup was also understated; no more than what she needed to sustain the illusion that she was a junior in college rather than a sophomore in high school. Lip gloss accentuated the lush fullness of her mouth, mascara called attention to her long-lashed, wide brown eyes. She had decided against any perfume other than that of fresh scrubbed girl and had left her thick brown hair styled in the simple, smooth curve she usually favored, with the ends swinging an inch or so above her shoulders. The people on Cedar took her for one more deb out for illicit thrills.

And for once, wasn't that exactly what she was?

Now, as she moved just slowly enough to observe her surroundings without becoming easy prey, she saw that her costume was indeed effective. A few wanted a closer look at her. Their come-ons were limited to crudely humorous one-liners as they moved briefly into her orbit. If quick, anonymous sex was all she wanted, she could have found something to satisfy her needs within yards of where she'd left the Harley. But she wanted more than that, and so the further she moved along the street, the more restless she became, uncertain if she would find what she sought after all. Gen decided to give Cedar Street two more blocks. If her hunt proved unsuccessful, she would follow her original inclination and bike into Manhattan to stalk one of the rave clubs.

The first block passed with nothing to offer. Then, almost at the end of the next street, she found the night's first real possibility. A dozen members of the Renegades, a local motorcycle gang, had gathered outside a bar. She slowed her pace to get a better look.

And for one of those dangerous young men, that was invitation enough.

He straightened away from the wall where he had been leaning and cut across her path, effectively blocking her progress down the crowded street. His intent was noted by his companions, who gave a few cat-calls and wolf-whistles to show their approval.

Gen approved as well. She liked the look of him: lean height, taut muscle, self-confidence bordering on arrogance. She figured him for nineteen, twenty at most. He was not flaunting gang colors, which might mean only that he was newly recruited into membership. Gen didn't think that was it. He looked the type to be here on his own terms, not someone else's.

His leather jacket was aged, cracked in places, and the jeans that clad a body Brad Pitt might envy were worn through at one knee. Her brothers tried for that effect, but scissors were no substitute for sharp-edged poverty.

Gen was further intrigued by the young man's coloring, which combined pale skin with dark hair and eyes to striking effect. The hair wasn't merely thick and black, it kinked into tight curls that hung just below his jacket collar without softening or feminizing features that, from broad brow to square chin, were blatantly masculine.

He looked exotic and raw, hot and dangerous: a lawless angel furloughed from Hell to tempt unwary young girls into wickedness. Girls like Gen. Still, she wasn't sure she was ready for someone who appeared to be quite this much of an outlaw. Her risks were of the calculated rather than the reckless variety. Gen was about to cut him down as she had the others when she caught a second look at his eyes. She had thought them black, or a dark brown, like her own. But as he came nearer, the street lamp above them cast enough light for her to see that they were a deep, startling, seductive indigo: eyes to die for.

That was the selling point: Gen wanted his eyes.

"You're on the other side of town from Blaise Heights, deb," he said in a smoky baritone that was almost as delectable as his eyes. Gen noted that he spoke like the people she was used to, like someone who understood language and didn't swallow his final consonants or rely on expletives to carry the brunt of his conversation, not what she had expected to find in a guy hanging out at a biker bar. As they stood together he sent his gaze over her in cool evaluation. The approval she saw in his look came close to insolence, yet there was wariness as well. She wasn't the first escapee from Blaise Heights to slum on Cedar, not the first 'blazing deb' to start a fire that might burn too dangerously bright. What she offered might not be worth the risks she brought. Gen couldn't help smiling. If he understood that, he wasn't stupid. She hated stupidity in boys.

"I know where I am," Gen told him, "and my name isn't Deb. It's Lisa."

"Right. Lisa." He smiled with just a hint of contempt, but did not challenge her use of what he clearly realized was a false name. The smile had revealed a set of white teeth unstained by tobacco. Gen tilted her head back to look up at him and smiled directly into his delicious eyes. Yes, she could definitely handle this.

"Know where I can get a drink?" she asked. As she finished speaking, the door of the bar behind them opened as some of the patrons of Ray's Place headed off to other pursuits. Another thirty decibels of hard rock to spill out onto the street.

"Ray's sells drinks," the lawless angel said. "I'm Jace. Let me buy you one."

His arm moved casually around her as they walked through the entrance. By the time they reached the bar, his hand was resting lightly against her hip. The gestures were not so much sexual as territorial. She enjoyed them.

Jace called to the bartender for two mugs of beer. Gen had a convincingly faked ID card should the bartender need persuasion to serve her more than a cola. He didn't. She wasn't surprised. Gen was one of those girls who mature early and can pass for seventeen by the time they reach twelve. During her first week at middle school, she had twice been mistaken for a new teacher rather than a new student. Recently, her ability to pass herself off as older had proved distinctly advantageous.

Jace paid for the beers and found a table. It was near a section of linoleum that served as the dance floor at Ray's Place and which had Gen longing for one of the rave clubs in Manhattan. Well, she hadn't wanted to waste the travel time.

They slipped off their jackets and hung them on the backs of their chairs. Jace's black T-shirt bore a silk-screen of the cover art from an album cut before Gen was born.

"Good album," she commented as she took her seat. "Did you like the sequel?"

"Yeah," Jace said as he scraped his chair closer to hers. "But it's not the classic the first one was." Gen could feel the heat of his body next to hers, feel her body reacting, warming, yielding.

"Then you wouldn't do anything for love?" she asked seductively.

"Depends."

She picked up the mug he had given her. Beer was not her beverage of choice, but she had an illusion to sustain. She braced herself, took a sip and made a welcome discovery. For beer, the stuff Ray's Place served wasn't bad. "Well, I like your taste in music and brew," she told him. "What else am I going to like about you?"

"Oh, I think you'll find plenty about me to your taste." His voice imbued the sentence with intense erotic promise. She wanted to know more.

"You hang with the Renegades?" she asked.

"When it suits me," he replied, smiling. "You into bikes?"

"When it suits me," she smiled back, lifting her mug for another draught.

"And when is that?" he laughed. "When Daddy's limo is unavailable?"

"More like when it's off-limits," she admitted.

"Strange time to keep it off-limits. Or aren't you worried about dangers like the Slasher?"

"Well, maybe I'll just find someone to take care of the dangers for me," she said. "What about you? Think that's a job you can handle?"

"Maybe *I'm* one of the dangers you have to protect yourself against," he said suggestively. Gen smiled and took another sip of beer.

An old song, something slow and moody, was playing. Gen moved subtly to the music, hardly more than a gentle swaying, as she sat drinking and looking around Ray's Place. Most of the crowd was either at the bar or watching the pool games being played at two tables on the other side of the room. As Gen took everything in, she was aware of Jace's regard, almost as if she could feel the cool gaze of those incredible eyes sliding across her flesh.

"Let's dance," he said after a moment. She gave him her hand and let him lead her out. There were only a few other couples dancing, but that was enough to crowd the small space and to give Jace all the excuse he needed to pull her intimately close.

He held her possessively, as if they were already lovers. Gen liked the feel of his body against hers, of his arms around her, his hands caressing her back. There was strength in those arms, allowing her an illusion of helpless femininity that, in small doses, she found arousing.

She moved against him like silk on skin—soft, smooth, sensuous. His reaction was immediate—an in-drawn breath, a tightening of the embrace, a slow fire kindling in the depths of his remarkable eyes. Gen laughed and pressed closer, lifting her head to tongue the rapidly beating pulse at his throat. Jace's hands caressed down her back to rest against her buttocks. Sweet. He lowered his head to turn his face into her hair, to search out and nuzzle her ear.

"What are you after, deb?" he whispered in that smoky, sensual voice that had drawn her from the first. "What do you want on Cedar?" The question was sincere, not coy. Jace truly wanted to know just how far a girl from Blaise Heights was willing to take her fantasy of freedom.

"I want you," she whispered back fiercely, desperate to communicate the depth, the reality of her need. Between fevered kisses pressed against his ear, his face, his throat, she continued. "Don't you know how hot you are? How wet you make me? I want your smoky voice and your tight body, and I want your gorgeous eyes."

Her frankness thrilled him. She could tell by the way he looked at her now, avidly, hungrily. His desire fed her own, and suddenly the night, early as it was, seemed too short for all the things she wanted to have with Jace. She stood on tiptoe to whisper a suggestion. He acquiesced, leading her off the dance floor. Gen put on her jacket while Jace finished his beer. As they left Ray's Place, Jace nodded good night to his friends. Then the two of them headed back up Cedar toward Grace Road and the parked Harley.

The Sportster almost ruined things.

"That's an awful lot of bike for a little girl like you," Jace observed coolly.

"Yeah, well it isn't exactly mine," she admitted.

"Didn't think so." He pulled her close, his embrace forceful, almost rough. His indigo eyes stared directly into hers, their expression that of controlled anger. "Straight up, babe: Does this damn thing belong to some boyfriend you're using me to make jealous?"

"Chill," she laughed. "It's my brother's. He lets me keep it for him while he's at college."

"Your brother's, huh?" he said, relaxing his grip. Jace cast a suspicious glance over the Sportster, a look not untinged with hunger. She knew he wanted to believe her, wanted an excuse to take the bike for a spin.

"My brother's," she assured him, pulling the key from her jacket pocket. Holding out the bit of metal, Gen watched his face, his emotions clearly reflected by his expressions. She saw the way uncertainty warred with desire, knew the exact moment when desire won out. Jace laughed ruefully and took the key from her hand.

Their ride was a continuation of the seduction started in the bar. With her arms wrapped around his rock-firm abs, Gen could feel Jace's excitement rise as the Sportster roared between his thighs and her own soft breasts pressed against his back. He guided the Sportster east on Grace Road until they came out on Laurel, turned south and opened up full throttle. The bike was a streak of black lightning on the roadway, flashing past Peerless Falls Road, Larch and Beechwood Streets until they reached Rose Arbor Road and headed east again.

He took the road all the way out to the edge of town, where houses were farther apart, and not a few were empty—the perfect place, Gen realized, for someone like the Slasher to lure victims. She shrugged off the thought and snuggled closer to Jace.

Jace had a studio apartment over the garage where he worked days. The entrance was up a set of iron stairs in an alleyway between a beer distributor and the garage. Gen liked the arrangement. Living quarters that small did not lend themselves to roommates. No interruptions or awkward questions, and no one to remember that a girl from Blaise Heights had been someplace she shouldn't.

It wasn't yet midnight. Dawn was hours off. Gen had all the time she needed to play with her new toy before she would have to sneak back home and pretend a continuation of the fever that had kept her from classes all week.

Jace hit the light switch inside the door, moved aside to let her enter and then headed off to the kitchen while Gen looked over the room. Double bed with throw pillows to serve as a couch, CDs stacked in one corner by the player, motorcycle gear stacked in another, furniture that was clearly rescued from his parents' basement. All of it was typical, expected.

The photographs, though—those were unexpected. And the books. Books in piles, books in heaps, books packed floor to ceiling in stacked plastic milk crates. Books in no discernible order, a volume of Byron's poetry on the shelf between a text on automotive mechanics and an anthology of horror stories. Gen picked up the anthology. Her own copy was almost as well worn as his. She put the book down on a stack of comic books and turned to consider the photos. While all of her peers decorated their walls with posters of rock bands or cult movies, Jace had hung the few patches of wall not supporting bookshelves with eight-by-ten photographs.

"You take these?" she asked, surprised. The photographs varied in composition: A picture of a deer gnawing tree bark on a snow-covered hill shared wall space with a shot of the town's mayor leading the Independence Day parade.

"Hobby," Jace said, handing her a beer. It was the same brand he had ordered at Ray's Place. She took a sip while Jace went to kneel by the CDs and flipped through the collection. Gen turned back to look more closely at the photographs. That of the deer was saved from smarmy sentimentality because it had a hint of brutality, capturing the survival imperative in the deer's tearing of the bark. The elements of the mayor's picture were more sly; somehow, the camera had caught him at a less than flattering angle, and surely the juxtaposition, in the background, of a campaign banner beside a grubby man with his belongings in a shopping cart, was not accidental.

"Some hobby," Gen said appreciatively.

"When I can fit it into my roster, I take a few photography classes."

"You're in school?" That explained a lot.

"Night classes at Falls County Community College," he responded. "This is my last term. I start at NYU next semester." He was still sorting through the CDs. "Anything you want to hear?"

She replied in the negative and walked up to another picture. "I like the way your shots seem to be, you know, like layers," she said as she examined it. The composition could have passed for a painted still life, red roses in an unadorned black vase on a wooden tabletop. A few petals had fallen on the surface of the table. You had to look carefully to see the hearse driving past the window at the edge of the wall behind the vase. She went on: "I mean you look at them and they seem to be about one thing, but you keep looking, and they're really about something else."

"Yeah, well, life is like that, isn't it? You can never be sure what's real and what's a front for something else."

Gen turned to glance at Jace and noticed that his face wore a closed-down, enigmatic expression as he looked back at her. Then he quirked a smile and went back to his search. For the first time since she had met him, Gen experienced a return of the uneasiness that had marred the evening for her at first. Maybe she had been too confident, had taken on more than she could really deal with. But, no, that was silly. She had to learn to rely on her instincts, and those instincts said that Jace could provide what she needed.

Jace, meanwhile, had found what he wanted. He rose and stretched, then removed the disc from its case and loaded it into the player.

"That go for you, too?" she asked softly, turning back to the photograph and assuming a light tone. "Hard-working college boy, are you really something else? Something . . . dangerous?"

He hit the start button on the player, and she heard the first familiar chords come over the speakers. As he had said, the first album was a classic.

Jace moved up behind her, kissed the back of her neck and took the half-empty beer can from her hand to set it down on a small table that stood nearby.

"Oh, I am all the danger you can handle," he said, his voice once again rich with erotic promise, dissolving the last of her doubts. She smiled and turned in his arms.

"I can handle a lot," she said and kissed his mouth, taking his lower lip between her teeth and nipping lightly.

She had him naked in moments, her lips never leaving his flesh while she undid buckles, snaps, buttons, slid his jeans down his hips, his shirt over his head. His hands moved as surely upon her body, and in a few minutes, she lay beneath him on the bed. She opened her thighs to him, experiencing a sharp moment of loss when he pulled away long enough to take a condom from a drawer in his night table. She eyed it with displeasure. Sex was new to her. Nick had been her first real lover, and that only a matter of days ago. Still, she had learned quickly and knew what she wanted—and that was to feel warm flesh and spurting seed inside her, not slippery latex. But she suffered the delay in silence and promised herself to make up for it later.

They had all night.

Their first coupling was urgent, feral, and the bed proved inadequate for it. They slid from mattress to floor in a tangle of quilts, pillows and limbs. It didn't distract them. Gen loved the weight of him crushing down on her, the pounding rhythm of his cock, the way he held her wrists immobile, the illusion of submission. As she felt him reach his climax, she pulled her head back so she could lock gazes with him as he came.

"You have the most beautiful eyes," she whispered just before he brought her with him over the edge.

When she could move, Gen retrieved her jacket, pulled a vial of coke, a mirror and a razor blade from the pocket and cut a few lines. After they had finished, Jace propped himself up on a pillow against the bed's headboard, pulling Gen over so that they lay breast to chest, her head resting on his arm.

"This has been nice," Gen murmured, tracing the outline of his pectoral with her left hand.

"Nice enough for you to be straight with me?" Jace asked as his right hand stroked the soft, cool skin of her flanks.

"What do you mean?"

"I'd like to know your real name."

"Figured you hadn't been fooled by my alias," she laughed.

"Figured you weren't trying too hard to fool anyone," he retorted. "One of the reasons I like you. Every now and then we get a group of 'blazing debs' slumming on Cedar, using made up names 'cause they don't want word getting out where they've been or who they've been doing. For sure, they don't want any of the guys they pick up to come looking for them at home. I don't play those games, so I usually don't get involved."

"But you got involved with me," she said, raising herself up on one arm to look into his eyes, to lose herself in the indigo depths.

"Yeah. I thought you might be worth the risk."

Gen had to laugh at the irony.

"I thought the same about you!" she explained. "I mean, I know the rep the Renegades have. I wasn't sure I wanted to get that close to one of them."

"I'm not one of them," Jace asserted.

"But they let you hang with them," she said, settling her head back down on his arm.

"Yeah, well, I'm good with bikes. The Renegades are what you might call regular customers at the garage. So, what made you decide to take the risk?"

"Your eyes," she said promptly. "Do you realize that you have beautiful to-die-for eyes? I saw them, and I knew I wanted them and I wanted you."

"Well, you've got us," he said, dropping a light kiss onto her temple. "So now, deb, what's your real name?"

"Gen. Genevra Burke."

Jace whistled. "Burke Communications?

"Daddy," she admitted. There was no reason not to tell him everything, now. And she was curious to see how he would react to the knowledge. So far he seemed mildly impressed, but hardly overawed. She was glad.

"What about you?" she asked. "Jace short for Jason?"

"Nah. My initials. Jonathan Alexander Cavenaugh."

"I like your name," she said.

"I told you you'd find me to your taste, Gen," he reminded her as he moved over her again, dropping slow kisses across her face and down her torso.

"You haven't *let* me taste you," she said teasingly, then gasped as he took a nipple between his teeth and bit lightly.

"Later," he said, reaching for another condom. She intercepted his arm, moving his hand to her breast, working to distract him. She counted on the beer, the coke and her own wantonness to make him forget the precaution he had been about to take.

The advantage to coke, Nick had told her, was that it intensified sensual pleasure while delaying gratification. He had been right. For more than an hour, Jace stayed hard for her, driving her to peak after peak, withdrawing once to spend an excruciating fifteen minutes laving her clit with his tongue, driving her to screaming euphoria before thrusting into her once more, starting the delicious spiral upward all over again. Gen was thankful he had no neighbors to hear the uncontrolled moans and cries of delight he forced from her. Surely the police would have been called hours ago otherwise.

But it wouldn't be really good for her unless it was good for him, too. She stopped concentrating on her own feelings and worked to bring him to completion. It seemed to take forever, but finally she felt his body tensing as a knife's edge of pleasure cut to his soul. This time when he released, he shot his seed deep into her womb, triggering her most exquisite orgasm so far that night.

"You are . . . incredible!" he gasped out afterward, as she snuggled back into his arms. He was asleep almost instantly, exhaustion winning out over the stimulus of the coke, at least for the moment. After a while, Gen eased out from under his arm, went to the player and changed discs, lowering the volume as she did so. The sequel had a lot going for it, too.

Returning to the bed, she contemplated her lawless angel. Everything about Jace pleased her—brains, brawn, stamina and those gorgeous eyes. He was such a find, absolutely delicious. Jace was the kind of young man with enough determination, talent and ruthlessness to make something of himself. Given a few years, and if she stuck with him, used the resources available to her to back him, he could develop into a major name in the arts. If not photography, possibly films.

It was a pleasant fantasy, and she indulged it as she watched him sleep. She must have drowsed as well, for she found herself coming awake when he left the bed.

"Want a beer?" he asked. She shook her head and burrowed more deeply into the bedclothes. She didn't fall asleep though, but listened as he moved around the apartment, using the bathroom, then changing CDs before heading to the kitchen. Gen heard his footsteps coming closer, but they stopped short of the bed.

"Wicked!" Jace said appreciatively. She opened her eyes to see him standing with his back to the room's one mirror, admiring a few lines of red welts she had not known she had raised.

"Oh!" she gasped. "I didn't realize—"

"Don't worry," he laughed. "I don't mind if you draw a little blood." He turned away from the mirror and came toward her again. "But let me see your hands." His voice had grown huskier, the smoky quality she found irresistible, more pronounced. Mesmerized, she lifted one of her arms out of the tangled covers and presented it to him. Locking her gaze with his own, Jace took her hand as he moved next to her on the bed and lifted it to his mouth.

"I want it back, Gen," he said softly. "My blood. I want to know what I taste like on you." He drew one of her fingers into the wet heat of his mouth and gently flicked his tongue along her incarnadined nail, all the while holding her gaze with his. In that moment, Gen understood the ease with which a Slasher could tempt victim after victim into folly, even those forewarned of danger. If Jace were the Slasher, which she knew—she *knew*—he could not be, she would in that instant have opened her veins and willingly poured out her life for the sake of the look in his eyes, the caress of his tongue against her flesh.

"Please," she whispered, not certain what she meant. Jace knew, though, for he abandoned her fingers to kiss his way along her arm, across her shoulder and up her throat to her lips. With gestures and murmured love-words he coaxed her onto her side and slipped down beside and behind her, lifting her upper leg over his hips, entering her in one smooth, sure thrust that took him deeper into her body than she would have believed it possible for him to go. Gen moaned softly. The position allowed his hands the freedom to caress her breasts and clitoris in slow, intoxicatingly seductive rhythms, bringing her to rapid, repeated release. Her first climax wasn't enough for him, for he kept up the assault until she was brought, impossibly, to the edge again. And once again before he allowed himself to join her in rapture. It was too intense, too much, and she drifted back to sleep almost at once.

She awoke hours later. Glancing at the clock on the nightstand, Gen realized she would have to leave soon. She hated the thought, not wanting to part from Jace, wishing there was more time. But there wasn't, and she would have to make the most of what she had.

Gen woke him with demanding kisses. "I have to go in a little while," she told him, "but I want to say good-bye."

He took hold of her arms and rolled her beneath him.

"Not just yet," he said. "I'm not quite ready to let you go." He hadn't exerted his full strength before, but he used it now to hold her still while his lips traveled once more down her body, seeking the molten core of her.

"Tell me again, Gen," he said as he nipped and licked at flesh made ultrasensitive by an excess of pleasure, "are my eyes to die for?" She moaned deep in her throat, writhing in his suddenly ruthless grasp.

"Please," she gasped, as she had earlier, "please." This time he ignored her.

"You promised I could taste," she pleaded. At that he relented enough to turn obligingly, so that his lovely hard cock was within reach of her greedy mouth. She ran her tongue around the tip, then sucked him deep into her throat, laving the ridge. He quickly grew so long and thick it was difficult to take him down to the root. Gen couldn't breath and didn't need to. What she did need was to have as much of Jace as she could get.

When he began to lose concentration on what he was doing to her,

Gen knew he was approaching his crisis. Her tongue now moved lovingly down the shaft of his cock, over the blue veins feeding blood to the engorged member. She took him as deep as she could, sucking harder, increasing her rhythm, then pulled all the way back, as if for a deep breath—

And let her fangs descend.

She did not traffic in pain. The twin, fine-pointed ivory purveyors of ultimate destiny she sank into the sweetly pulsing vein beneath her lips were also instruments of enthralling ecstasy. He did not realize, at first, what she had done, lost to everything but the incomparable pleasure she gave him.

And now Gen was soul to soul with Jace, mind to mind with him as well as flesh to flesh. With the blood came images, thoughts, emotions: a picture of Jace steadying his younger sister for her first solo ride on a bike—a fragment of last night's lecture in film class—a scene from the sticky breakup with a girl he loved.

And the blood conveyed his horror as, finally, beyond the delight she brought, the knowledge of what Gen truly wanted from him and the price he would pay for what she gave was borne in upon him.

Then she tasted his rage. And his lust. She shared the turmoil as his desire to push her away, to fight against her warred with his desire to offer himself up more completely. He wanted to hate her, to destroy her, to stop her—

And he could not stop himself from continuing to worship with avid tongue and lips the slick pearl of flesh she offered him.

Gen tasted every moment of his struggle.

Yes, my darling, yes, she cast the words into his mind as she let him feel her own pleasure, so that even as she experienced the sensations he knew as her lips and tongue and throat sheathed and caressed him, he experienced the effect of his mouth against her own femininity, felt her own building rapture.

For you, my beloved, my lover, my prey . . .

Ultimately he surrendered to the soul-stealing ecstasy only she could provide. His blood was as smoky as his voice, smooth on her tongue, and as she took it into herself, she experienced with him the appalling delight her final act brought him, shared with him the screaming, blinding, sheet-ripping orgasm, attaining her own and feeding it back to him as he spent into her mouth and she into his and she tasted, at long last, the mingled bitter-sweetness of his seed with the salt-spice savor of his blood.

The death-throe was the most profound climax: She lost consciousness as he yielded his own forever.

After a few minutes, Gen roused, greedily lapped the last drops away, then settled back on the bed. Jace's lids were closed over his marvelous eyes, and she dropped an affectionate kiss on each wax-pale surface.

Her time was nearly out. She finished the rest quickly. It took only a moment to don her clothing, get the few props she needed from her jacket pocket and scatter them across the floor. Her vial of coke was placed near Jace's right hand. If the police were called, she wanted them to attribute the death to an accident while under the influence.

To finish setting the scene, she got a glass from the kitchen, retrieved her beer from the table by the photographs and poured the last of it into the glass. Gen drank it off, then let the glass shatter on the floor. Picking up one of the shards, she did the necessary damage. Jace's left arm hung down from the bed, draining what blood she had left him in an artistic pool over the fragments.

A quick glance to assure herself that nothing critical had been forgotten, a final regretful kiss on Jace's cooling lips, and she was out the door, leaving behind a room rich with the scents of organic dissolution and reclamation, a room where autumnal death had gorged on new life and a lawless angel had taken his final fall from grace.

Gen took the Sportster and raced the sunrise west to Blaise Heights. Not that there was any danger. The myths derived from the facts about her kind had become corrupted, especially over the last two centuries. Just as her need for blood enhanced her sexual drive rather than replaced it, her need for night did not replace her ability to exist during the day. Sunlight couldn't kill her; it simply kept her from using all her powers, rendering her almost as vulnerable as those who hadn't changed.

No, the need for haste was simply a matter of keeping her unchanged and unsuspecting family from finding out she'd been gone all night.

One more stop before she could go home.

A dark silhouette against the predawn sky, Nick was waiting by the ruined fountain on the deserted Townsend estate. His mortal appearance that of a devastatingly handsome—and obviously wealthy—man in his late thirties, Nick was a business associate of her father's whom Gen had met during an otherwise innocuous supper party. Unsettled by her attraction to him, she had decided to stay out of temptation's way and avoid him completely, an exercise in futility when dealing with a determined Nick.

Nick . . . she wondered what name he had truly borne in that far distant time when he had first walked the earth. The original Greek form of the modern Nicholas perhaps? His dark beauty certainly had the classical Mediterranean stamp. Oh, she was curious about her paramour, but Gen knew better than to make her curiosity known.

"You decided to do it," he said approvingly, in that rasping, velvet voice that alone could seduce a blind woman, as his appearance alone seduced the sighted. He took her in his arms. No illusion, now, her submission. The arms holding her so tenderly could, at his will, become a crushing vise that would turn bones—even such bones as hers—to powder. Gen was no match for that strength.

Yet.

"And you? Did you set up the Slasher?" she asked.

Sardonic laughter. "The police will be bringing their killer to justice in the next few days. Of course they'll be too busy with that case, and the next victim, to pay much attention to a few easily explained accidental deaths."

He kissed her, and she tasted the blood of his kill on his lips—something young and sweet and wicked. Gen wondered if he could taste Jace's death on her, the smoke and spice of it, the struggle and surrender. Nick smiled down at her, staring into her eyes.

"I love your eyes," he told her, gazing deep into their indigo depths.

Unexpurgated Notes from a Homicide Case File

Judith M. Redding

Philadelphia Police Department Computer System
Log-on ID: Dash 5477   Password: XXXXXXXX

Case # 42681A	Eugene Brown, age 14, African-American
42681B	Derrick Brown, age 12, African-American
42681C	Malik Calliman, age 13, African-American
42681D	Anthony Toussaint, age 13, African-American

Officer: J. Teresa Dash, 6th Detectives   Badge No.: 5477
Reassigned from: Det. Thomas Powell, 39th district

Date: February 3

THE FOUR VICTIMS WERE FOUND IN the Delaware River near Pier No. 46 at 8:00 a.m., Wednesday, November 26. Per coroner's report, all four drowned. No drugs or alcohol were found in toxicology testing, although coroner's report notes that each victim had puncture marks on their forearms consistent with those left by a large-gauge syringe, and that each victim was missing approximately two liters of blood. Eugene Brown and Malik Calliman were found naked in the water; Anthony Toussaint and Eugene's brother, Derrick, wore only boxer shorts. The remaining clothing of all four youths was found on the pier itself, in neatly folded piles.

Coroner ruled the deaths accidental, noting that death was caused by drowning and hypothermia. The incident occurred two days before Thanksgiving. The case was reassigned from Det. Thomas Powell at the urging of the victims' parents and clergy, who have charged Powell (who is white) with racial bias. The parents of the youths believe their children were murdered (they cite the missing blood and syringe marks) and say that Powell showed no interest in further investigating this aspect of the case.

The personal effects of the victims reveal little: All four had subway tokens, housekeys, small amounts of cash, combs. Toussaint had a pager, which, per Det. Powell's notes, had been purchased for him by his parents.

All four lived on the same block of American Street; all attended St. Jude's Middle School. The Brown brothers were the eldest of four children in a two-parent, working-class household. Malik Calliman was the youngest child in a single-mother, working-class family. Anthony Toussaint was an only child in a two-parent household; both parents work; Toussaint's maternal grandmother lives with them.

The temperature on the night the youths drowned was forty-seven degrees Farenheit; the water temperature of the Delaware River was forty degrees Farenheit. All four died between 10:00 p.m. and 5:00 a.m. Coroner's report states that the combination of blood loss, water temperature and time in the water make it impossible to determine the exact time of death.

Question: Why were they at the pier so late?

Question: Why go swimming in the dark, in the cold?

Question: Why fold their clothes?

Question: Were they threatened in some way, and sought escape via the river?

Date: February 4
Re-interviewed parents of the deceased youths. No new information.

Toussaint's father, Leon, clarified that he bought Anthony a pager so that his disabled grandmother could contact him after school if she needed help or wanted him to run errands. On the night of their deaths, Eugene and Derrick Brown stopped by the Calliman and Toussaint houses, respectively, around 6:30 p.m. to pick up Malik and Anthony; all four planned to go to Lee's Variety Store on Second Street, one block away, and then to Videodrome, a video arcade two blocks from Lee's on Fourth Street. There was no school the next day. The Brown brothers had a 9:30 p.m. curfew; Calliman and Toussaint were due home by 9:00 p.m. Robert Brown called the police when the youths had not returned by 12:30 a.m.

Mr. Huang Lee, age seventy-two, verified that the youths visited his store on November 25 at approximately 7:00 p.m., purchasing sodas, candy and gum. Lee stated that the youths were regular customers and were courteous, easy-going boys. The back room of Lee's store is a Chinese herb store; Lee said he often hired Eugene Brown to help clean out his greenhouse and repot herbs.

Mr. Loftus Rooker, manager/bouncer of Videodrome, verified that the youths had entered the video arcade around 8:00 p.m. on the evening of their deaths. He stated that he and his assistant took them upstairs around 9:00 p.m. to speak with the arcade's owners, Johnnie and Eddie Byrd, after Rooker caught Eugene Brown and Malik Calliman trying to break open the cash door of one of the video games with a screwdriver.

Interviewed the Byrd brothers in their apartment over Videodrome. Both appear to be in their mid-twenties, with smooth, light brown skin, hair cropped to their skulls, prominent foreheads. Eddie is taller, more solidly built, wears a mustache and beard. Johnnie is thin, clean-shaven, baby-faced. Both wore silk shirts and linen trousers. Johnnie does all the talking.

"We yelled at them, took their names and addresses and sent them home," says Johnnie. "We would have contacted their parents the next day, except that they turned up dead and we didn't see much point." The youths had tried breaking into the games before, and the Byrds said they had "had enough."

The second-floor apartment is painted off-white and the main room has a green glass ceiling—the Byrd brothers grow geraniums, lots of geraniums; the apartment is suffused with their organic, green scent. According to Johnnie, they grow them for their mother, who runs a small *bodega* on Ellsworth Street. I asked if they grew the geraniums from seeds, and Eddie burst out laughing and said that geraniums can only be grown from cuttings. CNN runs constantly on the wide-screen TV. They say the police never contacted them, even though Johnnie had left a message for Powell stating they had seen the boys on the night of their deaths.

Date: February 5
Information provided by Officer Andrea Rose of Narcotics: The Byrd brothers are suspected crack dealers for their neighborhood and are the subject of an ongoing investigation. No charges have been filed. Rose suspects the Byrds of using the video arcade as a recruitment zone for teenage runners. According to Rose, the brothers are older than they look: Eddie Byrd is forty-one; Johnnie is thirty-nine.

A check of the Byrds' phone records for October and November shows no calls to Anthony Toussaint's pager number, nor any calls to 911 or the 39th.

Phone conversation with Dr. Deepak Mehta of the Coroner's Office: Although each youth was missing two liters of blood, that in itself would not have killed them, although it certainly helped to speed the effects of hypothermia. Mehta believes that all four lost consciousness due to hypothermia before drowning. He states that the syringe marks are not consistent with syringes used in intravenous drug injection, but resemble the puncture marks left by the large-bore syringes used when donating blood. Normal average blood donation per individual: one pint. Mehta noted that no clinics have *bought* blood or blood products since 1986, when the FDA started to regulate blood donations because of AIDS.

∿

Date: February 6

Re-interviewed Mr. Huang Lee. He does not believe that the youths would be involved in theft from the video arcade. He says that Eugene Brown was a "good boy" and noted that Anthony Toussaint was kept on a short leash by his grandmother. Malik Calliman was boisterous but polite, and Derrick Brown was quiet, followed his older brother's lead.

Lee does not like either of the Byrd brothers. He says that until recently, they purchased dried geranium blossoms from him. I told him that their apartment was like a hothouse and that they were growing geraniums exclusively. Lee seemed disturbed by this information and said that geranium blossoms are blood purifiers and are eaten like salad greens by those with blood ailments.

Date: February 12

Phone conversation with Officer Andrea Rose of Narcotics: Last night Andrea brought in a homeless fourteen-year-old boy under "Code Zero" (zero degrees Farenheit) policy. She picked him up a block from Videodrome. He had one hundred dollars in his pocket, which he says he received from Johnnie Byrd, who he said was a vampire. The teenager claims he allowed Johnnie Byrd to drink his blood in exchange for the money. The teenager had a syringe mark on his right forearm. The teenager refused to give either his name or a urine sample for drug screening.

Date: February 17

Four dead bodies found in a Northern Liberties crackhouse. The floors of the house were strewn with empty crack vials, used syringes, junk food wrappers. Three bodies were found in one bedroom, all apparently dead from drug overdose: one Caucasian male, approximately twenty-five; one African-American male, approximately twenty; one African-American female, approximately thirty. All three bodies had numerous syringe marks. The fourth body was found in another bedroom, African-American male, age undetermined, head almost completely severed except for a flap of skin. Above the mattress he was found on was the word *bloodsucker,* written in the victim's blood.

Date: February 18
ID on the decapitated body from the Northern Liberties crackhouse: Nathan Byrd, twenty-eight, cousin to Eddie and Johnnie.

Conversation with Dr. Mai Ling, of Chinatown Traditional Pharmaceuticals: Geranium blossoms were used in ancient China as a blood purifier and were referred to as "the vampire drug." She does not carry it and says it is no longer used in Chinese medicine, because more than minute quantities can cause seizure and large quantities can be fatal. According to Ling, some *botanicas* and bodegas still sell geranium blossoms, and the flowers are often used in Santaria rituals.

Date: February 19
Re-interviewed Byrd brothers. Both denied any drug connections to their cousin Nathan (Eddie described him as "that jerk") or with the homeless youth. Johnnie says he may have "given the kid a C-bill so that he could get a hotel room and something to eat, get out of the cold." Unlikely.

Date: March 5
Phone conversation with Andrea Rose of Narcotics: Homeless teenager who accused Johnnie Byrd of vampirism was found by Rose frozen to death next to a dumpster on Shunk Street near Third. His body was missing three liters (out of a total of six liters) of blood. A large-bore syringe puncture was found inside his right elbow. Coroner states that loss of blood would have hastened death by hypothermia.

Went to re-interview Byrd brothers. Loftus Rooker stated that they were vacationing in Bermuda.

The Brown, Calliman and Toussaint cases remain open. The parents are now pushing for the cases to be reassigned again.

Refugio

Terri de la Peña

L A NOCHE WOKE ME. HER MOIST nose nudged through the red-and-black Oaxacan blanket to my buried *cuerpo. Yo estaba dormida como una muerta.* I would have slept much longer if the dog had not begun to whine. But la Noche, my living, breathing alarm clock, knew I ought to be up and about.

"*Ay, por que no me dejas en paz?*" Slowly, I emerged from my woolen cocoon and met the ebony dog's amber eyes. "Why won't you ever let me sleep a few minutes more, eh?"

La Noche whined again. Then, keeping her steady gaze on mine, she backed away from me in the heavily draped bedroom and began to bark. Her noisy greeting caused my drowsy head to clear. I became conscious of other ever-present sounds. Sensing my gradual comprehension, the dog swung her *cabeza de loba* toward the covered windows, casting frequent glances in my direction.

No wonder la Noche was agitated. I heard helicopters—several—whirling through the twilit *barrio.* More trouble—a gang fight, a shooting, maybe a driveby.

"*Noche, no te apuras.*" I rose with reluctance and avoided the windows. "I know it's almost time for me to go."

After sundown, the crosstown bus, which circles the midcity to deposit elderly passengers at either the secular or the Catholic hospital and transports students to the community college, had stopped its run. On my way to work, I hurried along Seventh Street to Michigan Avenue, past the overgrown ivy fence of Woodlawn Cemetery, trying to keep out of sight of the hovering copters with their roving spotlights. Coastal fog swirled like evanescent phantoms, making visibility treacherous. Small and round, I did not want to be mistaken for a roaming *muchacho*. How would a helicopter pilot recognize my scurrying figure as a gray-haired *mujer,* not a baggy-pants, shorn-headed gangbanger? Wrapped in my full-length hooded Guatemalan poncho to guard against the evening chill, I soon aimed myself down Fourteenth Street and kept alert, wary of the increased police presence at the barrio's edges.

At the foot of the Fourteenth Street hill, the fog hung in moist patches. I paused for the traffic light near the bus stop. Barely turning, I noticed an African-American cop leave a knot of officers talking on the corner. I recognized her from times I had worked the ER. She was a strong, no-nonsense type, much taller than me.

"On your way to the hospital?" she called.

I nodded. "Another late shift."

"About two hours ago, there was a shooting on Michigan. You'll probably see the kid when you get to work."

I sighed at her remark.

She did not seemed fazed. "Don't understand why the crosstown bus doesn't run at night. Awful inconvenient for you, huh? Careful now, hear?" She moved on when the traffic light flashed green.

Pulling the poncho's hood closer around me, I crossed Olympic and went briskly past the half-completed mural on the Memorial Park gymnasium. Some taggers had recently flung their spiderlike *placas* on the west side of the building. I shook my head at the gang-inspired markings and kept right on going.

~

If you could ignore the *cholo* tattoos on his neck, arms and hands, the boy looked like *un angelito moreno* lying there so still in the hospital bed. Like so many Chicanos, he had beautifully long eyelashes, tapering at the ends like quivering butterflies. But *este vato* was no angel, not any more. He was a kid—once full of promise—who had somehow gone wrong. He had wound up a dropout, *un pendejo de primero*.

No one had closed the window blinds. The full moon shone through, illuminating the boy's face, adding to the pale glow from the monitoring equipment surrounding his bed. He was from the neighborhood, the next *calle* over: Mario Rosales, aka Chivo because of the sparse black hairs sprouting from his chin, like a poor imitation of a billy goat. He had been a sweet little boy, always laughing. After his father had deserted the family, he had changed.

His rosary-praying mother and sisters were camped in the waiting room down the hall. Some of his homeboys were there, too, all those rough-looking *chavalos* who used to play baseball on Eighteenth Street only a while ago. Nowadays they played with bullets and guns.

The corridor outside his room was quiet. Muffled voices drifted in down the hall. I checked Mario's vital signs and his IV. His breathing was measured, his eyelids slightly open. Yet, in his comatose state, he could not see me. He was unaware when I glided soundlessly to shut the door and returned to his bedside. He did not even notice when I leaned over him with the dagger's cold blade to make my mark, my own *placa*, on his young, immobile body.

Through the misty dawn I witnessed her approach, her topaz eyes piercing the foggy air. Gaining momentum, her ebony body sleek and supple, she hurled herself over the cemetery fence to welcome me. In her exuberance, her throaty voice punctuated the silent street. She nearly toppled me.

"*Ay, Noche.*" I noticed fresh mud on her tufted paws. Already she had smudged my white uniform slacks. I pushed her away in mock irritation. "Where have you been all night, eh?"

Barking with joy, she bolted around me, pulling at the fringes of my poncho, then breaking away again.

"Hungry? *Pues,* you'll have to wait till we get home."

Damp from my shower, I emerged from the bathroom. A single candle flickered by the bed and the pungent scent of burning sage filled my lungs. La Noche had kicked off the Oaxacan blanket and stretched herself out on the bed. She had shed her luxurious ebony coat—shape-shifter that she was—and reclined on her side. Her eyes were fiery, tantalizing, contrasting with her rich mahogany skin. As she watched me come closer, she licked her lips, her pink tongue teasing.

"Refugio," she murmured in her throaty voice, "did you bring it?"

I said nothing. The Guatemalan poncho was draped over the foot of the bed. I reached into its pocket.

"*Si, jefita.*" I held up the vial filled with the *sangre de* Mario Rosales. "*Aqui lo tengo.*"

Her amber eyes were inches from my dark ones. "I remember Mario Rosales," la Noche whispered with much satisfaction. Her lips were stained with his blood. "He used to throw rocks over the fence at me."

"When he comes back to the barrio, he'll be different." I stroked her thick black hair away from her forehead. "You went roaming tonight?"

"*Si.*" She wore a lupine grin. "I followed that *hombre* again, even chased him through the cemetery." She laughed, her sharp teeth gleaming in the candlelight.

I lay back and let the heat of her naked body warm me. "The man you saw before? The one who watches the taggers?"

She nodded, her little finger encircling my nipple. "*Lo mismo.* I think he's stalking them. He has a gun, Refugio."

I grimaced, not at her actions, at her words. "You saw it?"

"He keeps one hand in his jacket pocket. Some chavalos were tagging a fence near the cemetery, and this guy started going toward them, walking fast. I zoomed after him, darting between his legs—like I do with you—almost knocked him over. I snapped at his heels. The kids were pointing at him, cracking up 'cause he almost fell." Her eyes reflected her merriment. "He tried to kick me, but I was too fast. Then he took off running toward the cemetery. I chased him all the way to the other gate."

I lifted her chin and held it. "Ay, be more careful. He could've started firing at you or the kids. Someone could've been hurt."

She laughed again. "Refugio, he ain't got no silver bullets." Smiling, I drew nearer, ending her mirth when I covered her red mouth with mine.

La señora Rosales, a thin woman who appeared much older than her actual age of thirty-eight, waited outside her son's hospital room. Midway through my shift, I had come by to see how the boy fared.

"*El doctor* is examining him, doña Refugio," she said. Her narrow face was lined with concern. "Mario is awake."

"*Que bueno.*" I took one of her trembling hands in mine. "That's a good sign, Jovita."

"*Es un milagro.* I've prayed a hundred rosaries to save his life." She wiped her eyes with her other hand. "All I want is to take my boy home."

"*Puede ser que—*"

Through the partially open door, I heard Dr. Sorensen call. "Nurse Torres, would you come in, please?"

"*Con permiso,*" I whispered to Jovita Rosales. Brushing past her, I entered the boy's room.

Mario looked as pale as a flour tortilla. He offered a weak, though sheepish, smile on seeing me. "Hey, you're the old lady with that big black dog."

"That's right." I joined the doctor beside the bed. "Welcome back to the land of the living, Mario."

Dr. Sorensen gazed at me over his half-glasses. "You know each other?"

"Neighbors."

"Why you live in the middle of that war zone, I'll never understand," the doctor muttered.

"I belong there," I said without lowering my eyes.

He chose to ignore my comment. Instead Dr. Sorensen asked Mario to tilt his head to one side. "Since you're such good buddies, I want you to take a look at this, Nurse. Didn't this boy have several tattoos right here, and on his arms, and—"

"Yeah, and on my hands," Mario cut in. He held up his palms in dismay. "Aw, shit. What happened to all my—"

I lay a calming hand on the boy's scrawny shoulder. He grew quiet at once.

Dr. Sorensen was baffled. "I could've sworn—"

I took on my most professional tone. "I haven't been assigned to this patient, Doctor."

"He was covered with all manner of—and all I see now is a small cut on his neck. How most unusual," the doctor murmured.

My beeper emitted a shrill signal. "I have to get back to my station, Dr. Sorensen."

"All right then. I've simply never seen anything like—"

Mario leaned back, seeming fatigued. "Say 'hi' to your dog for me."

I paused in the doorway. "Come visit her, Mario. She'd love to play with you."

Sorting through the patients' hospital charts, I tried to ignore the incessant complaining voices emanating from the small radio next to Belen Gomez at the nurses' station. Talk radio always set me on edge, and I was already irked that Dr. Sorensen had foiled my plan to see Mario Rosales in private.

"Why do you listen to that pendejo talk show, eh? All those hateful people."

Belen, a light-skinned Mexican-American, was a recent nursing school graduate. She looked up from labeling blood samples. "I like to know what's going on, Refugio."

"Then listen to something else," I insisted. "All you hear on this damn show are anti-Mexican call-ins. All about taggers and gangs and 'illegal' immigrants."

"People who call in are anti-*immigrant*, not anti-Mexican," Belen corrected me with more than a trace of impatience.

"There's a difference?" I set the pile of metal charts in their slots beside her. "Listen, Belen, *tu sabes que* I was born in Mexico. *No me gusta oir esa cochinada.* I don't like hearing people say we're all a bunch of criminals."

"So turn the station, then. I'm not stopping you." Belen turned away. "You take things too personal, Refugio."

"You think keeping quiet will keep you safe? I never notice you disagreeing with anything Dr. Sorensen says about us." I paused by the counter. She pretended to be busy to avoid looking at me. "*Claro que soy* opinionated. I'm *vieja* and seen a lot, Belen. Trying to be a 'good Mexican' like you, trying to blend in, walking around with blinders on, won't guarantee you a damn thing."

Trudging home in the darkness before dawn, I felt weary, not from my shift, but from continuing to exist in a climate of hate and injustice. After almost six hundred years in this hemisphere, I found it ever more difficult to remain silent when confronted either by bigotry or denial of its prevalence. In my time, I had dealt with bigots of all types: *conquistadores*, revolutionaries, Texas Rangers, the U.S. Border Patrol, the LAPD, to name a few. Didn't Belen Gomez realize that brown people—Aleuts, Native Americans, Mexicans, Latin Americans, South Americans—were indigenous to this continent? No matter what anyone called us, we were *not* immigrants; we were here already. We met the boat, so to speak. Yes, I *did* take these things personally. La Noche would have left well enough alone; she had that luxury, choosing to live most of the time as a rambunctious dog. Maybe she had the right idea.

Belen and others like her in the barrio considered me an eccentric old woman, often too feisty for my own good. I had to remind myself that in the midst of a traditional Mexican-American community, my independent nature could arouse distrust, even suspicion. Far too many times in the past, I had had to move on, to leave a place where I had settled, because I no longer could fit in.

The biting winter wind sliced through my poncho. It howled and hissed through the towering eucalyptus ahead. I bent my head and held the edges of my hood to keep it from slipping to my shoulders. Approaching Michigan Avenue, I instantly felt a coldness in the air that had nothing to do with the weather. The black hairs on my arms rose in alarm. I stepped forward cautiously, sensing—smelling—an unwelcome presence.

Garbed in an olive windbreaker and faded blue jeans, he emerged from behind the auto repair shop. A stocky white man, he seemed unaware that I had stopped a few feet away. He lit a cigarette and gazed in the direction of the cemetery fence.

"Looking for something, señor?"

The cigarette never made it to his mouth. He dropped it.

"Damn, lady. What the hell you doing here in the middle of the night?" His right hand darted into his pocket.

"I could ask *you* the same question." I kept my voice steady. I knew la Noche was nearby. "You don't live in the barrio."

His eyes were furtive. "That where I wound up?"

I nodded, memorizing his thick neck, his chunky face.

With some defiance, he decided an old woman offered little threat to his well-being. "Ain't none of your business, mamacita." The hand in his pocket moved slightly.

I stiffened at his condescending tone. A low growl erupted from the oleander bushes behind me. La Noche darted out, snarling and barking. She reached my side, pausing to lick my hand before advancing toward him, her dangerous teeth bared. I followed her, my hand on her quivering back.

The man edged away. "You better put a leash on that bitch." He kept going backward across Fourteenth Street, his voice rising. "I'm goin' to clean up these streets, get rid of all the fuckin' Mexican trash around here. Your bitch'll wind up dead, too."

I cupped my hands to my mouth in order to be heard over the banshee howls of the wind. "Not in *your* lifetime, señor."

"You should've let me take him, Refugio. You saw his neck—so juicy *y sabroso. Ay, mujer,* it was making me salivate," la Noche grumbled when she snuggled into bed that night.

"When will you learn, *muchacha?*" I blew out the candle and lay next to her. "He isn't *ours* to take."

"You're the only affirmative action vampire I know, *esa*." Noche leaned over to lick my shoulder. "You'd rather have one of your protégés take him. Mario, right?"

"Unless time runs out." I sighed. "If it does, Noche, *ese hombre* is yours."

A few evenings later, I had my pruning shears in hand when the boy looked over the picket fence. "Hey, old lady, need some help?"

"*Como te va*, Mario?" I smiled as he undid the latch and came into the yard of the small rental house on Seventeenth Street.

"Still feeling kind of puny, but it's sure good to be out." He had stopped shaving his head, and the silly goatee was gone; his black hair grew in thick and black like la Noche's. "I dreamed about you, doña Refugio."

"*De veras?*" I snipped a rose off the bush for him.

He gazed at its blood-red center, inhaled its fragrance, pressed its velvety petals to his cheek. Then, trancelike, he ran his brown fingers along its sturdy stem. When he came to a thorn, he pressed one finger against it. Rich *sangre* surged forth. Mario stared at his bloody finger for a long moment. Raising his eyes to mine, he seemed motivated by a primeval instinct. I did not hesitate to partake.

"Now it's startin' to make sense why I don't want to hang around with the homeys," Mario said quietly.

With a quesadilla moon for illumination, he sat beside me in the backyard for hours that night. In plastic lawn chairs beneath the avocado tree, we were alone, becoming acquainted, as if I were his *abuelita* and he, my long-lost grandson. He had even phoned his mother to tell her his whereabouts; Jovita Rosales must have been astonished to learn her son was with me, rather than with the *vatos*. Bored with initiation rituals, la Noche had wandered to the cemetery to chase black cats and foil Tecolote, the resident owl, from catching squirrels. I had cautioned her about continuing to follow the prowling stranger.

"*Nuestra gente* have a very long history, *mijo*." I watched the smoke of the sage incense curl skyward. "You were chosen to join them, Mario. Remember that. *Si,* I know sometimes *esta vida* can seem stressful, even depressing. *Pero,* if you choose, you can live forever. You can be like la Noche and change shapes at will, you can stay young as long as you want. Me, I've decided almost six hundred years *es bastante.* When I hit the 600 mark en el año *dis mil,* I'm calling it quits. That's why I look the way I do; I really am aging."

"So is all that Hollywood stuff true? You can't look in mirrors, the sun blinds you, all that shit?"

"Mario, when has Hollywood ever been right about *anything*? Ay, don't believe those pendejo movies." I sipped my hot chocolate. "We do have to be careful about *some* things. Otherwise we're just like everyone else, except we live longer and need a fix once in a while."

He glanced at the nick on his finger and nodded.

"Like I was saying, mijo, I'm choosing muchachas y muchachos to carry on after me. There have been many before you—la Noche has been with me the longest. Mario, we have to make plans. Our people—*los Mexicanos, los Chicanos*—are in trouble these days. *Tu sabes*—all this *mugre* with gangs and drugs, *pinche* anti-immigrant laws, *todo eso.* That's why strong people are needed *en nuestra lucha.* Why should kids be lured into gangs when they can live forever instead? We need to motivate our young, Mario. *You* were in a gang. With your experience, you can help turn things around. You can offer new ideas."

Already his eyes had that prescient gleam; his mind leaped to formulate a goal: "Let's start a Neighborhood Watch, doña Refugio. That way, we can keep track of who's coming into the barrio. The homeboys get blamed for everything. Outsiders do lots of shootings and drivebys. Can we have a meeting at your house?"

"*Como no, mijo.*"

"This kid ain't goin' to boss me around, okay? He ain't *el jefe* here, Refugio. Don't know why you chose a *boy* this time." La Noche tore at a raw steak. She dipped one finger into its bloody juice and offered me a lick.

"The other muchachos will listen to Mario. They wouldn't pay attention to anything a girl—or an old lady—would say." I cut into my own barely cooked beef and wrapped a *tortilla de maíz* around a few chunks. "Remember when we lived on the Eastside and you shifted into a very sexy mujer?"

"I *am* a very sexy mujer."

"You *know* what I mean. Ay, Noche, it was counterproductive! You nearly got us arrested. *La gente en el barrio* thought I was a madam and you were one of my girls. *Es mejor que* you decided to be a real bitch during daylight hours."

"You're *so* funny, Refugio." La Noche's amber eyes glared, though her amusement shone through.

I blew her a kiss. "Besides, this way you don't have to spend money on clothes. And I like you so much better without them."

The neighbors, at first, seemed uneasy when they trickled through the gate and into my tiny house. Though I had lived there for years, I had rarely had company. Whenever la Noche was on the prowl, she would shape-shift into a leather-clad dyke, bring mujeres home overnight and invite me to partake. Most of the time, however, I relied on the hospital to meet my nutritional needs. The night of the meeting, la Noche was on her best behavior, greeting everyone with a tongue-on-the-side canine grin, wagging her bushy tail while begging for tortilla chips. Maybe I was mellowing, but I had to admit I enjoyed having a houseful of gente.

"*De veras es un milagro*," Jovita Rosales said to anyone who would listen. She gazed at her son with pride.

A pretty teenager, Suzie Garcia, giggled beside Mario. She told him about the *quinceañera* planned for her fifteenth birthday.

"So what's this all about, doña Refugio?" her father, Anastasio Garcia, demanded once everyone had crowded into the small living room.

Garcia, who owned the auto repair shop, was a barrel-shaped hombre with an officious air. On noting the pre-Colombian pottery and artifacts and the many votive candles to Tonantzin on the narrow mantle, Garcia seemed skeptical of my intentions. No doubt, he thought I was a superstitious old woman. He had no idea, I knew, that my pottery and artifacts were *authentic*, not cheap imitations.

"This meeting was Mario's idea," I said in my sweetest *viejita* voice. "Let him talk."

All eyes focused on the young man. Suzie Garcia already seemed smitten with Mario's sudden authority.

"I've told the cops this, and I want you to know it, too." Mario licked his lips and continued. "When I got hit, I was tagging the wall behind Mr. Garcia's shop. Sorry about that; it won't happen again. Anyways, the shooter was white. He came out of nowhere, and I think he's coming after all of us."

La Noche stretched out at my feet. She yawned, making a squeaking sound. No one laughed.

No one took Mario seriously either, at least not at first. He was known as a tagger, a vandal, reformed or not. Among the older residents, he needed to develop some credibility. Yet gunfire erupted the following night near one of the fast-food joints on Pico Boulevard. There were no casualties, though one of the vendors saw a white man sprint across Pico toward the community college. He must have blended in with evening students because the police found no trace of him.

About a week later, after Mario had helped me prune the back hedges, he and I took la Noche for an evening stroll. She was eager to do some serious tracking. The weather remained chilly, and since I had the night off work, I had suggested we walk together through the barrio to be sure the area was secure.

Several neighbors watering their lawns nodded as we passed by. Some raised their eyebrows at seeing Mario beside me. "*Tiene cuidado,* doña Refugio. You shouldn't be out after dark."

"The dog needs her exercise." I smiled as la Noche frolicked ahead. "We'll be all right."

Down by Seventeenth and Delaware, Mario spotted the homeboys from his tagging crew. He shouted to them. When they saw la Noche and me with him, they laughed and kept going.

Watching them, Mario frowned. "I think they're on their way to tag another wall of the gym, Doña Refugio."

"Let's keep our distance. Follow la Noche's lead."

Already the ebony dog trotted a short way behind the boys, far beyond us, her amber eyes fixed ahead. At Olympic Boulevard, she turned once in our direction, darted across the street and paused on the grassy median to sniff the air. Then she loped to the other side of the street, her body stretched into a stalking mode.

Mario and I hurried to catch up with her. We crossed Olympic and headed west. We had gone less than two blocks when we heard the shots. The tagging crew yelled, cursed, and some ran for their lives.

"Hey, Mario. That white dude's goin' crazy," one gasped when he ran past us.

"La Noche will hold him for you," I murmured, while struggling to keep up. "For him it will end tonight. For you, mijo, it will begin."

She had him against the gymnasium wall, below an unfinished portion of the community mural. Vicious teeth bared, la Noche snarled as she held the terrified man at bay. Three of the homeboys seemed transfixed at the sight. A gun and two cans of spray paint lay on the sidewalk. Mario kicked them into the street.

"Don't touch any of that stuff. You hear me? Get your acts together, *carnales*. I'll catch you later. Now, split," he demanded.

"Hey, man. He's yours, after all," one of the kids muttered. He signaled to his homeboys. They disappeared into the shadows behind the gymnasium.

Mario glanced at me.

I nodded. "Noche, that's enough."

She continued to snarl, her legs stiff, her hackles raised.

"That's right, mamacita. Call off your bitch." Though his voice trembled, the stocky man tried to maintain some bravado. "Never figured *you'd* get me out of a jam."

"You figured wrong, señor." I lay my hand on la Noche's back. "Your time is up."

His horrified eyes bulged when Mario began his attack. The stranger's scream split the night. Only la Noche's barking obscured it.

On a chainlink fence near an Amtrak station in California's Central Valley, I balanced myself, raven wings fluttering while la Noche alighted gracefully beside me. Her obsidian eyes flickered with amusement at my awkwardness. She uttered a throaty cackle and gave me a teasing peck with her bill. Never would she let me forget that shapeshifting came so much easier to her.

La Noche spread one ebony wing and began to groom herself. From my perch, I noticed a yellowing newspaper caught against the bottom of the fence. Its fading headline drew my attention. I swooped down to get a better look. Ever curious, la Noche followed me.

Vigilante Mystery Unfolds

The body of Stan Maxwell, a gun enthusiast and collector, was found on a grassy median strip of Olympic Boulevard in Santa Monica around midnight on March 26. He had been nearly decapitated. Police found evidence of animal fur and wolflike teeth marks on Maxwell's body. Authorities are investigating whether Maxwell was the so-called vigilante shooter who had targeted local Latino gangs. Police are searching for Refugio Torres, 59, a resident of the predominantly Mexican-American neighborhood where Maxwell's body was found. Torres is the owner of a black wolflike dog. Neither she nor her dog has been seen since the night of Maxwell's death.

La Noche poked the newspaper with the edge of her sharp bill. We gazed with satisfaction at each other. No one would find us, and Mario would keep the barrio safe.

I shook my shaggy throat feathers and gave a jubilant croak. La Noche's silken wings shone iridescently. Together, we took flight, soaring over the vast farmlands, heading in the direction of Delano.

Women's Music

Ruthann Robson

I POSE IN THE DARKNESS OF THE PRE-
performance stage and see her face
floating in the audience. Tonight, the
gig is one of several in San Francisco. I
remind myself that as soon as the pink
spotlight refracts off the sterling silver frets of my electric guitar and my voice reverberates through the
Echoplex stacked on the amps, I will forget her; forget
that she ever lived; forget that she ever died.

Sometimes I figure she is merely my personal but-
terfly, an embodiment of the stage fright every per-
former must conquer again and again. Other times, I
suppose that it is only natural that I think of Sammy
whenever and wherever I take the stage.

Not that Sammy was the one who taught me to
sing. No one did that. If that had been necessary, I still
would not be able to carry a tune. I was not a child born
into a life that could include something like voice lessons. I was a girl who sang every Sunday morning (and
Sunday night and Wednesday night) during the Salvation Army services. My mother often appeared in
the congregation to cry, especially if my repertoire

included "In the Garden" and she had consumed her usual beers and shots. Sometimes other women, and even a few men, cried as I sang. I stretched my soprano down into a raspy bass as I varied my register to fill the church, a small city cellar beneath a pawnshop. I watched the tears slide down the parishioners' faces, like the notes that slipped across the sheet music. I could decipher neither the tears nor the notes, but I was much more intrigued by the notes. I inched closer to Sergeant Haskins, the piano player, because she could translate those circles and lines and stylized flags into messages about where to press her fingers on the keys, where to press her foot on the pedals. There were times, however, that I found the mystery of her breasts bouncing under the worn fabric of her navy blue uniform equally enticing.

Often after Sergeant Haskins was finished pressing ivory keys and metal pedals, she would press my head against her lush breasts. "You sing like the silvery gates of Heaven," she would sigh. My voice box would feel like it had melted. Silver, silver, my own voice would whisper in my head. Although I had heard that the heavenly metal was gold, against her breasts I believed silver was the only possible salvation.

Still, I could not convince Sergeant Haskins to reveal the possibility of ivory heavenly gates and teach me to play the piano. She would laugh: "Your voice is a beautiful instrument of God; you should not suffer an instrument made by man." She did not press my head against her breasts when she said this. And she was not pressing my head to her breasts when she told another Salvation Army sergeant that she'd be goddamned if she'd teach that little white nigger to play the piano or else I'd be playing in a cathouse before I was seventeen. I heard her anyway. I leaned against the pawnshop gates a long time that night, just thinking about what she'd said.

If Sergeant Haskins would not teach me voiceless music, there were other women who would. The trick was to find someone who would do it for free. Just as there was no money for voice lessons, there was no money for piano lessons, or for a piano. My mother did not need to explain this to me, or to justify it with an appeal to God. She only needed to hum Patti Page ("Allegheny Moon"), Dinah Washington ("What a Difference a Day Makes") and Connie Francis ("Who's Sorry Now?").

She punctuated her impersonations with swigs from her beer bottle.

I finally settled on Gloria, an older girl from the more prestigious edge of the neighborhood. She was from Argentina, and her father was the band director at the parochial school for boys. Gloria played the acoustic guitar off the third-floor porch of a tenement, but we worked at imagining her as a lady with a lace mantilla strumming on an elegant European balcony. Gloria worshipped Joan Baez, who—as Gloria explained to me almost every time she mentioned the rapidly-becoming-famous singer/guitarist—was half-Mexican. When she was not talking about "Joan," Gloria showed me how to play chords, how to read sheet music and how to flat-pick a recognizable melody. When Gloria's parents gave her a heavy steel-string acoustic guitar made in Spain ("a lot like Joan's") and a box of tortoise-shell plectrums, Gloria gave me her old nylon-string guitar. She made me cut my nails before she let me try her new steel string, but she still let me try it. She was as patient as a Spanish saint while she positioned my fingers with precision, day after day.

Night after night, I slept at Gloria's house and she positioned her same nail-bitten hands around my fingers, although with less confidence. The wonderful thing about being a girl in America is the patina of innocence. After delicious rice and bean dinners, we slept together with her parents' blessing and my mother's gratitude. Gloria's parents were happy that she had any friend at all, for Gloria was shy and cross-eyed with perpetually greasy bangs and interested only in her guitar. My mother was glad I was not home to interfere with her stupor and not out on the streets inducing my own. So, Gloria and I, sinister schoolgirls, snuggled until sleep overcame us. She kissed me, and I let her, and I kissed her back. She slid her tongue in my mouth, and I let her, and I slid mine behind her teeth. Her fingers explored the wet accordion I hid in my underpants, and I let her, and I explored her. She pressed her tongue past my wet folds and hummed something deep that sounded like "Joanie," and I let her. I did not echo these acts. I was afraid it might ruin my voice.

I never sang for Gloria. I worried that she might cut off my access to an instrument, like Sergeant Haskins did. Or that she might imagine us as a duo: Joan Baez as two people. Gloria with her accomplished guitar, me with my heartbreaking vocal chords. But I knew even then that I did not want to be half of Joan Baez, or even all of her. Years later, one reviewer would christen me with another Joan, calling me the lesbian Joan Jett. One women's publication would canonize me by calling me a black Janis Joplin, and a rival periodical would enshrine me as a white Tina Turner. Forget my complexion, or even my sexual preference, I am unlike Jett or Joplin or Turner. I never sing about men; I never sing about heartbreak.

Before I ever learned to appreciate Janis Joplin's husky voice overpowering her all-male backup band, Big Brother and the Holding Company, before I ever heard Joan Jett singing "I hate myself for loving you" while her all-male band, the Blackhearts, jammed behind her, before I ever applauded Tina Turner, neé Annie Mae Bullock, shafting the abusive Ike, I wanted woman's music that was strong and solid and singular. Even when I only knew Gloria and the glories of her steel-string guitar, only knew Sergeant Haskins and her ivory gates to heaven, only knew that my voice was silvery enough to make alcoholics weep, I knew I had to make women's music.

When my mother went to the tavern to practice her vocation, I stayed in the two-room apartment and practiced mine. I plugged in her portable record player, strummed my secondhand guitar and sang along with Brook Benton about the evils of the boll weevil. I sang "Edelweiss" from *The Sound of Music.* I sang "Maria" from *West Side Story,* sometimes substituting Gloria for Maria as if it would produce more passionate timbres. I listened intently to Herb Alpert's *Tijuana Brass,* attempting to distinguish the instrument lines and compose appropriate lyrics, but I often got sidetracked by the album cover with the white woman wrapped in a seductive layer of whipped cream.

At every Salvation Army service with a music program, I continued to sing a solo, whether or not my mother was there. The Army was trying to enlist me with litanies of how I could sing the faithful to gates that were now described as pearly. On the more earthly side, the Army guaranteed me an audience for my voice three times a week and lots of time to practice. Perhaps if they had had more brightly colored uniforms and promised me piano lessons, I would have joined.

Instead, I kept devouring any type of music I could find, looking for women's music. Under the influence of Joan Baez and Gloria, I was practicing the sustained pitch necessary for singing "Amazing Grace" and the bar chords for strumming "We Shall Overcome," when I met Sammy. Sammy sang at one of the taverns my mother frequented. "You have to hear my daughter sing," my mother told me she had told Sammy. "You have to hear this woman sing," my mother told me. My mother seemed to talk to Sammy—and certainly talked about Sammy—as if Sammy were an adult. In fact, Sammy said she was only three years older than me; I figured that lipstick and a sequined dress can make all the difference.

I resisted meeting Sammy, afraid she would hate my voice or my guitar or the kid that I was. It was my mother who brought Sammy to the Salvation Army service one Wednesday night. Sergeant Haskins banged devotedly on the piano I now recognized as out-of-tune. I spotted Sammy in the congregation as I stood to sing my solo of the protestantly difficult "A Mighty Fortress Is Our God." It is not much of a tearjerker as hymns go, but several faces were wet nonetheless. Sammy's face was dry. And pale. Very pale.

Sammy was not wearing a sequined dress, but a black sheath that was a little too tight and—surprisingly—a little too long. She reminded me of Morticia of Addams family TV show fame, except that her hair was as white as my bleached underwear. It was cut bluntly, so that on each side of her face it curved like crooked half-smiles into her mouth. When her bare lips parted at my mother's introduction, I could see that Sammy had what cross-eyed Gloria and I called vampire teeth: jutting bicuspids in need of braces.

I thought Sammy was absolutely beautiful.

One look at this woman—and she *was* a woman, even without lipstick or sequins—and I was ready to give up Gloria, eager to abandon Sergeant Haskins. I have always been capable of unfathomable shallowness.

Sammy lived in a room over a tavern. Sammy wanted to put together a rock band, get a recording contract. Sammy had an agent, an eye for costumes, an urge to tour. Sammy slept in a man's size 17 white button-down shirt. She liked to bite hard at that softest spot in my shoulder when we made love. Sammy had a habit. Sammy's voice was decomposing as quickly as day-old shit in the sun.

We became partners. We soon had a backup band with drums and amps and electric guitars. We sang. We danced. We cooled out with the band. The boys talked about riffs and bass lines and stacks. I listened. The boys and Sammy shared drugs during rehearsals. I declined. I wanted not blur, but distinctions; not distortion, but clarity.

And I wanted Sammy, more and more. I wore ripped clothes, not because they fit our band's image, but because I wanted to display my beautiful love bites. I felt weak the mornings after we made love, but I struggled to recover and to bring her coffee. I was jealous of the attention she paid anyone else, even a stray kitten, even the newest guy in the band, the one who would be with us a week or two at most. We never could keep a drummer.

The more I wanted Sammy, though, the more she seemed to want only the blood in the needle. I watched her watch the red rise and fall in the hypodermic. It did have a certain seductive glare, like a thermometer under a tropical sun. But it made me nervous, and she knew it. "You just ain't ready," she said. I tried not to be embarrassed. I concentrated on Sammy's mouth, on our music.

Our band, which went through names faster than drummers, got gigs in more and more places, places we could call clubs instead of taverns. Our audience appreciated us by getting drunk on the dance floor and shooting up in the bathrooms. We got paid.

With the money we made, I paid my mother's back rent, bought a totally electric Fender and splurged on rice and bean take-out dinners. Sammy bought more and more heroin, fresh white roses every day and stockings with sequins sewn up the sides. I told Sammy the roses smelled as dead as her singing. Sammy told me I played guitar like a Salvation Army reject. We argued more often than not.

On stage, we blew kisses to each other. The specter of what our audience thought might be kinky sex aroused their applause. Sammy wore a white sequined dress that hugged her pale figure. I refused to wear sequins, but had a satin shirt with satin pants, both in too-tight black. We did not call ourselves salt and pepper, but the name came up often. We sang. I always sang louder. We danced. Sammy always danced harder.

During the mandatory keep-the-backup-band-happy intolerably long instrumentals with the sweaty drum solo, Sammy would shimmy and shake, but never strut. I took to picking up my electric Fender and crouching low into my silent chords. I was tolerated as long as I did not plug into an amp.

We changed the band's name to White Roses, at Sammy's insistence. We landed a gig at Trudy Heller's in Manhattan, a well-known hangout of record producers, according to Sammy. We were on the verge of success; we were on the verge of disbanding.

Then Sammy died.

It was Reef, our newest drummer, and the man I suspected of being Sammy's lover, who told me. He was an androgynous sort with long hair and girlish hips. He did not cry, although he sniffed a little. He told me Sammy had overdosed in the apartment of one of their friends that I did not know. I imagined her body, pale and streaked with blood. I tried to think of a question, a detail that would make it more real than a song lyric, badly sung.

I wound up writing lots of lyrics about Sammy, most of them bad if not badly sung. Especially bad was "White Roses," which I never sang, except in the shower. One song did make it to the stage: "Every Woman Needs a Dead Lover." It's one of my hits, if any title can be called a hit in the world of women's music.

The pink spotlight hits the sterling silver frets. I stand in a pool of silence, surrounded by applause. I strum and adjust the tone and volume controls of my expensive electric guitar. At the first chords, the audience stirs with recognition. My voice is distinctively sharp:

> *Every woman needs a dead lover*
> *To be a coldly perfect cover*
> *You can pick up a girl in a bar*
> *Drive her home in your car*
> *Tell her she's a cutie*
> *Lie that she's a beauty*
> *And say: Sorry, I can't love you*
> *It's something I just can't do*
> *The one I love is dead, dead, dead*

But let me stroke your pretty head
Safe and warm between my thighs
Let me come and close my eyes
You make me feel like I could die

I end with a short riff, crouching close to the edge of the audience. The women roar. Sometimes the mere sight of a woman playing an electric guitar is enough to make women yell with appreciation. It's like driving on a lonely road in South Carolina and seeing a woman working heavy equipment.

The song may be shallow and self-serving, as one feminist reviewer judged it, but every audience loves it, or at least they seem to. They also seem to love my equally shallow and self-serving attempt at conversation with almost a hundred women.

"It's great to be back in San Francisco."

JJ The women applaud themselves. I do not mention the fog that eddies around the streets, as if the whole city is nothing other than a set for a spooky movie. I do not mention the sun that never seems to shine, the earth that shudders with unexpected orgasms, the ocean that pounds on the shores, relentless and cold as death.

"Queer capital of the world."

The women applaud themselves again. I cannot see past the glare of the stage lights, but I can visualize the usual crowd: diesel dykes who like the hard drive of my guitar, lipstick lesbians who like the healing bruise of my lyrics. There are women with their lovers, women looking for lovers, and women trying to forget lovers. And all of the women in the audience, in at least a little secret part of themselves, wish they could be me. The women with shy voices and little ambition, the women who watched their brothers play guitar as they took up the clarinet, the women who croon from the depths of their diaphragms and play air guitar as they clean their apartments. The women of my audience.

Before I leave the stage, I want to satisfy each of these women as if I had invited her home for the night instead of making her purchase a ticket to a concert hall. Mostly, I want to make love with my electric Fender, a lighter version of the one I had in the days of White Roses. It is my guitar who is my lover, the lover who will never die. If I smash her, I can replace her. She cannot take up with a male musician unless I sell her.

My last song is always political, still always more rock-vibrant than ballad-like. This year I am singing an African freedom song. I am dark enough to ensure a good review.

I sing the song as slowly as possible. I never want to leave my spotlight of safety. The set always ends. I bow and wave and set my guitar down. I leave it there, and walk, alone, off the stage.

Backstage there will be hand-lettered invitations and bottles of liquor, flowers and plants, a few crystals and lots of photographs of women posed shirtless on their motorcycles with their phone numbers written across their breasts. The more adventurous women show up in person, bribing their way past the security guards (I insist upon women) and often spending the night with the equipment managers (again, I insist upon women). San Francisco is no different.

There are some great local women's bands that Gloria, my childhood friend and now my manager and agent, has heard about from one of the women now backstage, a rather sultry radio DJ. Gloria wants us to check them out, although I suspect she is actually more interested in checking out the DJ. But I am lethargic, overdosed on my own ego. After a concert, I try to shake my despondency in a hot shower, try to rest my raw voice, try not to sing to Sammy.

It isn't that I never take advantage of my opportunities. I select the reticent ones, the ones who stand off a little to the side of the fray, trying to convince themselves that they are brave. I treat them well, take them to dinner, try to talk with them. They often seem surprised that I am not stupid, that I've read a book or two. Later, I take them back to my hotel room. The sex is often mediocre; I struggle to make it scintillating. I mark them with my mouth, a bruise where I have sucked their flesh, either neck or breast. Love bites, they call them. It gives them something to remember. Occasionally, one will apologize that she is menstruating, attempting to deflect my hand from her tampon. But I will pull the string, toss the cotton cylinder and then kiss her stomach, very gently, without any teeth at all. She will be a bit nervous when my tongue reaches her blood, but I never, never bite, and soon she relaxes, letting me taste and taste. I no longer worry that this will ruin my voice; now it seems to make it stronger.

Tonight, I look around at my prospects. Among the photographs, phone numbers and other flowers is a vase of white roses. I like the dramatic act of throwing it to the floor. The women who travel with me expect this, although they do not ask for an explanation and none is ever given. It happens every so often, some woman who could not possibly know that of all possible seductions, this is the least likely to succeed. Or sometimes I think that Gloria gets the white roses; she thinks post-performance flares of energy might prevent depression.

As I grab the vase, I notice a card hanging from a noose of white string around the thorny stems: *You've come a long way, baby. Love from the old days. Always, Sammy.*

Couldn't be, I reassure myself. There are lots of women in the world named Sammy. But are there lots of old days, lots of long ways? Still, the white roses are just coincidence. Could have been red; these were probably discounted.

I ask Gloria about the vase in my hand. She stares innocently; how would she know? she says, she was on stage with me. I ask some equipment managers. They look offended as I demean their responsibilities. I ask some security officers. They point at one another.

"I thought you'd recognize me," one security woman says. She has short, graying brown hair and red lipstick. Incredibly pale skin. Her breasts twist under the cheap fabric of her dark blue security uniform. Then she smiles her smile.

"I thought you were dead."

"I'm not," she says simply.

I wait for an explanation, looking at this ghost from an afterlife where peroxide is apparently unavailable.

"I suppose it's kind of ironic now," Sammy says. "The guys thought you weren't sexy enough."

"Because I wouldn't fuck them like you did," I say because I feel like I've earned the right to be as cruel as I want.

"No. I think it was the way you danced," she answers. "They thought you would hold the band back or something."

"What does that have to do with your being dead?" I feel like smiling at her, but I force myself not to.

"Well, if I were dead, you'd quit. Lose interest. The only reason you were in the band was to be close to me. You wanted to play the guitar as good as a guy so you'd impress me."

"I didn't quit," I protest to this ghost, this security guard, like I still care what she thinks. Then I turn on her, "Why did you go along with it?"

"I had my reasons." Her smile. I am embarrassed by how young I must have been then, how easily bruised.

She seems embarrassed, too. "I came back and looked for you," Sammy explains. "I asked your mother, but she said you were gone."

"I was," I say, but do not tell her where I went.

"Well, I just wanted to tell you how sorry I am. Real sorry."

I wonder if she lives with someone, man or woman.

"All the women I know think you're just great," Sammy continues. "Really admire you. Don't believe me when I say I knew you way-back-when."

"That was a long time ago," I interrupt her. This is pitiful. Not her, but the way I still feel drawn to her, like I want to dive into her body and rest there for eternity.

"Not so long in the scheme of things."

"I guess not," I admit.

"How about we have a drink and talk about old times?"

I think she must not be living with anyone. "I still don't drink," I answer, and then, stabbing again, "And you, still shooting up every five minutes?"

"No. Not anymore. Not since I accepted what I am."

"So, no more men?"

Sammy shrugs, changes the subject: "How's your mother?"

"Dead." Dead as I thought Sammy was. Dead as dead. But it is never my mother's face that floats from the audience while the stage is still sheathed in darkness and my fingers tense for the first chords of my trademark opening song. It has always been Sammy's pale face, its jutting white halo, its dilated pupils reflecting sequins. It has never been anything like the beige flesh that bubbles above her navy blue uniform, underneath mousy hair ridged with attempts at curls.

Looking at Sammy, I try to decide which song will open up my next show, tomorrow night across the bay in Berkeley. A small intimate club. I think I'll try something new. Perhaps something previously unrecorded, something in plaintive minor chords. A solo. There will be no time for rehearsal. My professional but still unsullied voice amplified but not distorted. My virgin Gibson semi-acoustic cello guitar. Something slow and slightly sad. Like a song a lonely woman would sing to herself in the shower.

"Go get yourself two tickets for tomorrow night's show from the backstage manager," I tell Sammy. "And make sure you bring a woman as your date."

"I thought you would be my date," she says.

Same old Sammy. Confident when we sang together that her voice did not sound like shit, even though it did; and confident now that she doesn't look like shit, even though she does. Maybe it's her confidence that makes me say "Sure." Or maybe I just wanted to see that smile. Or maybe I'm just an idiot, to pick some worn-out security guard when I could have any of the dozens of fresh young women lingering backstage.

"One ticket then." I am casual. She rewards me with her vampire smile.

It is the smile that occupies my ceiling. I can hardly sleep the next day for thinking about her. I am restless, pacing around my hotel suite that seems too large and sunny. I take shower after shower, closing the curtain tight, creating a steamy coffin. I order room service, twice. No food satisfies. I pick up my acoustic guitar, try some new arrangements, but the strings sound more eerie than any audience would tolerate.

I curse myself, curse her. Why does she reappear now? Just when everything is going great. I know I'm at the verge of breaking into the big time, beyond the women's music circuit, into the mainstream. And even if I don't, I already have a damn good career. Enough money and enough admiration. And the chance to sing and play my guitar, the only things I've ever wanted.

Or the only things I could articulate. There is something else I want. Something to satiate some emptiness at my core. I can barely tolerate the cliché, but I also can't explain the lack. Maybe it's spiritual. I've even thought of going back to the Salvation Army to sing. Have even slipped into a service or two in some depressed town or another. I've tried tarot and rolfing and yoga and a chiropractor and every sort of sex and even, just a time or two, heroin. And, saluting my mother, some Wild Turkey and some margaritas heavy with salt. But nothing fills the void I call Sammy.

Maybe not even she will. That's the risk of seeing her again. Oh, why the hell did I agree? I'd go take a walk, but even the ground clouds of this San Francisco evening hold too much brightness. I take another shower, sing to myself.

Finally, by twilight, Gloria comes to my room. I have dressed and undressed seventeen times. Now I'm wearing black jeans and a black ripped T-shirt. Black boots. A wide silver belt. No jewelry. Like I just threw it on three minutes ago, which I did.

"You look like death warmed over," Gloria says cheerfully. She must have had a better day than I have, must have found the DJ intriguing.

"Thanks a lot. Should I change?"

"No, it's not the outfit. That's the same. But you seem different, really. I hope you don't get that damn flu. I worry about you. All your high-risk behaviors, don't think I don't know about them. I hear things. I'm your manager; I have to know what the hell you're doing. You know, you should really get tested."

"Oh, Jesus, not now."

"Okay, okay. But are you sure you're all right?"

"Yeah," I mumble. "I'll be fine. Get me on stage."

Gloria quickly looks around my room. For a needle or a bottle or a woman or something to explain my condition. Satisfied, she directs our entourage through the streets of Berkeley to the club. She is even more satisfied when we get there. There is a line outside, pouring out of the door and down the long block, where it bubbles into a crowd at the corner. Inside, it is standing room only, Gloria informs me, kissing me on the cheek. I look past her, to the white roses scattered on the floor, near the stage entrance. I look past her, but don't see Sammy.

Can't see her in the audience either. But I know she is there in the dark. Can feel her. Know she is not one of the women screaming, throwing her shirt onto the stage. Knows I sing only for her. And tonight, it is not my Fender that I'm fucking.

Backstage, it's over. Our drummer is still red with sweat. My voice is hoarse. Gloria is exuberant, hugging everyone. Whispers in my ear: "Major deal. Major deal." I see some guy from the industry trailing around after her, like she trailed around after him last month.

I feel dizzy. Like I need a fix, only I'm not sure of what. Or I am sure, but won't admit it. That bitch. That bitch. I don't see Sammy anywhere.

"That was great," some reporter says, sidling next to me, touching my T-shirt with her hot hand. Her press badge perches on her left breast, jutting out like a bicuspid.

"She likes an intimate audience," Gloria interrupts and then is gone again, winking.

The reporter smiles her unremarkable smile. I could have her, I think. I could bed her so easily. A slip of the tongue. A stretch of the mouth. But I can tell she would be too timid to bite hard enough. I can tell she would not be proud to be bruised. I excuse myself.

A sequined dress intercepts me. Some brutal blonde, pale and ethereal.

"That was stunning," the woman says. Then she smiles her Sammy smile.

She is the one who is stunning. And I am simply stunned. She had been standing backstage the entire time, leaning against some pole that looked like it could not support itself, never mind a human body.

"Sammy?" I half-ask.

"You were expecting someone else?"

"Yes, as a matter of fact. A rather mousy-haired security guard that I met last night."

"Oh," Sammy laughs, "that was just a test."

I am suddenly angry. "What is this, the Frog and the Prince?"

"Wrong fairy tale, darling," she breathes, taking my hand. Her fingers are smooth and cool. I can only forgive her.

"Dinner? Gloria told me there's a pretty good Italian place not far from here."

"Italian? We should avoid all that garlic, we'll be happier later."

"Then you select, you live around here now."

She takes us to a Russian restaurant on College Avenue. She orders borscht and salts it before she tastes it. I mimic her. We stir our food. We sip our vodka martinis. I have never been hungrier, less able to eat.

She drives me across the Bay Bridge, back to my hotel. I don't remember having told her where it was. We sit in the bar, for hours. We sip drinks that she orders. She orders more, allowing the others to be removed, virtually untouched. She walks me to my room, as if I have invited her.

I pick up my guitar. Sit on the bed. She sits next to me. My fingers caress the steel. Her finger traces my mouth. Inside my lower lip, then touching the tips of my teeth.

I am very still. Only my hands move across the body of my guitar, the neck of my guitar.

Her finger across my cheek. Behind my ear. Under my ear. Parallel with my jaw bone. On my neck. Dancing.

I can hardly breathe.

"We don't have to if you don't want to."

I think that I have said this, but then it seems she is waiting for an answer as if she has.

"I want—"

She closes the hotel room drapes. The first flickers of dawn, the last lights of the city, all erased.

I reach for her sequins across the darkness. The single zipper. The music of it is like sex itself, both secretive and simple. I smell her thickness. She smells the same as she always has.

But not everything is the same. She was once the one who reached for me. Her kisses were sloppy then, her motions jagged. And I was more compliant. Without the confidence to take what I wanted, who I wanted and how. Without the audacity to pretend I knew. No, not everything is the same.

I feel her strain against her passivity. I push my knee between hers, then up, higher until I hit the bone, where it feels like all the solids are seeping out. Some sticky wet spreads through the leg of my jeans. I wonder vaguely if she is menstruating; that must be the thickness I smell. I long to taste it, to drink it, to have it stiffen on my cheeks. Soon, I promise myself, knowing I must go slow so that I do not startle her, knowing I must do nothing that will make her change her mind about giving me this gift. About coming back.

But she is already moving beyond me. Against my leg, wet and chafing, under and over. The sound in my ear is a howl, but whispered. It cannot be misunderstood. She is only calm for a moment, her sounds still reverberating, when her mouth is on my earlobe, then lower. Her teeth catch my flesh. My skin swirls between her lips until my whole body is caught in some whirlpool. My own teeth bang against each other, lonely in their shaking.

The word *orgasm* appears on the edges of my consciousness casting for an explanation, but then quickly recedes, embarrassed by its paucity. This must be something different. Less like falling and more like ascending, less like death and more like being born.

By the time I wake, I've lost a day. I expect to see Sammy sitting in my room, somewhere. Instead, it is Gloria.

"We've been worried about you, kid."

"I'm fine." I rush to the bathroom, greedy for the mirror. I look for one of Sammy's notorious love bites, but my skin glimmers, translucent and unbroken.

Terrified that it has all been a fever, I search the room. The hotel sheets are certainly a bloody mess. The silver sequined dress is spread on the night table, over the phone. I slip into it, not surprised that it fits.

"It's you," Gloria exclaims. "You can wear it on TV. I got you a spot on a music awards special!"

It isn't the promise of some transitory fame that makes me smile. It's Sammy. And my knowledge that we will be together longer than fame, longer than forever.

Twelfth Night

Victoria A. Brownworth

THE NEW ORLEANS NIGHT WAS tentacled with fog—fog slithering through the tiny streets of the French Quarter, each swampy arm embracing the clots of tourists that laughed and staggered and caroused along the narrow slate sidewalks, the wet gray cobblestone of Jackson Square.

The fog reminded Miranda Kent of the thick fingers of mist that would reach up out of the deep, lush forest outside Kigali, in the impossibly green hills of Rwanda. *Kigali.* That was last year. The soldiers at the airport—French and Belgians, she had written in her news reports, sent over the wire—orchestrating the coup. And then the slow turning of the tide, the creeping escalation. It had only taken a few days really. The Hutu takeover, the Tutsis slaughtered, hacked to death with machetes. There had been body parts on every roadway as she had edged toward the border and Zaire. It had been too dangerous to take photographs by then, but she could not forget the pictures she had snapped in her own lens, the staccato notes she had taken as she rode over the roads at night, listened to the sounds of screaming, wondering if the jostling was caused by debris in the road or corpses.

She had been one of the last ones out. Had witnessed the cowering UN troops hiding their pale blue berets, terrified they would be murdered, too. The last news stories from Kigali had been hers. And when she'd arrived in Zaire, the first reports from her Goma refugee site had been hers, too. Her editor expected a Pulitzer this year. "Guts alone will win it for you," he'd told her. "You were the only reporter with the stomach to stay. I don't know how you do it." When cholera invaded the camps at Goma, she'd stayed for a few more weeks, tending the sick at night. Then she'd traveled downriver to write about the bodies floating up in Lake Victoria, about the thousands of bloated corpses polluting the water and the fish, about how a million people had been murdered in a month's time.

And then it had been off to a new assignment. *A rest*, her editor had told her. *Tuzla*. "It's in Bosnia," he told her. "But it's not Sarajevo. You'll be able to get water without getting killed."

Now, in the French Quarter, in her favorite city, the only sound was laughter and shouting, the occasional muffled notes of music from some bar or jazz place as a door opened and closed. The dense, damp scrim of fog had edged in from the river soon after dark—hours ago—and it was nothing like Kigali, really. Miranda stopped on the corner of St. Anne to let a particularly rowdy pack of revelers pass by, on their way, she presumed, to Bourbon Street and some strip club passing for a jazz joint. The clock in St. Louis Cathedral began to chime and with the eight bells came the realization that she was, as ever, late.

She stood for a moment and turned toward the sound of the carillon. It had been so many years since she first stood on this same corner, first heard the bells, first inhaled what was then the most foreign place she'd ever been. Nearly two decades since she had first seen the steamboats toiling up the Mississippi, the river whose name she had learned in a jump-rope game as a child, the river that gave her her first taste of oysters. No bodies floating downriver, here. No beheaded babies or hacked-off limbs or disemboweled women with their breasts slashed to bits. This river was the river of her dreams, not her nightmares.

It had been twenty years since she fell in love with New Orleans and all things foreign, twenty years since she'd come here from the North and learned all the things that had led her back here now, on a real holiday for the first time in two years. Back to the place where she had once come, anonymous, knowing no one. Back to the city that had taught her how to live, that had taught her how to deal with death.

It was twenty years since her first Twelfth Night, her first Mardi Gras, her first Easter Mass at the cathedral hulking behind her, tolling out the time. And almost as long since she had last seen her old friends, the three women she was late meeting now, the women she had come of age with here, on these streets, in this city, back when they were all fresh-faced and young and full of plans to change the world. Twenty years—back when she had never been anywhere foreign, when this was the most foreign place on earth. Back when she knew nothing of places like Kigali or Tuzlà or the many ways that people can be made to suffer and to die. Back when the future—hers and that of her friends—had been as evanescent as the mist in these gas-lit streets.

Miranda breathed deeply, drawing in the stale fog-tinged air, which smelled of tourist piss and the river and a hint of chicory wafting over from the Cafe du Monde across the square. It was a warm night, even for New Orleans in January, but Miranda shivered slightly as another passel of tourists jostled by her. She anchored her beaded evening purse under her arm and drew her black velvet theater coat around her. It wouldn't do for her to get mugged by some rowdy Alabama boys out for a night of fun when she had such an important reunion. She knew all too well how ineffective the New Orleans police could be in an emergency.

Stepping out of the way of a tipsy couple staggering arm-in-arm on their way to the next booze joint, she turned toward Royal Street and hoped her friends would remember she had never arrived anywhere on time.

It was twenty past eight when a flushed and slightly damp Miranda walked briskly through the cobbled courtyard that led to Vivienne Ng's little house. Candlelight glowed through the lace-covered front windows and in the momentary quiet Miranda stopped, wondering if this was how the Vieux Carré had seemed on another Twelfth Night, the one Dolores had told her about one autumn as they ate blackened alligator stuffed with oysters and pearl onions in a bungalow off the Gulf on Grande Isle. With the creamy lace covering the French windows and the amber shimmer of the candlelight beyond, the flicker of the gaslight just above her head, lighting her way into the courtyard, it could as easily have been 1895 as 1995, could easily have been even earlier—the years of Jean Lafitte perhaps, or the Napoleon who never came to live in exile here, as he had planned, in the house that was still her favorite cafe.

As she let the shiny brass knocker fall once, twice, against the black cypress door, Miranda thought how little time changes things, how only the specifics of history are there as signposts to remind us of where we are, who we are, what year it is.

She could hear laughter and the lilting sound of chamber music beyond Vivienne's door as she stood looking out over the courtyard at the bougainvillea bunched against a far wall, climatis ambling above it. New Orleans had always been full of heady scents for her. Coffee, food, and everywhere, something floral. It had all been part of the foreignness. So new, so different, so—yes—intoxicating. How had she stayed away so long, she wondered now. *God, I love it here,* she breathed quietly into the fog-limned night. *Maybe I won't have to leave.*

"We *knew* you'd be right on time, *chérie.*" Vivienne's vaguely French accent lilted over Miranda's shoulder as the door suddenly opened behind her, laughter following it. Miranda whirled about, the velvet coat flaring out around her.

"Y'all know how I never could disappoint my women." Miranda put the full force of her Southern accent, unused in two decades, into her words as she threw her arms around the slender Vietnamese woman who stood before her.

"Get in here, girl, you lettin' all that swamp gas in." The voice behind Vivienne was Justine Duffet—Vivienne's lover for the past twenty-three years—big and handsome, her skin nearly as dark as Vivienne's blue-black hair.

"Oh, *do* stop standing around in the doorway, y'all. You Northern girls never know winter when you see it." Luna St. Croix flounced up to the doorway, yanked Miranda unceremoniously through it and shut the door with a force that set the brass lizard knocker banging. "Now take off that wet thing y'all got on and come over here and have yourself a *drink*. Just like you to keep us all waiting twenty years for you to show up. Never did wear a watch."

Luna was already across the room, standing beside a tiny alabaster bar covered with various bottles and a large crystal ice bucket, mixing Miranda a drink.

"You don't even know what I drink, Missy Thing," Miranda laughed as she extricated herself from the damp velvet coat and handed it over to Justine, who held it at arm's length as if it were a dead animal and left the room with an exaggerated look of revulsion on her face.

"Still drinkin' those silly cloud things, for sure, messin' up good gin with gooey French syrup—am I right?" Luna's description of the drink Miranda had invented in her days as a bartender at one of the sleazier watering holes in the Quarter brought another round of laughter from the group.

"That's a Saint Cloud, and Cointreau is not some 'gooey French syrup' but a lovely, light, orange liqueur." Miranda attempted her best *haute* attitude, but Vivienne was chuckling.

"You'd think we'd seen each other yesterday, *chérie*. You sound just the same—like the old days," she said softly. "Let me look at you."

Vivienne led Miranda over to a big plush sofa the color of lichen and held her at arm's length. Miranda looked at Vivienne, still beautiful at fifty, still beautiful after all she had seen in her childhood in Saigon, still beautiful after being sold into prostitution and fleeing, with a tiny baby whose father she couldn't even imagine, at twenty-two to France and a year later, to the States. Her daughter, Minh, lived in France now, was a reporter, like Miranda. Minh had reinvented herself in Paris, where her mixed race wasn't a constant reminder of her mother's past. Miranda passed information back and forth between mother and daughter. Minh and Vivienne hadn't spoken in years.

Yet none of the pain showed on Vivienne's lovely sculpted face. She wore silk pajamas of the sort Miranda saw in Asia. Teal embroidered with red and fuchsia birds, the high neck accentuating the soft wing of black hair that swept back over one eye. Once again Miranda thought of the timelessness of some things. Vivienne looked much as she had twenty years earlier when Miranda had worked for her.

But what would Vivienne see when she looked at *her*, Miranda wondered. How much would they each reveal to the other tonight, Twelfth Night, that most revelatory of nights. Not just a drunken brawl and bash, like Mardi Gras, but the end of the Christmas season and the beginning of the days of Carnival. Throughout the city, the richest families in New Orleans were giving parties New York society couldn't imagine. Miranda had chosen Twelfth Night especially for this visit. It had been on Twelfth Night that she had met Dolores, on Twelfth Night that she left New Orleans for El Salvador, on Twelfth Night when her life had changed forever.

Sometime after she had first come to New Orleans she had had her cards read by some old Creole woman on a side street near the vegetable market. Miranda wasn't sure why she had answered when the woman called to her, whispered, *"Chèr, come on, chèr, let Mama Laveau tell you what she see."*

And the cards *had* told her. Mama Laveau had shivered as she turned the worn cards over, tried to send her off, waving her hands at Miranda as if she were shooing away a swarm of insects, dismissing her. But Miranda had demanded to know what the cards meant, and Mama Laveau had sat back down at her little table, sighed deeply and told her all the cards held, had hissed at her like the fat pythons Miranda would later see in the jungles of Latin America. "Death stalk you, girl. Death in a mask, Death on Twelfth Night, Death in a girl, Death gone lie between you legs and tell you it not Death. You won't find no escape, girl. No escape."

Miranda had been frightened. Sweating in the afternoon heat, startled when thunder broke out as it did every afternoon in the summer in New Orleans, drenched to the bone later as she walked through the teeming rain hearing Mama Laveau's words. "No escape. No beatin' back Death. But the cards tell me *you can teach him a lesson.*"

Mama Laveau had been right. About everything.

And now it was Twelfth Night again, and Miranda was back with the women who were her oldest friends, the women who read her stories from around the world, the women to whom she sent long letters and cryptic postcards from all the worst places on earth, the women she wanted to come back to—if she could.

Luna ambled over with a tall, fluted pink glass filled with cloudy liquid. "Now remember, these drinks kick ass, girl. And we got *lots* to talk about. Like for one, how come you are the only one of us who looks like you just got a face-lift?" Luna handed Miranda the glass. "Here we all thought livin' that hard life was gonna give you gray hair and a shit-load of wrinkles, and you look like you did the day you left here. So what, you found the fountain of youth in some rain forest somewhere? What's your secret, girl—'cause some of us sure could use it." She patted her full cheeks and pushed her fingers up against the crow's feet that pinched the corners of her eyes.

Vivienne turned toward Miranda and looked at her hard. "No face-lift, eh, *chérie?* Something else, *non?* That's why you came back after all this time away—not for Justine's *étouffée.*"

It had been twenty years since Vivienne had first read Miranda on that first day they had worked together. Miranda had come down from the North, fresh out of college and newly signed to a two-year stint in the domestic Peace Corps, VISTA. Asthma had kept her out of the Peace Corps, kept her from the first assignment to a country near Rwanda. She had been angry, certain that the experience of changing the world that she envisioned could never be achieved so close to home. She had arrived with no money and a lot of attitude, and Vivienne had read her with a swiftness and sureness that had amazed her. Vivienne had taken her out to lunch, gotten her drunk as only New Orleans lunches can, and told her a little about Saigon, a little about France and a little about how change really gets created.

Miranda had worked hard for Vivienne, and Vivienne had introduced her to Justine and Luna. And Luna had introduced her to the foreignness of New Orleans, starting in her own bedroom. Now Miranda looked at them all, these women who were more like family to her than anyone had ever been, except perhaps Dolores. She looked at them—at Justine readying the table for another of her fabulous dinners, at Luna, still the plump coquette with her long red hair and her too-tight skirt, at Vivienne, her sage mentor. These were the women she had come to because she wasn't certain where else to go, if she could go on now, without Dolores. If she could continue to live the life she had been living for twenty years since she left New Orleans for the world she so desperately wanted to change, the world Dolores had shown her.

"Listen, ladies, I have *not* been in this kitchen all day so you could gab while the soufflé goes flat and the shrimp gets dry," Justine called to them from the doorway of the dining room. "Now get your fat little butts—not you, Vivienne, you have a delightful little butt—in here and eat this fabulous meal."

Luna linked her arm through Miranda's, and they followed Vivienne to the table. The room was simple and elegant. The table was a stark black wood, and Justine had set their places with lace-edged linen placemats. The centerpiece had Vivienne's touch: a single branch of cymbidium with a small surround of pussy willows. It was an odd combination no one else would have considered, yet the drama of the baby orchids was offset by the simplicity of the little furred stalks of wood. Again, there was another facet of Asian culture that Vivienne refused to have bred out of her by her adopted country. Miranda thought of Minh with a pang. Vivienne didn't know her daughter had even altered her name, removed every trace of her Vietnamese heritage. As she looked around the table, looked at Vivienne kissing Justine's hand, thanking her for the exquisite meal, looked at Luna, still the liveliest woman she knew, Miranda was certain she had come to the right place for advice, was certain the risk would be worth it. These women would tell her what to do, just as they had two decades earlier; they would help her to move on without Dolores.

Dinner passed languidly, each new culinary delight receiving its appropriate due. Luna regaled them all with tales of her latest boudoir escapades. Justine updated Miranda on life in New Orleans and the many new restaurants she would have to try while she was in town. Vivienne told her about where the best new untouristy spots were for the kind of jazz and zydeco Miranda liked.

It was close to midnight when Justine brought out dessert and a sweet wine and suggested they settle into the living room and light a fire. "After all," she said, "it is Twelfth Night, and there's magic in the flames."

As Justine laid a small fire of cypress and cedar, Luna poured herself a brandy and arranged herself on the small damask-covered loveseat next to Miranda.

"Now honey," she fairly purred into Miranda's ear, "it is time for you to tell us your Twelfth Night tale, your deepest secret, your *raison* for being here in this town after twenty years of postcards, letters and the occasional transcontinental phone call. Something is *up* with you, child, and even if you do look twenty-five while the rest of us girls is gettin' ready for the rockin' chairs, there is trouble in your eyes, and we want to know what it is."

Luna leaned forward and lifted the lid on a small cinnabar box that lay on the coffee table in front of them. Justine shut the lid before Luna could remove what was inside.

"Let's hear what Miranda has to say first, Luna," she chided. "The cards will tell her what to do *after*."

Luna repositioned herself on the loveseat and sipped her brandy. Vivienne stretched her legs along the sofa, her feet propped on Justine's lap. The three women looked expectantly at Miranda. No one spoke for a time, and the only sound was the low lilt of a Schubert quintet and the crackle and hiss of the fire. A trio of candles burning in long brass sticks on a side table and the glow from the fireplace provided the only light. It was dim in the room, almost dark. The skin and hair and satiny clothes of her friends all shimmered in front of Miranda, and she felt for a moment as if she might faint.

"Tell us your secret, Miranda," Luna repeated and patted Miranda's thigh.

"Yes, *chérie*," echoed Vivienne, "that is why you are here, *non?*"

Justine stared at her, hard. In the dim light, Justine's features were hardest to discern. *She's darker than the Tutsi*, Miranda thought, briefly. *Darker than the Algerians, darker than the Guatemalans, darker than—* A series of images flooded her consciousness, faces like Justine's, skin the color of night. She thought of Dolores, of Dolores's *café au lait* skin, different from Luna's Creole olive, different from the blue-black sheen of Justine's. Dolores, her lover, her guide, her companion. Dolores, who was gone now, forever. Dolores, who had taught her how to live her life, and now she had no one to share it with except these three women who suddenly terrified her more than any battleground or war zone she had visited in twenty years.

The heat from the fire was making her blood pulse, her heart beat faster than it should. *Too much wine,* she thought. *And I shouldn't have had the gin.* She stood, then, and walked to the window closest to the fire, unsure whether she was simply going to take the air or flee into the night, away from these women, away from all they knew about her, away from the secret of Twelfth Night. She reached out a pale hand and turned the little brass handle of the window and flung it open onto the courtyard. Wisps of fog crept over the sill, and the scent of bougainvillea was thick in the night air.

She breathed deeply, closed her eyes, thought of the last place she had been before this, a small town outside Ahùachapan in Guatemala, near the border of El Salvador. *Not a hot spot,* her editor had told her, *but they've been doing things there, things I want you to check out.*

She had checked out those "things," the quiet little horrors that were going on in that border town. She had called Dolores before she had gone. Dolores said they would meet later, in Costa Rica, take a little vacation, she said. "The waterfalls at night are spectacular, *chérie.* And there are plenty of places to eat nearby."

But Dolores had surprised her in Guatemala, and something had gone wrong. They had been caught, and Dolores had been killed. Miranda had escaped into El Salvador, but just barely. A bitter irony, she thought, El Salvador, where she had started out twenty Twelfth Nights ago.

No one had spoken when she opened the window, and no one spoke now as she stepped across the sill and walked out into the courtyard. If there was a moon, she couldn't see it through the fog in the gas-lit night. *What to say,* she thought, her heart still beating fast with the memory of what had happened to Dolores, of how the *junta* had mistaken the two women for guerillas, how when Dolores had tried to stop them they had shot her over and over, how one young *capo* had decided this *norteamericana* must die and had taken his machete and sliced Dolores's head clean from her beautiful long neck. How they had all looked when her body began to change and Miranda had known she would be next.

No, there is no moon tonight, she whispered into the bougainvillea. *And these are the only friends I have left.* She turned and walked back toward the window. It was time to share her Twelfth Night secret. In the near distance she could hear the carillon chime at St. Louis Cathedral. Twelve times. For Twelfth Night, for midnight, for the hour when the secrets of the night begin to be revealed.

Only Vivienne looked up when Miranda came back in from the courtyard. Luna was curled in the corner of the loveseat, dreamily swirling brandy in her glass and tapping out the counterpoint of the quintet on her thigh. Justine was sunk deep in the shadows of the green sofa, and Miranda was again startled by how the darkness of her skin triggered such a rush of memories—not just Kigali and Goma, though they were the most recent—but also the time she spent in the Transvaal, before apartheid was over, when the police hippo cars and the necklacing were still going on with horrifying regularity. Suddenly all those faces passed over the shadowy head of Justine and Miranda heard herself utter a small gasp. The mass of faces stilled, the dark head shot from the shadows into the glowing amber light of the candles on the table nearby.

"You all right, girl? Get in here with us, and shut out that fog." Justine's voice was solid, solid and deep and warm. There was no threat in it, none of what Miranda had just seen. Justine patted the space on the loveseat across from her and next to Luna. "Come and sit with us, talk to us," Justine said so softly that at first Miranda thought she hadn't really spoken, that the voice was only in her own head. For a moment, the lilt, the southernness of it, reminded her of Dolores. *Was she hearing Dolores, was Dolores talking to her, telling her to take the risk, talk to these women, tell them everything?*

Justine spoke again. "Luna, honey, get this girl a drink. Something heavy and red, to put the blood back in her cheeks. There's some nice port under the bar—get her some of that." Vivienne turned toward the sound of Justine's voice and stretched her arm up over the back of the sofa. She motioned languidly to Miranda. Luna got up without her usual flounce and headed toward the bar.

Miranda crossed the threshold of the window and shut it tight. The handle was damp from the fog, and pinpricks of moisture beaded the lace curtain. She walked around the back of the sofa. She stood behind the little mahogany table and watched the candles flicker and then steady as the air from the window settled into the room. She raised her hand above the trio of candlesticks and then drew it back.

"I want to tell you why I came home," she said. In the near dark, standing behind the table, she thought she must look ghoulish—her face more like a Halloween mask than one from Twelfth Night. Her voice sounded hollow even to her, and as the *scherzo* portion of the quintet began, she thought there was also a hint of melodrama in her words. The light, the fire, the room, the silence of her friends—again she felt as she had when she'd stood outside waiting for Vivienne to answer the door: That this could be any moment in history, any time before this, a century or even two before. All the times Dolores had told her about, had taught her about. But she wasn't here to talk about the past. She was here to talk about the future.

Luna broke the spell. "Come on, *chèr*, drink this wine and sit yourself down next to me. I'm startin' to feel like we're in some kind o' time warp here—everything slow but the music. If y'all don't talk to us soon, we are gonna be *fast* asleep. Now tell us what's goin' on with you. It's some woman, isn't it? 'Cause I know your work don't get you like this or you woulda been back here about a week after you left."

Miranda laughed a half-laugh. "Yes and no," she said as she took the glass from Luna and slipped between the table and the loveseat to sit in the chair that faced all three of them. Luna shrugged and put her feet up on the space Miranda had occupied earlier. Vivienne sat forward and stared at Miranda, reaching her slender hand across the coffee table toward her. "It's okay, *chérie*. You are like family to us. No matter what it is—and I know you would come back here only if it was very bad and you needed us—we will take care of you." Her voice lowered a bit as she repeated, "You know we will take care of you."

I would cry if I could, Miranda thought, and took a long draught of the port. The fire blistered slightly beside her and she felt suffused with heat. She imagined what they all saw when they looked at her. A young woman of twenty-five—except she was soon to be forty-six, would have a birthday a week before Mardi Gras. As she leaned into the plum-colored damask of the chair, she envisioned herself as they saw her—very little changed from when she'd left here twenty years earlier on the eve of another Twelfth Night. She *had* been twenty-five then, when she left town with Dolores and drove along the Gulf, stopping at Grand Isle for a feast with Dolores and then driving on to Texas and Mexico and down deep into Central America. "I will show you Carnival, *chérie*," Dolores had told her. "And then I will show you the world."

It had been Twelfth Night when Dolores had begun to show Miranda the world, and every Twelfth Night since they had met, somewhere—El Salvador, Afghanistan, the Transvaal, Algeria, Iraq, China, Indonesia, Northern Ireland, Burma, Thailand, Mozambique, Somalia, Haiti, Rwanda, Bosnia. This year would have been a holiday—Costa Rica. Hardly any killing there. But then Dolores had come to Guatemala instead. Guatemala, where there was altogether too much killing. And now Dolores was dead, too.

What do they see, when they look at me? Miranda asked herself. *That girl*, she thought. That girl who left with the Creole woman Luna hated and about whom Vivienne had said, "Whatever you want, Mira, but be careful." Justine had warned her, too, told her to watch cooks who use too much spice in the food. Justine had been closest to the truth; Miranda remembered the long feast on Grand Isle, the alligator that Dolores had caught herself with a wire snare, the alligator she insisted on preparing herself while Miranda drank icy white wine on the screened porch at sunset.

That girl, Miranda thought. The same girl she was now, twenty years later. Almost. Not quite. *But that's what they see*, she thought. *They see me as still young.*

The fire illuminated Miranda as she sat in the big wing chair. She was taller than the rest of them, six feet in low heels—only a few inches taller than Justine, but nearly a foot taller than the tiny Luna. And she was white. Very white. Not like Luna, who was half Creole, half Irish and had the red hair to prove it. Miranda looked like she had walked out of a snowbank. Her hair was an arctic blonde, the color every bottle of peroxide tried to imitate but never could. It waved softly to her shoulders, in baby-fine tendrils that curled dramatically on nights like this one, when the air was damp and thick. She was a large woman, but graceful. Not fat, or even round like Luna. Just big—buxom, they'd called it in the fifties. *Like an Iowa farm girl,* Dolores would whisper to her, Dolores whose coffee skin looked so dark next to her own. *I like big girls,* Dolores would say as she pulled Miranda down into their bed. *I like a girl who can make my blood run hot.*

That was what they saw tonight, these friends of hers: a twenty-five-year-old woman with the experience of someone quite a bit older. A tall, voluptuous young woman in a claret-colored silk dress that hugged her high breasts and draped long and flowing around her full hips, grazing her ankles. A pale blonde woman with dark gray eyes and a mouth whose lips always seemed slightly parted, in a sensual, seductive way. Tonight Miranda looked striking in her dark moiré dress, a single strand of garnet beads around her neck, long garnet earrings dangling almost to her shoulders, a thin band with a blood-red stone on the ring-finger of her left hand.

"What do you see when you look at me?" Miranda asked of no one in particular. "Do you think I've changed since you saw me last—or do I look the same to you?"

Luna answered almost immediately. Her voice was strange, quizzical almost in its tone. It wasn't the strident Luna or the sarcastic Luna or even the seductive Luna. There was a hint of fear in her voice as she turned to Miranda and said without a hint of irony, "You look exactly the same as when you left. Except you don't really look very—" Here she stopped, searched her brandy glass for the right word.

"—Alive." Justine moved out of the shadowy recess of the sofa, the amber satin of her shirt shimmering in the firelight. "You look like you seen a ghost, honey, and just can't shake it."

Vivienne spoke last. She had taken a long thin cigarette out of a square green box on the table and was lighting it, slowly and deliberately. "I've seen this look before, *chérie,*" she said, a slight bitterness in her voice. "I grew up with this look in my country. My mother, before she was killed, my aunts, before they were killed. They had your look, *chérie*. Death, when it stalks you, when you live in its arms day after day, gives you that look. I thought—" and here she paused, turning her face away, toward the fire, her face glistening just a bit around the corner of her right eye "—I thought that was why Minh left. Because I had that look." Justine reached over and squeezed Vivienne's shoulder.

Vivienne said, "It's no woman, is it, *chérie*? It's your work. It's where you've been since you left. You cannot live with death and survive. Not even as a visitor. It was all the dying that killed my mother. When the village burned, she just died. Death just picked her up with everyone else. There were no marks on her, you see. It was all the dying. *Mort.*"

What had she expected to tell them? Miranda wondered. *What had she expected to ask them?*

"It's more than that, though, am I right?" Luna sounded more like herself now. More sure, a touch sarcastic. "There is a woman, isn't there?"

"Could I have some more of this?" Miranda held her empty port glass out to Luna. Then she began her story.

There had been a woman, she told them. The same woman. The woman she had left New Orleans with twenty years earlier. There had only been that same woman since. Until recently. Until she had been in a tiny village on the Guatemalan border of El Salvador, outside Ahùachapan, covering a story about how the *junta* had been stealing and selling the babies of native women and blaming the kidnappings on the guerillas.

The details came slowly. Time and again she wished she could cry, could scream, could explain to these women who would understand what it meant to her when Dolores was murdered, how she herself had almost been killed, too.

But there was more. There was so much more. And they knew there was more, because when Miranda told them about Dolores, about Guatemala, about how they would never spend another Twelfth Night together, Vivienne said, "But that is not the story you came to tell, is it *chérie*?"

No, Miranda thought. The story she had come to tell had begun twenty years earlier, and it wasn't over yet. The story had passed before her earlier that evening, as she had looked at Justine's face and seen the faces of so many victims pass across it.

"No," she said aloud. "No, that isn't the story. You were right. All of you were right." She spread her hands out to include the three of them. "You were right when you warned me about Dolores twenty years ago, and you were right in what you said tonight. I have," she looked at Vivienne, "spent too much time in the arms of death. And I am not," and here she paused, looked at Justine, saw only her old friend and decided it was time, "quite alive. In fact, I am *not* alive. I have not been alive since the day after I left here twenty years ago."

She sat back in the chair. In the firelight, the wings surrounding her fluffy white hair looked like a bloody halo. *It would take them time to understand,* she thought. *It would take them time to understand what she meant. That she was dead.*

The music had stopped. No one spoke and the fire sizzled, fanning the sweet, almost cloying scent of cedar and cypress out into the room.

"I warned you about her." Justine, her strong arms wrapped now around herself, shook her head as she stared at Miranda. "We see these—women—here, you know. Everything comes through this town. Everything."

"And you were right, Justine," Miranda responded softly. "She was everything you thought she was. She was Death itself. She fed me, and then she taught me how to feed."

There. She had really said it now. There was no mistaking her meaning, no misconstruing her words.

"*Vampire?*" Luna said it in a whispered query. "You're saying Dolores was a vampire and she made you a vampire and *that's* what you've been doing for the last twenty years—*killing people?* Are we supposed to believe this, honey, or are you really taking us for a longer ride than ever before?" Her voice was louder, her tone now slightly acid. "Didn't you tell us once you wanted to save the world? I believe *vampires,*" and here she paused for sarcastic emphasis, "are murderers. Am I right?"

Miranda had expected to be stung by this kind of response, had been afraid this would be what they would all say, even Vivienne. But she felt oddly cool. Her heart beat calmly in her chest—the calmest it had been all evening, in fact. Luna's words did not upset her; in fact, they relieved her. She knew what to say, she knew now how to tell her story.

Miranda turned to Luna. "Justine believes me. Vivienne believes me. And you believe me, too, I know you do—it was in your voice when I asked you how I looked to you. You were afraid. And you, Luna, are never afraid. You believe me. I am—" she looked into the blue edges of the candle flames, "—dead. Or, if you prefer," a hint of irony tinged her voice, "*undead*. If it makes you feel any better, Luna, it didn't happen here, in New Orleans. It happened on Grand Isle. On Twelfth Night. After eating a small alligator and rémoulade followed by a raspberry soufflé that would have done Justine proud."

Miranda turned toward Justine. "It was the first time she cooked for me. It seemed so decadent, so romantic. We even wore feathered masks—for Twelfth Night, you know." She could hear the wistfulness in her own voice, the echoing grief, the loss of Dolores. Had she come here to bare what was left of her soul or to find another companion? She wasn't sure. And as she looked at her friends, she wasn't even sure if she was safe.

But it didn't matter, now. If Justine got up and walked into her scrupulously well-organized and well-stocked kitchen and got out the elephant garlic and the silver tongs and a stake of mesquite wood, she wouldn't fight it. If Vivienne and Luna held her down while Justine sent her into the limbo Dolores now lived in, she wouldn't fight it. She had come here because she wasn't sure how to go on. If her friends couldn't tell her, if they decided to kill her, well, she laughed—lightly, bitterly, out loud—*I can live with that.*

"You—none of you, not even you, Vivienne—have seen the world I have seen. You've read my stories, you've seen the photographs. On the evening news you see the video footage, when there is footage, when there is someone like me—and there are others like me out there, a few, not many—to take it. Someone, as my editor always tells me, *with guts for brains.*" Miranda breathed deeply, inhaling the heady scent of the fire, now dying down. She took another long sip of the port and looked up into Luna's questioning face.

"Yes, the wine reminds me a little of blood." She shifted her gaze to the glass, stared into it, watching the firelight reflected in it, tried not to see those faces again as they swam before her on the surface of the wine. "Blood tastes dangerous—or perhaps it is that I have only tasted it in dangerous places. It's thick. And sweet. And just a little spicy. Like Turkish coffee, or real Swiss hot chocolate, like Justine makes."

When Miranda returned her gaze to Luna, she saw the range of emotions on her pretty olive face—fear, revulsion, *desire*. *Luna*, she thought. *Luna will be my companion. Just like when I first came to this town.* Suddenly Miranda felt safe. Suddenly she knew the risk had been worth it.

"How do you justify the killing, Mira?" Justine's voice was even, not judgmental, curious. "You *do* kill, don't you? I mean, you have to kill to survive, don't you? Or is that just part of the myth?"

How odd this is, Miranda thought. *We are talking about this as if it is some different sort of diet, as if Justine had just asked her*, "And how did you lose all that weight?" She sipped again at the warm port. She was hungry suddenly.

She began, "There is always blood where I am—blood in the houses, on the streets, in the rivers. Blood pulsing out of body after body, one life after another on the verge of extinction. I do not have to kill—there are so many to do it for me. However, I *can* save some of them. I can offer some of the victims—not my victims—life."

Miranda held her glass out to Luna, who took it wordlessly. Miranda fingered the small red stone on her left hand. She continued, "Anything worth anything has a price. Dolores taught me that. *You* taught me that, Vivienne. There is so much suffering, so much fear. I have saved young children, made them what I am, given them back a chance at life."

Miranda waved her hand in the air, a dismissive gesture. "Oh, I know it's not the kind of life you would want for them. But they can't have that kind of life, and it's not because of me. I hate blood, I hate the carnage. But I've learned to use it." She smiled a half-smile, a *La Gioconda* mixture of irony and determination. "I've learned to make all the blood work for me. Remember how angry I used to be? I learned to use my anger for change. I've taught myself how to create change. Vivienne," Miranda turned toward her old friend, "you know what I mean. I have seen such fear at the moment of death. And I can take that fear away. I can change it."

Luna held out a fresh glass of port. Miranda took it, closing her fingers around Luna's, looking up into her smoky eyes, eyes that held no fear now—and no contempt either.

"I came here because I had lost Dolores, and with her I had lost my sureness—my sense of mission, I guess you would call it. I needed to feel safe, to be away from blood and bullets for a time. I needed to feel warm and secure. And the only way I could feel that was to tell you. And what better night than Twelfth Night, the anniversary of my death. Or my new life, depending on who is writing the story."

Here Miranda stopped. She set the glass down on the table before her and lifted the lid on the small cinnabar box. Inside sat the Tarot, nestled in a black muslin bag. Justine reached out her hand, as she had earlier, when Luna had gone for the cards.

"I don't think it's time for those, yet, honey. I think there's a few more things we need to talk about here." Justine's tone was firm but kind. Miranda sat back.

The room was nearly dark and very still. The candles had burned down almost to their wicks. The fire was little more than glowing embers. They all seemed to notice the dark at once, but Miranda sensed no fear from any of them. Justine got up and opened a drawer in the little table that held the candles. One by one she replaced them. But instead of the slender buttery tapers that had burned there before, these candles were green, red, black. Miranda saw Justine was taking no chances with death sitting so close by.

"You are *such* a butch, Justine." Luna's throaty voice was flirty. They all knew what Justine was doing. Protecting her woman, her home, her friends, herself. Justine let out a small sound that had just the edge of a laugh in it as she laid a long strip of cypress on the dying fire and sprinkled something that she had taken from the drawer on top of the wood before she stoked the fire.

"You know I don't want to hurt you, Mira, but I'm not sure exactly why you've come, what you've come *for*. I just want to keep things friendly." Her back was to Miranda as she spoke, and all Miranda could see was her broad shoulders, the shimmering amber fabric seeming to glow like a huge ember in front of her. When Justine stood again, she walked behind the sofa and put her hands firmly on Vivienne's slender shoulders.

"Tell us more about what happened, *chérie*." Vivienne's voice echoed in the still room, louder than she expected, than any of them expected.

"Do you mean my work or do you mean Dolores?" Miranda felt hot again, and dizzy. Justine knew what she was doing.

"Tell us how it happened. How you continue."

Miranda explained. Explained how she had met Dolores at a Halloween party where there had been real voodoo and other things Miranda had wanted to know about. "They were friends of *yours*, Luna," teasing the other woman just a little.

There had been months of long talks, dinners, kisses. Dolores had disappeared periodically and then returned. Miranda hadn't been completely clear what it was Dolores did for a living. Only that she was a writer, and that they shared the same view of the world.

But Dolores was older—as old as Miranda would be now—or at least that was how old she had looked. Miranda learned later that Dolores had been in New Orleans for many years. That her mother had been a Tchopitoulas Indian and her father had come from Spain. Dolores had met her fate one night long before Napoleon ever dreamed of coming to Louisiana.

Dolores wanted to take Miranda away from New Orleans. "You love this city too much, *chèr*, you need to see the world. Make some change." And that was when the kisses and talks led to the long Twelfth Night of secrets revealed.

"She didn't force me," Miranda explained. "She gave me a choice. And I chose her. And I chose a life that would make it possible for me to do my work without fear."

Then Miranda told them what she had seen in twenty years. The bombings in Belfast. The starvation in Mozambique, Somalia. The coups in Haiti, Thailand, Burma. Apartheid in South Africa. Civil war in Rwanda and Bosnia. The covert wars in the hills of El Salvador and Guatemala.

"My life can only be at night, but my work is at night," Miranda told them, her voice rising over the sudden hiss of the flames beside her.

"But all that is terrible in the world, all that is truly noteworthy, all that keeps us barely separate from the marauding animals in our natures happens at night, in the terrible, evil dark. Board meetings and stock market shifts and inaugurations happen in broad daylight, but coups and massacres—the knock on the door by the secret police, the piling into the cattle cars to the crematoria—these things happen after dark, before dawn, while respectability and conscience sleep. So you see, I can do my work very well indeed, because my world is now the same as theirs. Killers do not prey in the light. Never in the light."

Miranda stopped, reached for her glass. Her hands shook slightly, but the queasiness was gone. Justine wasn't out to get her; she only wanted to have some control over her. Whatever she had put in the fire had no lasting effects. Justine only wanted her to know there was more if it was needed.

"What do you want from us, *chérie?*" Vivienne sounded tired. It was past two, Miranda could tell from the sound of the night in the courtyard. She was hungry. She'd had too much wine. She would have to leave soon.

"I want what I have always wanted. Your friendship, your love. I want to know I can come here and be with you all and be safe. There is no one with whom I can be safe, now that Dolores is gone. You see, I don't spend time with the others. We don't share the same—" she paused, trying to find the right emphasis, "—politics."

When Miranda leaned forward to look deep into Vivienne's black eyes, the garnet earrings swung into the glow of the firelight. They looked like drops of blood cascading down her pale neck, dripping onto her claret dress. Miranda said, "I want a companion, but I won't take any of you if you do not want to come. I can wait. Dolores waited years for me, and then I was indirectly responsible for her death. But if any of you—" she waved her hand, the one with the spot of blood-red stone on it, "—want to join me, I will tell you what I know. I will tell you that I have learned a great deal about seeking justice. More than I ever learned from working with you, Vivienne. There is a great deal to be done out there. There are people who deserve to die, like the men who killed Dolores, and there are people who deserve the chance to do what I do—to try another way. To remind those who sleep at night what happens in the dark."

Now she stood. The Tarot cards still lay in their box. "I don't think the cards hold the answer for me now," she told Justine. "I think I got the answers I came for."

She took her glass into the kitchen, opened the refrigerator and took out a bottle of mineral water. Twisting off the top, she poured it into the glass. Port had thickened in the base of the globe, and as she drank the water, she stared at it, reminded of how hungry she was, how there was a killer who had been stalking women along Decatur for several months and how she knew now where he spent his nights.

She walked back into the living room. Luna was holding her theater coat. "I'll walk you back to the hotel," was all she said. Justine looked away, then said, "You are always welcome here, honey, as long as you know the rules." She stooped to snuff the candles.

"*Et tu*, Vivienne?" Miranda asked.

"Give my love to Minh when you're in Paris, *chérie*. Tell her I miss her." Vivienne's sad eyes met Miranda's. She stood and put her slender arms around her, holding her with a fierceness Miranda hadn't felt since Dolores.

"Thank you for a lovely Twelfth Night, *mes amis*," Miranda said softly. She kissed Vivienne on each cheek and held out her arms to Justine, who hugged her briefly, but with the same strength as Vivienne.

"I'll call, y'all," Luna said as she followed Miranda into the courtyard.

The door closed quietly behind them both. The brass lizard knocker glowed faintly in the gas-lit courtyard, and the air was thick with scents.

"I have something I must do first, Luna," Miranda said as she put her arm around the smaller woman's shoulders. "Why don't you meet me back at the hotel?"

"Why don't I come with you," Luna said, reaching her long fingers up to Miranda's cheek. "It's been a long time since you were here. Things have changed. You may need a guide—especially at this hour. A girl can't be too careful in this town, not after dark, not on Twelfth Night."

∿

The fog was dense now, and Miranda could barely see Luna as she walked ahead and out of the courtyard. Miranda stood still, smelling the air, remembering Dolores, remembering all the other Twelfth Nights. The muffled sound of the carillon chimed in the distance—one, two, three. The night was passing. Through the fog, Luna stretched out her hand to Miranda.

"It's time to go, honey." Her voice was muted by the night, but the air around Miranda was redolent with her scent.

They would go together. She would have her companion. She would be safe. Miranda didn't need the cards; she had come to her own epiphany—fitting, on Twelfth Night.

There was no moon tonight. But there was Luna.

Backlash

Nikki Baker

Friday, October 16, 8:32 p.m.

EADS TURN AS CASSANDRA'S pager begins to scream; the head waiter at Nick's Fishhouse frowns toward the table. Quickly digging the plastic box out of her bag, Cassandra glances down at the numbers coming up on the display. Across the creased white table linen, Luther's clay-brown face is frowning, too, in sullen disappointment: "Can't take you anywhere."

"Work," she tells him, her warm seafood salad getting cold.

Cassandra is thinking that of anyone, she should be disappointed. Luther, if anyone, should understand about her work. Isn't that why she is with him, because they are the same—ambitious, she thinks, recalling his days on call for felony review, when his pager used to set him upright in the bed at all hours of the night? Hauling his ass down to the PD to see if somebody's collar was good enough to hold. Patient steps toward where he was going. Now Luther is first chair at the State's Attorney; they only call him in when they need a big gun, a tough conviction or a pretty-faced black man to put some other sorry brother out for good without the *Sun Times* crying racist. And here comes Luther, smooth-talking to the papers, big and handsome, natty in his double-breasted suits, having made it.

Cassandra can't help but smile, remembering the swaggering way Luther first brought her here, how he asked for the date as if he were doing a beat cop like her a favor, showing her something. "Ever been to Nick's? Now, girl, that's a place." Swollen-up smug, the maitre d' pulling out the table so they could slide across the corner booth he'd told her was so hard to get. He took her home in the same brassy way. Invited himself in for a drink that ended in her bedroom—patting the empty space beside him, legs splayed out rumpling the comforter, tasseled Italian loafers looking like two canoes on size elevens. She'd joined him on the bed, mostly curious and climbing and never really sure of who was jazzing whom.

Now here she was three years later, having made detective, night law school. Not bad for her mother's nappy-headed child. Six days on and two off, rotating shifts, and a precious free weekend every six weeks. Nights like this one playing hooky while her partner Lonnie picked up her slack.

"You know I can't help it." Cassandra turns the pager off, drops it back into her purse. She takes Luther's hand across the table, rubs the fingers in her own.

They will come back next week for a belated anniversary celebration. Shacked up three years, longer than she had expected it to last. *Three years.* He says, "I'll drop you off."

Cassandra calls the dispatcher from Luther's car phone so coolly that to listen to herself she wonders sometimes if she's alive anymore or just going through the motions, this job, this man, traded up from sweet, slow nights and the touch of smooth, soft skin to blood that doesn't even begin to pump when her pager calls her after some everyday sidewalk horror. Except this time the dispatcher gives an address that could straighten out Cassandra's hair, save her the trouble once every eight weeks of a touch-up relaxer. She is tingling at the back of her neck just like the first time. 643 Eddy. Cassandra used to know someone at this address, hopes she doesn't anymore, slamming the car door and shouting back over her shoulder at Luther, "Don't wait up."

Friday, October 16, 9:03 p.m.

From the corner of Halsted and Addison, Cassandra walks the four blocks west to Eddy. She doesn't have to check the address in her notebook to find the house, wouldn't have to consult the chicken scratch she took down from the dispatcher even if it were not for the body wagon and the black-and-white blocking the alley. This is Booker Robie's building, the four-flat brick with the shambling wood porch. Cassandra and Booker used to ride together when she was starting out, late summer of 1985, when Cassandra was assigned to vice. She and Booker cleaned out all that shit going on under the Belmont El tracks.

Cassandra walks up the blue-gray, chipped-paint stairs, past a uniformed cop who sits smoking on the steps, and through the open door into the marble entry under the stairwell. Four sets of mail boxes built into the wall-box and, on the opposite side of the hall, a panel of buzzers. Cassandra reads down the list of names. Celebrezi, Cohn/Raab, Robie/Lind, Hamilton.

Lind?

Cassandra mounts the stairs and starts up the flights. Somehow she is not surprised all the action is on the third floor. The investigation team is taking pictures down the hall from Booker's apartment, from the vantage point of the doorway, the apartment next door, the stairs. Lonnie is already there. The five-day growth of beard he wears, the bulk of his body under two sweatshirts and a trench coat, reminds Cassandra of a bear. Waving her over from the tidy little foyer, Lonnie's looking sick, so there must be blood. His mouth is tight and grim between his moustache and the scraggly underbrush that covers his chin. He nods at her stiffly.

"It's Booker." Lonnie points toward the back end of the railroad flat where Cassandra knows there will be a living room.

"In there," Lonnie wets his lips, rolling one over the other.

Down the hall, Gary Lally smiles with an undertaker's cheerfulness. "Ain't pretty," he advises. Lally comes to these for fun, listens on the dispatch in his car. The other cops let him, even though they are supposed to limit access to the crime scenes. As Cassandra walks past Lally toward the open archway that ends the hall, she picks up the smell of raw meat, dying blood and fresh shit.

Booker Robie is lying on his couch, stripped down to his shorts, naked legs hanging catty-corner over the edge, his neck sliced open. One cut, clean and deep. The ashen brown skin gapes away from the gray dead muscle underneath. But Booker's face is painted over with a calm expression. A checkered red-and-white woolen stadium blanket is on the floor in a heap near his feet, as if in leaping up he had thrown it off of his legs. His eyes are blank and staring. Opposite the fussy overstuffed couch—not Booker's taste—the TV is still going and there is an open beer can on the floor, upright and undisturbed.

Cassandra stands over the body, watching the medical examiner's investigator work in Booker's open mouth; she clasps her hands behind her back self-consciously as he pokes with a finger in a latex glove at the fuzzy white stuff growing over Booker's tongue. *Not Booker anymore, just meat.*

Her hands still locked together behind her back, she starts her walkdown of the room. She will do this once to get its feel and then again with her notebook, writing her observations independently of Lonnie's, writing everything—the color of the couch and Booker's boxer shorts, the position of his beat-up combat boots kicked off beside the coffee table—navigating the trail between Booker's television and his stereo, estimating the distance between the couch and the kitchen.

In a flat like this, some old law used to mandate that there be two openings in case of fire. She can see the second door from where she is standing, probably opening from the kitchen onto a rickety wood back porch in lieu of a fire escape. Booker would have been able to see it and anybody coming through it at the first sound without getting up from the couch.

In the kitchen, Cassandra tries the back door. *Locked.* There is a window above the sink, no screen, and a wooden sash wide open. The wrought iron security bars are bent back away from the window and hang broken. In this old brick construction, though, the ground is forty feet below. Through the open window Cassandra can see the evidence team's man looking for footprints and ladder marks. Forty-foot ladder, Cassandra thinks, *good luck*.

From the door of the kitchen she can see the pattern of Booker's blood on the cotton rug, how it sprayed when he was cut, his heart pumping it out in pulses, making arcs on the pale, tight-woven rug. She sees him cut from behind, then how he must have stood up in horror. The second overlapping trail of blood is shorter. She looks for its path to waver as he fought, but strangely there are only the two distinct lines and the drying puddles on his shirt, as if somehow the bleeding stopped or the blood was caught and carried away. *To where?* The staring eyes and the mute parted lips don't tell Cassandra anything.

She bends again to look at Booker over the shoulder of the investigator, the one Lonnie calls an "exacting young man." She's watched him work before, Colin Conn, thorough and quiet. After a while she asks him, "Well?" barely noticing Lonnie standing behind her, watching too.

Conn's slim shoulders rise just slightly, hands still working. "Somebody cut him."

They have come with the stretcher now.

Conn is pulling at his rubber gloves. "The white stuff in his mouth is a real bad case of thrush." The gloves come off inside out and he holds them at arm's length to drop them in the trash, then he shrugs again. "If I were to bet, I'd say he had AIDS."

Cassandra watches Lonnie's face go stiff. "What makes you say that?" she asks, her own face nearly as rigid as Lonnie's.

"The yeast going crazy in his mouth." Conn points toward Booker's collar offhandedly. "The purple mark there looks like Kaposi's sarcoma to me, but they'll have to biopsy it at the lab."

Cassandra can see another purple lesion on Booker's chest, under his open denim shirt.

Lally has heard them. Now he is whistling, "Shit," through his teeth. "God damn. I just saw him last week, man."

They all saw Booker just last week. At Bobby Tarrington's sergeant's party, Booker got drunk and pulled off his polo shirt on the dance floor, waving it around over his head like a flag. Then, there wasn't a mark on him. Lally is pacing all around the body, stopping every once in a while to blink stupidly into the dead face, as if he's expecting Booker to sit up and explain it to him, all the time whispering, "Shit. Shit. Shit."

"Have a little respect, man," Lonnie growls.

Cassandra doesn't say anything. She wonders aloud if there is anyone they should call.

In the corner near the hall, a short blond man is crumpled by the wall, crying, his jacket balled up in his hands. The police go in and out of the room, passing him as if he were a piece of the furniture.

"What's he doing here?" Cassandra asks.

"He lives here." Lally blushes, suddenly more red-faced than usual. "The boyfriend, I guess." His voice is goading as he points at the man, "Name's Nathan Lind. He found him." Lally shakes his head. "Jesus, you think you know a guy."

Gary Lally rode with Booker for two years. It surprises Cassandra that he's just now figured out Booker was gay. *The boyfriend.*

"Shut up, Gary," Cassandra says.

But Gary keeps on talking, "You work with a guy, you know? Play ball, shower with him even; you'd think he'd have the decency to warn you he's a fag."

"What's it matter now," Lonnie says. "Man, don't you have any place you're supposed to be?" Lally's cheeks color again.

They are all watching Nathan Lind cry, slumped against the wall. He is slight and skim milk–pale. Booker could break him in two without even meaning it. But Cassandra thinks, a sharp knife, a trusted lover and stealth. It wouldn't be the first time—or the last. "So, where was Mr. Lind when all of this transpired?" Cassandra says, asking Lonnie. "Do we know for sure they were an item?"

Nodding, Lonnie takes his notebook out of the pouch in his sweatshirt. The letters on the front spell Villanova, where his oldest kid, John, plays basketball. Lonnie reads from the spiral-bound steno pad, "Nathan Lind, roommate," eyebrows raised, "two names on the lease. Says he was out getting Chinese at a place called Two Happiness on Southport. He was gone maybe forty minutes. This is what he comes home to."

Lonnie has already called Two Happiness Restaurant and confirmed the call-in order at eight-fifteen and the pickup twenty minutes later. Cassandra can't help but smile; Lonnie is way ahead of her, seems like he's always way ahead without even trying, but he lets her run the show if she wants.

"Lind says he walked to get the food. If he didn't, he could have cut Booker and waited around to call us or he could have cut Booker before he left." Lonnie glances at the man in the corner before he offers, "I don't think so though. One cold-hearted bastard who could do a guy and then go get carry-out."

The couch is blind to anyone who came in from the hall, but Booker was a big guy. Whoever killed him tried to take his neck off, and Cassandra doesn't think Nathan Lind looks up to it.

"Listen," Gary Lally is standing behind her, kibitzing hard. "What I say is, where's the blood?" A gash deep as the Mississippi in Booker's neck. Lally figures there ought to be more blood, but it's not on the floor or soaking into the heavy brocade pattern of the couch, and it's sure as hell not in Booker anymore.

Cassandra looks at Conn. "We've got the word of a talented amateur here. What's your expert opinion, Mr. Conn?"

Conn shrugs. "Could be a quart or so low, now that you say so," he admits. "I can't say for sure until I sit down and do the official report. It could all just be coagulating there in his butt."

Cassandra asks, "Any idea of who else could have done this?"

Lonnie flips the notebook closed, "Guess that's what they pay us to find out."

Two hours of questioning, and Cassandra has found out Nathan Lind is a junior professor at University of Illinois Extension, and he and Booker have been together for three years. Mr. Lind has never had so much as a speeding ticket, and he can't get a full sentence out without falling apart. It is almost dawn when Lonnie drops Cassandra in front of Luther's house, the modest brick bungalow he bought from his mother before she died. He has left the porch light burning for her.

"Somebody waiting up," Lonnie speaks his vowels soft-mouthed, unhurried. "Uh huh," Lonnie says, "he better watch you, girl. If I were twenty years younger, he'd have a reason."

In Lonnie's voice is Cassandra's imagined father barely remembered, already old when she was born to a wife twenty years his junior, long dead by the time Cassandra could have known him. The voices of her girlhood talking, jumbled around Saturday night card tables, voices drifting on the breeze of summer nights through the projects, three small rooms and open, screenless windows over battered sills and long, dirty shards of cracking paint. Voices barely remembered, maybe never even there when Cassandra was a girl and people called the projects "homes," a neighborhood. "No shame in being poor and honest," her mother said. Clean, cheap housing for people trying to do right.

Cassandra opens the car door and then, surprising herself, turns back, reaches across the seat, catches hold of Lonnie's familiar spare tire under his sweatshirt as she hugs him. Before they moved in together, Luther told her that Lonnie stopped him outside of Daly Plaza and asked his intentions, saying, "You don't treat her right, and you've got to answer to me."

Cassandra says, "If you were twenty years younger, Lonnie, I couldn't keep up with you," as she closes the car door. Usually he would watch her all the way to her door, but the street is quiet. Lonnie's car pulls slowly away, and Cassandra feels a chill run through her neck all of a sudden, lets her eyes pan across the hedges by the front door. *Someone's there.* Her heels click against the asphalt, running up the driveway, keys out, all the time kicking herself for her silly superstition. It's the thing with Booker that's made her jittery, the proximity to death, and still she holds her breath all the way inside the screen door. *Don't turn around. Just get the key in the lock.* When the knob turns, Cassandra can finally breathe out again. Inside, pulling the door shut behind her, all the apprehension is gone. The eyes she imagined watching her are closed now, and all she can feel is dirty from Booker's, the sweetish smell of his apartment still hanging in her nose and her hair.

Cassandra drops her clothes all the way down the hall as she undresses. She can hear her heart until the nearly scalding water drowns it out, beating its own pulse on her back. The steam opens up the tightness in her chest, and she stands right under the shower spray, letting the water fall over the gathers in her plastic flowered shower cap.

Cassandra wonders about Booker and the little man slumped in the corner of his living room, white and thin as smoke. Delicate as the things that draw people together, as fragile as she and Solange. Cassandra is wondering if Solange will be the med tech on this case and, if she is, what they will say to each other.

From the hallway Cassandra can watch Luther sleeping, his breathing heavy and broken by a rattle in his chest, the remains of a cold he has been fighting. She watches him for a while and then slips across the cold wood floor into bed, spooning her body against his back. He murmurs her name in sleepy recognition, sighing, makes no protest as she raises her hand to touch his neck. Cassandra imagines how easily she could slit his throat.

Saturday, October 17, dawn

Cassandra dreams of blood that flows in rivers under dark watching eyes until the river is no longer blood anymore, but churning muddy water. The eyes are hers. She can see Booker Robie and Nathan Lind dancing waist deep in it, tongues darting and meeting between full parted lips, bodies rocking together, oblivious, slowly making eddies in the lazy river. Then the bodies and tongues are hers and Solange's. Then Cassandra is dreaming of making love.

Saturday morning comes five hours too soon. But before Luther is awake, Cassandra is up and on her way to meet Lonnie at the office. Her shift doesn't start until 4:00 p.m., but she and Lonnie agreed last night: Fuck the overtime.

Lonnie's already got the ME on the phone. He's nodding and taking notes. When Cassandra comes up, Lonnie begins a simultaneous translation.

According to the ME, Booker's corpse was a walking encyclopedia of opportunistic diseases, with a chest full of pneumocystis pneumonia, along with the thrush and skin cancer, which would have killed him if whoever it was had been any slower about slitting his throat.

"So where'd all the blood go?"

Lonnie grunts, "Ask him yourself." Working his gum with a sideways jaw, he hands over the phone. Not two months ago, Lonnie stood right there taking money he'd bet on the department softball playoffs from the watch commander singing, "Man, you see that boy run around those bases? Hit it beautiful." Booker had hit it out of the park and was home so fast you'd wonder if his legs had ever touched the ground.

Cassandra asks how long it would take someone to get that sick, as sick as this corpse the ME is going on about.

"AIDS pneumocystis is insidious." There is a hopeless shrug in the ME's voice as he tells her how it gradually fills your lungs with water and bugs until you don't remember when you started having trouble breathing, just that all of a sudden you can't breathe. "This guy was so far gone, I wouldn't wonder if he got out of breath going to the john," the ME says. "This man had been sick for a while."

Cassandra flips the pages of her notebook. This is not what Booker's partner said. She turns to Lonnie, covering the phone with her hand. Nathan Lind claims never to have seen the thrush in his lover's mouth before. "Who'd be looking," Lonnie countered last night on the ride home. Nathan Lind says they both tested HIV negative when they got together three years ago, and there's been no fooling around.

Lonnie is nodding, jaw twitching against the gum. Cassandra remembers the catch in Lind's throat as he said this, the deep breath and his nodding head, as if he's cataloging his doubts, carefully putting them away.

"People fool themselves," Lonnie says. "Happens all the time." Lonnie knows. He's a man with a new, younger wife and a fresh divorce. Cassandra watches him write out the support check every month at the desk they share at Town Hall, twenty-third district. "You play, you pay," Lonnie says. Conventional wisdom: Gay murders are hard when there's a closet, so many layers of acquaintances, circles of friends that don't overlap. Lonnie wants to put Booker's death down to tricking, or a lover's quarrel when Nathan Lind gets wind that Booker's been slipping around, down to the Levi's and leather sidewalk sale at Belmont and Halsted, where boys are as easy to pick up as carry-out Chinese food, looking for something harder, streetier, younger.

Cassandra's been there. Not to Belmont, but further north, to a women's bar called Chardonnay, making new, one-night friends at the bar, underneath the driving pulse of the white-girl dance music. Calling Luther from a strange apartment, "Don't wait up." Luther is willing to take Cassandra at face value as long as he doesn't have to look like a fool in public. Lonnie figures, who's to say what happened when Nathan Lind finds out Booker's brought something nasty home.

But the bent-back bars. Lonnie says they could have been that way for ages in a rental flat. Nathan Lind could have bent them back himself. No footprints on the back porch or in the soft flower beds under the window. No sign of forced entry. Lonnie says, Lonnie says. Cassandra thinks Lonnie doesn't know shit about this thing. Not about Booker, or about her.

"Where'd all the blood go?" Cassandra asks, and the ME tells her to check the luminol report, if anybody did one. "Damned if I know. It sure as hell wasn't in the body."

Just for fun Cassandra pulls all the unsolved homicides for the past year and reads the case files. It takes her all afternoon, but she finds five junkies cut with a sharp, thin knife.

At five o'clock, when Cassandra pulls her car back into her own garage, all she would like to do is sleep. But Luther meets her at the door in tuxedo pants, his fingers closing off the links of his French cuffs, his kiss smelling like cologne and toothpaste.

"Remember? Drinks are at six-thirty," he says and orders her to hurry up.

Cassandra has forgotten the fundraiser for Joe Reilly, who works with Luther at the State's Attorney, who the Democrats are running hard for Cook County Circuit Court judge. Black tie optional, and Luther always takes the option; he is like a woman with his clothes. He has laid hers out on the bed, the little black dress that makes Cassandra hold her breath, a gentle reminder not to be too tired for this affair. She will dress to complement him. Luther owes Joe Reilly. Cassandra owes Luther. She is ready by six, every hair in place, pressed into submission by the heat of a curling wand. This is the way Luther likes her, looking good and clean like someone's smart Pill Hill wife, as if no unpleasantness has ever touched her. The lie of beautiful clothing—put it on and become somebody else.

Saturday, October 17, 7:30 p.m.

Cassandra takes the Manhattan Joe Reilly has brought her, smiling, always smiling. She imagines how worn her smile must look by now. Luther is bullshitting amiably, playing straight man to Joe Reilly's manic party standup. "O. J. who?" says Luther.

Joe is roaring, "You're on the jury!"

An explosion of laughter. Cassandra can feel her face laughing, too, as if this were the first time she had heard this sad, sick chestnut. "Hold on, hold on," Joe is saying, "I've got another one." His voice drones on, another layer just barely heard over the other glad-hand din.

Cassandra's smile stretches wider and thinner until she feels as if her mind has left her body here to cover its own obligations. Her mind is roaming, wandering to Booker's body on his couch. To Nathan Lind. To Chardonnay and to a black woman across the room who Cassandra realizes she must have been watching for a long time now.

The woman is tall. Her hair is short and reddish. Mariny, Cassandra's mother would say with distaste, and nappy, tight, dense clumps pruned down close to her yellow scalp. Framed by her hair, the lightly freckled face is striking, set in planes and angles with deep hollow eyes. Old eyes, they seem to suck the light down into their flat black pupils, and look slightly off, sunken into this fresh unwrinkled skin. She's ten years younger than Cassandra, twenty-six, maybe twenty-seven, muscles tight under her green dress. The clinging fabric dances as she walks, from the coat check to the bar, lightly touching backs to part the crowd, followed by Cassandra's gaze. On this yellow woman in the green silk dress, the dead black eyes promise warm oblivion. Over a tall iced drink, they flick across Cassandra's, stop, hunting something like recognition long enough to make Cassandra count the months, wondering how long it's been since she was with Solange. Hand on his elbow, Cassandra asks Luther if he knows her.

"Why?" Luther is still laughing, shaking his head no. "Am I in trouble if I do?"

Cassandra bends her forehead to meet Joe's and whispers, "The light-skinned black woman, talking to Eloise Gough in the corner."

"Marilyn Peel." Reilly knows everybody. Chewing a miniature quiche he tells her, "Used to be a records clerk for night narcotics court, pulling up files. Ambitious." Reilly wags a finger, smiling as if this is a dangerous quality in a woman, eyebrows raised toward Luther significantly. "Very ambitious girl."

"Must be," Luther says, "to show at one of your fundraisers."

"Hey," Reilly parts his hands, pushes back the air agreeably. "She's with the Rape Crisis Advocate lately. They always send people to these gigs."

"Really," Cassandra tells him. "I must tell her how much I love her dress."

Joe Reilly looks again and smiles appreciatively. "She does look good for as sick as she's been." When Cassandra asks him, Joe shrugs it off; he doesn't know, pneumonia or bronchitis, tuberculosis. "I don't know—something chronic, on and off for years."

At eight o'clock Cassandra leaves her purse with Luther and slips out to page herself from the lobby phone. Cassandra tells Luther she's got to go and steps into the hall of the Chicago Club in time to ride the elevator down with Eloise Gough, a public defender who dresses like she's in private practice. "Rich old man," Luther whispered when Cassandra asked him. Eloise and Cassandra worked together when Cassandra worked vice. Eloise is nice enough. Tonight, half lit, she smiles at Cassandra as if she's an old friend.

"And how are you?" Eloise asks. "It's been a while. Too long," talking rapid-fire. The black woman she was talking to? Nobody, someone from narcotics court, she thinks. Left a while ago, for health reasons. Waving her hand, Eloise can't keep track of all the people she meets. In seven floors with no stops, Eloise has managed to say three times how she wants to have Cassandra and Luther by their new place. Eloise will call next week. No, she's sure she has the number, really; voluble bullshit, the oil that greases the wheels between Luther's machine connections. Cassandra still marvels sometimes to be riding on it, the machine that is going to take her where she wants to go.

A loose-limbed young man with a razor cut down to his caramel-colored scalp, the valet comes around the front with Eloise's hunter-green Range Rover before Cassandra can hail a cab. His eyes slide up to meet Cassandra's and then away, back to the keys he holds out to Eloise. Eloise puts two folded dollars into his open hand. "Can I drop you any-where?" Eloise asks halfheartedly.

"No need." Cassandra is going to see Solange Orstowski again.

Saturday, October 17, 10:30 p.m.

Eloise Gough's Range Rover is parked with all the doors wide open at Blackhawk and Larabee streets, half a block from her half-million-dollar townhouse, three blocks from the Cabrini Green Housing Project—somebody's 1950s fantasy of high-rise living for the less fortu-nate, turned into a slum stacked on top of itself. A community where the old used to watch over the young, now turned into a gang culture crammed into three blocks of gunfire and dissolution.

The rain streaks the cab windows as Cassandra looks down the block of new townhomes painted cheerful colors to set them off from the aging red brick and concrete, as if to make people forget that Cabrini Green was new once upon a time. Developers have been build-ing and yuppies snapping up these high-priced homes for a decade now, waiting for this nearly lakefront property to come back and those X-shaped red brick project buildings to die into rubble under a city wrecking ball. Cabrini Green is already half empty, whole floors un-occupied, the apartments not re-released when the tenants vacate, just waiting for urban renewal. Cassandra hasn't been over this way in years; no need. Cabrini Green is Area Three, Bob Hasty's stomping ground. The lazy sack has got the watch commander convinced that another cut throat has to do with Booker, so now this belongs to Cassandra and Lonnie.

Cassandra tells the cab driver to pull up behind the evidence van. Somebody is already snapping photos down the street. Cassandra watches the police photographer for a while as he walks a little way and turns to focus, and snap, snap, snap. His strobe flash freezes moments in the falling rain. The fancy car is a mess. So is Eloise Gough, nothing Lonnie's going to like. Cassandra is thinking that for once she has managed to get here before Lonnie, still in the cocktail dress and heels she was wearing to Reilly's party. Solange lives at Sheffield and Webster. But Lonnie's coming all the way up from Merrynook. Must be swearing too, a homicide a day for the last three days of a six-day shift and all the overtime they need authorized for once, cursing coming out in the rain from a warm bed. So is Cassandra, no time to shower, still damp from sex. She remembers Solange rolling over dozy-eyed as her pager went off, remembers being both sorry and glad. Sorry to leave Solange, but glad for something truthful she can tell Luther when she gets home tomorrow morning. Seems like everything with Solange is mixed emotions. They have been on and off for two years now, neither one seeming able to let it alone. Solange can't let go of Cassandra, and Cassandra can't let go of her ambitions.

"Take some risks in your life," Solange says. White-girl talk from a place of white-girl comfort. Cassandra has taken enough risks in her life already. What she wants now is the sure thing from a kit, readymade, the institution and the privilege guaranteed, because the rules change for people like her. Just when you think you're ahead of the game, they go and change it on you. "You think I've had it so easy?" Solange screams, her off-blonde hair loose and wispy-ended at her shoulders. It hangs in her face like the fur of some fancy, thin-faced dog. This is how Cassandra likes her best, tough veneer scraped off, a little distraught. "Fuck you then," Solange says. "What do you know about how things have been for me? Fuck you."

"All right," says Cassandra, "Fuck me. Yeah, that's all right with me."

The light, cold rain falls steadily, beading up on the shoulders of her long wool coat as a uniformed officer leads Fred Gough by the arm. He looks lost and broken. "Husband," the cop announces, surprised when Cassandra's face shows recognition.

"We've met."

Fred Gough remembers. Joe Reilly's New Year's party. He takes her outstretched hand and pulls her into a bear hug, clumsily holding her too long, hands rub up and down, too far down her back, smoothing the fabric of her coat.

Over his shoulder, she can see a uniformed cop who has a chunk black boy by the collar of his Chicago Bulls' starter jacket, trying to catch Cassandra's eye. The boy is struggling, chest heaving, "Aw, man, I didn't *do* nothing. Man, fucking Jesus," snatches of words coming out on each breath.

"I never should have moved us down here," Fred says, breath liquor-sweet. "So much crime." Cassandra nods. What can she say? Finally, he lets Cassandra go.

She backs away, telling him how sorry she is, thinking Fred must have stayed home—she doesn't remember him at Joe Reilly's campaign party—making a mental note. *Be sure to find out where he's been.*

The uniformed cop waves Cassandra over, still hanging on to the kid in the starter jacket, holding him so tight that he's almost lifting the kid off the ground. Across the street, Lonnie's climbing out of the blue Nova his wife usually drives, walking toward her and the boy and the cop.

"Man, I ain't *done* nothing," the boy is complaining. Up close, the back of his jacket is streaked with blood, like he's sat down and rolled in it, but there's not much of it anywhere else, clean hands and shiny amber baby-face. The hands are working helplessly. "Man, let me loose." He's looking from her to Lonnie, twisting his neck back at the uniformed cop, his body whipping like a pinned snake, eyes moving so fast the light behind them seems to flicker like a candle's flame.

"This the perp, man?" Lonnie's looking sideways.

The cop shakes his head.

"Then let him go," Cassandra tells the big white officer. It's a thing she has about the cops in Old Town, stopping black kids for nothing but being poor, keeping the world safe for drunken tourists on their way from Second City, baggage of identity. She would like for it not to bother her, this beefy cop with the black kid flopping by his collar, held up like some trophy fish he's caught. "Go on, put him down."

When the cop drops him, the boy lands hard on unsteady feet. He catches himself, straightens, rolls his shoulders. Turned loose, attitude seems to flow back into him until he's puffed up, smart-mouthed again. "Yeah, man, hands off, all right? Like the sister say, you know I was the one called you-all in the first place, see."

Cassandra's got her notebook out. "Shut up," she says to the kid. "I'm not your sister. What's your name?"

The uniformed cop is talking for him in that Bridgeport voice Solange can do just perfect when she wants to make Cassandra laugh, "Kid's name's Joe Jackson. He says he was just passing by minding his p's and q's when he finds this lady. Sees her in the back seat of the car all slumped down." The uniformed cop looks down at his own notes, "Eloise Gough. Her throat is cut. There's blood everywhere."

"That's right," the boy puts in. He's preening his fade, nodding, casual. "I just found her there, and I'm calling you guys like the good Samaritan, see."

Sure of himself now, until Cassandra asks him, "Joe, what's the blood all over your jacket?"

The cop is smiling. But Lonnie's got his forehead all lined up with fatherly concern. This is how they will play it tonight, she is hard and Lonnie is soft.

"What about the blood, Joe? That lady in the car is dead." Cassandra makes her voice a threat as Lonnie drops a heavy arm across the boy's shoulders. "Tell me about the blood, Joe," Cassandra picks away, the big white cop beside her smiling his want-to-get-ahold-of-the-kid-again smile and the kid jumpy-eyed, as if he's wishing to run like water, slip away back into the broken cracks of the street.

Hard and soft. "Just tell the truth," Lonnie's voice strokes. "It's going to be all right." His arm holds the kid like a thick leather strap.

"I ain't *done* nothing." The boy is yammering. She can feel him measuring the distance to the boxy projects down the street, calculating if he can get there, but Lonnie's got him under that arm. In the minute of silence he is gauging Lonnie's weight, deciding not. His shoulders slump a little. "So, all right, man, the ride is fine," he says, edgy. "The keys are just hanging there, so I just thought I'd sit in it you know, fine ride and all. I'm sitting there, it's dark and it be *smelling* funny, so I turn on the light, and there's blood all over." Tears have started to come up in his eyes. They run down his face without breaking the rhythm of his story, stress tears, not sadness, face twisted up with the excitement of violence close enough to touch. "There's blood all over the place," says the kid, "and the lady, she's cut bad in the back, right, so I freak. I didn't do nothing." He lifts his shoulders, spreads his arms a little way, tears still rolling out over an even voice. The boy wipes his nose, asking, "If I'd have done something, man, would I have stopped you-all like I did in the street?"

"We're going to take your statement officially," Lonnie tells him.

Now Cassandra is waiting for the kid to shrink away from Lonnie's arm. But he doesn't. The kid's warming under it, relaxed, as if Lonnie's passing something that the kid needs through his touch. "We'll call your folks when we get to the station, and then I'll give you a ride home," Lonnie says. His voice is easy. "All right?"

Lonnie is beautiful to watch with kids and animals, boys. Somehow he is less good with the girls, as if their involvement in drugs and sex is somehow more wretched, dirtier. He cannot bring himself to put an arm around them, cannot bring himself most times to look at them, dirty, pregnant, a baby on each hip and not old enough to vote, as if the fall of a woman is longer, too far down to even try to help her up. Booker was like that, too, Cassandra remembers, when they worked vice together. He said once of the young black women, "Just have 'em spayed, like cats and dogs." Cassandra had to chalk it up to something else—grief, exasperation—so she could keep on liking him.

"Town Hall station?" asks the kid. "Yeah, all right, man. I've been there before."

They leave the kid to the uniformed cop and walk a little way down the street together. "You think he did her?" Lonnie asks, jerking his head back at the kid stubbing his toes on the sidewalk.

There is not near enough blood on him. "Have you seen the car?" Cassandra asks. Lonnie nods, face going ashen.

The car is a mess. It looks like someone cut Eloise's throat, pulled her over the front seat and into the back to finish the job, blood all over the inside roof and dashboard, the back of the front seat a mash of fingerprints, as if somebody finger-painted her blood all over the tan interior. The prints are mostly Eloise's from flailing, or the boy's as he scrambled to get the hell out. Eloise's throat is a grinning slash, skin drying at the ends, like lips pulled back for a smile.

Cassandra has one hope: a smeared handprint in blood on the calfskin leather of the back passenger's side door, as if someone were bracing himself. A hand belonging to a small man or a big woman, its pressure distorted, hard for the AFIS print computer to read. The evidence tech says the thumb looks good, and the boy said he was never in the back seat, but they will print him tonight and find out. Cassandra walks with Lonnie to his car. Even if she knows they're both thinking it, it makes her feel smarter to admit it first. Maybe Bob Hasty isn't such a lazy shit. This thing with Eloise Gough does look a lot like Booker.

Monday, October 18, 1:35 p.m.
Cassandra watches the ME's hands work inside the Y incision made down Eloise's body. The arms of the incision form a V of flesh from each shoulder to just beneath her breasts, met by a stem that runs down below her navel. The ME flips the V roughly over her face, as if to spare her the sight of her own dissection. Lifting the broken ribs and breastplate, he breaks the block of organs and sets them carefully on the small metal sample tray above the examination table. As he weighs them, he is humming something muffled and tuneless through his mask, noting almost as if in passing their shape and condition into the dictation recorder. He sections lungs that seem too heavy for her size, eyes the white pustules, pokes at the water-swollen tissue with the tip of his scalpel, pronouncing, "Bad pneumonia." He sticks a needle into the heart for a blood sample, but not much comes up. His syringes take tissue as well as fluid when he pulls back the plungers, and he swears softly.

Cassandra would like to feel outrage, feel something, but she has seen too many autopsies, done double-duty since Lonnie hates them, can't stand blood. Cassandra has seen enough autopsies to know that the clean, drying cavity that Eloise's organs have left isn't normal, her arteries free from the thick, black, puddled blood. "No blood." She believes she is thinking until she hears her own words.

The ME shrugs, "I just work here," and then goes on to the stomach, reducing Eloise Gough to parts, sectioned and cataloged. What fluid she has washes down through the holes on the shiny table and away.

The cause of death is a wound with a sharp, thin object to the carotid artery of the neck, a switchblade, a straight razor—that, or AIDS-related complications. The ME shakes his head, hard pressed to say which. "Flip a coin," he says when Cassandra tries to pin him down. "If you tell me this woman was walking at 8:00 p.m. last night, I'll have to believe you, Detective."

After Booker, the ME would like to call the Centers for Disease Control about the lack of blood and the weird pneumonia. "Yeah. Have at it," Cassandra says.

At five, when Cassandra gets back to her desk at Town Hall, Lonnie's got the fingerprint report and smiling wide as if he's told himself a joke. He's got his feet up on the desk and his hands crossed over his belly like he's ready for a nap. "The cause of death is either a cut throat or AIDS," Cassandra tells him, "same as Booker." She tells him the ME wants to call in the CDC around it, maybe it will help. Lonnie is nodding, slow and easy with the grin still painted on his face.

"You work around here anymore?" Cassandra asks, and he stirs just enough to slide a print report across the desk to her as she sits down. It says the thumbprint they found in Eloise's car doesn't belong to Eloise or the boy, but to someone named Shawna Jones. Cassandra doesn't have time to ask if he's got the case file and the LEADS report before Lonnie slides them over to her side of the desk as well. Now they are both smiling, stupid and delighted.

"So what does the Law Enforcement Agency Data System have to say about our girl Shawna Jones?" Cassandra asks Lonnie.

Now he's got his palms locked behind his head, reared back on two chair legs. On the Chicago-only background check, Shawna Jones, alias Shawna E. Jones, Shawna K. Jones, Janet Fish, FiFi Jackson, Mary Brown is worth ten pages. It's prostitution mostly, and possession, heroin, but there are two assaults, one with a straight razor. Lonnie can't stop smiling as he tells it. Booker busted this girl when he was starting in vice ten years ago at least, Lonnie says; his name shows up as the arresting officer a couple times.

"Those are just the high points." Lonnie closes his notebook. Looking at his watch, he rocks his chair back onto four legs and swings his feet to the floor again. "I'm knocking off."

He's been here since eight this morning, massaging the fingerprint technicians. Cassandra came in for the autopsy at two o'clock and will stay on to cover the rest of their shift until midnight, wearing the beeper so she can cut out if anything comes up. When Lonnie walks out, Cassandra thinks the spring is back in his step. She hasn't seen that since the papers came through on his divorce.

Cassandra orders in vegetable fried rice from Two Happiness and settles down behind the desk, hunched over the stack of printouts, to eat it out of the paper carton. She's looking for Booker's name on the arrest report and reads down the stack until she sees:

City of Chicago/Department of Police/1121 South State Street
Indent. Section   Chicago, Illinois 60605
CRIMINAL HISTORY OF SHAWNA JONES   F/B 1 a A aaa
     1 a A aaa

DATE OF BIRTH	17. Sept. 55
NAME & ADDRESS	DATE OF ARREST/ARRESTING OFFICER/CHARGE
Jones Shawna	2. Feb. 75, Goodin 23rd dist., Prostitution
822 Montrose	Released w/o charging
17. Sept. 55	
Jones Shawna	9. Mar. 75, Robie 23rd dist., Prostitution
822 Montrose	
17. Sept. 55	
Jones Shawna	17. June 75, Robie 23rd dist., Agg. Assault,
822 Montrose	20, July, XX, Judge Holt, 2 years, Jail.
17. Sept. 55	

The rest is the same, with the final arrests listed as homeless. After 1987, the record stops. Shawna Jones has been wanted for parole violations for twelve years. In the file, her grainy picture has pale tan skin and flat black eyes. It nags Cassandra with familiarity, and Booker Robie's name as the arresting officer puts her there, too, working vice at Town Hall station, could make this Shawna Jones any girl, fast-talking, lipping off, flipping off the cop cars riding up Sheridan past the broken ruins of what used to be the suburbs when Chicago was newer. *Why Booker? And why Eloise?* Cassandra is turning it over with the pictures in her mind of his grinning neck splayed out on the spotless couch, thinking no girl could come in, cut Booker's throat and carry off all the blood, no girl could get that close, thinking how Eloise Gough could barely stand to think of Cassandra's black ass in her fancy car. *How? And why either one? Why both?*

While thumbing through the stack of reports, Cassandra sees it, not all of it, but some. Eloise Gough was the public defender, not good enough then to get Shawna Jones court supervision, not in Holt's courtroom. Booker Robie and Eloise Gough got Shawna Jones two years at Dwight Women's Prison.

Cassandra thinks she can see Shawna now, heroin-thin with dirty reddish dreads, her black, pin-point eyes darting around crazy in booking, as if she could get to a way out if she could only see it. They stop to hold Cassandra's eyes. *Sister.* Eyes pupil to iris, blank black screens, sucking light. They will ask for everything you have if you don't look away. *Sister, spare some change.* Make you want to keep your hands in your pockets, on the strap of your purse. *Want a date?* Sheridan and Montrose. Their short, short skirts in late November, no stockings, their asses hanging out. Hanging out, hawking what they have, pressing hard against the splitting seams of cheap, light fabric. Booker hated that about vice. *Want a date?* at six in the morning, breath puffing out. Booker hated those women. *Ought to have 'em spayed like cats and dogs.* The offers hang, condensing in the air. Leaned up on car doors. Not selling, not really. *Have 'em spayed*, Booker said, *save their kids some tragedy. Because those junkies, they're not people anymore. They're just trash.*

The cheap brown girls are Maxwell Street, clawing and scraping, trading the only thing they've got for whatever it is they think they need. Used and secondhand, trades. *Maxwell Street.* For a moment, Cassandra is a girl again, linked between her brother's hand and her mother's, biggest to smallest, their Goodwill clothes, thin coats flying out behind them, like the ragtag knots in the tail of a kite. Cassandra walks past the tables of junk lined up along the dirty street, skipping like a scrap of gutter paper in the wind. *Trash*. Her mamma stops to buy them knockoff designer jeans and shoes so cheap that their stiff leather cracks on the first wearing. In the dead black eyes Cassandra sees herself less lucky, hard-faced, full breasts pushing at the front of a filthy T-shirt hung down over a short, short skirt. Cassandra thinks how funny memory is and how you can invent a whole person, a whole connection out of circumstance. So many girls that their faces blur. Maybe Cassandra doesn't remember this girl Shawna Jones at all.

No, Shawna Jones owns the eyes Cassandra is suddenly considering, black as well, like swirling water deep enough to lose yourself. The eyes belong to Marilyn Peel, Rape Crisis Advocate's office. They come to Cassandra often now as she lies beside Luther, waiting for sleep, or as she makes love with Solange. They seem to ask her in, saying *come with me for a little while*, as seductive to her as the junk is to this Shawna Jones. The anthracite eyes are everything, beginning and end.

Cassandra turns the pages of her calendar to another obligatory fundraiser before she realizes that she is thinking how much she would like to see Marilyn Peel again. She calls the number information gives her and waits for the answering machine to pick up. The mechanical message delivers a voice as hypnotic as the eyes, and Cassandra drops the phone back into its cradle, turns the pages of her calendar back to today.

The desk clock reads 6:30 p.m. Luther gave her the desk clock when she started law school, to break her habit of being late. "We can't have you running on CP time." Cassandra doesn't want to run on Colored People anything. Cassandra wants out of the minors, onto the fast track. She's been taking one course each quarter at John Marshall, the boot camp of law schools. After three years, she's into her second-year courses. Course number ten, week number three, starts at seven tonight down on Jackson and Plymouth. Criminal Law, and she hasn't done the reading. Cassandra can just make the class if she leaves now.

Monday, October 19, 6:30 p.m.
John Marshall Law School is at 320 South Plymouth. From Town Hall station it takes Cassandra forty minutes on the 32 bus down Clark. She

gets off at Madison by Marshall Fields and walks the rest of the way, down State, past the filigree ironwork tarnished green above the entrance to Carson Pirie Scott, south toward the old Monodonak Building. Years ago, she took a course in design to satisfy an elective for her degree in elementary education, and architecture styles and schools now come to her vaguely. Cassandra wonders if the law will be like this when she finally gets out, just so many forgotten facts. At Plymouth, John Marshall Law School is in a tall, thin 1920s brick building with crumbling brown tuck pointing, spruced up since the Bar Association moved next door. Big new picture windows have been installed in the front.

Cassandra opens the glass doors and mounts the stairs to the fifth floor where the second-year classrooms are. A couple of streaked windows on either side of a blackboard look out on more dirty brick. These classrooms get you ready for the penal system, dark and dismal. There are long fluorescent lights overhead, rows of tables—slabs of pale, plasticized, fake wood set on hard, thin metal legs—beige armless chairs with stiff plastic backs and shovel-blade seats. Cassandra is crammed almost shoulder to shoulder with all of the clerks, shop girls and paralegals who would like to be lawyers someday, but who don't have the luxury of skipping a regular paycheck to do it. She is starting to recognize the members of her cohort now, making special study-friends. Cassandra is too ambitious to have too many who are more than nodding acquaintances.

Poured into the hard plastic seat, hunched over the table near the front, Cassandra wonders if she was smaller fifteen years ago as an undergraduate, or just more stupid, more uncomplaining. She is cataloging her missteps: elementary education, work study, her first lover, Lynette Devereaux. Growing up in low-rise projects, Cassandra was saving herself, unwilling to risk pregnancy and paralysis, being trapped in the life her mother had for one night's pleasure, and came to college a virgin, too stupid to know what it was she liked. Lynette Devereaux taught her, taught her not to be impressed when a slick, sharp-dressing guy took her out to some place where Tony Bennett might be singing, taught her who Tony Bennett was. Cassandra asks herself what she is doing with Luther and his self-conscious climbing.

Another misstep? She doesn't think so. Luther's going to take her out of the PD. He's going to get her started where she's going: state's attorney, mayor's aide, appellate judge.

Tonight Judge Holt is the guest speaker. Cassandra knows his story, feels superior to the other students, having shaken his hand the night before last on Luther's arm. She catches his eye while he talks, and he smiles his recognition, his legendary eye for faces. Luther briefs her beforehand, a head for names. Make a good impression, Luther says, Judge Holt is a hard case. Cassandra is glad he smiles at her as his gaze slides down the rows, telling war stories, saying how he gave some worthless bastard this or that.

There in the front she sees Marilyn Peel, flagging herself with raised hand, waving it slowly every so often. The judge points, and Marilyn stands to talk, the sonorous voice from the answering machine, and flawless skin as smooth as a painted doll's. "Excuse me."

Marilyn Peel as if Cassandra has summoned her up. *Be careful what you wish for.* Cassandra remembers Joe Reilly's laughing summary of her, *an ambitious girl,* and wonders how she could have missed her in these dull evening classes filled with shop girls. Marilyn Peel's skin shines like a translucent veneer over warm blood; in her neck a vein is ticking. "Excuse me, Judge Holt, but to what extent do you think it's appropriate for you to use your discretion in sentencing?"

"I beg your pardon?" the judge asks.

"What is it that makes you especially qualified to sit in moral judgment?"

"Somebody has to." Judge Holt is still smiling, still conversational. He is easy with the answers, used to hecklers.

Cassandra can feel Marilyn Peel starting into a story of too few privileges, too few breaks. Cassandra is thinking, too many what-ifs. If she could, Cassandra would tell Marilyn Peel not to go there.

Judge Holt is waiting, fat with privilege. "Don't do the crime if you can't do the time." Holt cuts her off, playing to the crowd, tough like the nails-and-bones television cop who costars with a parrot, some actor who got his start playing one of the Li'l Rascals. There are titters in the back of the room, but Marilyn Peel will not sit down. Cassandra feels her embarrassment hotly as Judge Holt squints at Peel over the first row of faces. "Don't I know you, miss? I feel sure we have met somewhere before."

Marilyn Peel offers her name, narcotics court. Rape Crisis Advocate's office.

Holt rubs the pink dome of his head, neck to chin to forehead again, rubbing it pinker, if this is possible. He thinks to himself, slack-jawed, with an expression that makes him look slow. "No, that's not it." No, Holt is not slow. The interchange takes less than half a minute. "I don't think so, that's not where," he says.

No one else says anything. Holt's eyes widen slowly, blink and then narrow again. He makes an uh-uh-uh sound before he smiles. "Ah, I remember now," finger paused across his lips. "Miss Peel, did you say?"

The words *cat-and-mouse* run through Cassandra's head, and she's sorry somehow, not even sure if it's Marilyn Peel she's sorry for. Cat and mouse. Hot-faced and embarrassed that Marilyn Peel is black and looking foolish as Holt plays with her.

"Why don't you see me after class, Miss Peel." Then Holt is on to other things. *After class.* Marilyn Peel nods. And the class resumes. "Let me tell you," Holt says, "about my first murder trial."

The show is over, and the class bends back over its notes. Watching Marilyn Peel in profile, Cassandra can see she wears the hint of a smile.

At nine-thirty, Cassandra watches Marilyn Peel walk up to meet Holt at the podium. Marilyn Peel has taken her time arranging her things, but Holt is waiting, his pink face lit with something nasty and sure. Cassandra has taken her time, too, packing up the battered Coach briefcase she carries, letting the rest of the class spill away down the dingy hall. Marilyn Peel and Judge Holt are talking in low voices by the steps up to the podium as Cassandra walks past them through the open door.

Tuesday, October 20, 5:35 p.m.
The phone rings Cassandra out of a deep, short sleep, then all of a sudden it stops. Awake now, she can hear Luther padding down the hall, a

knock, and then a sliver of light through the cracked bedroom door.

"Babe," Luther says, "you awake?" Luther ought to know by now. Day one of Cassandra's three days off she sleeps in, sleeping all day, trying to get back on regular hours after working evening shift. Now she's awake. He tells her, "Phone for you." Luther doesn't know who it is. "A woman," he says. This is always an accusation somehow, and he closes the door just hard enough to make Cassandra wonder if he's slammed it.

Cassandra picks up the phone by the nightstand, the back of her neck tingling. It's Solange on the other end. "Hang on a minute, I'll get a pen," Cassandra says, before Solange can talk. She is willing her not to talk, not yet, because Luther's taken to lingering a while on the other line before he puts it down. Cassandra waits a few minutes more in silence until she hears Luther hang up the extension. Then she tells Solange, "I thought I told you never to call me here." Her voice sounds fierce even though she is whispering. She wonders if Luther notices her whispering in the other room, wonders how much he listens at all. "I love you too, baby," Solange says, even-voiced and sassy even against her anger. Cassandra wonders if there is anything she can say to put Solange off, that will kill their thing. "Relax, baby, this is business." Solange tells Cassandra that Judge Holt was found in Dearborn Park last night, throat cut and not a drop of blood in him. "I just thought you'd like to know."

"Jesus," Cassandra says, thinking *Holt gave Shawna Jones two years.* Now he turns up dead in Dearborn Park, out of Cassandra's area and no goldbricks down there like Bob Hasty. No telling when they would have put it together enough to let her or Lonnie know at the PD.

"So, I'll be seeing you, Detective," Solange says, then whispers, "I love you, Cassie."

But Cassandra can't answer her, can hardly hear her. Cassandra can hardly breathe, puffing out "Jesus," no way to get another breath to take its place. "Jesus Christ."

Solange says, still sassy, "I don't think he has a thing to do with this."

At Town Hall station, Gary Lally is hanging around the lobby as Cassandra heads up the stairs to her desk.

"Can't stay away, can you?" Lally says.

"No more than you can. I don't follow body wagons," she says, "they follow me." Body wagons, three in four days, and she can't find Lonnie at any of his usual haunts.

Three hours later, she has cleaned everything off her desk except the file mugshot of Shawna Jones, black junk-head's eyes staring empty, dreadlocks standing up like Topsy. After a while Cassandra takes the photo to the copy machine and runs it through, blows it up. Now she's got an eight by ten, takes the bottle of white-out from her desk and paints the dreadlocks out, like doodling, paints Shawna Jones bald, blowing on the thick, sticky white-out until there is only Shawna Jones's pale, yellowish skin standing out from the white page. Cassandra makes a copy of the bald picture. With the side of her pencil lead she draws in tight, nappy curls of hair, and when she's done she knows she is looking at a picture of Marilyn Peel.

Marilyn Peel, Shawna Jones, strangely paler. But the same woman. In the arrest report there is a list of ten-year-old wrongs. *Eloise Gough got Shawna Jones two years at Dwight Women's Prison.* Booker, Eloise, Judge Holt. Cassandra realizes that this was the first time Shawna Jones did time.

Cassandra wonders if Marilyn Peel is really enrolled at John Marshall at all. When she calls, the registrar says Marilyn Peel is really a student, a first-year student with no business in Cassandra's criminal law seminar last night. Cassandra gets on the phone with Bernice in Driver's Services at the Secretary of State, a middle-aged sister, hair pressed into an old-style poodle, a million dye-black rings all over her head. Bernice does hair on the side. Cassandra sees her sometimes herself, pays her thirty-five dollars in months when things are tight for a touchup that would cost her fifty at her regular salon. On those nights, Bernice tells stories of when she used to do hair on the Southside before she got her thing with the city, but she got tired of working Saturdays like a dog for the church crowd.

"You need your hair done, honey?" Bernice asks, glad to hear from her.

Cassandra tells her no, just information, asks if Bernice will run a name right quick. Cassandra can hear her punching away on her keyboard, calling up the identification file.

Then Bernice is reading. There are six Marilyn Peels. Four are white. One was born in 1935. The last is Marilyn M. Peel, born in 1955. Lists her address in the 2000 block of Clyborn. This is the one Cassandra wants.

From the cellular phone in Luther's car, Cassandra calls the home number Bernice gave her for Marilyn Peel. The same smooth-voiced machine gives its message, ending in a long, high-pitched beep. Cassandra hangs up.

The Rape Crisis Advocate's office is north at Montrose, but traffic is light driving north up Western and then cutting back east. It's getting dark the way night comes in the fall, suddenly, the sun dropping back over the buildings on the West Side. Cassandra is driving away from the sun, toward the darkness, and by the time she gets to the Rape Crisis Advocate's office at 8 p.m., she needs her headlights on. The woman behind the desk looks as if she might have been a missionary in another time, dry and earnest in her sensible shoes, crazy-eyed with conviction. The plastic plaque beside her phone says her name is Anne. Cassandra asks for Marilyn Peel, and the dry white woman shakes her head, chiding her. "The volunteers aren't supposed to give out their last names," she adds. "It's not safe."

Volunteers. Cassandra is wondering now what Marilyn Peel does for a living since she left narcotics court and why, if she doesn't have to work days, she's in night law school with the rest of the wage slaves. An ambitious girl, Joe Reilly called her. "Is she in tonight?" Cassandra asks again.

The woman, Anne, looks down her roster grudgingly, leafing through sheets of paper tacked down on a clipboard, and determines that Marilyn hasn't come in for her shift. Pinch-faced, she consults a tinny-looking drugstore watch. "That's not like her at all," she says, almost to herself. Then the phone is ringing again. She answers it, talking slowly and calmly, puts the receiver back in its cradle and lets her sour gaze settle back on Cassandra.

"May I ask why you need her?" Her tone is like crackling twigs.

Cassandra drops her eyes, mock shyly. "She helped me," Cassandra lies. "I wanted to talk to her again because she helped me so much." Cassandra lies so smoothly that she startles herself with how easily the words come. It startles her how she would like to see Marilyn Peel again, even with all of this. Cassandra would like to be wrong about Marilyn Peel, Shawna Jones, whoever she is.

This Anne crackles at her, "May I tell her you've called?"

"No need," Cassandra tells her. She is nearly out the door before the woman can ask her name.

Driving back down Western until it meets Clyborn, Cassandra reads addresses. The 2000 block of Clyborn is desolate, no sidewalks. Gray buildings fading into grayer streets, the asphalt fractured into a million potholes. Cassandra slows the car to a ten-mph crawl, saving Luther's suspension. The address that Bernice gave her for Marilyn Peel is the address of the Lands' End Outlet Store, nothing residential in sight, just the shambling steel of burned-out warehouses.

Cassandra parks by the crumbling curb on the other side of the street, thinking that maybe there is a loft, something back here, cheaply rented if all Marilyn Peel does is volunteer work and law school. Cassandra can hear her shoes on the gravel as she walks up to the padlocked fence. She shakes the gate, and it gives way easily, swinging free where someone has cut the lock. Behind the gate there seems to be nothing anyone would want fenced, but still there is the sound of dogs. Walking up the gravel road that leads to a shambling warehouse, Cassandra can hear the dogs getting louder, and then she can see them behind another gate, huge black dogs, snapping at the chainlink when they see her, hungry and white-toothed. Cassandra stands for a while, watching them throw their bodies up against the fence. She knows she won't get to see whatever they are guarding and starts back down the gravel drive, walking in the gullies of stale tire tracks to the first open gate and then farther to the crumbling roadside.

As Cassandra stands by her car, it begins to rain. She can still hear the dogs' furious barking. On Luther's cellular phone, she calls Marilyn

Peel's home number again. This time she leaves a message. Then she heads back to the office to write it up.

Wednesday, October 21, 1:00 a.m.
When Cassandra finally pulls into her driveway, the house is dark. The porch light she has left on for herself is out, and something feels off in the house as she turns her key in the lock, steps onto the thick jute mat in the entryway. It's there in the shadowy living room, by the floor-length drapes drawn closed across the picture window. Not the rising and falling of her own chest, now pumping fast and uneven. The sound is measured in and out, barely audible even in the still, dark house, coming maybe from the folds in the pleated drapes. *Did I close them?* Luther's told her a million times, his mother's pride, those custom drapes. Cassandra hears the sound of someone else's breathing, thinks, *Where is Luther?* Panicked, her blood in her temples pounds with her heart. *Where's Luther?* Cassandra hears a voice from the living room read her mind.

"He's not here," it says.

Cassandra can tell it is Marilyn Peel, sitting on the couch, part of a vague aggregation of shapes that seem to flow comfortably into the shadows that drape the room. *He's not here.* Cassandra remembers Luther is traveling tonight, on his way to Washington for a prosecutors' convention; she's thinking that she doesn't have to protect him, thinking she could take care of whatever this is if only she could see better, just get the lights turned on, wondering what else Marilyn Peel knows about her and why she has contrived to know it.

Marilyn Peel repeats the taunt, "I said your man's not here," in the calming seductive tones Cassandra remembers from her answering machine. "Lucky for him," Marilyn adds. Cassandra believes she can feel her smiling.

"What are you doing here?" Cassandra asks, her hand still feeling its way down the wall, feeling for the light switch.

"My dogs said you were looking for me," Marilyn Peel says. "Here I am."

Touching the ribbed plastic, palm closing over the switch, the other hand sliding slowly across her ribs, Cassandra thinks *she is crazy.* Cassandra's hand pushes back the fabric of her jacket noiselessly, reaching for the holster under her arm.

"I can read your thoughts, you know," Marilyn Peel says. "They come to me like scents through the air. I can smell your fear, hear the pulse singing in your blood." Cassandra can feel her fingers trembling on the switch, on the trigger, all keyed up as she tries to locate the woman from the sound of her voice, place her well enough to get a clean shot. Cassandra wonders if Marilyn Peel has a gun.

"Do you find me beautiful, Detective?" Marilyn Peel teases her. "You shouldn't. I'm your death."

"And why is that?" Cassandra's own voice sounds tight and pinched, and she wonders if Marilyn Peel can hear this inflection, hand on her own gun, thinking Marilyn Peel has got to be stone crazy to come here. *Keep her talking.* "Why is it you want to kill me?" Cassandra's hand is on her gun, wet-palmed.

"Not want to, have to."

Cassandra is thinking, *I can smell your fear, hear your heart.* Cassandra can hear her own heart, too. Right hand on the gun, the other fingering the light switch, thinking, *this is it.*

Marilyn Peel says, "Go ahead and try, Detective."

The voice is still coming from the same direction. Cassandra throws the switch and shoots at the sound. As her eyes adjust to the brightness in the room, they focus first on the hole she has just put in the plaster where the sound was, chest-height in the wall. Marilyn Peel sits on the other side of the couch, calmly as if she has dodged there in plenty of time, the lamp behind her lighting her taut, translucent skin, like a bulb showing through a thin yellow shade. But paler now, without the healthy scattering of freckles, Cassandra thinks and remembers what Eloise Gough said in the elevator. *Looks good for as sick as she's been. Sick, my ass.* To have moved that fast, Marilyn Peel must be as strong as a horse.

"Go ahead, Detective, try again." Marilyn parts her lips over long, white incisors and cranes her long, thin neck to watch Cassandra. "Try again."

She has no gun. But Cassandra is pointing hers, "You just stay there,

Ms. Peel," right hand braced now with her left for accuracy, working her way along the wall, toward a chair on the opposite end of the draperies, getting closer, taking better aim. Cassandra lies, "There doesn't have to be any trouble."

On the couch beside Marilyn Peel's crossed legs, the reels of a small, black tape recorder are turning with a straining, scratchy sound. In the time it takes for Cassandra to notice it, look away with her gun still pointed, Marilyn Peel has somehow gotten behind her.

Her arms wrap Cassandra up like band steel. They bend Cassandra's own arms across her back and twist until the gun comes out of her grip and Cassandra is screaming. Marilyn Peel's hand on her wrist is as cold and smooth as a snakeskin, and her breath on Cassandra's neck smells foul as they dip together, Marilyn Peel stooping low to sweep up the gun from the carpet before she walks Cassandra to the dainty straight-backed chair by the drapery pull.

"Sit down, Detective," Marilyn Peel advises her.

"What's the tape for?" Cassandra asks.

"Posterity. Judge Holt was the end of it, and when they come across your carcass tomorrow, someone will play it and they'll know why. Now sit down, Detective," Marilyn Peel tells Cassandra, twisting her arm until tears come up in Cassandra's eyes and she eases herself down on the chair. When she's sitting, Marilyn Peel hands her back her gun. Cassandra closes her hands around the butt and stands to aim, but somehow Marilyn Peel has gotten across the room already, back to the couch in seconds.

Cassandra braces anyway, aims and shoots, hits air and plaster for the second time. Marilyn Peel has moved again so fast that Casssandra can't believe her eyes are not playing tricks on her. But there is another bullet buried in the wall, making two above either side of the couch, like bookends.

"Jesus," Cassandra says.

Marilyn Peel advises her again, "Sit down, Detective, unless you're really a slow learner."

Cassandra lets her knees drop her down on the chair.

"You know, I was going to let you go," Marilyn Peel tells her.

Cassandra is thinking maybe if they talk long enough Lonnie will miss her on her shift. Maybe he'll come. Cassandra, feeling her stomach flop, says, "You killed Booker Robie, didn't you. And Eloise Gough and Judge Holt," what ought to be a question and isn't.

"Yes," Marilyn Peel says, baring her disturbing teeth, "but I was going to let you off out of sisterhood. I was watching you the night I did Booker. You felt me there in the bushes by your door, deciding."

The gun is useless in her lap, and Cassandra can hear herself asking, "Why did you kill them?"

"You could call it a backlash," Marilyn Peel tells her. "What goes around comes around," she says now reflectively, as if she is talking to herself. "All right," she says, "I suppose the least I could do is tell you what you haven't guessed. This you couldn't guess," she laughs as she starts to tell it, unhurried, so that the pitch of her voice seems to take Cassandra into it, closing her mind to the questions she would like to ask, until there is just the sound of Marilyn Peel's voice, her dead black eyes and the long shadows the lamp behind her makes in the room.

Marilyn Peel says, "I was twenty-six in 1983," and Cassandra is falling into her eyes.

"I was living on the street and tricking for junk. Other junkies mostly, sometimes I would roll them, cut their throats and take their stash. One night I hit big for me, a guy who had maybe a thousand dollars' worth and I went back under the El to shoot." She is telling about the cold, wet fog and the chill of the rusting El tracks, settled back against the rusting metal so that Cassandra can feel the damp, can smell it and the rotting wood underpinnings of the tracks. "I remember how the junk was sweet, singing in my veins like new blood." Cassandra is transported there by the liquid pupils until she can feel it, too, the touch Marilyn Peel describes on her shoulder, as if they are connected. Cassandra feels the pain as Marilyn Peel tells of its coming, dull through the music of the junk and then louder, Marilyn Peel says, although Cassandra is unsure that the words are actually spoken. "It came up," Marilyn says, "like a roar until I couldn't hear the junk anymore. All I could feel was the beating of my heart pouring out through my neck. He was biting me. I could feel his heart, too, as if its pulse came through his teeth, beating calm and steadily while mine was pounding crazy, fighting death. Then my heart slowed down to match his rhythm, then slower. It quietly drained away while his heart became louder." Cassandra can hear the sound of her own heart hammering. She can feel its blood. "Yes," Marilyn says, "I felt if I allowed the sound of my heart to become too faint I would die. I had the razor in my hand, so I cut him, jabbed and cut with the razor until I could feel him let me go, and then there was only my heart beating deep and heavy again. Even the sound of the junk was gone."

Marilyn Peel tells dead-voiced how the man fell back into the gravel under the tracks. "I kicked him hard and turned to run, but something stopped me. Instead of running, I watched him working there for his breath. I watched the lesions come up on his face, all mottled and purple, watched his body jerk and twitch as he lay there in the dirt. That was when I ran."

Cassandra is watching, too, the purplish lesion coming up on Marilyn Peel's face in the dim light, growing. Another lesion starts to bloom on her forehead.

"The Kaposi's." The drone of Marilyn's voice breaks, stops mid-sentence. The break is what Cassandra needs to wake from the lulling dreaminess Marilyn Peel has put on her. "The Kaposi's, is it coming up again?" Cassandra's watching Marilyn's long, thin fingers circle the blemish on her cheek. "I find recently I have to feed more often to keep them from coming back. It's just another sign that my time is almost over, the desperation with which I have to pursue food now, the energy I have to expend to just keep myself alive. The desperation reminds me of the one who made me, and of who I used to be."

She sighs, breath rattling through her chest, then her voice continues. "He was a vampire, too, but I watched him die of it. I watched him die, made sure he was dead with my straight razor in his chest, and then I ran. That was a Saturday night. Back in my room, I saw his face come up over mine in the mirror, covered with the purple marks, running in sweat. There were two deep puncture wounds on my neck. I was sure I was tripping, had to be. I stuck some toilet paper on the bloody marks and slept through Sunday and Monday both. On Monday night I woke up and the marks on my neck were gone. I didn't want junk anymore. I didn't know what I wanted, but I was hungry, so I went out into the street and cut another junkie." Marilyn Peel tells Cassandra that's when she knew what she wanted was blood.

"Blood is easy to get, easier than heroin and cheaper emotionally. When I stopped needing the junk, I found I could get other things as well: money, education—at night." The pale pleated drapes bell out between them, and Marilyn Peel stands to close the window, reaching under the billowing fabric to slide the triple tracks shut with a smack. "I found it was nearly impossible for me to stay awake in the day; when I tried, the light burned me. So I got my GED at night and then went on to college in criminal justice at University of Illinois. Criminal justice had a special interest to me. When I got the job at narcotics court, my life was different than I had ever imagined it. I believed what had happened to me was a gift from God. Now I know the gift was from somewhere else."

"Why did you kill Booker and Eloise and Judge Holt?" Cassandra asks again.

"Because there is no rehabilitation for me and no redemption. All I know is that to live I must eat, and now I must eat more frequently to replenish the blood that the disease in my body is killing. And I must hurry and tell you this, Detective, because I can feel myself getting weaker even while we are sitting here. Though not too weak to beat you across the room. AIDS accelerates death in everything. It accelerates the rate at which I must feed, and now I must kill more and more frequently in order to replenish the blood."

"Why kill them, Shawna?" Cassandra whispers.

She watches Marilyn Peel stiffen at the old name, then repeat it, repeat it almost smiling, as if it is someone she used to know. She says, "Shawna Jones was a junkie. She died with her desperation twelve years ago. My name is Marilyn Peel now."

"But why kill them now?"

"Because Marilyn Peel is dying. Soon she will not be able to feed frequently enough to make it through the day. I killed them because Marilyn Peel is not immortal, only cursed, and Shawna Jones was cursed by them before I came to this."

Cassandra doesn't believe in vampires, but she believes in the power of the mind. If this woman believes she's a vampire, maybe whatever will stop them will stop her. Cassandra's watch says 6:30 a.m. Sunrise was maybe fifteen minutes ago. The curtain pull is only inches away. Cassandra remembers Marilyn's voice: *I can read your thoughts.* Cassandra doesn't think so.

She is working her hand along the side of the chair toward the tasseled curtain pull.

Cassandra's fingers touch the cord.

"Am I boring you?" Marilyn asks. "Someplace else you'd like to be?"

Cassandra pulls the cord, throwing open the curtains, and the new light cuts through the room like a river between Cassandra and Marilyn. Cassandra answers, "As a matter of fact, there is," hoping that what stops vampires in B-grade movies will stop Marilyn Peel. Her hand is on her gun again. Cassandra stands, gauges the distance to the door, walks slowly backward.

But Marilyn Peel doesn't move from the shadows by the couch. Instead she stands, squaring her shoulders toward the light that streams thin and crisp through the open drapes. She pauses, bowing her head as if she is praying. Then Marilyn Peel steps into the light and lets it cut her like a laser. As the light falls across her foot, her leg succumbs to fire. Flames lick up her slacks. For a moment, Cassandra is transfixed by their sudden brightness. Marilyn Peel's skin burns away as she walks though the light, into the flames that now consume her arms and legs. "Roll," Cassandra yells at her, tossing the afghan throw from the back of Luther's reading chair, but Marilyn just stands there. Flames shoot from her head like the red dreadlocks she has cut away. The only sound is a hiss, like that of dry, burning wood. No smell as Cassandra watches Marilyn Peel crumble into dust. The afghan throw is gone, too, flared away into a fine white pile of ash. Walking toward it, Cassandra's steps make a wind that sprays the ash until the pile is gone. Then there is nothing but the sound of the tape recorder still lying on the couch, near the indentation where Marilyn Peel sat, framed by the two bullets stuck in the wall. *Posterity.* Cassandra ejects the plastic cassette and holds it up to the light. Smoke fumes from the plastic casing, and the thin tape starts to burn.

Her service revolver is on the floor by the chair, two shots fired. Cassandra knows that eventually there will have to be something for the file.

Contributors

MEREDITH SUSAN BAIRD is the author of the satiric novel *Romancing the Romaine—The Adventures of Valentine Willowthigh*. Her short stories have appeared in several anthologies, including *Out for Blood*, and she has won numerous awards for her short fiction, including first prize at the Philadelphia Writer's Conference. A twenty-two-year resident of Southern California, she now lives in Malvern, Pennsylvania, with her husband and eight cats.

NIKKI BAKER is the author of the Virginia Kelly mystery series, featuring the first African-American lesbian detective. Her novels *In the Game, The Lavender House Murder* and *Long Goodbyes* have all been nominated for the Lambda Literary Award for Best Lesbian Fiction. Her short fiction and nonfiction have appeared in numerous anthologies. A lifelong Midwesterner and former resident of Chicago, she currently lives in the San Francisco Bay area.

TONI BROWN is an African-American lesbian writer. Her work has appeared in the journals *Sinister Wisdom* and *Common Lives, Lesbian Lives* and has been anthologized in *The Poetry of Sex: Lesbians Write the Erotic, The Body of Love* and *Lesbian Writers*.

JAN CARR is the author of the novel *Harem Wish*. She has also written many books for children, including two new picture books, *Dark Day, Light Night* and *The Nature of the Beast*. Her journalism has appeared in *Playbill, Stagebill, Theater Week, Variety* and *Writer's Digest*. She lives in New York City with her partner, Stan, her young son, Charlie, and their two cats.

JOANNE DAHME is the author of two science-fiction novels, and her short stories have appeared in several anthologies, including *Thirteen by Seven*. She holds a bachelor's degree in civil engineering from Villanova University and a master's degree in journalism from Temple University, and heads the Public Affairs Division of the Philadelphia Water Department. She lives in Philadelphia with her husband and son.

DIANE DEKELB-RITTENHOUSE's shady past includes stints as a factory worker, tarot card reader, medical technician, designer of telecommunications terminals and, in a dark and desperate hour, candidate for political office. A native Philadelphian, she abandoned a flourishing career in Manhattan as an unemployed bellydancer/actress/punk-rock lyricist for the joys of wife- and motherhood. She is the author of numerous science-fiction and fantasy tales and lives with her husband, underground comic book writer W. E. Rittenhouse, and their daughter in Levittown, Pennsylvania. Her day job is on the staff of a local college, where she also leads a union and teaches courses in genre writing.

TERRI DE LA PEÑA is a native of Santa Monica, California, where her family has lived since the early 1800s. Her novels *Margins* and *Latin Satins* are assigned reading in Chicana/o studies, women's studies and lesbian and gay studies courses in universities throughout the United States. Her short-story collection, *Territories*, is forthcoming from Third Woman Press.

JUDITH KATZ is the author of *Running Fiercely Toward a High Thin Sound*, winner of the 1992 Lambda Literary Award for Best Lesbian Fiction. Her second novel, *The Escape Artist*, will be published in fall 1996. She lives in Minneapolis, where she teaches women's studies and creative writing. "Anita, Polish Vampire, . . ." is her first vampire story.

MABEL MANEY is an artist whose work has shown throughout the Midwest and California. The author of the Nancy Clue and Hardly Boys mystery series, her novels *The Case of the Not-So-Nice Nurse* and *The Case of the Good-for-Nothing Girlfriend* were nominated for Lambda Literary Awards in several categories in 1994 and 1995. Her most recent novel is *The Ghost in the Closet*, and her short fiction has been anthologized in various places, including *Girlfriend Number One*. She lives happily in San Francisco with Miss Lily Bee.

JUDITH M. REDDING is a Philadelphia-based independent filmmaker whose films and videos have shown in the United States, United Kingdom, Canada, and the Netherlands. The film and video editor of

Deneuve magazine, her writing also appears in numerous newspapers and magazines in the United States. She won a 1994 NEA grant for screenwriting, and her short video, *Mondays*, won third prize/experimental in the 1994 Visions of U.S. Home Video Competition.

RUTHANN ROBSON is the author of *Another Mother*, a novel about a lesbian who is an attorney, a mother, a lover and a daughter. She is also the author of two collections of short fiction, *Eye of a Hurricane* and *Cecile*. She has lived throughout the South and now lives in New York.

SUSANNA J. STURGIS has been courting Lilith, Medea and other dark muses for many years. She lives on Martha's Vineyard, where she takes long walks with her dog, dabbles in theater and makes her living as a freelance editor.

JOYCE WAGNER is a writer and actress, formerly of Chicago and now living on Martha's Vineyard. Her work has appeared in *The Joy Page* and *Perihelion*. Her Barbie doll is angry and refuses to speak to her.

LISA D. WILLIAMSON enjoys scuba diving and racquet sports when not in front of her computer. She is the author of a mystery novel, *The House That Jake Built*, featuring sleuth Valerie Duncan, and has won several awards for her fiction. Her short stories have appeared in several anthologies, including *Out for Blood*. She currently lives in the Philadelphia suburbs with her husband and two sons.

LINDA K. WRIGHT is an African-American writer of poetry and fiction and an officer of the Meridian Writers' Cooperative. She has won numerous awards for her poems and short stories and is the 1995 winner of the Charles Johnson Fiction Award. Her work has appeared in several anthologies, including *Thirteen by Seven*, *Hen's Teeth* and *Out for Blood*. She currently lives in Malvern, Pennsylvania, with her husband.

About the Editor

Victoria A. Brownworth is a Pulitzer prize-nominated, syndicated columnist for the *Philadelphia Daily News* and *Deneuve* magazine. Her work appears in numerous queer and mainstream publications, including *The Village Voice, Ms., The Advocate, Spin* and *Out*, and she teaches writing at several Philadelphia-area colleges. She is the author of seven books, most recently *Too Queer: Essays From a Radical Life*, and the editor of three, including *Out for Blood: Tales of Mystery and Suspense by Women*. She lives in Philadelphia.

Selected Titles from Seal Press

Sweat: Stories and a Novella by Lucy Jane Bledsoe. $10.95, 1-878067-64-8. The elusive sanctity of sport. The exquisite rewards of risk. The adventure that is contemporary lesbian life. *Sweat* will tempt you from your comfort zone.

All the Powerful Invisible Things: A Sportswoman's Notebook by Gretchen Legler. $12.95, 1-878067-69-9, paper; $20.95, 1-878067-70-2, cloth. A beautifully written memoir of self-discovery and an eloquent chronicle of outdoor life. Legler writes of the complexities of being a woman who fishes and hunts as well as the more intimate terrain of family.

Listen Up: Voices from the Next Feminist Generation, edited by Barbara Findlen. $12.95, 1-878067-61-3. For the first time, the voices of today's young feminists, the "Third Wave," are brought together to explore and reveal their lives. Topics include racism, sexuality, identity, AIDS, revolution, abortion and much more.

Closer to Home: Bisexuality and Feminism, edited by Elizabeth Reba Weise. $14.95, 1-878067-17-6. A dynamic anthology of essays by and about women who are bisexual, this collection breaks new ground in feminist and queer discourse.

The Dyke and the Dybbuk by Ellen Galford. $10.95, 1-878067-51-6. A fun, feisty, feminist romp through Jewish folklore as an ancient spirit returns to haunt a modern-day London lesbian.

Latin Satins by Terri de la Peña. $10.95, 1-878067-52-4. Full of humor, tenderness and salsa, this novel tells the story of the lives and loves of a group of lesbian Chicana singers in Santa Monica, California—the irrepressible Latin Satins.

Disappearing Moon Cafe by SKY Lee. $10.95, 1-878067-12-5. A spellbinding first novel that portrays four generations of the Wong family in Vancouver's Chinatown by one of Canada's most celebrated authors.

Seal Press publishes many books by women writers under the categories of women's studies; fiction; mysteries; translations; sports and the outdoors; young adult and children; self-help, recovery and health; and parenting. To receive a free catalog or to order directly, write to us at 3131 Western Avenue, Suite 410, Seattle, Washington 98121. Please add 16.5% of the book total for shipping and handling. Thanks!